"Vérant immerses readers in the sounds, smells, and tastes of a professional kitchen, with a cast of sous-chefs, old friends, and a gruff but handsome mushroom forager along for the ride. Francophiles and fans of Mary Simses and Roselle Lim will adore Sophie's journey."   —*Booklist*

"A great story line, strong writing, plus a handsome French 'hero' and lovely descriptions of France make this debut women's fiction book a sure winner.... A charming, feel-good French romance that transports you out of your everyday life and into the heart of France—a delectable read."
                                                        —*The Good Life France*

PRAISE FOR

Sophie Valroux's Paris Stars

"A *deuxième plat* of Sophie? *Délicieux!*"   —KJ Dell'Antonia,
                    New York Times bestselling author of *The Chicken Sisters*

"A culinary delight. One can't help but root for this ambitious young chef as she overcomes unimaginable obstacles to reach for her dreams. With heart and charm, author Samantha Vérant delivers once again!"
                    —Nicole Meier, author of *The Second Chance Supper Club*

"Captivating characters, mouthwatering food, and a hint of romance . . . this picturesque novel has it all."   —*Woman's World*

"Chef Sophie is at it again with her passion for food—which will make you wish you could hop the next flight for France—and her desire to have it all. . . . Vérant pulls off *Sophie Valroux's Paris Stars* with all the grace and style we have come to expect from this talented author."
                                        —Barbara Conrey, *USA Today*
                                        bestselling author of *Nowhere Near Goodbye*

"Vérant is a masterful storyteller with a special knack for weaving mouthwatering menus into her storyline."   —Lori Nelson Spielman,
                    New York Times bestselling author of *The Star-Crossed Sisters of Tuscany*

The
Spice Master at
Bistro Exotique

SAMANTHA VÉRANT

BERKLEY
New York

BERKLEY
An imprint of Penguin Random House LLC
penguinrandomhouse.com

Copyright © 2022 by Samantha Vérant
Readers Guide copyright © 2022 by Samantha Vérant
Penguin Random House supports copyright. Copyright fuels creativity, encourages
diverse voices, promotes free speech, and creates a vibrant culture. Thank you for
buying an authorized edition of this book and for complying with copyright laws
by not reproducing, scanning, or distributing any part of it in any form without
permission. You are supporting writers and allowing Penguin Random House
to continue to publish books for every reader.

BERKLEY and the BERKLEY & B colophon are registered
trademarks of Penguin Random House LLC.

Library of Congress Cataloging-in-Publication Data

Names: Vérant, Samantha, author.
Title: The spice master at Bistro Exotique / Samantha Vérant.
Description: First edition. | New York: Berkley, 2022.
Identifiers: LCCN 2022025627 | ISBN 9780593546000 (trade paperback) |
ISBN 9780593546017 (ebook)
Subjects: LCGFT: Romance fiction. | Novels.
Classification: LCC PS3622.E7325 S68 2022 | DDC 813/.6—dc23/eng/20220602
LC record available at https://lccn.loc.gov/2022025627

First Edition: December 2022

Printed in the United States of America
1st Printing

BOOK DESIGN BY KATY RIEGEL

To Mom,

thank you for always encouraging me

to follow my dreams

AUTHOR'S NOTE

As an American expat living in France, and now French too (but with an accent that's apparently "cute"—and possibly interpreted as an insult), I've made friends from all over the world—one who actually has a spice dealer, and another who cultivates exotic spices, flowers, and plants in her garden. I've traveled extensively (when I could), mostly all over France and Southeast Asia, where my taste buds come to life and the scents and flavors transport me. Juju is my extra-large cat. Though he's nearly twenty pounds, please don't tell him he's fat; he's big-boned and, on a new "regime," he likes his new diet of green beans and croquettes. His eyes are yellow, not orange. I hope he doesn't sue me for using him as a character. Thankfully, he can't read. As far as my own mother is concerned, she does "sage" rooms, teaches yoga, and likes hang drums, the latter leading to a *very* bizarre Christmas. Although she's never been a sex therapist, my mom did give me the eye-opening illustrated book *Where Did I Come From?* (written by Peter Mayle) before my younger sister was born.

WARNING: This book contains delicious descriptions of food (don't read while hungry), a bit of magic (whether it's real is up to you), and it does get extremely hot in Kate's kitchen (and maybe elsewhere).

The Spice Master
at Bistro Exotique

ACT ONE

The only real stumbling block is fear of failure.

In cooking you've got to have a what-the-hell attitude.

—JULIA CHILD

CHAPTER ONE

A Temporary Distraction

DREAMS MANIFEST WITH a vision and obtainable goals. And mine have always been clear. Food is my life—my calling, my raison d'être—better than sex, better than anything.

I get lost in sensual experiences when I prepare a meal—the way the juices run all sticky and sweet on my hands as I cut fresh fruits like an orange or a fig, the way the flavors dance on my tongue when I taste my fingertips, the way salty and sweet fresh oysters kiss my lips at first, followed by a lustful intoxication when they slide down my throat, or the way a fragrant soup heats up my entire body, my soul.

Foreplay is the preparation, and the climax comes with the finished recipe, bringing all the senses together while balancing flavors. Food is passion in its purest form and one of the reasons I became a chef.

As I tenderly fold the dough for my sourdough bread, my hands caressing the slick and smooth form much like a lover would, I look up, taking in my pristine kitchen—the polished prep station, the stoves, all my tools of the trade—and I can't help but to let out a proud squee.

Holy guacamole—preferably hand-crafted tableside with a mortar and pestle—I am actually opening up my *own* restaurant in Paris, and my culinary offerings are going to rock people's minds and taste buds. Bistro Exotique—*my* restaurant—will finally unlock its doors to the public in four short days and I'm going to share my passion with the world, satisfying the most discerning of palates while invoking all the senses.

I huff out a laugh, hoping my neighbors didn't hear my cries and moans for more garlic last night. More! More! Garlic! Or when I'd gasped out "Pound it" and "Harder," as I smashed whole peppercorns with a mallet. At the very least, nobody would have heard anything unsavory and, surely, they'd understand that dreaming up recipes keeps me tossing and turning with unbridled inspiration all night.

I've been in the kitchen since 6:00 a.m., the dough is on its final rise, which gives me half an hour to get to Marché Saint-Martin— one of Paris's last historical covered markets, with its original stone entries from the late 1800s still remaining. I lightly spank the mound, loosely cover the beauty with a kitchen towel, and then wash my hands before heading to the front door and locking up. Meandering slowly, it will take me eleven minutes to get to the market, but I push myself into speed walking, wanting to be the first in line when the doors open at nine.

On the way, I'm reminded of how much I love this neighborhood and the location, with its lively cafés, cheaper rents, and the canal— a haven in the summer, boasting dances on its banks, festivals, and cultural cruises for Parisians and tourists alike. Add in the poets on their box stands, the fishermen, and the picnickers—it's people-watching galore. Although there is a ton of foot traffic with *les flâ-neurs* (people wandering and observing), this haven is surprisingly calm.

Not in the best of shape, I'm breathless when I reach my utopia, my playground of seasonal delights, immediately running up to Fabian, my fish vendor, panting heavily. He loops his thumbs into the straps of his denim overalls and rocks back and forth in his thick black rubber boots.

"Kate, are you concerned about the delivery?" he asks, his caterpillar-like eyebrows raised. "Don't worry. It's all good, and we're all crossing our fingers for the success of your restaurant. You don't have to check in."

"I'm not worried. I want to test out a new recipe. I dreamed about it last night. A ceviche." *Pant, pant.* "Do you have sea bass?"

"I do."

"Is it fresher than fresh?"

"Of course. Practically off the boat. How many?"

"Just one for now," I say, catching my breath. "But I may need more on Friday if the recipe works out."

"Should I empty it? Filet it?"

"Yeah, that would be great, save me some time."

"Give me a few minutes," he says.

"*Fantastique! Formidable!* Thanks and I'll be back." I pull out my list, holding it up. "More fresh ingredients to catch."

Fabian grins and turns to take care of my order, knife in hand.

Being in the market always transports me to another dimension, another time and place—each ingredient conjuring up memories. For a moment, I stand in front of the glass, staring at the fish, breathing in the briny and salty scents of the ocean, and I'm back to my roots in California, bodysurfing the waves in Malibu and feeling the sand sticking in between my toes as I walk back to my towel, the frothy water lapping and crashing on the shore. I'm suddenly licking my lips and craving fish tacos covered in a Baja sauce. So many fish in the sea, so many ways to prepare them.

Too bad I haven't been by the ocean in years, but I chose cutting blocks over surfboards. Such is the life of a chef. And I have no regrets.

At least I live by Canal Saint-Martin, a glorious 4.5-kilometer-long waterway lined with ancient chestnut trees. I'd never risk jumping in it—who knows what kind of diseases lurk under the surface? But I have skipped stones into the water like the character Amélie did in the movie of the same name from the safety of its elegant iron bridges.

A woman passes by me, saying *"Excusez-moi,"* and I come back to the present.

To clear my head, sometimes I try to guess who would eat what. What would she eat? Meat? Vegan? Vegetarian? Pescatarian? More important, would her taste buds be open to spices? I call this research ocular reconnaissance. The woman meanders toward one of the butchers and points to a goliath-sized leg of lamb—definitely a carnivore. I wonder how she'd prepare her meal—perhaps with slices of garlic stuffed into the meatiest parts of the top, slow roasted with rosemary, with potatoes on the side, the juices, the herbs, infusing into everything. Served with a mint sauce? Or is she the type who colors outside the lines and does something less traditional? The woman pays for her purchase, tucks the large package into her polka-dotted wheeled shopping caddy, and catches me gaping at her. With a visible shudder, she shoots me a death glare, understandable since we're not at a café where it's okay—even expected—to people watch.

Sometimes my research puts me into uncomfortable situations.

I offer an awkward smile and turn on my heel, racing around the stalls, from the stinky cheeses to the produce, inhaling every scent, falling in love with all the colors, picking up the ingredients I need along the way for my dish—namely juicy mangoes, succulent limes, and enormous avocados I can barely fit into my palm.

Finished hunting and gathering, I make my way back to Fabian. He hands over a butcher paper–covered package with a wink. "I'll put it on your account."

"Merci," I say. "You're the best."

I stuff the fish into my now full wicker basket and speed walk back home, hoping I don't trip. Yoga and swimming I can handle. Running? Not so much. I've fallen a few times, plus the jiggling hurts my boobs—my chest is a blessing and a curse. On that, I should probably stop humming *I'm bringing booty back* while skipping my way through the maze of stalls.

I'm in a great mood—giddy, hopeful, and optimistic. The sunlight filters through the trees, illuminating the sidewalk in a hazy, golden glow and reflecting on the wicker basket bursting with the colorful ingredients now resting by my feet.

Although I'm eager to create the dish, testing this recipe will have to wait a few more minutes. It's the end of May, and, for once, the rain has subsided, the sky is clear, and I want to get a photo of the restaurant, capture the magic of the moment for posterity.

I stand across the street from my future, gazing at the crisp charcoal-gray awning, hung up a few days ago. Emblazoned with the logo a friend of mine had designed, the name sparkles in the sunshine, the symbol a hummingbird. It's perfection.

Right when the economy picked up, after a major crush—with restaurants closing left and right—I'd swiped in like a vulture, getting a fabulous deal on the space in the trendy tenth arrondissement, and signed the lease on the spot. I can't beat the corner location, which faces the canal on one side.

Not only did I get a good deal on the space for the restaurant, my five-hundred-square-feet one-bedroom apartment in the same building came as an added bonus. My place isn't big, nor is it fancy, but it has everything I need save for a washer and dryer. Thankfully, my restaurant has one, I'm the boss, and we're closed on Mondays. It's a win-win.

With a wicked grin on my face, I take the first shot. The way the light flickering on the silver wings of the bird sparks up my heart, zapping me like a virtual defibrillator. I fight the urge to spin around and dance on the street or raise my hands into a celebratory fist pump.

Well-heeled Parisians, hipsters, and youngsters surge by me like salmon swimming upstream, rushing off to work or to school or wherever else they may be going, some giving me odd glances with raised brows while I stand on the corner, clicking away.

Of course, after living in Paris for thirteen years, I know the sidewalk comes with a unique set of rules: (1) Stay on course. For example, a couple or group of people walking toward you from the other direction should move to let you by if there isn't space. You hold your ground. (2) Don't stop suddenly, or you risk being slammed into because Parisians walk fast. (3) Watch where you step. Although a bit better since I'd first moved to the City of Light at the age of fifteen, land mines of dog crap still littered the paths. (4) Don't stand in the middle of the sidewalk during the rush hours. Even the sweet little old ladies will run right over you. (5) Last, and probably the most important rule of them all, never smile. People will think something's wrong with you—especially if you're by yourself.

Not usually a rule breaker, I can't stop myself from losing a little control; I smile wider until a man barrels by me, his elbow jabbing into my left rib, and my phone tumbles onto the ground. I scramble to grab my lifeline to the world before somebody smashes it into a million pieces or kicks it into a sewer grate, noticing his designer shoes—Prada. He's about to walk on without an apology, not one *désolé* or pardon. Nothing.

My phone slides on the pavement. It's an iPhone—one I bought secondhand but still expensive. I'm blocking his path, crawling on my hands and knees like a squirrel on Red Bull. (I've seen this happen. Trust me. Run. Or risk a potential attack.) The screen seems to be okay, but this guy should have one shred, one tiny ounce of politeness. Instead, he turns to walk away.

"Hey, you! You could have broken my phone," I yell in French.

"You shouldn't be standing in the middle of the sidewalk during rush hour," he replies with irritation.

"Oh yeah? And you shouldn't be—" I say, looking up and taking in his appearance.

So damn hot.

My throat catches. Words do not form. He's sexier than the ceviche I'm planning on making—slick and smooth, cool and hot. Confession: I may have a problem binge-watching rom-coms and steamy romances, hoping for my own meet-cute. If they happen in the movies, why not in real life? When I'm not in the kitchen, I watch them all, inhaling the happy endings—from *Sleepless in Seattle* to *Pretty Woman* to *Sixteen Candles*, the latter so politically incorrect and cringe-worthy today but made up for with the drool-worthy hotness that is Jake Ryan.

Something about this guy reminds me of Keanu Reeves, with his razor-sharp cheekbones, mildly unkempt black hair that nearly touches his shoulders, two-day scruff, penetrating hazel eyes, and, from what I can tell—dressed in a casual but elegant fitted black suit—a buff body. I may have developed a slight Keanu obsession after I saw him in *Always Be My Maybe*, the story of him being the temporary love interest of an ambitious chef. Even though he played a douchebag version of himself, he was funny and hot as hell.

Normally, I only salivate over recipes, but this feast for the eyes is clearly an exception. Food is my first love, and I'm not looking for the real thing at the moment, but there's nothing wrong with a temporary distraction.

"I just wanted to take a picture," I say, pointing to the restaurant.

I'm still on my knees, looking up into his beautiful face. There is a halolike glow around his head, making him appear absolutely heavenly. He coughs as I swoon. Instead of apologizing or returning my twitchy smile, my two-second fantasy scowls, turns on his heel, and mumbles, *"Putain de touriste."*

And screeeech. Record scratch.

Maybe it's the way I'm dressed? Granted, no Frenchwoman would dare wear food-encrusted Crocs, a torn sweatshirt, and stained cargo shorts—at least, not in public. A scrunchy holds my frizzy blond hair in a messy ponytail. Dusted in flour, I'm a hot, sweaty mess. And, sure, nobody on this planet has ever referred to me as a fashionista, but, in my defense, I have dirty work to tackle—like testing recipes and scrubbing down the industrial stoves until I can eat off them.

"Can you move?" he says, pulling out five euros from his wallet. He holds the bill over my head. "Here, this should help."

My fantasy evaporates like dry ice on a summer day in the hottest of deserts. I shoot him daggers with my eyes and swat the bill. He actually thinks I'm homeless?

"I don't need money."

"Could have fooled me," he says, his eyes making an unabashed loop over my outfit, and then pockets the bill.

Under my breath, I mutter, "*Quelle bite.*"

What a dick.

"I heard that," he says in English, his lips pressing together into a thin line. "Crazy tourist."

"You speak English?"

"Yes, and it's obviously more refined than your limited French."

The lilt in his affected voice, the precise English accent that would normally have me drooling, echoes in my head when I snap to. How dare he? He crashes into *me* and then launches insults like grenades? Bye-bye, meet-cute, this prince in disguise is as ugly as a toadfish.

"*Je ne suis pas une touriste,*" I reply defensively, getting up and straightening my posture. I am quite proudly *almost* French, having spent nearly half my life here. I nod my head in silent affirmation. I'd become naturalized shortly after receiving my diploma from Le Cordon Bleu eight years ago. I think I say the latter out loud.

"*N'importe quoi,*" says *Anti*-Keanu, his upper lip lifting into another nasty sneer. He looks over his shoulder. "*Si vous n'êtes pas une touriste, vous êtes folle.* Should I repeat myself in English?"

This guy hasn't seen my knife skills, the way I could filet him like the sea bass in my basket. Now, *that* would be crazy.

He swaggers down the street before I can come up with a witty retort like "I may be crazy, but crazy is better than being a pretentious jerk" (and insanely good-looking, but I'd never admit that to him). Plus, he's already turned the corner, and Paris is such a big city I'll probably never see him again. Good riddance. Snorting back a huff, my eyes latch on to my restaurant, and I take in a deep breath. Anti-Keanu is *not* going to ruin my day.

Thanks to my road map and my inner voice (who occasionally

swears or comes up with ridiculous expressions), though I may question my sanity, I've never doubted my capabilities as a chef.

Slap a red beret on my head, put me in a striped shirt, and call me anything you damn want to. I know who and what I am. And one thing I'm most definitely not is a tourist. What I *am* is a chef in Paris, the City of Light. Nothing is going to snuff out my glow.

CHAPTER TWO

The Strangest of Strangers

I LIFT MY PHONE to take one last photo of the restaurant when a sleek black Mercedes pulls up, blocking my shot. A capped driver jumps out and steps to the back to open the rear door. One designer-clad foot follows the other and, finally, a woman emerges. Quintessentially French, she's wearing large black sunglasses that cover half her face and a red dress with a wild floral-and-butterfly pattern, her lips painted bright scarlet. Unlike me in my dirty Crocs and flour-covered clothes, she exudes a refined elegance. She places an enormous gray cat wearing a studded rhinestone collar with a matching leash on the ground, and I'm finding it extremely hard not to gawk. The cat is a silvery gray, almost blue, and its fur reminds me of feathers. The woman is light on her heels, practically floating.

As she and her monster-sized cat cross my path, the subtle scent of jasmine fills my nose, and I'm rendered immobile, almost in a trance, until a sloppy wetness saturates my left shoulder, splattering up to my cheek. A grayish-white splotch drips down my arm. A coo aids me in finding the culprit, or rather culprits: two pigeons the size of small turkeys blinking at me with beady evil eyes.

"Be careful." I point, shaking my finger in warning. "You just might end up on my menu."

Maybe I am certifiable. I'm talking to birds. At least I'm not expecting them to talk back.

"*Ça, c'est un gage de chance,*" says the woman. She stops in front of a building and turns around, the cat doing the same.

"No, it's not a token of luck at all," I mumble, grimacing. "It's bird crap."

"*Non*, it's good luck," she responds with a lift of her thin shoulders. "Very good luck."

"Pardon?" I ask, flabbergasted.

When forced, some Parisians will speak English, mostly in restaurants or in other areas of the service industry, but not willingly. I get it. I used to tremble in my Crocs when I didn't have a strong grasp of the language. I've bastardized so many French words I've lost count. *Une poule* (chicken) and *un pull* (sweater) sound exactly the same to me. I obviously need chicken, not a sweater, when I'm at the food market, but that doesn't stop my vendor from laughing. Don't get me started on *foi* (faith), *fois* (time), and *foie* (liver)— pronounced the exact same way but understood in context. Aside from my horrible accent, having two people speak my mother tongue in one day is beyond bizarre. Blinking back my astonishment, I continue, "You speak English?"

"*Mais, bien sûr,* I do. I studied abroad." She shakes her head from side to side, proudly, her chin-length bob of straight black hair gleaming in the sun like silky ink. From her bag, she pulls out a silk scarf, handing it over. "Here. Wipe your arm. And you can keep it."

"Merci," I say, a bit perplexed. Why is she being so nice? As I clean off pigeon *merde*, her cat's huge orange eyes meet mine. Averting my gaze from the cat's, I lock on to the label on the scarf. It's got to be a knockoff. People definitely did not give strangers Hermès accessories. "I can have it cleaned and return it to you."

She pops her lips. "No worries at all. I have hundreds, possibly thousands." Her statement sounds like a question enunciated with perfect intonations—pristine and proper. She smiles again, revealing perfectly white teeth. "My gift to welcome you to the neighborhood."

"Merci," I say again, politeness being the most important of the French tenets. When you walk into a boulangerie, or anywhere else, you always greet the people with a *bonjour* and leave saying *merci, bonne journée*. "How did you know I live in the area?"

"You're opening up the restaurant. I've been watching you from afar. I'm so glad we crossed paths and we could finally meet. In fact, I was going to stop by later this afternoon."

I didn't know if I should be scared. "You've been watching me?"

"My atelier is just up there." She waves a manicured hand to a small wooden sign on the second floor of the ornate building: *Madame Lin-Truffaut's Comptoir aux Épices et Parfums du Monde* (Madame Lin-Truffaut's World Spice and Perfume Counter). Underneath the name, the words read "by appointment only." A phone number isn't listed. "I am a spice lady, scent master, and herbalist—the best in all of Paris, perhaps even the world," she continues, raising her chin proudly. "I help people tap into their senses."

The cat's giant orange eyes blink as if it understood every word she'd uttered. I blink too. I like the idea of cats. They're cute and funny in those wacky YouTube videos when they scoot across the floor on their bellies like furry ninjas or pop out of boxes. I simply don't like anything small and furry and there's a very good reason for that.

When my mom, Christine—who now insists I call her Cri-Cri—and I first moved to the hip and trendy fourth arrondissement, Paris came with some beautiful discoveries . . . along with unexpected surprises, like the time I discovered a cat curled on the front stoop of our building and then quickly realized it wasn't, in fact, a cat. Scarier than Stephen King's diabolical clown It, I'd tried to cuddle an extra-large rat. After the monstrosity leaped onto my shoulder, digging its claws into my back, Mom, being Mom, burst out into laughter.

"You've always wanted a pet," she'd said.

Not funny. I have the scar on my arm to prove it.

"This is my cat, Juju," the woman says, noting my obvious confusion, maybe even my fear. "He's my good luck charm."

"Uh, yeah," I say, backing away ever so slightly. "That's some collar. I love the rhinestones. *Trés chic.*"

"Rhinestones? Don't be silly. I buy all his accessories from a jeweler. His collar is from Catier. As they say, diamonds are a cat's best friend."

My upper lip twitches. Nobody has ever said that. And I'm pretty sure she means Cartier.

She blows the cat a kiss, and I swear, if cats could smile, this one does, his giant face twisting with love or hunger.

"He's huge," I say, watching his tail flick a bit menacingly.

"He's a rare French breed, a Chartreux. He's just, how do you say? Big-boned?" She chortles out a laugh. "I really should put him on a regime like the *vétérinaire* said. He weighs nine kilos. Can you believe it? I strain my back when I try to pick him up. But he really doesn't like *les haricots verts* or *les courgettes*. He's quite the gourmand."

My head spins with confusion. I wonder, *What cat would like green beans and zucchini?* as I convert the math in my head. Her cat weighs around twenty pounds. And, apparently, he hates vegetables but adores his bling.

She clasps a hand on to mine. "Your name is Katherine Jenkins, *oui*? And, *alors*, you are American," she says without question.

How'd she know?

"Please, call me Kate, madame. I'm also French now too. For almost eight years," I say, hoping she doesn't suggest I go on a diet like her cat, who is now pressing his nose against my ankle. Maybe he wants to eat me?

Another confession: after moving to France, I'd gained the "French freshman ten"—in kilos, not pounds—and it never came off. The food was just too good, and I'd discovered there was more to life than kale salads, wheatgrass smoothies, and eating raw foods (my mother's staples), and the other reason I became a chef. My goodness, I loved every ingredient, every fish, every meat, and every vegetable. Don't get me started on the cheese, breads, and desserts, my downfall into a hedonistic culinary world.

The woman scrunches her nose and places her sunglasses on the top of her head, her eyes glittering almost as dazzling as her cat's collar. She offers a sweet grin. "Call me Garrance, not madame. We are friends now, Kate."

I wonder her age. Forty-five? Sixty? I'm beyond intrigued with this woman. First, strangers in Paris aren't quite as friendly as this; they're more reserved, in the strictest sense, and it takes months or years for them to open up, or even talk to you. Second, she's dressed to the nines and so put-together and elegant, I'm wondering why she's even taking the time to speak with me. I twist the hem of my stained sweatshirt, really regretting my choice of outfits.

"It was nice meeting you, Garrance," I say with a smile, and point to the restaurant. "As you can imagine, I have a lot to do to prepare for the opening."

Garrance's gaze flickers down, and I realize I've offended her.

Another French rule: once a conversation is initiated, it's rude to walk away. Don't get me started on the dinner parties that last until the wee hours of the morning. After an awkward silence, I try to put the discussion back on track, make amends. "You should come to the opening party. It's on Friday night."

"We'd love to. Merci."

"Great," I say, and then place the focus on her. "What kind of spices do you sell?"

Her posture straightens, and her eyes sparkle like topaz—a hint of green in the brown hues. "The most precious of them all. The magic kind."

"Magic?"

"The kind you don't find anywhere in the world except for at my little atelier. I don't sell to anybody, but I like you. Your aura—it's orange, like my son's." She gives me the once-over. "Although yours, I'm sad to say, is a bit faded, not really as bright as it should be."

"Like your cat's eyes," I say, my words spouting off like a drippy faucet before I can clog them.

Her lips curve into a smile. "I do think of Juju like a son, but Charles came from my loins. He's a chef, like you." She pauses when my mouth twitches with confusion. "My son, not the cat." She blinks and then laughs. "You can stop by my atelier, see if there's anything of interest. I may have some things that will help you with your endeavor."

A breeze blows, bringing the scent of her perfume to my nostrils. Along with jasmine, a whisper of another captivating aroma I can't quite place nearly makes me lose my train of thought until she clears her throat.

"Thank you, but unfortunately I don't have the budget to take on any more products."

"I never said I was *selling* you anything," says Garrance, tilting her head to the side, clearly assessing my words and doubt. Her fingers flutter toward the restaurant, her full lips pinched into a frown. "The old proprietor did not want my help either. And then look at what happened."

Curiosity bites me on the ass. "What?"

"He got wrapped up in a wine Ponzi scheme, owed some very bad people a lot of money. The business failed, and then he just disappeared." Her breath comes out in a whoosh and she whispers, "Poof."

This conversation is getting stranger by the second. "I don't understand."

"Bad investments. Bad people," she says pointedly, and then shrugs like it's no big deal. Her eyes lock on to an apartment above the restaurant. Thankfully, it's not mine. "But what's done is done. The gendarmes think there may have been foul play."

I gulp. "Murder?"

"Perhaps. But no body was found, so no murder." After an extreme moment of awkward silence, Garrance pops her lips again and points to my awning. "You *must* change that. I implore you. Bring some light and life into the neighborhood. Charcoal gray is so very drab." She places a pensive finger to her lips. "A piece of sage advice: You should change to a red awning for good luck and success. Or, at the very least, green for harmony and growth, money and wealth."

My god, my mother would love this woman. I'm sure they'd talk about new age symbolism or superstitions or whatever for hours. Too bad I don't subscribe to mystical mumbo jumbo at all.

"Right," I say. Although craft butcher paper covered the floor-to-ceiling windows, I know what waits for me inside the bistro, and I love every design element I've chosen. "Merci. Nice to meet you. Bonne journée. I'll see you around."

Garrance turns on her heel, the cat leading her. Before opening her door, she says, "I'm looking forward to the opening. Thank you for the invitation."

"Yes. See you on Friday," I respond with a hesitant smile.

She waves a hand to the sign on her shop. "Bonne journée, Kate. You know where I'll be if you need me."

Out of the corner of my eye, I notice a blue delivery van has pulled up in front of the bistro. They're in the process of using some make-shift contraption to pull up a stand-up piano to one of the apartments above the restaurant—the one Garrance had locked her eyes on, the one a man could possibly have been murdered in. The whole effort looks quite precarious, the piano dipping down to one side, nearly sideswiping my awning.

After a shudder, I pick up my basket of goods and race across the street, fumbling for my keys. Before I enter the bistro, I look over my shoulder. Garrance and her cat no longer stand in the spot I'd just left them. Just as I'm about to open the door, one of the deliverymen screams. *"Merde! Merde! Merde! Bougez-vous. Maintenant!"*

Shit! Move now!

And then I see why. One of the ropes attached to the piano has snapped and is thrashing around in the air like a whip, almost slapping my face. The piano creaks and groans, about to collide into the side of the building. The workers are doing their best to pull the remaining rope. Extreme fear and panic washes over me. I'm praying: *Save my awning.*

Shocked, I stand immobile as people dart off the sidewalk right into the street. My primal instinct to take cover, to get to safety, doesn't kick in. I'm stuck like I'm in a horror film and the people in the audience are screaming, "Run! Get away from the killer! He's right behind you!"

But I don't move. I just watch, frozen.

The piano crashes into the side of building and then smashes down, right onto my beautiful charcoal awning, ripping it off the wall. The thick canvas fabric flutters to the ground, the dismembered keys clank with the breeze, a horrific nightmare of a melody. The workers scramble, jump into the truck and tear off, dirt and debris spitting from the tires.

This can't be happening. Garrance's words about the last owner of the restaurant churn in my brain: *The business failed, and then he just disappeared. Poof!*

Part of me wonders if somehow Garrance is behind the destruction, the timing too impeccable, especially after she'd voiced her opinions about the awning and her laissez-faire attitude regarding the former tenant's disappearance. Still, she didn't seem to be a *total* psychopath, just an eccentric gossip with a creepy orange-eyed cat.

My fingers fly to my temples, and I will my heart to stop racing, making a mental note to google Garrance and the previous tenant. Shaken, I grab my basket of goods and open the door to the restaurant, mentally kicking myself for not getting the license plate number of the van and freaked out by almost meeting my fate.

No, the piano crashing down on my awning is *not* an omen of failure.

I will survive. And, more important, so will my restaurant.

CHAPTER THREE

Today's Special:
Jerk (with a Side of) Chicken

T HINK, THINK, THINK.

What am I going to do? Where do I start? I want to scream. But in the face of disaster it's best to remain calm. I can deal and remain positive. I wasn't crushed by a piano, and only one side of the terrace is unprotected now. I still have the entrance and the side. But if I don't get the front portion covered facing the canal, the best seating, I can say goodbye to a lot of business.

Lists are my life. Without them, I'd never get anything done. I have clear goals, marking up the destinations like a Metro map—miss your stop and you're screwed. I know how to get from point A to point B and onward—with grit and determination. As the events from the morning swim around in my brain, I pull out my moleskin notebook from my bag and glance at the first page as I always do. Although this notebook is new, the first page always starts out with my mantra:

Mise en place:
Prepare everything in advance—my ingredients, my life, my dreams.

Point A began on my fifteenth birthday, when my bohemian mother—a purveyor of yoga, the chakras, and all things new age—told me that when the winds of change blow your way, one has to decide which direction you want it to take you and that sometimes you just had to go with the flow to float into bliss. I usually ignored her "profound" wacky statements until, very nonchalantly in her sing-song voice, she'd announced that she was leaving my father so we could ride the breezes of freedom with the wings of hummingbirds and I needed to pack my bags.

One week later, with a lot of grumbling about me insisting I spend summers and school breaks with Dad, Mom and I moved out of our swanky beach house in Malibu with floor-to-ceiling windows to a two-bedroom apartment above a boulangerie in the fourth arrondissement of Paris, right in the heart of the Marais, and also where I had my incident with the rat. Mom positioned the move as a vacation, telling me that she and Dad simply grew apart, wanted to live separate lives, but they still loved each other and loved me.

Thirteen years later and we're still here without my dad. The divorce, as Mom put it, was easy and almost painless, like ripping off a Band-Aid. Honestly, Dad, with his head stuck in business deals and making money, didn't have much time for me anyway unless he was instructing me on the finer points of the stock market and making sound investments. At first I missed him, but save for a couple of family vacations I rarely saw him anyway.

Mom and I had embarked on an adventure filled with a reckless abandonment I'd never experienced in California. Paris was new and exciting—the busy streets, the historical sights, the smell of the fresh-baked bread and *viennoiseries* like chocolate and almond croissants wafting into my bedroom window every morning. I'd realized my life in the States had starved me of my appetite, and I wanted to fill up, eat, and inhale life in one single gulp.

I still remember the moment I tasted my first buttery crois-sant and drooled over an epic coq au vin. I remember all those mo-ments my taste buds were awakened by a symphony of delectable flavors—all the cheeses (more than a thousand), the sauces, the decadence—and I knew I wanted to become a chef. Mom supported that decision, telling me that I was a formidable woman who could do anything she set her mind on.

The proof is right here: *my* restaurant.

Thankfully, I followed my dad's advice, and, having invested wisely over the years, my portfolio grew. Along with my dad's sti-pend (a.k.a. guilt money), I put myself through Le Cordon Bleu, worked at the top restaurants for six years, climbing the ranks, end-ing up at the now Michelin-starred Cendrillon Paris, and I'm more than ready to strike out on my own.

But the pressure is on because my lease came with a huge caveat. I have six months from the opening of the restaurant to get things on track, to make the restaurant a success.

Taking a deep breath, I survey the space. Perhaps I really did luck out that the former tenant disappeared, after all. He'd left al-most everything behind, and I only needed to break down one wall for the slightly-open-kitchen concept I'd had in mind so our diners could become a part of the culinary experience, as well as purchase a few things like new barstools with an iron base, decorative items, and new glassware, dishes, and silverware. Along with repainting the walls, refurbishing the formerly black leather banquettes to a choco-late brown, and updating *les toilettes*, everything else just needed a little TLC. The wooden tables needed to be sanded and restained dark—almost black—for a more tropical vibe and the ceramic-tiled floors regrouted, buffed, and polished.

My eyes leap to the pristine white walls decorated with tasteful art of fruits and vegetables I'd consigned from a local gallery, to the natural stone–colored tiles with varying French patterns in gray, to the hexagonal-shaped bar (one side a wall), to the globe lighting adorning the ceiling, finally landing on my pièces de résistance—a rustic buffet with a marble top with tiered iron shelving and a matching sideboard.

Before today, everything had been running so smoothly—not one glitch—all inspections passed, all licenses in order, all the thick French bureaucratic tape cut. I just need to adapt to this messed-up situation. I pull out a stool at the bar, sit down, and write.

1. Put perishable goods in the refrigerator
2. Sourdough! D'oh!

Merde. How long has the fish been sitting outside? Garrance and now this debacle have really thrown off my schedule. I scramble up from the barstool, throw the whole basket into the walk-in cooler, divide the dough into loose rounds, covering them quickly, and return to my seat. I check those babies off. Done!

3. Find out who owns the piano
4. Call the police and file a report
5. Call up the insurance company for the awning and get a replacement
6. Test the recipe
7. Go over all lists

I look down at my phone and sigh. Cri-Cri (a.k.a. Mom) has called me at least a dozen times. I've been meaning to call her back but keep putting it off.

8. Find out what happened to the previous tenant
9. Google Garrance
10. Call your mother

Obviously, I have my priorities. Nodding with satisfaction, I lock up the restaurant and then make my way to the awning killer's apartment. I know which one it is because it's two floors below mine. After stomping up the steps, I find myself in the hallway of the first floor—not to be confused with the ground floor, which is known as the *rez-de-chaussée*. Somebody is sobbing—bawling, really—their cries like a flock of erratic seagulls.

Hesitantly, I knock. There is no answer. I bang on the door, and it creaks open. I'm here, and I'm not backing off.

"Pardon, monsieur? I hope I'm not disturbing you," I half yell the words in French, although they are a lie. I totally want to disturb him.

A wild-looking man in his mid to late fifties dressed in a plaid cotton shirt and faded jeans with holes in the knees looks up from a crouched position on the floor. His long hair is tied into a ponytail, and his eyes are tinged red. He bumbles toward me, snot dripping out of his nose, his cheeks tear-stained. I take a step back as he races toward me, his hands gripping and pulling at his hair.

"My piano, my life! Everything I've worked for is gone. Gone! Gone! Gone!" He catches his breath, wipes his nose with the sleeve of his shirt, and then takes a good look at me. "You are the American with the restaurant? Downstairs? I've seen you around but we haven't met. I'm Oded."

"I'm Kate," I say, and quickly put the niceties of this introduction to the side because I'm here for a reason. "Um, I wish we'd met under better circumstances." I pause. "Your piano kind of destroyed a portion of my awning."

Oded sinks to his knees and grabs my hands, the holes in his torn jeans ripping more. "I'm so sorry. I should have known not to buy the piano from Leboncoin, but it was cheaper than anybody else. They offered the delivery, and they were all I could afford."

I feel bad that he's been scammed. Like Craigslist, sometimes one found great deals on Leboncoin, but it also came with its share of unsavory swindles.

His upper lip twitches, and he releases my hands from his grip. "I'm a musician, *vous voyez*?"

My eyes sweep his apartment. Although it's sparsely furnished, with only a chair in the corner, a couch that's seen better days, and a couple of vibrant, patterned cushions on the floor, it's bigger than mine, with a Juliet balcony and floor-to-ceiling windows.

"At least you're not struggling," I say. Hint-hint.

"Oh, I got a good deal on the place—practically free—because somebody..."

His words trail off with a gasp, and I flinch. Garrance hadn't minced her words earlier. As much as I didn't want to believe them— *poof*—a man had really disappeared.

Oded breaks down again, his breath ragged. I place a tender hand on his shoulder. I feel terrible for his distress and the loss of his piano, but not as bad as I feel for my awning.

"I'm so sorry you're upset," I say. "But I'm kind of upset too. The restaurant is my dream—"

"I understand dreams," he says with a nod and a sniffle. "Playing music is mine, but my piano is now dead. How can I help you fix this?"

"I need the name and number of the delivery company," I say.

"I don't have it," he says. "It's not a company. And the number they gave me isn't working. I—I—I just tried calling."

"Somebody has to pay...," I say, my voice trailing off. I gulp. "The awning cost me more than six thousand euros."

I'm met with a blank stare until I clear my throat.

"I'm so sorry. I don't have that kind of money. If I did, I'd give it to you," says Oded with an animal-like sob. "I'm hoping to find stable work soon, but nothing has come through yet. Do you have insurance?"

Of course I have insurance. I have everything—expect for my awning. The last things I want are umbrellas with liquor logos—not the vibe I'm going for. I have a vision. Right about now, I want to burst into tears and I bite down on my bottom lip to keep it from quivering.

Oded stands silent, assessing my obvious distress, and then he rubs his eyes with his knuckles. "Let me make you some mint tea? We can talk about this. Find a solution."

"I'd love some, but at the restaurant. I have to call the gendarmes."

Oded wrings his hands, worry creasing his brow. "The gendarmes? I—I—I didn't do anything. This isn't my fault."

Good grief. This situation isn't my fault either—unlike the time when I nearly burnt my former Malibu home down while trying to flambé shrimp when I was twelve (I was obsessed with the Food Network) and my parents had to pay a fortune to redo half the kitchen. My dad was beyond furious. My mom argued I was only getting in touch with my artistic side. Still, as bad as I feel for the man, somebody has to face the repercussions, take responsibility.

"I need to file a report. And we need to figure out a way to get the sidewalk cleaned up."

"I'll do it," he says, his bottom lip quivering. "I'll have a friend help. But why the police? I don't want to get into trouble—"

"You won't. You're a witness, and the police need to assess the damage. I'll need it for the insurance claim." I turn toward the steps, stop, and look over my shoulder. "Are you coming?"

"Okay," he says. "Let me grab the tea."

Oded's heavy footsteps echo in the marble-tiled stairwell, one clomp after the other, and I keep checking over my shoulder to see if he's going to bolt or if he's following me, so I don't notice the person in front of me until I bump into them. Anti-Keanu. I let out a surprised gasp, and the hair on my arms bristle. What the hell? This day can't get any worse.

"*Toi*," I say, my eyes narrowing into a glare.

"The crazy American tourist," he says, his nose pinching like he smells something bad.

I take in a breath and surreptitiously try to whiff my armpit. I'm a little stale, but I don't stink. "I told you, I'm not a freaking tourist. What are you doing in my building?"

"You live here?" he asks, a look of surprise, maybe disgust, registering on his face.

"Yes, and I'm opening up the restaurant downstairs. Which is why I was standing on the street trying to take pictures of it when you slammed into me and almost broke my phone."

I don't know why I'm explaining this to him. Maybe because he smells delicious. Like vanilla, a bit musky, and something citrusy too, the scents invading my nostrils. This hallway is definitely too small. And it's also placing me too close to him. His jacket is draped over one arm, and the sleeves of his shirt are rolled up to the elbows. I'm trying to make out the tattoo on his forearm, to no avail. If anything, he looks even hotter than he did this morning.

No, no, no, I can't go there with Anti-Keanu.

"If I broke your phone, I'll pay for it," he says.

"It's fine."

"Then I don't see the problem," he continues. "As for your restaurant, good luck. I have a feeling you'll need it."

"Why?"

"Because you're so . . . so, what's the word? Basic. Like American bread or that horrible cheese. Bistro Exotique? Is this your idea of a joke?"

Oh. No. He didn't.

I hear him mumble, "Alors, I'm definitely not eating there," before letting out a huff. "You should really get the sidewalk cleaned up. It's dangerous. Not exactly good for business, non?"

I clench my teeth and hiss, "You think?"

Oded creeps up behind us. "It's my fault. My piano crashed into the awning. Killed it."

Anti-Keanu scowls. He raises his hands, and my eyes shoot to his toned, honey-colored arms.

"I don't even want to know what happened," he says. "Can you please let me pass? I just want to get into my place."

It's my turn to be surprised.

"Wait. You live here too?" I ask, and he nods with a disturbingly wicked smile, his eyes wide, and his posture straightening. "What apartment?"

"Why do you need to know this?"

"So I can avoid you."

"I'm on the second—the entire floor, so if you don't want to run into me and exchange such excruciating painful pleasantries again—"

"Don't worry. I'm going to keep my distance."

"*Bon,*" he says.

I find myself locking on his face. Damn. For such an asshole, he's so sexy.

"It's rude to stare," Anti-Keanu says, breaking me out of my thoughts.

"We live in Paris," I say, lifting up my chin. "Café culture. We people watch. Maybe you're the tourist. Maybe you're . . . you're . . . the basic one."

Yeah, I really ripped him a new one. He just lets out a low, acerbic laugh.

I hate him. Detest him to the moon, stars, and back. Of all the dumb luck, his place is directly below mine. To think, after this morning's encounter, I'd hoped to never see him again, and now I'm probably going to run into him and his nasty attitude all the time. Sometimes big cities become way too small—unlike his giant ego and obvious contempt for me.

He shrugs and waves a dismissive hand. "Now that that's sorted out, can you step aside?"

Livid, I move, taking in a deep and angry breath. Damn him and his vanilla scent as it engulfs my senses, permeating the entire hallway as he passes. I look over my shoulder. It doesn't help he has a really great ass. I collect my thoughts. He *is* an ass. I stomp down the stairs, Oded following.

I mutter, "Bonne journée, bastard."

A FEW HOURS later, the police have come and gone. I take pictures of the destruction before Oded and his friend clean up the sidewalk as best they can. With a hearty *mmmpf* I can't control, after shaping my dough and nestling the rounds in proofing baskets, I call Alex at the awning company.

"*Donc.* I'll have one of my technicians stop by the space this morning. There will be good news if we can salvage the frame, but unfortunately we cannot replace the charcoal gray as the fabric is out of stock for many months."

I remain silent for a moment, assessing the situation. This poses a problem of magnificent proportions. The piano destroyed the largest portion of the awning, where I can seat at least fifteen covers facing the canal. Summer terraces are the bread and butter of Parisian café life. The coming months will be the busiest, not to mention August with the influx of tourists. My heart stutters.

"We need to find a solution, please."

Alex continues with a chipper tone, "Don't worry. I have one. A customer recently canceled an order and the dimensions of your restaurant are nearly identical. We can make some adjustments if you're open to changing the color."

"But I can't change just one side to another color. That would be aesthetically unpleasing."

"Alors, if you want design continuity, my suggestion is to replace all three sides."

"The entire thing?"

"Yes," he says.

I grunt. "What color?"

"A dark emerald green. And we can print your logo and install it on Friday. I'll pick up a check this afternoon, *d'accord*?"

"A check?" My hand slaps my forehead. "For how much? What about my insurance?"

"I'm afraid you'll have to take it up with them." He pauses. "If we can salvage the frame, it will be half the price."

After hanging up with Alex, I swallow back a gulp and call the insurance company, my head pounding, the kind of ache that radiates in your eyes.

"Madame, the awning is retractable, oui?"

"Oui."

"Alors, I suggest you retract it the next time you or other people move things."

"But—"

"I'm sorry but we cannot cover this. Bonne journée."

The line goes dead. I'm out three thousand euros I could have spent on plants—my mother's advice, which I was seriously considering—or any other last-minute add-ons. This day is deteriorating faster than butter in one-hundred-degree heat.

CHAPTER FOUR

All Keyed Up

I FEEL LIKE I'VE been run over by a truck. Or like a piano crushed me. Although my energy is zapped, I decide to test the ceviche—get the mise en place of my life on track. Right about now, I need some confidence back, to prepare.

I cut off the bottom tip of a mango to balance it on my cutting board. Then I cut the meaty cheeks off, adjusting my knife when it hits the pit, and strip off the sides. I make lengthwise and crosswise cuts into one of the halves, careful not to slice through the peel. I'm about to invert the fruit so it sort of looks like a hedgehog and makes it easier to use all the mango goodness, when a burning odor wafts up to my nose. Confused, I look around. Not one burner is on. This ceviche is served raw, and I haven't started baking the bread, as it is still proofing.

Frantic, I wipe the sticky juices off my hands with a dish towel and bolt into the dining room, finding the source of the smell: my mother. She's waving a bundle of smoking herbs tied with a string and chanting. Bohemian chic, like always, she's dressed in one of her long flowing skirts with a Dharma wheel pattern and a white shirt, her long, silky gray hair, threaded with strands of white, down.

"Mom, what in the world are you doing?"

She looks at me with furrowed brows. "Kiki, I told you not to call me Mom anymore. We're both adults now."

"And I told you to stop calling me Kiki," I say, and she shimmies her shoulders, her lips twisting into a wicked grin.

"Our names rhyme. It's cute."

"Not in France. And you have the better nickname, *Christine*."

She twirls. "It's Cri-Cri now, not Mom or Christine. And I really don't understand what's so wrong with Kiki."

Somebody sedate me. "Mom, you know the problem," I huff, and she snorts.

At the age of six, my mom gave me the children's book *Kiki Dances* and I adored the story, keeping the tattered copy on my bookshelf, where it still rests today. When I was twelve, I'd decided Kiki was short for Katherine, and I insisted everybody call me by that. The name stuck until we moved to Paris, when, at the age of fifteen and on my first day at ASP (American School of Paris), I'd introduced myself to the class.

"Bonjour. I'm originally from Malibu, California. Uh, my name is Katherine Jenkins, but most people call me Kiki," I'd said, and the entire classroom burst into laughter.

With my cheeks flaming red, I'd tried to recover. "What's so funny? Kiki is short for Katherine, and one of my favorite children's books was *Kiki Dances*."

The laughter came harder. The teacher placed her hand over her mouth to hide her shocked amusement. I wanted to die. I mumbled, "I really don't understand why everybody is laughing."

Mark, one of the boys who didn't laugh at me, said, "*Kiki* is slang for 'dick' in French."

Oh.

My eyes went wide, and after I collected my mouth off the floor, I said, with an embarrassed laugh, "Well, that obviously doesn't work. Uh, call me Kate."

Throughout the following years at ASP, the obnoxious penis jokes popped up and "Kiki Dances" took on a whole new meaning with wiggling forefingers placed under the pants of the boys—as if I didn't get it. On the plus side, with no beach-body Malibu babes wearing bikini tops and shorts that rode up their asses in sight, I'd found a group of like-minded friends, including Mark, my first boyfriend and still one of my best friends to this day.

Don't let the name "American School" fool you. Sandy-blond and über-preppy Mark was from Australia, and more than half the students came from other countries, some of them French—a lot of them kids of diplomats. Plus, my classmates were foodies and not on starvation diets. Thanks to all the lavish dinner parties their parents threw, my taste buds were exposed to delights from all over the world, and the inspiration for the concept behind Bistro Exotique was born.

"Fine," says my mom. "I'll stop you calling you Kiki."

"Finally. You still haven't answered my question. Why are you saging the restaurant again?" I wave my hand in front of my face, thinking I probably shouldn't have given her a spare key. "You already did, and it stinks."

"After you told me what happened today, we have to get rid of the bad energy once and for all." She snuffs out the burning-sage bundle into an ashtray and steps over, wrapping me in the tightest of hugs. "I don't know what I'd do if something happened to you."

"I'm fine."

"You are more than fine! You're a dynamo!"

Her gaze meets mine when I roll my eyes, and then it darts to the walls.

"Where is my art? I thought you were using my pieces."

Uh-oh.

Growing up, my mom, a wacky sex therapist with three books to her name (*Unleashing Your Inner Tiger, Orgasms Are Zen,* and *The Vagina Code*), wanted to teach me about owning my body and freeing my mind. It was always so humiliating when I had to explain my mom's fixation with "cucumber" and "flower" art to friends when they came over. Still, as much as she embarrasses me, I do love my mother and her wildly weird ways. I just wish she'd tone her enthusiasm down by a notch or maybe ten thousand.

"M—Cri-Cri, I made a deal with one of the neighboring galleries," I say. "It's good for business. I get a commission if they sell. Your paintings are in my apartment."

I don't add: *in the closet, hidden where they belong and nobody can see them.*

She sighs and then nods. "Ah, oh well, but I think they'd be excellent conversation pieces."

Believe me, growing up they definitely were.

She winks when I wince and walks over to the butcher paper–covered windows, ripping one of the panels down. "Let's let a little light into this place. Let people take a sneak peek as to what's in store for them. Give them a taste." Mom turns to face me. "Like flirting."

"After today, I may be flirting with disaster," I say.

"Why don't you just close the electric shutter like the other windows?"

I sigh. "Because it broke last week, and the landlord hasn't fixed it yet. They probably never will, and, knowing my luck, a gang of thugs will loot the place."

"Don't be such a pessimist." Her hands flutter to her chest as she looks out the window. "I'd flirt with that." She waggles a pointed finger. "Go! Go! Go outside!" She eyes me up and down. "But maybe change your clothes first."

"Not going to happen."

I walk over to the window to see who or what has captivated her attention. And it's him—Anti-Keanu pacing on the street while talking on his cell phone. I shoot him the finger, whether he sees me or not I don't care, and, as I face my mom, I mumble, "He's the biggest dick I've ever met. And, even worse, he lives in the apartment underneath mine. I really don't want to cross paths with him ever again—"

She tilts her head to the side and lets out a giggle. "Ah, you're the woman on top. If I were your age, I'd definitely want to run into that. Nothing wrong with a big—"

I slap my hand to my forehead. "Mom! Seriously?"

"Cri-Cri," she responds.

I should be used to her word vomit and oversharing, but I'm not. When I was eighteen, she bought me a "surprise" present. It was a rabbit—and I'm not talking about a cute, furry creature with lopsided ears and a twitchy pink nose. No, my mother had gifted me a vibrator—totally inappropriate, especially since I was still a virgin—and told me I could name it. After all, I'd always wanted a pet bunny. She may have scarred me for life.

I may be a food whore, but at twenty-eight years old and with a mom like mine, this could come as a shock, but, in my mind, I'm still a virgin. Semantics. Closing yourself off is what happens when your mother tells you to open yourself up.

"Cri-Cri, I'm focusing on the success of my restaurant."

"What about your heart? You haven't dated anybody since Michael. You're young, you're beautiful—"

Damn. She just had to bring up the one and only real relationship I'd had that ended in disaster.

"My true love is the kitchen. I don't need the distraction of a relationship or flirtationship right now, especially with a jerk," I say, and my mom growls, such a weird gurgling sound I'm thinking she might be part coyote.

She taps the window. "That man is so handsome. And I think he's interested in you. He's eyeing the restaurant now. You know what they say, right? The way to a guy's heart is through his stomach and, well, his appetite for other things—"

"Gah." I throw up my hands in frustration. "If you think he's so good-looking, why don't you go flirt with him?"

Let her meet the devil incarnate face-to-face and see for herself.

"Because I have principles. He's way too young for me. I'm not a cougar."

"But you haven't dated anybody in years." I want to say *since Dad* but don't. She'd already pulled on a raw nerve when she'd mentioned Michael. No need to bring up the past again.

"I'm keen on the idea, but I haven't met anybody I want to spend time with." She rolls her shoulders. "Anyway, enough about that. I can see you're tense. I've always told you that when the winds of change blow your way, you have to decide which direction you want them to take you, and sometimes you just have to go with the flow—"

"To float into bliss."

Mom stops laughing and smiles. "You remember that?"

"I remember everything you taught me."

Though some of her lessons I'd truly like to forget. Every position in the Kama Sutra and then some.

"Good. And I want you to be happy. That's my biggest lesson. I'm so proud of you. Now, what were you preparing in the kitchen—can you can alter the recipe for me? I'm starving."

Good grief. I know where this conversation is headed even before I open my mouth.

"When are you going to admit that you're not actually a true vegetarian? I mean, you eat turkey on Thanksgiving—"

"It's tradition and everybody gets a day off. It's in the rule book." She winks. "By the way, I forgot to tell you, I'm pescatarian now. I need more protein in my diet. And fish don't have feelings."

A moot point. I'm not going to argue the ways she validates her ever-changing personal choices. She's hopped on every trend—Keto, Paleo, Atkins, and even gluten-free and vegan until she realized she couldn't eat all the buttery French breads and flavorful cheeses.

"Stop looking at me like that," she says as she scrutinizes my face and posture. "What were you making?"

"You're in luck. I'm testing out a new recipe," I say. "A ceviche with sea bass."

"Sounds delicious." She rubs her hands together. "Can't wait."

"I'll whip it up in an instant," I say, heading into the kitchen. I slam my knife into the sea bass, skinning it, and then slice the fish into pearlescent slivers. While it marinates, or rather, cooks in lime juice, I set to preparing the rest of the ingredients, chopping and dicing. A few minutes later, I combine all the ingredients in a large bowl, adding in the mango, avocado, cucumber, herbs, and spices—hot like my mood but offsetting the heat with more lime juice. Finally, I plate and garnish with cucumber in the smallest brunoise cuts, and cilantro, returning to the dining room with our meals. She's at the window again, and I'm hoping he's not there.

"What are you doing?"

"Just people watching," she says. "I'm wondering if there are many couples out there like the new clients I'm teaching about tantric sex. Such a sad story. The man is a premature ejaculator. Can you imagine?"

When it comes to her food choices and her practice, I think she's taken a hypocritical—not a Hippocratic—oath.

"No, I can't. And I also can't believe you're telling me this. What about doctor-patient confidentiality?"

She shrugs. "I didn't tell you their names. Paris has more than two million inhabitants, and more than seven million people in total if you include the surrounding suburbs. It could be anybody." She smiles. "Let's eat."

We sit at one of the tables by the now slightly uncovered window.

"I have amazing news to share. My publisher bought my next book." She claps her hands with excitement.

I wait for her to settle down and she continues.

"Unfortunately, they aren't going with the title I proposed, which was *Your Vulva Is Not a Volvo*, but I adore the new one."

I set my fork onto the plate. Vulva? And Volvo? Her grin stretches across her face and, instead of telling her what I really think, I have to be supportive. "And the new title is?"

She beats her hands onto the table in a drumroll.

"Stop being so dramatic."

"*The Chronicles of a Voracious Vulva*." Mom beams from ear to ear, her blue eyes lighting up like sparklers. She forms her hand into a claw, swiping it down like a cat. "Grrrr-row. Don't you love it?"

I choke on my tongue. No. Not at all. But I don't tell her I think it's horrendous because she's clearly happy. And I love her smile when it's all lit up. I'm also used to being extremely uncomfortable with her work. Instead, I say, "Who buys books like these anyway?"

"A lot of people. You should see my advance. A high six figures. Very high." She shimmies her shoulders and winks. "Everything will work out. It's kismet and karma." Mom takes a bite of her meal and looks up, mumbling with her mouth full. "Kiki, this is sex on a plate. I think I just had a foodgasm."

I let out a snort and sit back in my chair. "You need to stop making everything about sex."

"Ha! Not with something this good. And sex is life. If I hadn't had it, you wouldn't be here." She bangs her hands on the table, emulating the scene in the restaurant from *When Harry Met Sally*. When she's finished, she laughs like a wild hyena and meets my eyes. "I'll have what I'm having."

I sit stoic with my arms crossed over my chest. "Not the phrase."

"Come on, Kate, lighten up."

Granted, I'm used to her wackiness and, according to her, I'm wound up tighter than a bad facelift—rigid, stiff, and completely unnatural. Maybe she's right. Sometimes I wish I could be as free-spirited as she is. But I'm not.

"I'm just being me."

"And you are the best you." She shoves another forkful into her mouth, chews. "This, this is delicious."

I take a bite of the ceviche, and the melody of flavors is like a symphony in my mouth—all the flavors merging together—sweet, sour, hot, salty, and, yes, it *is* foodgasmic, but I'm not telling her that. My thoughts meander to Anti-Keanu and his perfect lips, and I can't help but wonder what his mouth tastes like—sweet, minty, savory?

Oh no, he got into my head and I'm so not going there. I just want to crawl into bed and forget the events of this day.

Mom pulls out a deck of gold foil cards with extremely detailed illustrations from her purse—this one classic, the art blending symbolism and icons. She must have at least twenty at home.

"Cri-Cri," I huff. "I really don't want a Tarot reading."

"Too bad. You're getting one." She slaps the deck on the table. "You know the drill."

"I don't believe in this mystical stuff."

"I do. The cards are simply meant to guide you. And by the look.

of it, you need a little guidance." She flips her hair over her shoulder. "Humor me. Split the deck."

With an annoyed sigh, I'm about to cut the deck into thirds when Mom coughs. "Tap the deck first to instill your energy into it. Then shuffle them. And then cut them into three piles."

I do as I'm told. Mom spreads the cards across the table like a fan. "Focus on the cards and choose the three that you feel most drawn to."

The cards are not calling to me, but I pretend like they do, choosing one in the middle and one from each end.

"Now, think about the question you want to ask."

"When is this going to end?"

"Kate, be serious."

"I am," I say, and Mom shoots me the stink eye. "Fine. I'm thinking about my question."

Will my restaurant succeed?

"Good." She flips the first card over and frowns. "Oh my, it's the ten of swords—this card indicates disaster."

"My life?"

"Don't be silly. Maybe the next one will be better." She gasps, "The tower," and clears her throat. "Well, the third card should be the charm." Her lips pinch together. "Death."

"Great, thanks for the reading." Shit. These are three of the worst cards imaginable—nothing good is going to come out of this.

Mom shimmies her shoulders and then straightens her posture. "Let's move on to the tower. So, while the card often means something is going to shake up your world—it's more of a warning to prepare you for a disaster. Which is why I like the death card for you."

"Put an end to my misery already. Kill me now."

"Stop being so morose. This card is symbolic of an ending, to focus on new beginnings, to make changes or you're headed for self-destruction." She leans forward. "You have to bring renewal and transformation into your life."

"You're right," I say, and Mom jolts.

She places her hand over her heart. "Who are you? And where did you put my daughter?"

"I need to evolve. Failure is not an option." I stand up and grab our plates. "And, on that, I have things to do in the kitchen. Thanks for stopping by."

Picking up on the not-so-subtle hint, she sets down her fork and stands up. She kisses me on the cheek. "I know you're busy, Katie-Bug. I'll see you at the opening. I'm so excited."

Like a tornado of energy, my mom races to the front door, her hair blowing in the breeze. After she leaves, the restaurant still smells of burnt sage, and I decide to leave the door open to air the place out. The last time my mother had done this, it took four days to get rid of the stench. Before I head back into the kitchen, I sit at the bar with my moleskin notebook to look at the remainder of my list.

8. Find out what happened to the previous tenant
9. Google Garrance

I sigh—no need to call my mom now—and add:

11. Call landlord to fix the electric *volet*
12. Bake the bread

The landlord can wait. It's time to google the previous tenant, knowing I probably should have done more research when I signed the lease. I know the name of the former restaurant, Les Endives, so I start there. Article after article pops up. One, in particular, catches my eye. I skim it, latching on to the facts.

Chef Jean-Paul Beaufort was born in Marseille, moving to Paris at the age of sixteen, where he worked in the restaurant industry for twenty years until he struck out on his own with his flagship restaurant in the tenth arrondissement, Les Endives. Well received in the neighborhood at its start, offering French classics at a moderate price, Les Endives was poised for success.

When the prices of his menu went up, along with a pricier wine list, a new client base infiltrated the bistro, some of them, according to a witness, rather unsavory. Soon, rumors circulated that Beaufort was victim to a wine Ponzi scheme to the tune of one million euros and fell into serious financial trouble, connecting Beaufort to mobsters in Marseilles.

The police have treated his disappearance as a case of murder, but his fate is unclear.

I can't believe what I'm reading. What Garrance told me is true. Time to google her. A couple of articles pop up, spouting off the same thing. My heartbeat slows down to a throbbing pulse as I read.

She's a widow and a prime shareholder of the Tenang Resort group—the average room running around fourteen hundred euros a night in twenty locations around the world, including Paris, and she's one of the wealthiest woman in France—exact worth unknown. I learn that her husband, Peter Lin, born in Jakarta but raised in Singapore, died in a plane crash two years ago along with Garrance's father.

I click through more articles, surprised to find out that her son is a Michelin-starred chef who disappeared from the culinary scene two years ago—around the time Garrance's husband and father met their fates. Words like "elusive" pop up in every article. There are no photos, which I find quite odd, especially for a Michelin-starred chef.

Before I can dive into more research, I hear light footsteps and look over my shoulder. As if on cue, Garrance swaggers into the restaurant with Juju, now wearing a blinged-out ruby-red collar. A shiver shimmies its way down my spine. I close out of the browser and clasp my phone, straightening my posture and on full alert. Perhaps I'm super paranoid, but something about her doesn't add up.

"*Coucou!*" (hey, there), she says.

"Garrance, bonjour," I say with trepidation. "I, uh, wasn't expecting you."

"Sorry to barge right in. The door was open." She makes her approach, her skirt swooshing. "I was so sorry to see what happened this morning. Are you okay?"

"I'm fine. Thank you for asking." I clear my throat, wanting to test her. Depending on her response, I'll know if I should be worried. "You'll be happy to know that the new awning will be emerald green."

Her hands flutter to her chest, and she gasps. "What a wonderful choice!"

"Not mine," I mumble.

Her head tilts to the side. "At any rate, as mentioned, I'm here because I wanted to check in to see if you were okay, and I'm glad to see you are. Also, I brought you something. They're the finest of *salicornes*, green beans from the sea, from Brittany, *très exotique*. I thought you'd adore them."

She holds out a large bag and, without even opening it, the scent envelops me and I'm no longer in the restaurant. I'm running by the ocean, powdery sand sticking in between my toes, waves crashing around me as I dive into the sea with reckless abandon. The water swells into a froth, whipped like freshly made Chantilly. My body glistens with water droplets. A man sweeps me into his arms—Anti-Keanu—and we're kissing just like in the scene in *From Here to Eternity*, the tide surging. I'm almost mouthing the words "I never knew it could be like this. No one ever kissed me the way you do," when I finally snap out of this creepy, scent-induced trance.

"Merci," I say, wanting to stay on her good side. She could be working with the Mafia and I don't want to *poof*—disappear into thin air.

Garrance straightens her posture, eyes me curiously. She places the bag on the bar. "Use this as you see fit. I'll see you at the opening. We're really looking forward to it."

I can't find three simple words: *Please don't come.*

"Oui," I say. "See you."

With his orange eyes blazing bright, Juju swishes his tail as if to say *Stupid human*, and then they are gone. Once I gather my wits, I get up from my seat and I'm about to throw her box of killer sea green beans into the garbage when I think: *Keep it, it could be evidence of her involvement with the previous owner's disappearance and more.*

CHAPTER FIVE

Mayday. M'aider.

TODAY HAS TO be better than yesterday or I'll snap.

After jumping out of the shower, I brush my hair, tying it back in a messy bun, and throw on a pair of fitted sweatpants and a clean T-shirt. I still have dirty work to tackle, and this outfit is better than yesterday's.

In the past, you'd never see a woman on the streets of Paris wearing workout pants because it's assumed you'd been working out and, if so, were unhygienic. Today, more and more ladies are bopping around town in stylish track pants, thanks to high-end designers like Gucci, Lacoste, and Chloé embracing sportswear, women choosing comfort and style. The fashion world calls this look "athleisure" and it's occasionally paired with a cute cardigan, ballet flats, and a wide headband. Which, after yesterday's comments from my mother and Anti-Keanu's attitude, is exactly what I'm going to do.

As I snake down the stairwell, I peek into the landing of the second floor: the coast is clear—no sign of the beast. I breathe out a sigh of relief and race down the steps, open the front door, and scramble to the sidewalk, eyeing the destruction before I head into my space.

I squint, trying to visualize the look, thinking a dark emerald green wouldn't be too bad. Although not my vision, the color might be nice, and I just have to adapt to the situation—get my mise en place in position, prepare myself for this setback because it's completely out of my control.

Before I unlock the front door, my eyes focus on Garrance's shop. In the window, white curtains flutter. Juju's collar sparkles in the sunlight, and bright orange eyes meet my gaze. He licks his chops. Her sign sways in the wind. Madame Lìn-Truffaut: She's not a spice master; she's a master of disguise. Red manicured nails grip the curtain, and Juju's tail swishes. I turn around quickly and enter the restaurant.

The butcher paper my mother pulled down from the window flaps in the breeze, thanks to my leaving the door open. I grab a roll of tape from behind the bar to patch it back up. People can experience the magic of this space when I'm good and ready. I'm not ready now. And damn it. Why hasn't the landlord fixed the electric shutter? I make a mental note to call them. Again.

It takes me a few minutes to find the edge of the tape (why does it always stick like that?) with my short ridged nails, and I'm about to seal the paper when every hair on my body bristles. Two hands surround hazel eyes like binoculars, peering in. I recognize those sexy eyes, that chiseled jawline with the perfectly trimmed two-day scruff.

I jump back, startled, as he gestures for me to come outside.

What the hell? I am so not expecting this. In my head, I prepare myself to not let him get under my skin.

I stomp out of the restaurant and onto the sidewalk, placing my hands on my hips. "What do you want?"

He shuffles his feet. "I wanted to apologize to you for being so rude yesterday."

And now I'm completely floored.

"Thank you," I say, a flame of hope lighting my chest.

He eyes me as if he's expecting me to say something else. But I didn't do anything wrong.

"Apology accepted."

"Good. We're neighbors, and we should try to get along." He shrugs and offers a sly smile. "So could you do me a favor, neighbor, and stop playing your awful music and singing along with it? I can hear you through the vents quite loudly."

I want to die. Sometimes to unwind, I'll open a bottle of wine and dance and sing along to Ed Sheeran. On repeat. I didn't think anybody could hear me. But he obviously did. Merde. My cheeks grow hot. I have to change the subject. "Did you want to come to the opening of the restaurant?"

"Non, merci," he says with a smirk. "Your meals might be as horrifying as your voice—"

I shake my head, immediately put on the defense. "My voice isn't bad. And my dishes are amazing. And you're being totally rude again."

"I'm just telling you like it is," he says, turning on his heel. "Keep it down. Okay?"

Shaking my head, I watch him swagger down the street in his designer clothes and I'm more angry right now than I am embarrassed. I yell, "You being nice? It was a trap! Apology no longer accepted!"

He turns around and blows me a kiss before walking on.

Every muscle in my body tightens like wound coils.

Forget about him. Forget about his stupidly beautiful face. He's not worth my salt or, for that matter, my pepper. I have more important things to do, and thinking about him is not one of them. I dance my way back into the restaurant, singing "Push It," my voice loud and clear and, no, I don't think it's bad.

* * *

IT'S NOW NINE in the morning and I'm waiting for my sous-chef, Natalie, a classmate from Le Cordon Bleu and coworker at my former restaurant Cendrillon Paris, to arrive and help me prep and cook all the meals for the staff's tasting. She should be here any minute, and the rest of the team is set to arrive at 2:00 p.m.

A few months ago, we trained the staff with the ordering system for three intensive days, and I'm hoping they remember everything they'd learned, as Saturday will be the first day of actual service.

As for hires, I'm keeping it light: one roustabout (all-around kitchen guy whose duties include dishwashing), a mixologist, and three servers for each service, who will share the task of playing the host or hostess. The restaurant can seat fifty to sixty covers, including the terrace, but I'm starting off with forty, and will work my way up to full capacity when I'm ready.

To calm my deep-fried nerves, I set to making the panko-encrusted lime-and-coconut calamari I'd discovered while vacationing in Martinique with my parents when they were still married—one of the planned appetizers I've developed with my own spicy twist—a whisper of hot serrano chili powder, and served with a roasted garlic-lime aioli. Unfortunately, the aromas of lime and coconut are not making me feel better.

I'm chopping up cilantro when Natalie slinks into the kitchen. We exchange *les bises*, kissing each other's cheeks. She pulls away, her mouth twisting into a grimace.

"Is something wrong?" I ask, and she nods. "Are you sick?"

Instead of meeting my concerned gaze, she focuses on the floor and taps a nervous foot. "Sick with guilt."

My knife clatters on the prep table. "What's up? You know me; you can tell me anything."

"You're not going to like it." She places one hand on her hip. "I can't work for you. A start-up restaurant is too risky."

Anger and panic flame in my neck. "And you couldn't have told me your concerns sooner? Like weeks ago?"

"I didn't have the offer weeks ago." She pauses. "Chef Monica gave me a promotion. I'm staying on at Cendrillon as the new sous-chef."

The gravity of this situation sets in. I bite down on my bottom lip knowing that by the pinched look twisting her face, there isn't anything I can do or say to convince her to stay. The traitor. I should have known better.

And *bam!* Like Emeril, my day just got worse.

"You're leaving me high and dry? A day before the opening?"

She turns to leave, her long ponytail whipping my face. "I'm sorry if you hate me and never want to speak with me again, but I have to look out for my career. And the path for my culinary future isn't here."

And then she's gone, leaving me wrecked and stressed. I rub my temples, my cheek. What am I going to do? How could she have done this to me? I want to throw up. I set to looking over my lists and prepping—frantic, trying to convince myself I can manage on my own. It'll be tough, but I can do it. I didn't come this far to fail.

BY NOON, I'M still reeling from this unexpected sucker punch, and I'm hunched over at the bar, tempted to drink. But I'm not about to lose my mind—no, if anything, I'm staying in control. I'm in somewhat of an angry trance, mumbling every swear word under the sun, when Oded walks into the restaurant holding an elegant blue-and-white star-patterned ceramic dish with a matching lid.

"I hope I'm not disturbing you," he says, and I eye him warily.

"You're not. I have a few minutes. But please tell me that you are not trying to poison me like Garrance. She gave me a bag of something very suspicious yesterday." I correct myself when his eyes go wide. "Salicornes—green beans of the sea."

"I don't know who Garrance is or why she gave you salicornes. But this is my apology for the awning—a peace offering of sorts." He points to the dish and sets it on the bar. "I know you're a chef, and I wanted to do something nice for you."

I can't remember the last time anybody cooked for me—if ever. This is a surprise—hopefully a nice one.

I lift up the lid and inhale the aromas of what looks like a flaky pot pie, dusted with powdered sugar, the top scored in a crosshatch pattern. And holy moly, mother of the gods, I'm embraced by heavenly scents. Spicy. Sweet. Savory. Delicious. I commandeer a fork, take a bite, chew, and then swallow. Three layers of flavors infused with chicken, egg, and almonds melt on my tongue, the finish topped off with whispers of orange blossom, saffron, ginger, cumin, and turmeric. "This is absolutely incredible. What is this delight?"

"Bastilla," he says with a proud smile. "It's a typical recipe from Morocco, where I'm originally from, usually made with pigeon, but this one is made with chicken. My mother's recipe. It's also called pastilla."

"Are you a chef?"

"No, but my parents had a restaurant, and I helped them out when I was younger." Tears sparkle in his eyes. "As I told you the other day, I'm a musician." He gulps. "One without a piano."

"I get your distress. I can't imagine not having my knives," I say, and his eyes go wide.

"Ah, I'd want to murder me too," he says with a wheeze. "Again, I'm so sorry."

"Stop apologizing. Not your fault. I don't want to kill you, especially after tasting this," I say, locking on to his sad gaze. "What kind of music do you play?"

"Mostly classical, but I can conquer anything. I'm self-taught, know my way around every instrument. Some people call it a gift," he says, straightening his shoulders with pride. "I believe I told you that music is my life."

Returning his smile, I say, "Food is mine." I clear my throat and nod at the dish. "Did you want some?"

"Non, merci, it's for you. Like music, food brings people together, oui?"

"Yes, yes it does," I say with a slight frown. My fork clatters on the bar.

His eyes widen with worry. "What's wrong? Is it the bastilla?"

"No," I say. "It's wonderful. Other things are bothering me. I don't want to bore you."

"You can talk to me," he says. "If you want to. Sometimes we need to let things out and not hold them in."

Needing to unload, I tell him about Anti-Keanu and how I think wacky Garrance is behind the destruction, how she could be part of some kind of Mafia. Then I tell him about how my insurance won't cover the awning, and his face crumbles into a concerned frown.

He huffs. "Our neighbor is rude, that's true, and this Garrance may be odd, but it wasn't her piano. It was mine. She didn't have anything to do with it. It's my fault. I'm so, so sorry. What can I do?"

"For now, nothing," I say. "I'm dealing with it."

"I can't live with that."

I point to the bastilla. "This was your mother's creation?"

"Yes. Why?"

"How about sharing the recipe with me?"

"I'll gladly share the recipe, but that's not enough," he says, shaking his head from side to side. He takes in a breath. "Look. I don't have the kind of money to help you pay for the awning, but I can help you out whenever you need it for free. I can run errands. Maybe coordinate and unload the deliveries in the morning?" He points to the outdoor seating. "Or set up the terrace? I want to help."

Mayday. Mayday.

The phrase comes from the French verb *m'aider*, meaning "help me," and, boy, do I need help. I realize Oded could be a solution—at least temporarily.

My words come out in a whoosh. "I have a *huge* favor to ask of you."

"Anything," he says. "I owe you."

I begin, and then, with a shaky voice, explain what just went down with Natalie. "Can you help me out in the kitchen? I know you can cook," I say, holding in my breath, watching his reaction. "Don't feel obligated. You can say no. I'm just grasping at straws here. I don't know what to do—"

Oded clasps onto my quivering shoulders like a dad trying to calm down his keyed-up daughter. "Save for a couple of auditions, I don't have any events planned for a few weeks." He winks and nods his head enthusiastically. "Sounds fun. I'm in. It's been a while since I've worked in a professional kitchen. Now, tell me what to do, Chef."

A sense of relief snakes through my entire body.

"Thank you so, so, so much," I say, and he smiles, "but just re-member you signed up for this. Well, there's that, and I'm paying you." He's about to argue with a "Non, non, non," when I cut him off. "I'll still need help setting up the terrace, and maybe you can run the occasional errand. Deal?" I stick out my hand, and he takes it.

"Deal." He pauses. "Are there uniforms?"

"There are," I say. "But they're not stuffy."

I head over to the locker and grab an apron and a baseball cap, both imprinted with the logo of the restaurant. As I hand them to Oded, he smiles and says, "I have a good feeling about this."

That makes one of us. I'm not sure what I'm feeling. Panic and fear aren't the best of ingredients. But I'm doing my best to swallow them down.

I breathe out a sigh of relief. "Good. We're going to start with my version of tacos, the tortillas made with duck fat." I pause, look at the ceiling with remembrance. Fish taco Fridays—like the ones I'd had in Malibu. "One thing I miss from my days in the States is good Mexican food. They don't have it here."

"Mexican? But we're in France," says Oded.

"Yep, I know, but this dish has a French twist." I laugh. "I guess I should call it Frexican."

His eyes twinkle. "I'm liking the sound of this already—very unique."

I grin. He didn't call my dishes or me basic.

With the Natalie problem handled, I'm about to tackle my list—like finalizing the menu and sending it on to my graphic designer friend so I can print them out—when I pull out my phone, glancing at it. A couple of missed calls and texts await.

> DAD: I'm sorry, honey. Can't make it to the opening. I have a big deal coming up. Proud of you!

A wave of disappointment washes over me. He's never been truly present in my life—kind of there as a kid but definitely not as an adult. The last time I saw him was four years ago, when he was closing one of his huge deals in Paris. We spent a whole fifteen minutes together before he rushed off. Over the years, I've gotten used to being let down. But this time stings more than the others. I call my mom.

"Dad blew me off again," I say.

"Figures."

"Seriously, why did you leave him? And move us here?" I lean forward, gripping the phone. "Tell me the truth, not the watered-down one you always tell me."

Growing up, Mom and Dad never fought. There was always a lot of laughter. You'd think we were the perfect family. Mom always gave me straight answers about sex—but not much about anything else. And I really didn't need to know that much about the clitoris or voracious vulvas or Petey the Perky Penis.

"We just grew apart, had different dreams and goals. When he first started making mountains of money, he changed, got wrapped up in all that flash—the fancy cars, the big house on the beach, the designer clothes, but I didn't change with him, and I think he was embarrassed of me. So we agreed to follow our separate dreams."

"A dream that clearly doesn't include me," I say.

"Some people have different goals," she responds. "He loves you, but . . ."

"He loves his deals more," I say.

"I'm sorry, sweetie, but some people change, and sometimes it's not for the better. His priorities are just out of whack." She gulps. "I'd do anything for you, and I'm so damn proud of you. I love you so much—"

"Thanks, Mom," I say. "Love you too. I've got to go. See you at the opening."

With a sigh, I hang up and scroll down to the next text from Caroline, the first French friend I'd made in France. We are polar opposites—she's gorgeous and slim with slick chestnut hair, and is a full-fledged fashionista. Currently working at Maison de la Barguelonne, one of Paris's largest purveyors of luxury brands, she's been begging to dress me for the opening.

> CARO: Why aren't you picking up? I have to talk
> to you!

> CARO: Seriously, Kate. Call me back asap.

I dial her number and she picks up on the first ring. "What's going on?"

She wheezes. "I c-caught—" She gulps and then continues breathlessly. "I caught Hugo cheating. With his pants down. Screwing one of the models from the show in the corner of a dressing room. The engagement is off."

I suck in my surprise. "Merde."

Caro has been wedding planning for months, enlisting me, her faithful friend, as the maid of honor. Knowing her the way I do, she needs to scream and vent and doesn't want advice or pity. The same way she was for me when my boyfriend Michael broke up with me right after we'd had sex—the reason I still deny the loss of my virginity. I just need to listen to her, be a friend without judgment. "I don't know what to say, but I'm here for you."

"I know. Which is why I'm coming over. He stayed in a hotel last night, but that cheating, lying bastard is moving his stuff out of my place tonight, and I don't want to be there when he does because I might kill him." She lets out a sad laugh and says, "Hold on." I hear her mumble to somebody about a new line of dresses. "Look, I have to get myself together before a meeting so I don't act like a psychopath." She pauses. "And, no, before you ask, I haven't been crying. I'm too angry for that."

"Got it." I pause, thinking about what she'd done for me after my big breakup. We'd gone to this rage room where they supplied baseball bats and a variety of things—plates, computers, whatever—to break, thus releasing stress and pent-up anger. "Do you want to go to that place where we can smash stuff and scream? Could be fun?"

"Non, I have zero energy for that. I just want to decompress with you," she replies. "Alors, I'm coming over to your place after work, around seven, and we are going to eat like pigs and drink like fishes. Okay?"

"Sounds like an excellent plan."

"Love you, Katie-Bug."

"Love you too, Caro-Bear. See you tonight."

The line clicks to a close, and I feel terrible that I felt sorry for myself. Caro's problem is way more serious than mine. I can fix an awning, but a broken heart takes a long time to heal, and I'm speaking from experience. Perhaps my mother didn't scare me away from sex and opening up my heart: Michael did.

With a huff, after checking off everything on my list, I stuff a couple of bottles of wine in my purse. Needing to stay clearheaded and in control, I'm not sure I want to drink, but friends don't let friends wallow alone, and tonight we're going to let loose, if only for a few hours.

CHAPTER SIX

All Night Long

I'S A LITTLE after seven, and I'm waiting for Caro, who is notoriously a half hour late, sometimes more. The evening is warm, and I open up the windows. A nice late-spring breeze flows into the apartment, bringing a strong scent along with it. I lean slightly out the window, hear the clatter of knives, the sizzle of a pan coming from the apartment below. I sniff the air: garlic and onions. Anti-Keanu must be cooking and using the perfect ingredients to describe his personality.

But then a new scent wraps around me, and it smells so good—sweet and fragrant. I close my eyes, trying to figure out what he's making. Instead of conjuring up a recipe, I'm lost in his embrace. Strong hands pull me close. I'm staring into his beautiful lips, his eyes and—

The doorbell rings.

Get a grip, Kate.

With a shudder, I buzz Caro into the building and open my front door. Damn Anti-Keanu. I have to stop fantasizing about him. Maybe the fact he doesn't pose a threat is the reason why he pops into my thoughts? He can't hurt me because never in a million years would we be together.

Caro barges into the apartment. She hangs a garment bag onto the closet door. As usual, she looks fabulous in a fitted black skirt, a pale pink silk blouse with lace insets, and heels so high I wonder how she walks in them. She slams the door behind her. "Men! I hate them!"

Was she reading my mind, or what? "Me too," I say. "What's going on with Hugo? Are you okay?"

"I don't want to talk about him until we have some wine." She heads into the small kitchen, sniffing the air. "Something smells delicious. What did you make? I think I'm gaining weight just smelling it."

"I didn't make anything," I say, and close the window. "My jerk of a neighbor is stinking up the whole building." I pause. "I thought we'd order in Chinese from Fangs like the good ol' days."

Caro raises a manicured brow. She opens up a bottle of wine. "They deliver?"

"Uber Eats."

"*Oh mon dieu*, yes!" She shuffles through the cabinets and then pours two glasses of pinot noir, handing me one. "I haven't had their veggie moo shu in such a long time. Let's splurge and get the dumplings too. My treat. You are really my bae."

"True, and I love it, but nobody really uses that expression anymore."

"Alors, let's come up with a French version," she says, tapping her chin in thought. "*Avant tout le monde*. You're my ATM." She blows me a kiss.

"Um, no, I'm not a cash machine," I say, and we crack up. "How about fam. You're my fam—short for *famille*."

She kisses me on the cheek. "*J'adore ça*. You are like a sister to me."

Caro and I met a few days after my mom and I had moved to Paris. She lived in the apartment next door, and I didn't think somebody as cool as her would want to be friends, but the second she found out I was American, we became inseparable, attached at the hip. We had more in common than I thought, namely our taste in music, movies, and TV shows. Plus, she loved hanging out at my place and laughing at my mother's so-called art.

After ordering our nostalgic meal, we settle on the couch, kicking off our shoes. "What's that weird thing?" she asks, pointing to the polished steel, dented spaceship-like monstrosity set on my coffee table.

"It's a hang drum," I say. "My mom gave it to me a few months ago."

Caro hits the drum a few times. The sound is tranquil, mysterious, a bit haunting, and fills the room, reverberating in my chest. A warmth, a silence, a joy envelops my body, a bit like meditating.

"It's mesmerizing." She tilts her head to the side. "How is Cri-Cri, anyway?"

"The same—wacky as ever. She's threatened to play her drum at the opening. Oh, and, I caught her saging my place the other day. Again."

"Why?"

"To get rid of the bad energy."

"Send her over to my place," says Caro with a huff. "It needs to be super-saged. I'm going to burn all my sheets." Her eyes narrow, and she takes a sip of wine. "Tell me. What did you really think of Hugo?"

Did she want an honest answer? What if they got back together? We've been down this road before in our early twenties, and I'd gotten supremely ticked off when she'd warned me about Michael. "I didn't really think about him."

"Kate! He's dead to me. He's canceled. Now tell me the truth."

"Well," I say, starting off hesitantly, and Caro motions for me to carry on, "he was a little too polished, maybe a little skeevy and a little pompous—"

"Beyond pompous. Do you know he took longer to get ready than me? And you know how long it takes me." She snorts. "All that hair gel, every strand in place. And, ouf, he wore so much cologne. I'm better off without him. And I now have my bathroom back."

"What are you going to do about the wedding?"

"Cancel everything." She frowns and gulps down a sip of wine, her brown eyes losing their former luster, darkening.

"I'm sorry," I say, clasping onto her hand. "How are you coping?"

"Ah, I could be better. I want to stuff my face with cheese and chocolate and drink champagne while I'm curled on the couch watching romantic comedies on Netflix on my iPad."

I know she likes big screens, especially when binge-watching shows. I also know she never drinks alone. "Not your enormous TV with high def?"

"The *connard* is actually taking it." She sniffs. "Of course, he paid for it, but still—"

"Oh, *putain.*"

"Oui, putain." Caro lets out a breath and then sips her wine. "I've already deleted or ripped up every single photo of him. That felt good, even though I've wasted four years of my life." She lets out a sad laugh and then tops of our glasses. "You know what? I don't want to talk about him anymore."

"Got it," I say. "But if you want to cry—you know you can ugly cry in front of me."

"I know, but I can't. I think I'm still in shock." She grabs my hands. "Tell me what's going on with you. It feels like an eternity since we've hung out. I need to laugh tonight."

Where do I start? The past few days have been less than amusing.

I take in a deep breath and begin telling her about Anti-Keanu and the strange spice lady with her creepy cat. Laughter ensues.

AFTER CHOWING DOWN our moo shu and updating Caro, I open up another bottle of wine. Caro turns on the stereo, linking her iPhone to my Bluetooth speaker. Soon, we're clomping around the apartment to the music we listened to as teens—Britney Spears, Beyoncé, and, for good measure, a little Billie Eilish. Both of us love pop music and rom-coms, the cheesier the better. As Caro wiggles her butt, she spills her glass of Pinot on the floor.

"Whoops, sorry about that."

"Don't worry. I've got it."

I race to the kitchen for a stack of towels—a bonus of running a restaurant. While I'm cleaning up, the music changes and we're singing the lyrics to Taylor Swift's "We Are Never Ever Getting Back Together" at the top of our lungs, Caro beating the hang drum. Somebody pounds on the door. I dance over to the entry and open it, my eyes narrowing with confusion the moment I do: Anti-Keanu.

"Oh, it's you," I say.

He's wearing gym shorts and a tight T-shirt, both highlighting his glorious muscles, his tattoo—inked black and an intricate design of a lotus flower. I gulp and meet his gaze, blinking.

"It's me, neighbor."

"Here to offer up another fake apology?"

"Nope," he says, shaking his head. "Something else." He holds out a ball of white fabric, stained red. "You ruined my one-thousand-thread-count duvet."

"I'm sorry?" I don't really hear him because I'm staring at his mouth.

"Finally, an apology from you," he says. "And you should be sorry."

"For what?"

"Do I have to repeat myself?" he asks and I nod. "You ruined my duvet."

"Oh, please. How could I have ruined it?"

He points to the glass of wine in my hand, and then, over my shoulder, to the towels. "Perhaps with that. Your drink seeped through the floor. You owe me a new duvet or nine hundred euros."

Caro joins me, her eyes darting from side to side, assessing him and me. He crosses his muscular arms across his fabulous formed chest and for a moment I'm thrown for a loop.

"No way," I huff. "It's not my fault the floors are porous. Take it up with management."

He glowers. "Maybe I will. And maybe I'll have you evicted."

"Good luck with that," I say with a smirk. "You know how French laws work."

His threat is empty. When it comes to real estate, the laws in France protect the renters, not the owners. Even if he starts the eviction process, it could still take up to three years to get rid of me.

"Alors, then I'll report you to the police," he says, and I raise my hands, palms up, as if to say *For what, you douche?*

He sneers and continues, "For a noise violation and ruining personal property. This is your second warning—"

"Maybe I'll report *you*," I say, pointing at him.

"For what?"

"Ruining my day. Twice."

"You're crazy."

He said the c-word again. This time I do come back with a retort— one I'll later blame on Caro for drinking more than our fair share of wine, save for the glass she spilled, and putting me in this ridiculous confrontation. "You don't know me. Maybe I *am* crazy. I'd sleep with one eye open tonight."

Caro nudges me in the ribs and whispers, "I can't believe you just said that."

With a look of utter disgust, he turns on his heel and storms down the hall.

"Wait, neighbor," I call out. "I don't even know your name."

"Not telling you. You just threatened my life." Looking over his shoulder, he meets my eyes and says, "I'm serious. I will report you. So I suggest you keep your music down and stop clomping around. And definitely stop singing. You both have terrible voices, like howling hyenas. And it's definitely killing me. Believe me, I couldn't think of a worse way to die."

I slam the door shut. Caro is hunched over with laughter, wheezing. "I take it that was Anti-Keanu. Maybe *you* should report him."

"For what?"

She waves her hand dramatically like a fan. "For being so extremely gorgeous."

"Not funny," I say, although I'm thinking the same thing.

We plop onto the couch, me livid. "I hate men," I say, turning the volume down on the stereo. "Okay. I take it back. I don't hate *all* men. Oded, my neighbor, the other guy I told you about, is sweet, and he's also a lifesaver."

For a moment, we sit in silence.

Caro pours us another glass of wine, and we clink glasses. "At least we have each other forever and ever." She nods to the closet. "And, don't argue with me, but I brought you something exquisite to wear to the opening."

Ugh. The opening. I still have so much to do. I finally unzip the garment bag Caro had brought over. I gasp as I stroke the silk before pulling it out from the plastic. Curious, I check out the label: *Madeleine Bouchard*. Holy haute couture! This dress probably cost more than two thousand euros.

I set the dress on the couch and eye my best friend. "Caro! I can't accept this," I say. "It's too expensive."

"You can and you will," she says. "I didn't pay for it. It's a perk of working at Maison de la Barguelonne. Well, there's that, and it's from last year's summer collection." She pauses. "I hope you don't mind."

"Mind? It's glorious. And beggars can't be choosers!"

"Try it on."

"On it."

I scramble out of my track pants and T-shirt, quickly pulling the dress over my body and zipping up the side. This shimmering gold and navy luxurious design surely came right off the runway. The dress hits right above the knee, and the tie at the neck with the ruffled edges around the V-neckline make my waist look thin, downplaying the size of my enormous breasts, though they still look amazing.

"It's a perfect fit!"

"Twirl," she orders, and I do. "I knew you'd look absolutely fabulous."

I grin. "What would I do without you?"

"Well, you'd probably be wearing something horrific at the opening."

"True," I reply.

Caro's cell buzzes. She glances at it and blows out a sigh of relief. "He's gone. And I should get going too. Honestly, I'm spent."

"Do you want to crash here?"

"Non, that's okay," she says, standing up. "I think I need some time to process everything on my own."

I'll give her space if she truly wants it. "You sure?"

"I'm sure." She hugs me and then kisses my cheeks. "Love you, Katie-Bug."

"Love you more, Caro-Bear."

After Caro leaves, I sit on the couch, feeling stuck. I want to do so much more for her but know that she'll ask when she's ready. Sometimes people need to sort and categorize exactly what they're feeling before letting somebody else in. She's one of those people who needs to be ready to let go of her emotions, and I am one too. I just hope she doesn't hold everything in for too long.

I'm stripping out of my gorgeous dress when I hear a woman's laughter, followed by a man's deep and throaty voice. I throw the gown on the couch and shimmy into my sweats. A bang. A dish breaking? Is somebody having fake movie sex? Close encounters of the uncomfortable kind? My answer comes when animalistic moans echo in my apartment. They're coming from the vent, so I know they're coming from Anti-Keanu's apartment, and whoever is making the noise is definitely not in pain and she's definitely not eating. His words have the hairs on my arms standing on end.

"I'm going to lick the chocolate off every inch of your beautiful body, every curve."

"Oui, oui," says the woman with enthusiastic moans.

My face grows warm. I shouldn't be listening, but I can't help myself, and I'm rendered immobile. Why is the sound so clear? Is he by the vent? Inside of it? Granted, he's unbelievably hot, but he's also an asshole—I wonder what kind of woman would want to be with him.

Not me. Hell no.

I seriously need to invest in a noise-canceling headset—the best on the market. I don't care what it costs.

Annoyance overtakes me as her squeaky sighs and gasps fill my apartment. This salacious dude really needs to curb her enthusiasm.

I've had it. I throw my square-heeled boots on and jump as hard as I can.

Silence.

I'm about to head to bed when hard knocks pummel my floor. Not that I'm Ms. Maturity, but he's stooping to these kinds of tactics? What did he do? Grab a broom? I yell into the vent. "I'm going to report you."

"Go ahead," he yells back. "And good luck with *that*. As far as I know, amazing sex with a beautiful woman isn't a crime."

The squeaks and sighs start up again. The moaning and thrashing and the banging echoes in my apartment, this time louder.

"Don't stop. Don't stop."

"Baby, I'm not going to."

"Please, give me more. Deeper."

"Do you like it like this?"

"Harder."

I feel dirty listening, but I'm completely transfixed, I can't move. I'm also a little turned on, imagining his lips on mine, his vanilla scent. I'm also wondering if he's purposely being loud because of Caro and me. Did we piss him off that much? And he has to prove a point? One thing's for sure, this building has excellent acoustics. The banging and moaning goes on for a good half an hour, and I'm wishing I didn't understand French.

Finally. Silence.

I'm about to brush my teeth and then get some much-needed sleep when the sexual Olympics start up again. "Oui," comes the woman's moan. "Oui! Oui! Oui!"

I put in earplugs and pull my pillow over my head. Along with worrying about the opening, this is apparently going to be a very long night.

CHAPTER SEVEN

Bang, Bang—He Shot Me Down

Thanks to my awful neighbor, I've barely slept a wink, his sexcapade lasting for hours and then again in the morning. Seriously. Does the guy run on Energizer batteries? Is he *that* insatiable? I'm thrashed. Tired beyond all belief. I'm even hallucinating, envisioning his smug face. Such a pretty face.

Stop. Thinking. About. Him.

I throw on my boots, and as I get ready for the day, I stomp around the apartment. "Sleep through this, Anti-Keanu." I'm tempted to River Dance but want to save my energy.

Rude, crude, and despicable, he's not worth my time or aggravation. I have way bigger fish to fry. I slap my cheeks, trying to get back to life before another day sets in followed by a very important evening. Tonight is the opening, and I'm a little bit nervous but excited all the same. I pull out my list, going over every last detail, knowing to prepare for the unexpected and maybe come up with a plan for the perfect murder.

1. 6:30–8:00 a.m.: food deliveries (me and Oded)
    2. Tear down the butcher paper covering the windows, confirm final guest list
    3. Prep all dishes (me, Oded, line cooks)
4. 9:00 a.m.: linen deliveries
5. 10:00 a.m.: set up the terrace (Oded)
    6. Desserts (me), continue prepping
7. 2:00 p.m.: staff to set up the dining room
8. 4:00 p.m.: staff meal
9. 5:00 p.m.: shower and get ready
10. 6:00 p.m.: Last-minute preparations (get ready for them)
11. 7:00 p.m.: Go time, welcoming speech

After this final point, my list gets longer—each recipe accounted for with me slaving in the kitchen and then popping out to mingle with the guests. Press repeat. I'm not going to wear spiky heels like Caro suggested but ballet flats. And, yes, I'm definitely wearing my apron over the fabulous dress she'd given me. But, for now, I'm comfortable in my sweats and a T-shirt, and I pull my hair into a messy bun. Before leaving the apartment, I scribble out a nice-sized check for Oded and check my phone.

> MARK: I miss you! 😟 We're so busy and we don't
> hang out that much anymore. Looking forward to
> the opening. Can't wait to see you.

I let out a sigh. I haven't spent much time with any of my friends ever since I became a chef. When I worked at Cendrillon, I barely had time for myself. But I'd worked my way up in the brigade, and I'd paid my dues—part of the payment was having no social life. I used to be the glue, the girl melding everybody together, but we all lead separate lives now. Caro, the fashionista, and Mark, sweet Mark from Oz, now a hedge fund manager at a huge bank. I scroll to the next message, happy my friends are up at this early hour and just as driven as I am.

> CARO: Before you ask, I'm fine. I'm going to buy a
> new TV and binge-watch French romances after
> the opening.

> ME: But there are never happy
> endings...

> CARO: Exactly. How's the hot neighbor? Any
> word from him?

And now I'm thinking about Anti-Keanu again.

ODED IS ALREADY in the kitchen when I arrive. Last night, I'd given him a key, and he's already loading crates of fruits and vegetables into dry storage. "They came early," he says. "Good thing I was here. I think they were going to leave everything at the front door."

I race up to him and wrap him in a hug. When we pull away, he steps back, a look of surprise registering on his face.

"Really, it was nothing. Didn't sleep much last night." He grimaces. "That nasty neighbor we met in the stairwell? I heard him last night through the vents. And, let me put it this way, this building needs some serious insulation."

"I heard him too. And I'm going to kill him." My eyes go wide. "Any ideas on how I could get away with it?"

"Please don't do anything rash," he says with a chuckle. "I'd rather cook with you than visit you in prison."

"Can we just come up with some possibilities for my sanity? I mean, my knives are always sharp." I pull out the check from my pocket. "Joke aside, this is for you."

Oded's eyes bug out as he looks at the amount. "This is too much."

"No, it isn't. You've been here for me."

"But my piano killed your awning."

"Hmmm. There's a thought. We can drop a piano on him." I narrow my eyes. "Can you order another one?"

"I hope you're *not* serious."

I pinch my thumb and forefinger together. "Just a little bit. It's kind of fun to think about. Plus, I'd look terrible in an orange jumpsuit, and I think I'd gag from prison food."

"You had me there for a minute."

"As for the check, you are keeping it. You're saving my ass, and I don't know what I'd do without you," I say and he flinches. "Sorry for swearing. Sometimes I can't help it." I take in a breath.

"Maybe you can put the money toward a new piano," I say, and then burst into laughter. "But you better tell me about the delivery so I can retract the awning."

"I don't know what to say," he says, a lone tear sliding down his cheek. His hands grip mine. "You're one in a million, Kate." He grins, giving me a light pinch on the cheek. "We have work to do. The fish and meats are set to arrive. Tonight is your big night!"

Oded and I are in the process of setting up the terrace when Anti-Keanu races out of the building toward a taxi. After placing a suitcase in the trunk, he turns and sees me gawking, his smile so smug I want to slap it right off his stupid face. Before he jumps into the cab, he raises his hand into a salute. I shoot him the finger, my arm waving like one of those weird balloon men outside a used-car lot. Anti-Keanu circles his finger at the side of his head in the crazy motion before jumping into his cab and driving off.

Good riddance. Don't come back.

Oded's middle finger is raised when I turn to face him. "What?" he asks. "Solidarity. I don't like the pompous guy either." His eyebrows lift up, a serious expression. "Will you need help disposing the body?"

I'm silent, my spine rigid. I'm thinking about how crazy this is. This guy, this jerk, who I don't even know from Adam has gotten under my skin, and I'm acting like a petulant child. I laugh so hard I almost fall down, until Oded's hands steady my wobble.

"See, I can be funny too," he says, blurting out a laugh.

"Your comedic timing is impeccable."

"Speaking of time—"

"Right," I say, snapping back from my fantasies of the many ways to get rid of Anti-Keanu to the present. "I have work to do."

"*We* have work to do."

"Sure you don't want to run?"

"Never," he says.

AFTER THE FOOD deliveries, Oded sets to prepping with the two line cooks while I wait for the linen delivery outside to get some fresh air and clear my head before madness sets in. I'm leaning against the frame of the doorway, breathing in and out, when a van pulls up. I greet the driver with a hearty bonjour that makes him jump with surprise. He pulls out a dolly, loads the boxes onto it, and then gives me a look that reads, *Lady, I haven't got all day. Where do I put these?*

"Follow me," I say.

He unloads the boxes and produces a clipboard, thrusting it in my face. "Sign here."

I scribble my name with a swoosh. "Merci. Bonne journée."

"*De même*," he replies gruffly, and races back to his truck.

Somebody is clearly not happy with his job.

I can't wait to see the linens, set them out on the tables, or maybe roll in them. I find my pocketknife behind the bar and open the first box, giddy with anticipation. My knife cuts into the tape. I lift up the flaps, and then I scream like a banshee, "No! No, no, no, this can't be happening!"

Oded races out of the kitchen. "Kate, is there a problem?"

"Yep, yep, yep. There is. A huge one." The French oftentimes emphasize words three times to drive a point in. I'm being very precise. "Look! Look! Look!"

Oded rubs his eyes, confused. "At the napkins and tablecloths?"

"Yes!"

His eyebrows furrow with confusion. "They're nice. I love the color—nice and vibrant."

"They. Are. Yellow. Tweety-Fucking-Bird Yellow."

"Tweety?"

"Titi," I say, using Tweety's French name. "From the cartoon."

"Oh," he says, scratching his chin.

I mumble, "I always wished Sylvester would have eaten that obnoxious bird." My shaky finger points at the box. I meet Oded's concerned gaze; he obviously needs an explanation. "I ordered white. These are not white."

"If it's really an issue, call up the service and have them exchange them."

Right—I could do that. "Sorry, I'm a bit stressed out. I'm not thinking straight."

"No worries," says Oded. "Every problem has a solution."

I race to the bar to grab my purse, the contents, of which, scatter on the floor as I search for my phone. My jaw also drops to the floor when I speak to my vendor.

"I'm sorry, madame, but we can't change the linens this week. You must have checked the wrong box."

"I didn't check the wrong box."

"Ah, but you did. I have the order on my screen right now. Canary yellow. Perhaps you made a mistake? Polar bear white is just below this."

It *is* my fault. I'm doing too much. I didn't pay attention. How can I run a restaurant when I overlook details like this?

She continues, "If you want polar bear white, change your demand for next week's shipment."

"Merci," I manage to choke out, and then I collapse on the bar, my arms wrapping around my head.

Warm hands lightly grasp my shoulders. "Yellow is lively. It's not so bad. And, at least there is good news," says Oded. "They're installing the new awning now. And, if you're open to hearing this humble man's opinion, I think it's great. The color—"

"Brings light and life into the neighborhood."

Damn Garrance. I want to blame her for the delivery mishap even though I know it's my fault.

Oded slaps my back. "That's the spirit." He points to the kitchen. "Shouldn't we start cooking?"

"Yes! I can control my recipes," I exclaim. "See, weird, we've just met and you know me so well. Are you, by chance, my personal Yoda? Or Mr. Miyagi?"

"I don't know who you're referring to, but I understand. Music is my way. Food is yours. It's the way we deal with our emotions, our passions." He rocks on his heels, grins. "And I'm thinking you need to filet some fish." Oded's eyes shoot to the floor, and he sucks in his breath. "I didn't know you had a cat. He's beautiful. Nice collar."

I freeze and slowly look down. Oded is crouched on the floor and petting Juju, whose purrs resonate like a loud motor. His orange eyes meet mine. My mouth hangs open. I'm thinking Garrance is really messing with me, what with the awning, the Tweety-yellow napkins, and now her creepy spy of a cat.

"I think you may feed him too much," says Oded.

"That isn't my cat," I say, every muscle in my body tensing. "And I don't know how he got in here."

Oded waves a hand toward the entrance. "The door is open."

"Yes, but he lives across the street on the *second* floor."

"Well, obviously, he didn't teleport himself here," he begins, and I'm thinking it's quite possible until Oded continues. "He probably snuck out. Cats are wily creatures. I had six growing up. One knew how to open doors—"

Enough said. I'm keeping everything locked—the restaurant and my apartment. I'd have a serious heart attack if I found Juju in my bed, sharpening his claws before he sinks them into my neck. Maybe that's how Jean-Paul Beaufort met his fate? Then again, a cat couldn't dispose of a body.

Juju saunters toward me, tail swooshing. I back up until I'm cornered against the bar. I'm sure he can sense my fear. "He obviously likes you, me not so much. Can you grab him before he claws my eyes out? And take him back to Madame Lin-Truffaut's spice shop across the street?"

"Sure," says Oded, holding back a laugh. "I've never met a person who is afraid of cats."

I grunt as Oded scoops up Juju and heads for the door. While he's walking away, Juju's crazy orange eyes meet mine, and he blinks slowly. A possible death threat? I'm going to be sleeping with the fishes?

With my mind swirling, I head back to the kitchen, barking out orders to the line chefs. Oded returns a couple of minutes later, holding out a small brown bag. "This is from Garrance. You should see her shop. It's amazing—so many spices and plants. What an interesting woman." His eyes widen and his eyebrows raise as if he's impressed. "She's very elegant too."

Oh no. Garrance has bewitched Oded. I'm not stepping into whatever trap she's setting me up to fall in. I walk behind the bar and throw the bag into a garbage can. Oded pulls it out. "It's grains of paradise, the finest kind. You don't throw gold like this away."

He peeks into the bag, and I swear his face glows—purple, red, and then green. A strange feeling, a scent washes over me—perfumed like pepper, heat and earth. I'm now running in a wild field bursting in vivid hues of greens. Anti-Keanu pulls me to the ground and . . .

Oded clears his throat.

What the hell just happened?

I turn on my heel to head into dry storage. "I don't want it. You can keep it."

"But," he argues, "we could use it in a sauce—"

"Nope," I say. "Just nope. They're yours."

He sets the bag down on the counter, and I glare at it.

BEFORE THE OPENING party, the staff will taste all of the entrées, the first small course, as well as desserts. I return from the walk-in cooler, setting a crate on the prep table, the aromas of the sea wafting up to my nostrils, briny and fresh. I pull out a fish, run it under water, and begin scaling, the back of my knife peeling away the thick layer of scales, silver and black slivers flying everywhere. It feels good to get this pent-up energy out. I pull out my list, writing down: *Keep it together, Kate.*

By the time Oded, the two line cooks, and I have prepped the tasting menu, the dining room has been set up. Once everybody settles onto the barstools, I clap my hands together. "Is everybody ready?"

I'm met with a resounding oui, applause, and a couple of fist pumps. "Any questions before we begin?"

"Where's Natalie?" asks one of the servers.

"She had a change of plans and won't be working at the bistro," I say, fighting back my fury and nod in his direction. "This is Oded, and he's our interim sous-chef."

A few confused brows raise, but no questions are asked. Good. The crisis has been averted, and I'm so over drama. After all, bad luck happens in threes, according to Mom, so good things must be waiting around the bend.

I smile, hopeful. "Let's get to it. Tonight will be different from Saturday's service, as we're only serving smaller portions. With that said, you'll circulate with trays, making sure everybody gets a taste of our exotic offerings." I pause, handing out menus. "Oded and I have prepared all the main courses on the menu, and we're doing a full tasting today. I hope you brought your appetites."

"I'm starving," somebody says, and the room fills with laughter.

"While we try the offerings, I'll explain what goes into each dish—how it's prepared and all the ingredients. I suggest you all take notes and study them before this evening's service." From the bar, I pick up notepads, pens, and printed menus, handing them out. "After that, we'll run through the ordering system again, and I'll answer any questions. Then, we'll taste the entrées and desserts, and go over everything again before Saturday's opening to the public. Sound good?"

"Oui, Chef!"

"Great! Let's get this party for your taste buds started! Everybody into the kitchen!"

My cell buzzes—once, twice, three times. And then again. I pull my phone out from my pocket. "I should check this."

My eyes blur as I read through an onslaught of disappointing texts. I can't focus on the names.

> Sorry, babe, can't make it tonight. Flying off to Zurich. Will make a reservation when I come back. Good luck.

> Kate, I wanted to be there for you, but I'm dealing with family issues. Catch you on the flip side.

> Something came up. Can't make it.

> Tried to get the night off. Can't. Sorry, I'll make it up to you. You've got this.

> I'm on bed rest. Can't leave my house. I'm so, so sorry. Being pregnant sucks the big one.

> Sick as a dog. Will stop by next week. Bon courage!

> It's going to storm tonight. Can't make it.

With each message, I feel the blood rushing my face, especially when the "influencer" cancellations roll in. Stunned, I look up from my phone. "Oded," I say, "this isn't good."

"What?"

"All of my friends are flaking out on me. The press too." I gulp. "Nobody is coming."

"Nobody?"

"In the loosest sense of the word." I rub my eyes. "I was counting on sixty to seventy people, and I'll be lucky if we have twenty—you, me, the staff, my mom, and Mark and Caro." My bottom lip takes on a life of its own. "I ordered way too much—especially shellfish."

Oded pinches his lips with concentration. He looks up, raises a finger. "Can I invite a few people?"

"Of course," I say.

"Fantastique! I'll be right back."

As he races out the door, I want to scream, "Wait! What are you doing?" but he's already gone. I meander into the walk-in cooler to chill out, watching the air from the heat of my breath spiral in whooshes. All I can do is hope for the best, to keep calm and cook on.

CHAPTER EIGHT

Shut the Front Door

IT'S 5:00 P.M. and thunder rattles the windows, torrential rain following a few seconds later, pelting the glass. I'm expecting the Wicked Witch of Western Europe and her gang of evil cats to thwart my plans. Everything is prepped, including the staff. But I'm not ready. After checking my phone, I turn to Oded, my stomach twisting into knots so tight I think they'll be impossible to unravel. "This is bad. Nobody is going to come tonight."

He hip-bumps me. "It'll be fine. The people who matter in your world will be here. Go, get yourself together. I looked at your list. It's after five. And, seeing that I'm not tonight's shooting star, I can handle the rest of the preparations."

I mumble, "Shooting stars are dying stars. They sparkle, lighting up the sky in glory, then they fizzle and burn in a glorious moment, and then they're snuffed out."

Oded grasps my shoulders. "Sparkle for a moment. This is your time to shine. So you've had to face a few obstacles. That's life. And nobody can control the weather. If you want a rainbow, you have to deal with the rain."

"Wouldn't it be great if we could control the weather? Just vacuum all the storm clouds away?"

"Not possible." He points to the door. "Go."

I want to argue with him, but I know he's right. My neck is covered with sweat. I smell like fish and duck fat. My hair is matted down onto my forehead and falling onto my shoulders in seaweed-like clumps. I'm gross.

AT 6:00 P.M., the weather has let up and the sidewalks steam in a billowy white—ethereal and creepy. Oded and the staff wipe down the chairs and tables on the terrace.

"Kate," says Oded. "You brushed your hair. You look nice."

I'm about to thank him for this backhanded compliment when my mom materializes from the thick fog. "Kate, honey, I'm here early to help you out." She claps her hands together. "This is so exciting. I'm so proud of you. You look absolutely radiant."

"Merci, so do you," I say, noting the large sack she's carrying. "What's in there?"

She scrunches her nose and then takes in Oded's presence. Her lips twist into a sly smile, and her hand shoots out. "*Bonsoir*, I'm Cri-Cri, the mother of this amazing chef." She straightens her posture, her chest sticking out ever so slightly. "And you are?"

"Enchanted to meet you," says Oded, flashing a grin. When they release hands, he swipes his hair back. "You are way too young to be Kate's mother though. I thought you were sisters—"

Both of them laugh a little too loud and for far too long, their gazes locked. I think they're flirting, which is off-putting and kind of endearing at the same time. I didn't know Oded could be so charming. I'd have to warn him about my mother.

My mom gulps back her laugh and snorts. "You are too kind."

She hooks her arm into his, escorting him inside. "Now, tell me, how do you know my Kiki?"

Oded jumps at the word, and I huff, "Mom! Stop."

"Oh, sorry," she says, quickly correcting herself. "How do you know my Kate?"

Just skin me alive already.

ONE BY ONE the guests arrive, and aside from a few people I'd attended school with, along with Mark and Caro, I'm wondering who half the people are. I'm hoping some of them are press. I try to mingle, but it's kind of awkward while my mom cozies up to the bar, Oded by her side. She's playing the hang drum, her head thrown back in some strange trance, her body swaying rhythmically. Oded is completely captivated by her. I can tell because he's staring at her, not even blinking. I tap Oded's shoulder. "Who are all these people?"

He clears his throat, lifts his hand. "People from the neighborhood. I stopped by the local bar and the boulangerie—"

"Isn't he the sweetest?" says Mom, breaking out of what looked like an out-of-body experience, and bats her eyelashes.

Oded grins and turns toward her. He shrugs. "She wanted more guests. I did what I could."

Although I'm happy Oded pulled through, I can't stop my thoughts of what a failure I am. Even my own dad blew me off. Everybody did. This isn't the vision I'd had for the opening.

"Cri-Cri," I say curtly, "I asked you *not* to bring your hang drum."

She blows out air from her nose in a huff. "People are enjoying the hypnotic sound. Aren't they, Oded?"

He grins. "They sure are. You're very magnetizing."

My mom goes back to beating the hang drum, and it's almost

like I've become invisible. I feel like I've been sucked into an alternate universe, one I want to climb out of. Just beam me up, Scotty.

"Gah! I don't have time for this. I'll see you in the kitchen, Oded."

"Mm-hmm," he mumbles. "I'll be there in a minute."

I'm supposed to give the opening speech in fifteen minutes and then start the service. Anxious, I'm looking toward the door when Garrance makes her entrance, the scent of jasmine infiltrating my nostrils with every step she takes toward me. She's wearing a flowing black silk gown that ties at the neck. She's also carrying Juju, who is wearing an intricately studded emerald collar. The restaurant goes silent, all eyes on the newest guests. Caro races up to me and grabs my arm. "I recognize her. She comes into the showroom at least once a month. She's absolutely fabulous." She pauses. "So is her cat. How do you know her?"

I'm about to respond, but Garrance sashays over before I can.

"Kate," she says. "You look lovely. Thank you so much for inviting us."

"I'm sorry," I say with irritation. "I didn't know you were bringing Juju."

"Oh, is this not a cat-friendly bistro?"

"Uh, no, it isn't." I try to come up with excuses to ask her to leave, but Juju is staring me down. Plus, I don't want to piss her off.

"Will it be dog-friendly?"

"Of course," I say. "This is Paris."

She *tsks* and strokes Juju's head. "Oh, then I don't see the problem. Juju is a dog in a cat's body." She raises her eyebrows and continues before I can argue about allergies and dander. "I'm going to say hello to a couple of people I know." Garrance whispers, "It was very wise of you to invite people from the neighborhood. I'm wishing you the best of luck tonight." She turns to walk into the motley crowd and then looks over her shoulder. "The new awning looks beautiful, by the way. Emerald green—such a royal color—symbolizing luck, freshness, and abundance."

I'm left speechless as she totters away on her heels. Caro elbows me. "I can't believe you know Garrance Lin-Truffaut. And that she's actually here."

"I didn't want her to come," I say just as Mark saunters over.

He and Caro greet each other, Caro stepping back with an appreciative nod. "Oh my, Mark, I barely recognized you. You've changed since university."

He looks down at his polished shoes and shrugs. "No more braces. Contact lenses—"

Caro squeezes his arm. "And you've clearly been working out." She turns to me, eyes Mark. "Any chance of the two of you getting back together?"

"Caro, Mark and I are better off as friends. Our first kiss when we were fifteen was hella awkward."

"True," he says. "Plus, I've been dating Eloise for three years. We're moving in together. I'll always love Kate as a friend." He lifts his shoulders. "Sorry Eloise couldn't make it. She's on rotation tonight. But enough about me. I want to know who that strange lady is with the cat."

"She's not strange," says Caro, "though it is very bizarre that she's here." She raises a manicured brow and whispers, "I can't believe I didn't put two and two together when you told me about her. I can assure you that her cat's emeralds are very real—so are the diamonds and the rubies. She commissioned custom pieces at Maison de la Barguelonne and named them Catier."

Mark snorts. "That is probably the weirdest thing I've ever heard."

"I agree," I say, my eyes following her as she flitters and floats her way around the room, making a beeline toward my mother.

A few seconds later, she and my mom are laughing like old friends as if they'd shared an inside joke, and tapping the hang drum, Juju sitting on my mom's lap.

"My mother and Garrance are clearly hitting it off. I don't trust her. I should probably intervene—"

Caro latches on to my arm. "Don't worry about it. Madame is beyond eccentric—"

"I really didn't want her to come," I say with a sigh. "But she's here." I lift my shoulders. "I think she's connected."

"Yes," says Caro. "To the most powerful people in France."

"Definitely a mobster."

"Don't be ridiculous," says Caro. "Just look at her."

Oh, I am.

"I guess it's time to get this party started." I tap my glass of champagne, take a deep breath, and wait until I have everybody's attention. I nod to the servers, and they bolt into the kitchen. "Thank you so much for joining us for the grand opening of Bistro Exotique. Tonight, we've prepared small tastes of what you can expect from our menu. And we have something for everyone—vegan, vegetarian, pescatarian offerings, and, of course, this wouldn't truly be a French bistro if we didn't have meat for all of you carnivores," I say, this last phrase met with laughter. I wait for the chuckles to die down and continue. "Please, enjoy yourselves tonight and if you have any questions, just ask me or one of the servers. *Merci. Merci beaucoup. Santé.*"

Garrance's scent wafts over me and so does a sense of calm. For a moment, I'm catapulted into the gardens from my childhood, to the California jasmine climbing the trellises. I'd watch the hummingbirds and breathe in the ocean air. My eyes blink open and I shake my head to clear it. As much as I want to, I can't take a trip down memory lane right now because I don't trust Garrance and I have to get in the kitchen.

It's eight, and it's time to prepare the filet mignons encrusted with pepper, sliced and served with an Israeli couscous salad with almonds, feta cheese, cherry tomatoes, roasted red peppers, preserved lemons, braised fennel, and artichoke bottoms. Funny, when I'd first made this meal for Caro, she didn't believe me when I'd presented the dish and told her it was couscous, having only experienced the fine or medium grains at Moroccan or Algerian restaurants. Regardless of the name, Israeli couscous is more pasta-like and not crushed, but delicious all the same, and I love the texture—especially when making a Mediterranean-infused creation that celebrates the flavors of both spring and summer.

While Oded preps the salad, I sear the steaks, and an aroma hits my nostrils—more potent than pepper—with a hint of floral notes, hazelnut, and citrus. I don't think anything of it, because my recipe is made up from a mix of many varieties of peppercorns—black, green, white, red, and pink. Maybe I'd added in a fruitier green? I set to slicing, and Oded plates the dish in small glass bowls—a little salad with a slice of steak on top—a toasted almond and mint garnish. We're ready to go.

"Service," I say, slapping my hand on the table.

After my servers, Theo and Angèle, race in to grab the trays, I survey people eating as they circulate around the room.

"I feel like I've just tasted paradise," somebody says.

"The crust on this steak is perfection," says another.

"Now, this—this is exotic. So much flavor."

My mom's voice rises above the din. "I want to eat the steak so badly, but I can't. I'm a pescatarian. Ooh, but the fennel tastes divine with the Israeli couscous salad—so sweet and delicious and licorice-y, especially with these wonderful spices."

Garrance catches my eye. She winks and mouths, "*Tu vois?* My spices are magic."

Confused, I taste the steak and, as I lick my lips, I'm immediately transported with visions of Anti-Keanu and me embracing, so real it's like I'm there. He's unzipping the side of my dress and pulling it over my head. He kisses my neck, and his tongue gently licks my clavicle. My body is covered in spices—peppery and floral. I'm in a bed of flowers, now naked, his tongue exploring my body. A tribal drumbeat surrounds us, and my body rocks to the rhythm, to his touch. My neck grows hot, covered in a thin sheet of perspiration—

I snap back to the present when Angèle taps me on the shoulder and asks, "When are we serving the next course?"

After gathering my wits and my breath, I notice that the people congregating in the restaurant all have this glazed look, like the one I must have had when I tasted the dish. Something is amiss. And I think I know what it is.

"In a minute," I say, holding up my finger. I storm up to Oded. "Did you use the grains of paradise in the seasoning?"

"I did," he responds. "I thought they'd be a nice addition to the mix. You can't waste gold like that."

"No, you can't," says Garrance, my mom nodding in agreement.

Livid, I race to my station, grab the jar of remaining crushed peppercorns, and empty them into the trash can, followed by the remaining grains of paradise. No matter how amazing and transportive they are, I'm never, ever using Garrance's spices because these strange sensations can never happen again. With my heart racing the way it is, the feeling of euphoria, I'm convinced she creates more than spices and scents in her workshop—probably a drug dealer specializing in ecstasy—not that I've ever taken the drug myself, but I've seen people on it.

As I take in a deep breath, trying to place all the paranoid thoughts and the anger swirling around in my mind on the back burner, I set to plating the next dish—the ceviche, along with the vegetarian option. Oded joins me.

"Are you mad at me?"

"Put it this way, I'm not happy," I say with too much force. "But I'll get over it."

His face pinches into a puppylike frown, and he looks at his shoes. "I just didn't want the spice to go to waste. People loved it."

They did. And I don't like it.

"It won't happen again," he mumbles, placing the garnish of fresh herbs onto the ceviche.

"Good." I bang my hand on the counter, and Oded jumps. "Service."

The servers scramble into the kitchen, grab the trays. Standing within eye- and earshot of the dining room, I watch and listen as people eat, my tension running high. I brace myself on the counter as the words echo in my ears.

"Mmm, this is wonderful, but the other dish was better."

"This is missing something. I just can't put my finger on it."

My heart races, thumping in time with my pounding head. This is all Garrance's fault, not Oded's. She's setting me up. For what exactly? I don't know.

Oded clasps a soft hand on to my arm. "Kate, please don't be mad at me."

I know Oded only did what he thought was right. It's true that grains of paradise are coveted and the steak tasted amazing, but there's something off with Garrance's spices. People don't react to food that way, and all the dishes are just as good.

I meet his concerned gaze. "I know how talented you are, and I told you to get a little creative in the kitchen. I'm mad at Garrance. She's trouble."

"I think she's quite interesting."

"Maybe," I say, "for a potential criminal."

"Criminal?" he scoffs. "A lady like that?"

"Exactly. Never judge people on first impressions," I say with a huff. "Ready to get started on the next plate?"

Oded eyes me curiously.

Finally, the evening comes to an end, and one by one the guests leave, kissing me on the cheeks.

An older, burly man with a full gray beard, a curled mustache, and the clearest ice-blue eyes I've ever seen calls me over. "I'd like to make a reservation." He taps the wood. "This table right here, by the window."

"Sure," I say. "When?"

"For every lunch service. And dinner too. Under the name Pierre Lavigne." He lets out a sad sigh. "I'm glad the restaurant is open again. Coming here will keep her memory alive. Thank you. And thank you for inviting me. My wife and I used to come here every day when Jean-Paul Beaufort ran the place." He pauses. "Do you know what happened to him? One day, he just up and disappeared—"

I'm about to reply when Garrance waves goodbye and blows me a kiss as she swooshes to the door carrying her monster of a cat.

Worry creases my brows. I have to find out what she's up to.

CHAPTER NINE

Save the Drama for Your Mama

IN THE MORNING, I'm greeted by a cloudless sky and Oded's smile. It's the first day of service, and I'm going to try my best to put last night's disappointment behind me.

"The storm clouds have passed," says Oded as he sets up the tables and chairs on the terrace. "It's a beautiful day." He points to the sun. "Tu vois? Every cloud has a silver lining."

"Too bad I don't have the playbook," I say.

"You don't need a book for positivity," he says, tapping his chest with a sturdy finger. "Good things come from within."

I know he doesn't pick up on what I'm inferring. In France, they rename films and the book *The Silver Linings Playbook* changed to *Happiness Therapy*, which with the way the French pronounce it, sounds like *A Penis Therapy*—as pointed out by my mother. Sometimes the "h" makes all the difference. But I'm not getting into this with Oded.

"You're right," I say, humming a couple of bars of "I Got Sunshine." "I'll try to be more positive."

He pats my back. "That's the spirit! And you've got a lovely voice."

"Really? I'm not tone-deaf?" I ask, thinking about Anti-Keanu's insult. Howling like a hyena?

"No," says Oded. "If there is one thing I'm a master of, it's the melodies found in music. You can definitely hold a tune."

Oded's tone and facial expression tell me he isn't lying to be polite.

"Why, thank you," I say with a little curtsy.

Across the street, the canal sparkles in the sunlight. Fishermen dot the banks, jockeying for the best spots. I have no idea what they catch, but I do know I wouldn't eat fish from this polluted waterway. Perhaps the fishermen just catch and release. At this time in the morning, the sidewalk is clear, just a couple of runners and a few people making their way to the park or the boulangerie or wherever they're going. A man stops, eyes the large printed menu hanging framed on the wall. "*Vous êtes ouvert pour le dejeuner?*"

"Oui, oui, oui," I respond with a bit too much enthusiasm. Like most bistros, our lunch menu offers à la carte options, including salad choices—one vegan—and a fixed price menu; an entrée (starter) and *plat* (main course) or a plat and dessert for twenty-two euros; or an entrée, plat, and dessert for twenty-eight euros.

"Ah, bon," he says, scratching his chin. "The ceviche sounds interesting. I'd like to reserve a table on the terrace for four people if possible. The name is Grégoire Martin."

"*Parfait*," I say.

I nod and make a mental note to enter his name into the reservation system.

While waiting for deliveries, Oded and I finish setting up the terrace, Oded whistling "Pour Moi La Vie Va Commencer" by Johnny Hallyday—the beloved rock star oftentimes compared to Elvis Presley. Lung cancer took Hallyday's life in 2017, but he's forever etched into the hearts and memories of the French.

"Pour Moi La Vie Va Commencer"—"For Me Life Will Begin." It's the perfect song. I smile and hum along. Things are looking up. Seriously, what else can go wrong?

A truck pulls up—it's one of Fabian's guys with my glorious seafood order—oysters, shrimp, spiny lobsters, salmon, and sea bass. He jumps out of the cab and unloads the crates. Like Fabian, he wears denim overalls, one side unbuckled, a gray T-shirt, and thick boots. Standing before me, he hands over the slip for me to sign while Oded carries the bounty into the walk-in. I look over the list, my throat catching.

"Where's the sea bass?" I scan the order and my throat locks. "I didn't want langoustine. I wanted langouste. And I didn't order scallops."

"Oh," he says. "We won't have any more sea bass until next week. He thought scallops would be a fine replacement. Didn't Fabian call you?"

I pull out my phone. Three missed calls. I curse myself for putting the ringer on silent so I could get a decent night's sleep. This is bad. Langoustines, like crawdads, are not like langouste, spiny lobsters, at all. Did I make this mistake? Along with the sea bass ceviche, lobster served with a lemon risotto is one of my specialties.

"Can you take the langoustine back? And get me the langouste?"

He holds up a finger, pulls out his phone, and speaks in rapid-fire French. His eyes meet mine, and he holds out the phone.

Fabian's voice pounds in my ears. "I'm sorry, but you checked off langoustine. I just looked at the order. Unfortunately, all of our langouste are accounted for, but we can get them to you next week. As for the sea bass, I couldn't get any in at the last minute . . ."

His voice trails off as I try to come to grips with this conundrum.

"Kate," he says. "I'll see what I can do, but I'm not making any promises. Did you want to keep the scallops?"

"Oui. Merci," I say, cursing myself. "I'll be more careful next time. Bonne journée."

I hang up the phone and hand it back to the deliveryman. He leaves, and my eyes go wide with panic. I sit at a table, drumming my fingers on it, trying to come up with solutions. I could do shrimp with lemon risotto instead of lobster. I can make a carpaccio with the scallops, using the same ingredients for the ceviche, but slicing the mangoes and scallops thin. I can come up with something for the crawdads, maybe grilled with chili peppers and served with savory potatoes. What I can't do is have my graphic designer change the menu and have her send it to me at the last minute because she's on holiday. This will have to be on the servers and, once again, I know I have to adapt and adjust—get everything in order, which is becoming harder to do when my mise en place is completely out of whack. I've got to get my act together. We have twenty covers for lunch, including the kind Pierre Lavigne.

With a sigh, I set to preparing ingredients—shallots, cucumber, mango, and avocado—with a mandoline for the last-minute carpaccio. I'd placed a few of the scallops in the freezer for twenty minutes, so they'll be easier to slice by hand. Finally, after the scallops "cook" in lime juice, it's time to taste. I grab two small slate plates and place alternating slices of each ingredient on it, and then sprinkle a little chipotle chili powder, followed by some cilantro, and why not, edible flowers, pomegranate seeds, and a dash of pepper.

"Oded," I say, "come taste this, please. I'd like to know your thoughts."

He steps over to me with a fork and digs in. He looks up, eyes wide.

"Is something wrong?"

"Not at all," he says. "I don't know how to tell you this, but I guess I should. It's so fresh and so wonderful." He pauses. "It's better than the ceviche. The texture is much nicer, also the way the flavors come together."

"Really?" I ask, and he nods. I grab a fork and taste it. Oh my goodness, he's right, and I'm feeling quite proud of myself for turning lemons into lemonade. "I'm eighty-sixing the ceviche and putting this on the menu." I lift up my shoulders. "Now to test the flambé dish."

"Can't wait," he says, pointing to his now empty plate. "Especially if it's as tasty as this."

The pressure is on. I'm trying my best to remain positive, but I keep feeling twinges of panic in my gut. Last night's party didn't go as planned, and I can't help but wonder what else could go wrong.

Oded, noticing me spacing out, is picking up the slack with the rest of the preparations, especially after I start a grease fire when flambéing my shrimp. I stand numb as Oded grabs the dry chemical extinguisher, snuffing out the flames. The kitchen fills with curls of thick, white smoke and seeps into the dining area.

"Kate, what's going on?" he asks.

"I didn't turn the evacuation off," I say, and go back to preparing a new dish. "Sorry, I should know better. I'm a little out of it today."

Oded eyes me with concern. "Take a break. I can handle things."

"No, cooking helps keep me sane," I say, though I probably look like a wide-eyed madwoman about to have a nervous breakdown.

Angèle, one of my servers, barrels in, waving her hands in front of her face. "What happened in here?"

"Nothing," I say. "This is the smell of defeat and my dying dreams."

"Oh," she says, her nose pinching with confusion. "Anyway, there are some strange people here. That man? At table five. He ordered two meals and two glasses of wine," she says. "He's not with anybody. And he's talking to himself."

"He's probably talking to his wife," I say.

Angèle's eyes bug out. "Is she invisible? A ghost?"

"She's with him in spirit."

Angèle shudders. "He's creeping me out. And I'm not a fan of ghosts."

"Be nice," I say. "He's lonely."

Angèle rolls her eyes, picks up the entrées, and leaves just as Theo bounds into the kitchen. "Chef, three tables left."

"Why?"

"Because they didn't like the changes I proposed for the menu—everyone seems to have their hearts set on the lobster or sea bass and not the proposed substitutions." He frowns. "They yelled at me, wanting to know why they were put on the menu if they weren't available."

I rub my temples. "If you get any more complaints, offer any of the next guests a free entrée or dessert. Also, tell them that the scallop carpaccio is better than the ceviche—fresh and delicious."

"Okay," says Theo, slapping an order into the order trolley. "I have to get some drink orders in."

He leaves, returning a few minutes later. "Four more tables left."

This first lunch service is beyond disastrous. Aside from Pierre Lavigne and two other tables, all the customers left hungry, irritated, and angry. Theo and Angèle keep shooting each other odd looks. Oded's lips pinch with concern. It's three in the afternoon. With a sigh, I dismiss everybody until dinner service resumes. Over this two-hour break, cancellations roll in one after the other. My phone dings twice. I clench my teeth and open the screen. And there it is: a Google alert for a review.

The latest restaurant in the tenth arrondissement, Bistro Exotique, has some very interesting menu choices that sound completely delectable on paper, but that's as far as one gets—

none of the highlighted specialties were available at their opening lunch service. If you're looking for lobster replaced with crawdads or sea bass replaced with scallops, very small portions for an exorbitant price, and abominable service from an ill-trained staff, then you've found the right place. I'd stay away from Bistro Exotique until they iron all their issues out— preferably with a steamroller.

I let out an animalistic groan, the pain of the words sinking in and stabbing my brain.

People aren't even giving me a chance to prove myself. Of course there would be issues on the first day of service. It also would have been nice if this asshole of a food critic had alerted me to his or her presence, but that's only wishful thinking and never happens in this industry. They show up when they want to—like food ninjas. When are things going to start happening for me instead of against me? As my heart sinks into my stomach, I open the other alert, fearful, and nausea boils in my stomach: it's worse.

After disappearing from the Paris cooking scene months ago, authorities have found the body of Jean-Paul Beaufort, a chef from Les Endives in the tenth arrondissement. Police discovered the body in the Seine and said Beaufort's hands were tied to a rafter, the body so severely decomposed at first they weren't sure if it was a man or a woman. They are treating the case as murder. The new chef at Les Endives, now called Bistro Exotique, has been ruled out as a suspect, as the victim had ties to the Marseille Mafia.

This is bad. They mentioned the restaurant *and* the freaking Mafia in the same damn freaking article. I had been a suspect? What the hell? I don't cry. I don't scream. I don't yell. I can't do any of these things because I can't find my breath. I'm in shock. With my head resting on the bar, I tap the hang drum my mom left behind. *Think, Kate, think.* Failure is not an option. A loud knock jolts me out of my misery. I skulk to the front door, open it.

"*J'ai un livraison pour Kate Jenkins,*" says a man.

"*Oui, c'est moi,*" I say, hoping this guy isn't a hit man.

I cross my fingers behind my back, hopeful. Maybe Fabian pulled through? I could be comeback Kate if I have the right ingredients. Maybe I'll even offer a free cocktail to bribe people to the restaurant? I have to do something.

My heart sinks as the man rolls a dolly bursting with plants into the foyer—at least two dozen of them with waxy green leaves climbing up small wooden trellises, a few bursting with pale yellow flowers with lanced-shaped petals and hot pink stamens. These are rare vanilla orchids—some even producing pods—and are supremely difficult to care for. I inhale deeply, and my thoughts jolt to Anti-Keanu, his exact scent. We're suddenly running along the beaches of l'île de La Réunion and then rolling on the sand, the waves of the Indian Ocean lapping on our wet bodies. I have a vanilla orchid in my hair. He's kissing my neck—

"Well, that's everything," says the deliveryman.

"But I didn't order these," I say snapping to attention.

He shrugs, hands me an envelope, and leaves. Curious, I pull out a thick linen ivory card with gold trim.

Dearest Kate,

Thank you so much for inviting us to the opening. Juju and I had a wonderful time and really enjoyed talking with your mother. We also adored the ceviche. These orchids are small tokens of my appreciation—something exotic for your bistro. I noticed you

didn't have any plants. If you need advice on how to take care of
them, you know where I am.
All my best.
Your friend,
Garrance

My random fantasy has flipped me out. I'm mad at myself for losing control. I'm mad at my father for not making the effort to get to the opening. I'm mad at the review and the article. And I'm really wondering what the hell a wealthy woman like Garrance wants from me and, more important, what her exact link to Beaufort is. Regardless of her ties to the Mafia, I'm going to ask her to stay away from the restaurant and me.

After double-checking the kitchen, making sure all the burners and stoves are turned off, I lock up and bolt across the street, nearly getting run over by a cab. Garrance buzzes me up. I clomp up to the second floor and she opens the door with a smile.

"Kate, what a lovely surprise! I hope you received the plants."

"I did," I say. "Merci, but I'm very uncomfortable accepting such an extravagant gift." I want to add *Because I don't know you and think you're fifty kinds of shady,* but refrain. I don't want to end up on her hit list.

"Don't be silly," she says. "Come into my atelier. I'll make you cup of tea." She eyes me up and down. "You seem a bit frazzled, like you need to relax a little bit."

And now I'm wondering if she's going to poison me.

CHAPTER TEN

Spice, Spice, Baby

GARRANCE USHERS ME inside her workshop. Speechless, I crane my neck and look over her shoulder to survey the space. Every square inch is filled with exotic plants bursting with flowers and glass bottles in varying colors, one of them glowing red. I'm hit with so many scents, each one better than the next, and, due to complete sensory overload, I lose focus.

"Are you into witchcraft or something?" I ask, the words tumbling out. At least I haven't accused her of being a mobster. Yet. I don't want to end up sleeping with the fishes. Cooking them any which way? That I can handle.

Garrance laughs and puts a kettle on a hot plate. "No, but I do believe in the magic of scents and spices, how they can transport you." She nods to a jar filled with dark, flaky tea leaves. "This is vanilla tea, made from the same plants I sent you today."

I puff out my bottom lip. "I still don't understand why you sent them to me."

"I thought it was clear from my note. I wanted to thank you," she says, straightening her posture. "Well, there's that, and I always look out for my personal investments."

"Excuse me?"

"Kate, I own the building you live in; this one too. I could have asked you for a much higher rent, but I liked the proposal you sent in for the space—*très exotique* and your passion for creating recipes reminded me of my own with scents." She pauses as I'm visibly processing this information. "I told you the previous tenant didn't listen to me, but I'm thinking maybe you will. It's important to bring life and light into the neighborhood, not darkness. There's so much more I'd like to do, and I think we can do it together."

I don't even notice Juju snaking around my ankles until he meows. My fingers fly to my temples. "Right about now, I'm supremely confused."

"Kate, I know people, very powerful people, and I have a good head for business."

My spine goes rigid. "Are any of them tied to the Marseille Mafia? Because, if so, I don't want to become involved with them, so I don't want to be involved with you. I'm running a clean operation."

There, I'd said it. I may sound nuts or accusatory, but I'm not going to fall into whatever trap she's trying to rope me into.

She gasps. "Why in the world would you think that?"

"You told me about the previous tenant and the wine Ponzi scheme, his disappearance. They found his body, you know."

"Yes, I read about that this morning. So very sad. And no clues as to who did it." Garrance shakes her head as I narrow my eyes with distrust. "My darling, Kate, I've never been involved with unsavory types. My late husband, bless his soul, worked with my father creating the very exclusive Tenang Resort Properties—Tenang meaning 'tranquility' in Indonesian, where my husband was from." Her eyes focus on the ceiling. She whispers, "Sadly, I'm a widow, but a very wealthy one."

I'd pegged her all wrong. Feeling like a paranoid idiot whose imagination had gotten the best of her, I clear my throat and rock back and forth on my heels, making a mental note to stop watching true-crime documentaries.

"Have you heard of the Tenang properties?" she asks.

"No," I say, lying. "But it sounds like you've led an interesting life."

"I have. I suppose you'd like to hear about how I'm *not* connected to mobsters?" She lets out a sad chuckle, and I nod. "I met my husband, real-estate tycoon Peter Lin, in Singapore, where he worked with my father, Clement Truffaut, building up the luxury hotels, my father also a hotelier. A few years ago, both of them met their fates in a deadly disaster on a private jet. Now, my son, Charles, and I control fifty-one percent of the company my husband and father created." She offers a weak smile. "Over the years, my son and I made a few investments of our own—like your building. And this one." Her head dips down. "I've been a wife. Now I am not one. I am a mother, but it's a tenuous relationship with my son because he's closed himself off to the world. The one thing I have left is my creativity, and I need more out of life, tu vois?"

I shift in my seat. "I'm so sorry you had to face such huge losses."

"Life isn't easy, but I still try to make the most of it."

Garrance pours us tea in dainty porcelain cups decorated with a blue faience pattern of flowers. I feel at ease with her now that I know she's not connected to the mob, and I take a sip, letting the sweet vanilla, floral, and caramel notes soothe my nerves while hoping I'm not whisked away into another strange fantasy.

Garrance takes a sip of her tea and then dabs her lips with a monogrammed linen napkin. "This vanilla is from Madagascar. Have you traveled much?"

"A little bit—Mexico, Hawaii, and Martinique with my parents. Well, when they were still married. L'Îles de Maurice and Réunion with my mom. Um, when it was just me and my mom. But I haven't been anywhere in years—too busy cooking and building up my career." I eye a rack of glass tubes on the counter, lean back in my chair. "I wish I could travel more, get more inspiration, but I do like to experiment with ingredients from every corner of the planet."

"Yes, I remember every word of your proposal."

I cross my legs at the ankles. "How did you get involved with spices and perfumes?"

"Although I consider myself a tried-and-true Parisian, the reason I'm settled here now, I've lived all over the world, mostly southeast Asia, where I met my husband, a bit in North Africa, Sri Lanka, and even Brazil. I was in charge of creating the hotel group's signature scents—the soaps, shampoos, and perfumes—my infatuation moving toward cultivating spices and plants." She waves a hand toward her spices and vials. "I still create for the group when inspiration hits."

"Is it a profitable business?" I ask, regretting the words the moment they leave my lips.

"Kate, this is my hobby, my passion. I don't sell to anybody. This is for me, for my company, my husband's and father's legacy. And I'd like to help you too."

I'm having a difficult time understanding what she wants from me. My firstborn? "Why?"

"Please, don't take this the wrong way, but you remind me a bit of me when I was your age—full of hope and the desire to follow your dreams." She straightens her posture. "I saw a spark in your plans for the restaurant—a sense of adventure, of breaking free from the norm. The way you think about food is the way I think about spices and scents. We're both creators, and when I met you in person, I liked

your energy." She purses her lips. "Right now, I want to focus my energy on something positive." She chuckles. "Regardless if you thought
I was a mobster, I believe we share the same goals—connecting people
through sensorial experiences. Am I wrong?"

Still a bit embarrassed, I bite down on my bottom lip before re-
sponding. She's just summed up everything I want to do in one simple sentence. "You are absolutely on point."

Garrance winks as Juju jumps onto my lap. "It appears that Juju
likes you too."

Feeling out of sorts, I stroke the cat's head, look down at him.
He's weighing my thighs down, and I like the way it feels, all warm.
I also love his loud purrs. He's nothing like a rat. "The big lug is kind
of growing on me," I say, stroking his chin, and Garrance grins.

I set my teacup down on the carved wooden table, surveying the
space, the sheer elegance of all the ingredients—the beautiful litho-
graphs of flowers and insects on the walls. I wonder if there's a back
room. "Your workshop is amazing," I say. "Do you live here?"

"Good heavens, no. I live at one of our hotels in the sixth." She
lifts her shoulders and then stands, heading behind the counter. "I
do know the value of hard work, but I adore having my every whim
catered to. Now back to you." She opens a crystal vial, the facets of
the glass reflecting a kaleidoscope of colors on the walls. "Come,
smell this. I concocted this mix today. Give me your hand."

Confused, I step over to her, and she dabs a dropper into the
glass and brings it to my wrist.

"It's a *parfum*—a custom scent I created for you. We're going to
bring you some happiness, some joy. Now smell it. What do you
think?"

I bring my wrist to my nose—and I'm lost in a melody of
fragrances—sweet and musky. Almonds? Vanilla? Florals? A switch

clicks in my brain, a feeling of exhilaration rolling through my body in waves. I'm at a loss for words. Garrance really captured something special; she knows what she's doing.

"Do you like it?"

I smell my wrist again, my eyes wide. "Like it? I love it. What's in it?"

"A little frangipani, some ylang-ylang, a bit of almond oil, and a light sandalwood musk."

"Frangipani? From Hawaii?"

"It does grow there, and it's one of my favorites. But I discovered this wonderful flower when my father and husband were building a resort in Thailand, and I immediately incorporated them in some of my products. When I create my scents, it's like wine—but instead of taste, it's smell— the head notes, when you first apply the perfume; the heart notes, which is when the aroma fades ever so slightly; and the base notes, the scents that release as the perfume sits on your skin and warms up to the body's temperature—which usually takes about an hour." She claps her hands together. "Well, that is your lesson from me for the day. Now, I'd like to find out if our passions align the way I think they do. Tell me, Kate, when you cook, when you create your recipes, what are you thinking about?"

I tap my bottom lip with a pensive finger and then let out an excited breath. "Creating something out of this world, a dish that surprises you when you first taste it and surprises you more as each one of the flavors reveal its nuances."

She nods her head. "Exactly. If you can create meals the way I create my parfums, I think we can come to a mutually beneficial arrangement." She leans forward, a spark in her eyes. "What did you do with the salicornes I gave to you?"

I don't tell her I kept it for evidence. "I put them in cold storage."

"Good," she says. "If you're up for it, would you be open to making me a light dinner before your regular service, something not on your menu? With the salicornes."

I smell my wrists and decide to take on the challenge. "Of course," I say.

"I'm expecting to be impressed," she replies, and my heart races. Something in my gut tells me I can't blow this.

THIS IS NUTS. This is unexpected. And it's also thrilling and intimidating. For some reason or another, I want to prove myself to Garrance, not that I need her approval, but I kind of want it.

As Garrance and Juju sit at a table in the dining room with drinks (a glass of white for her, a bowl of water for the fuzz ball), I commandeer the bag of salicornes from the walk-in. What can I do with them? If anything, I have to keep the flavor intact.

I survey what else is on hand. I have fresh cod (a lovely, flaky white fish). Perfect. I'll bake this dish in the oven, wrapped in aluminum foil, served with rice pilaf and garnished with fresh herbs.

After preheating the oven, I peek into the dining room. "I need about thirty minutes," I say.

Garrance looks up from her phone. "That's fine." She eyes her watch. "I have forty. *Non plus*."

I nod. I'm sweating profusely, wanting her to love what I make, worrying about her reaction if she doesn't. After taking a calming breath, I get to prepping, slicing up fresh tarragon, the grassy floral fragrance enveloping me. I take two pieces of foil and set filets of cod on each one, followed by the salicornes. Drizzle a bit of lemon. A few razor-thin slices of garlic and lemon. A bit of salt and pepper. Paprika. Some *herbes de Provence*, my special blend. And, finally, the tarragon.

While the fish is baking, I make the rice, deciding to add a dash of cardamom and cumin. Soon, the kitchen smells like heaven, and I feel like I'm floating on my feet. It could be the aromas emanating from the oven, or it could be my wrists, the base notes from the perfume she gave me.

Finally, once the meal is ready, I plate it, adding edible violet flowers as a last-minute garnish. Before bringing Garrance her dish, I taste it. And, oh my, now I'm swept away into a fantasy of the sea—the same one I'd had before when she'd first given me the salicornes, but stronger, more intense. I'm running along the rugged beaches, and then I'm falling on the sand. I can hear the waves crashes, the calls of seagulls, the—

"Darling," says Garrance from the doorway. "I only have ten minutes."

"Oh, yes, sorry, sorry, sorry," I say, snapping to attention. "It's ready."

"I'm so looking forward to what you've created." She turns, and I follow her into the dining room, and after she sits, I set the plate down.

She eyes the meal and nods her approval. "It looks divine."

I sit with her at the table, my plate (already tasted) in front of me. But I can't eat. All I can do is watch as she picks up a morsel with her fork and gingerly moves it to her mouth, takes a bite. Her eyes close. She chews, then swallows. "Absolute perfection," she says. "I knew we were kindred spirits."

I let out the breath I'd been holding in. "I'm glad you like it."

"I'm sure you can do more with the rest I have to offer you—the best spices, the best ingredients in the world." She daps her lips with a napkin. "I have to get back to the hotel. I'd really like to help you with the restaurant if you're open to ideas."

My mind is spinning. I wasn't expecting her offer. I'm also wondering why she isn't finishing the meal if she likes it so much. "Can I think about it?"

"Of course, dear. I'm leaving for Jakarta in a few hours to meet with my son and see my late husband's family, but I'll be back in one week." She stands up. "One more thing, Kate, as you may recall, your lease has a special clause in it—a contingency."

I cough, and continue coughing, until Garrance hands me a glass of water. "Yes, I have six months from opening the restaurant to make it a success."

"No, you had six months from the *signing* of the lease. If things don't work out, my company has the right to take the space over. Starbucks is interested in the location and has just sent over a premium offer. Let's just say, I gave you the deal of a lifetime because I believed in you." She juts out her chin, raises a brow. "Simply put, I don't want another failure in the building."

I'm now completely blindsided.

My brain feels like somebody placed it in a pressure cooker and it's about to explode. I can feel my face paling. My hands tremble. "French laws protect renters," I say, wheezing.

"Usually, yes, but for apartments and homes. You signed the lease for the restaurant with our terms," she responds with a shake of her head.

My lawyer did not translate this clause very well. Closing the restaurant down would mean she'd be shutting down my dream. And I've spent so much damn money—almost all of my nest egg. This isn't fair. She has to be reasonable. I think I'm about to break out in hives. "But I was preparing the restaurant, planning everything, getting all the licenses for five months—"

"I know. Which doesn't give you much time. Regardless, I'd like to come to an agreement with you." Her eyes narrow, and she places a pensive finger on her lips. "Don't answer me now. Think things over. I'll be expecting your answer upon my return. On that, I have a few things to settle before my trip."

She turns to leave, and my legs are about to go out from under me. I brace myself by holding a chair. "Thank you for the orchids. And the perfume." I gulp, blinking back the tears welling in the corner of my eyes. "You'll have my answer when you get back."

"Yes, darling," she says, scooping up Juju with a slight groan. "Lovely lunch. Absolute perfection. I see big things in your future." She looks over her shoulder. "Between you and me, a Starbucks in this neighborhood would be an absolute atrocity. French culture is slowly dying, the cafés closing down left and right. I'm counting on you to make the right decision. Ultimately, this comes down to business."

And with those words, her skirt swooshes as she walks, the door closing behind her.

My head instantly fills with a checklist of all the catastrophic possibilities, the biggest one losing the dream I've worked so damn hard for. I drop to the floor, willing myself to not have a heart attack.

CHAPTER ELEVEN

Variety Is the Spice of Life

THE NEXT WEEK is beyond abysmal. We're lucky to serve three or four covers for each service, including Pierre Lavigne. Angèle quit after swearing she saw a ghost in dry storage, and, save for the dishwasher/busboy Albert, and Oded, everybody else follows suit. Nobody wants to work at a restaurant with bad reviews, bad karma, and no customers.

I sit back in my chair, deep in thought, thinking about Garrance's offer. I'm hesitant to place my trust in Garrance, but it's either listening to her or my wacky mom. When I smell my wrists, scented with the perfume she'd given me, I'm wrapped up in a cocoon of happiness.

I desperately need her help or I'll face a failure of epic proportions. If her perfume can calm my boiled nerves, her advice can surely save my dream. She is, after all, a success—at least her company is. It's after two, and not one table is occupied. We had only one cover today—Pierre Lavigne—and he just left. I'm going to lock up early because she should be home from her trip. I race across the street, leaving Oded to close up, and Garrance buzzes me into her building. I let out a sigh of relief. She's back.

"Kate, lovely to see you," says Garrance, and we exchange les bises, air-kissing each other's cheeks with a soft *mwah* after she opens the door.

As usual, she is dressed to the nines, this time Chanel (I think) and, of course, smells of jasmine.

"I hope you had a nice time traveling," I say, tapping my toes. I'm a nervous ball of energy. What if she rescinds her offer? I have so much riding on this. I want her help, need it.

She sighs. "A bit painful with all the reminders of my husband and my father, our life there, but wonderful all the same." She ushers me into her shop, points to a new batch of vanilla orchids and other exotic plants. "Plus, I picked up more of my favorites." She studies my face, grasps my hand. "How are things at the bistro?"

"Not good," I say glumly. "At all."

She gives me a knowing look. "I take it you've thought about my offer."

"I have," I say, my heart leaping. "And my answer is yes. I really need to do something. Big. I really need your guidance, if you're willing to give it."

Please say yes.

"Of course," she says. "But, you must understand, I'm not offering my assistance for just you. I'm also doing it for my son and me. And, to be honest, I haven't been this excited about anything in a very long time. I have a few ideas."

She's definitely piqued my interest. "And?"

"The first project I'd like to do is create a custom scent for the restaurant—special seasonal recipes to seduce people into entering the establishment, ensuring hunger and lust: vanilla, almond, and coconut; citrus and sandalwood; pepper, ginger, and chili. You'll pipe it onto the terrace and place it in the bathrooms, creating a magical atmosphere. A scent that transports you."

"I love it," I say. "The perfume you created for me does exactly that—it's like I'm calm and positive when I smell it."

"Good," she says. "But I have a feeling that you're not going to like the other things I have in mind." She pauses and raises a finger. "I'd like for you to close the restaurant for two—maybe three—weeks while we figure some things out. Then, we're going to redo your opening and invite all of my connections."

"Um, I know I don't have many patrons now, but I do have rent to pay." I don't add that only one customer regularly comes into the restaurant and, save for Oded and the dishwasher, Albert, my entire staff quit. Couldn't even give me a week to get my bearings and fix things. "And what about Starbucks and the clause?"

"Are you forgetting I own the building? I'm giving you a grace period to get things on track."

"But—"

"No arguments." She holds up a sturdy finger to shush me. "As for my other request, I'd like for you to work with my son, Charles, when he gets back from Singapore. He's missing kitchen life, and it will be good for him."

My eyes go wide, and she picks up on my trepidation.

"It's a small price to pay for my assistance. Do we have a deal?"

Why in the world would a chef of Charles's caliber want to work with the likes of me at a mid-priced bistro? Still, I don't have any other options. I nod slowly. Garrance seems to have faith in me, so I'm placing mine with her. "Yes. And merci. Merci beaucoup."

"Wonderful! We're going to have so much fun. Darling, I can't wait to begin." She crouches down and latches a leash on to Juju's diamond collar. After stepping into the hallway, she says, "Follow me."

I'm so confused. "Where are we going?"

"To the roof. I want to show you something."

She saunters down the hallway, Juju leading, and I stand rooted to my spot. Garrance looks over her shoulder, flashing a grin. "It's this way, Kate. *On y va*."

Hesitantly, I follow her up the steps to a metal door. When she opens it, I let out a gasp. A large dome glimmers in the sun. Garrance opens up another door, this one glass, and I'm rendered speechless as a plethora of scents and humid air hit me, wrapping me up in Mother Nature's embrace. I'm in the islands. I'm in heaven. And I'm on a roof in Paris. I need a crane to pick up my jaw.

"This is my climate-controlled greenhouse, my pride and joy."

This slice of Parisian paradise is filled from floor to ceiling with tropical plants like orchids and flowering trees, moths, butterflies, and bees floating from flower to flower—not to mention the exotic birds—cockatoos, parakeets, and a couple of parrots, their plumage in reds, greens, blues, oranges, and whites.

"*Gros con*," squawks one of the macaws, swooping closer to Juju, and then chants, "*Petite salope*."

Juju sits on his haunches and hisses as the birds join into a cacophony of swears. Garrance shakes her head. "I'm sorry about that. Charles taught the birds some very, very bad words."

"Oh," I say, taking in the space. I'm too gobsmacked to laugh about the fact that a macaw called a cat "fat asshole" and "a little bitch." The ceiling must be at least thirty—maybe forty—feet high. This greenhouse with its water system and solar panels must have cost a small fortune. I walk up to a lime tree—the small, vibrant green globes bumpy and patterned, almost brain-like. No, they can't be. "Are these kaffir limes?"

"Why, yes, I use the leaves to make oils for my scents." She pauses. "Charles uses them to cook with to replace bay leaves to infuse the flavor into his dishes . . ." Her voice trails off. "Or, rather, he used to." She meets my eyes. "Please take some leaves and some limes."

"I couldn't," I say, even though I want to.

"Of course you can. Don't be silly." She winks and walks over to a flowering tree. "I wanted to bring Asia and the tropics to me when I moved to Paris. So I did. This is one of the frangipani, or plumeria, as it's also called."

I walk closer to inspect the flower—five thick mostly white petals with a gradated yellow center reminiscent of a watercolor. "They're beautiful."

Garrance points to another tree with hot pink flowers at the far end of the greenhouse. "There's the other one." She closes her eyes. "They remind me of my Peter, our *lune de miel* in Thailand after we married."

"Do you miss him?"

"I do. Every day." She sighs and taps her chest. "But he's still with me. In my heart. I can't imagine if I lost my son too. No parent should ever have to experience that kind of pain." She swallows. "But, that's life, and this is mine. Come, Kate, there are other things I want to show you."

By her posture, I know this conversation is over. Maybe she'll talk with me more about her world and experiences one day.

We round the frangipani, coming face-to-face with two peacocks— one male, with magnificent iridescent plumage sparkling in royal blues, greens, and golden browns, not to mention the circular eye-spots, his crown a crest of feathers resembling a helmet. The female, although beautiful, has drabber plumage and a short tail.

Garrance beams as the large birds greet her like dogs. "Meet Yin and Yang," she says, and Juju rolls onto his back. "These two are the only ones who tolerate Juju and vice versa."

"Maybe because they don't call him names," I say with a laugh, and Garrance joins me.

"Kate, I wanted you to see my passion. In addition to my flowers, I grow everything here—ginger, lemongrass, hot peppers, black pepper, chilis, and more. As they say, variety is the spice of life." She picks a pepper off a vine. "This is urfa biber, a pepper from Turkey with notes of raisins, chocolate, and smoke when dried. Have you heard of it?"

"Yes, but it's hard to find," I say, intrigued. "And I've never cooked with it."

"You should. It might change the way you think about recipes. I have some prepared downstairs, and I'll give you some."

Still reeling from the shock of this oasis, the wrong words tumble out of my mouth. "How did you get all of this here? Isn't it illegal?"

She winks and walks over to the kaffir limes, picking a few and handing the rounds and leaves over to me. "I fly private. And a little bribery goes a long way. Now, come, we have some work to do. I already created a summer scent for the restaurant and would like your opinion on it."

She doesn't have to ask me twice.

THE FOLLOWING DAY, the scent Garrance has created is soon dispersed through the restaurant via an electric diffuser—the aromas of citrus, coconut, and ginger hitting me in waves. Ravenous, I set to making a roasted red pepper and garlic hummus, incorporating the urfa biber to see if it really makes a difference. I dip my finger into the dark purplish-brown flakes to taste, and I'm blown away by the earthiness of the flavors. I smack my lips, tasting undertones of raisins, chocolate, and maybe a little coffee.

Even though I've made a crudité platter with some pan-seared padron peppers sprinkled with sea salt and homemade garlic-infused naan, I can't help shoving spoonfuls of the hummus into my eager mouth. I close my eyes and find myself wondering if Anti-Keanu tastes this good—sweet, smoky, with a nice kiss of heat.

Before another strange and disturbing fantasy sets in, I shudder the thought of him off and then grab a platter to join Garrance in the dining room. She sits at the bar taking notes, Juju curled up on a stool by her side, and soon, we're to become culinary and drink scientists—Garrance's plan. She eyes the dish and smiles as I set it down.

"You used the urfa biber, oui?"

"I did."

"What do you think?"

"I'm sold," I say. "It's incredible. This spice is really going to kick all my recipes up a notch."

"You're going to create magic here," she says with a swift nod.

"I hope so," I say, my throat catching. "But what if I don't believe in magic?"

"You will, darling. With my spices and scents, you'll tap into all the senses, pushing them up an extra level, and bring on fantasies. Your meals will transport people." She swipes a chip into the hummus, eats it, and then dabs her mouth daintily with a napkin. "This is perfection."

Her confidence is infectious. I straighten my shoulders.

I clear my throat before I can tell her about the strange, food-induced fantasies I've been having about Anti-Keanu. "Music while we experiment?" I ask, holding up my remote, and she nods.

As we listen to a playlist I'd created for the bistro, the two of us stand behind the bar, facing a kit that Garrance "borrowed" from her hotel's lounge—incorporating dry ice, grapefruit juice, and edible bubbles.

"For the drink, I'm thinking we make a grains of paradise gin cocktail," says Garrance. "Kate, do you still have the grains I gave you?"

Palm to face. "I, uh, I . . ."

"You gave them to somebody?" she asks with a sly smile, and I nod.

"Oded," I say, leaving out the fact I'd thought she was trying to poison me. And that I threw them away in the garbage can after he used them at the opening.

"Don't worry. I have more," she says, reaching into her purse.

"Garrance," I say. "You're being so kind to me—"

"I'll do anything for my friends." She mumbles, "And I don't have many."

"What? Why? You're so interesting, so elegant. You have to be the life of every party."

"Unfortunately, people always end up wanting something from me," she says, frowning. "But such is the life of a wealthy widow."

My posture crumbles. I feel terrible taking so much from her. "I—I—"

Garrance places a hand on my shoulder. "Never asked me for anything. I offered. Your joy is bringing me joy. And I also told you I'm doing this for me too. My spirit, my love of scents and spices is re-awakened. I have so much to offer, to give, and I'm sharing it with you." She pauses. "By the way, I meant to mention this earlier, but your aura is brighter."

I look into her eyes. "I think yours may be too."

"See? We already have a mutually beneficial relationship." She lifts her shoulders. "In fact, I'll happily offer you the friends-and-family discount at any of my resorts."

I'd seen the pricing of the rooms. "Thank you, but I don't think I could afford it even with a discount."

"I'm sure you could afford *free*." She laughs when my eyes go wide and my mouth drops open. "I'm only offering because you didn't ask or assume. But my so-called friends did. And now they are no longer in my life."

I want to know so much more but can't ask because my tornado of a mom whirls into the restaurant. The moment she'd heard we were mixing it up and playing around with smoke and fire, she'd canceled her appointments and raced over. Mom throws her purse onto a barstool and claps. "This is going to be so much fun!"

Garrance sets to mixing the drink, placing it in a *coupe à champagne* glass. A few minutes later, we've managed to create a bubble on the top of the cocktail that smokes and dissipates when popped with a finger.

"I am blown away," says my mom.

Garrance mixes up two more cocktails. "Now, we have to taste it. Kate, we need two more smoke bubbles."

"On it."

I place a bubble on one drink, then the other. When we pop them, the smoke whirls around the glass and to our faces. This certainly feels like magic.

"This is so freaking cool!" I squeal and take a sip of my drink. I lick my lips and gulp back my surprise. "Plus, it tastes amazing too."

As we toast, Oded barrels into the restaurant and stands in the doorway. He's wearing a fitted black suit and looking very dapper. "I got it! I got the audition!" He stops, noticing Garrance and my mom, and blushes. Weird.

I race over to him and wrap him in a hug. "That's fantastic. I'm so happy for you, and now we have more to celebrate. Come, sit. Tell us all about it. I'll make you a smoke cocktail."

After Oded exchanges les bises with Garrance and my mom, he sits at the bar, and I'm about to mix up his drink when Mom says, "I'll do it." She places a hand on Oded's shoulder. "I told you the cards didn't lie."

"Oh my god, Mom, you gave him a reading?"

"I did."

"When?" I ask, and they both clear their throats. Something is definitely up between the two of them. "Have you guys seen each other after the opening?"

"Maybe," says my mom.

"Like a date?" I ask, and Mom shrugs.

"Why? Do you mind?" she asks, shooting me a sly grin.

"It's a bit weird," I say with a slight cringe. "Oded and I work together. If something goes wrong between the two of you—"

"We're just friends," says Oded. "We share something in common."

"What's that?"

"We're both emotionally invested in you and the success of your restaurant," says Mom with a tsk, and she continues mixing Oded's drink.

"I concur," Garrance pipes in.

Oded pops his lips. "At first I told Cri-Cri that tarot cards were the devil's tools, but she assured me there wasn't anything religious or witchy about them, that they were only used for guidance."

"What cards did you get?" I ask, curious.

"The star, the sun, and the world," he says, lifting his brows.

"Oh, you got all the good ones. Mine were abysmal," I say as Mom places a smoke bubble on his drink. He recoils, his eyes sparked with a dash of fear. "Pop the bubble and then tell us about your audition."

He does as he's told, and after the smoke from the bubble dissipates, he takes a sip and straightens his posture, his chin lifted proudly. "You are now looking at the newest member of the Ensemble Orchestral de Paris."

"For the piano?"

"Non," he says, taking another sip of his drink. "For the violin. I told you I was trained with many instruments." He grimaces. "I didn't have a piano to practice on, but I did have my violin."

My mom shudders as the sound system switches to a pop/rap beat. *Boom. Boom. Pow.* "This music is absolutely atrocious, Kate. It's not relaxing or exotic at all."

"I agree," says Garrance. "And I have an idea. Can I take you all to a dinner early next week at the lounge in my hotel? We can cele-brate Oded's new position, and there's something I want Kate to experience."

"You own a hotel? In Paris?" asks my mom.

"I do," she responds.

"Among others," I add. "All over the world."

Oded and my mom share a surprised look.

"Right," I say, lifting up my glass. "Let's toast to Oded."

Oded leans toward me. "Wait, Kate. I know I came bearing good news, but there's bad news too."

Oh no.

His gaze drops to his shoes. "I can still help you out in the morn-ings, but I won't be able to help you out in the kitchen anymore."

I grin. "I figured that much out. Don't worry, the restaurant is closed for two weeks, and Garrance's son is coming to save the day. And you don't have to help out in the mornings either."

"Yes, I do. It's a matter of—"

"Principle," I say.

"I'm just glad you're not mad."

"Mad? I'm thrilled to pieces for you."

"Garrance is a very interesting woman," he whispers. "And so is your mother."

A budding romance is definitely in the air. I'm happy the people in my life are coming together. The storm clouds have lifted, and I'm grasping on to all the energy, feeling extraordinarily positive too.

A FEW HOURS later, I close up the restaurant, a bit buzzed from test-ing the drinks, and when I round the corner, I barrel right into him. Anti-Keanu.

"Toi," I say with a slight stumble.

After giving me the once-over, he wheels his suitcase toward the entrance of our building and then looks over his shoulder. "Don't stand in the middle of the sidewalk."

"Is that a rule? I have one too." I waggle my finger in front of his face. "Don't dance with a bear."

He lets out a soft laugh. "What the hell does that even mean?"

I shrug and then slur, "Well, it is on my list of don'ts. I mean, a bear could kill you if it wanted to." I'm giggling and wobbling. "I might be a bear."

He already thinks I'm nuts, and I'm in the moment. I let out a growl, swipe out my hand like a claw.

"Very scary," he says, shaking his head. "Did you need help getting up to your apartment? You seem out of it."

Wait. I must be drunker than I thought I was. He's being somewhat nice. This is totally a trap, and I'm not falling for it. "No, thank you, I'm perfectly fine."

He raises a brow as my body sways. "If you say so."

I cross my arms over my chest. "I say so."

"Okay, then," he says, and then unlocks the door, leaving me on the street.

I watch him enter the building, laughter burbling in my stomach.

"You're always so serious, Kate," I whisper to myself and tap my chest. "Lighten up, like Cri-Cri tells you to do. Go with the flow. Float into bliss—"

So out of character for me, I tell myself to forget the rules, and then I dance on the corner, slapping my knees, in a full-on giggle fit. A couple walking by gives me a dirty look and crosses the street. I'd forgotten how fun it is to lose a little control—and, yep, I've lost it.

Once I gather myself together, I stumble up to my apartment, kick off my shoes, put on my pj's, and I open the window to let some air in. And damn him. He's cooking something, and it smells divine—smoky and sexy like him. I slam the window shut and crawl over to the vent. "I have another rule. Don't you dare make all your racket tonight."

I wait a few seconds. He responds, "Don't listen."

Ten minutes later, I'm about to crawl into bed just as I hear moaning.

"Don't stop. Don't stop."

"Baby, I'm not going to."

I pull out my earplugs and stuff them into my ears.

This is war.

ACT TWO

Always remember: If you're alone in the kitchen and

you drop the lamb, you can always just pick it up.

Who's going to know?

—JULIA CHILD

CHAPTER TWELVE

The Beast of Burden Is Back

IN THE MORNING, I'm in the kitchen playing around with some recipes, namely an urfa biber–infused sauce for my version of chicken-and-cheese enchiladas mole—balancing all the flavor profiles—taste, aroma, and texture.

Considering I'm not expecting anybody to come in today, I'm wearing tiny gym shorts from high school that kind of still fit and a tank top. Thanks to a torrential downpour, it's muggy and hot, the heat misting on the sidewalks outside, and when I turn on the stove, I'm sweating bullets. I'm considering buying an air-conditioning unit when *he* walks in, his eyes going straight to my chest.

"What are *you* doing here?" I flick my hand like I'm shooing away an irritating fly. "Go away."

He leans against the frame of the doorway, looking all sexy in his perfectly cut jeans and long-sleeved black T-shirt. "The front door was open. I knocked, but nobody answered, so I just came in." He gives me a once-over. "You look a little rough around the edges."

Oh shit. In hazy bits, pieces of last night's conversation swirl around in my head. I should probably be embarrassed, but I'm not.

Why is he carrying a sack of groceries? And why is a chef's coat draped over his arm? "You're not cooking here."

"Believe me, I don't want to."

"Then, get out," I growl, pointing with my knife. "In fact, I think you should move out of the building."

"No, little bear, I have something to discuss with you," he says, placing his bag on the counter. "I saw my mother last night."

I snort, trying to peek into his bag to see what ingredients he bought—probably piss and vinegar. He smashes the sack with his hand, closing it, and I jump back.

"That certainly didn't sound like anybody's mother. If it was, you have a pretty sick relationship. An Oedipus complex, perhaps?"

"That's absolutely disgusting," he says with an exaggerated scoff. "I went to the hotel, and I saw my mother, Garrance, last night. So if anybody is moving out of the building, it will be you. By the way, the Starbucks deal is quite tasty."

My knife clatters on the prep table. No. Anti-Keanu is Garrance's son? I should have asked her if she had a picture before I'd agreed to her terms. Plus, he'd hit me in my weak spot, threatening my livelihood. "You're Charles? You can't be. He's supposed to be sweet, kind, and talented. You're none of these things."

"Sorry to disappoint you, *gila*, but I am Charles," he says with a snort, and straightens his posture.

"Gila?"

"'Crazy' in Indonesian."

I glare at him. "No matter what language you're speaking, never call a woman crazy. It's a rule."

"It's rude to stare." He points a sturdy finger at me. "And you're going to stay away from my mother." He brushes his hair back, glares at me, pouts those sexy lips. "I'm sick of people like you trying to take advantage of her."

"What? For your information, I didn't ask her for anything; she offered."

"So, you just took her up on it?"

I cross my arms over my chest. "She insisted. Wouldn't take no for an answer." I don't add I really didn't have a choice.

"Then you're just another one of her pet projects. She's always taking in strays," he scoffs.

"I'm not a stray. And Juju is *not* a stray. He's a rare breed—a Chartreux."

"I don't like cats. And you're clearly a street cat."

It's time to launch into bitch mode 2.0. "I don't like *you*," I say, and then I mumble, "And I bet Juju doesn't like you either. By the way, your mother is wrong. Your aura is not orange like Juju's or mine. It's black and nasty, like your soul."

Way to rip a new one, Kate. I feel like I'm twelve years old, but he brings immaturity and snark right out of me.

"*N'importe quoi,*" he says. "I don't believe in that crap. I'm not helping you out in the kitchen. And unless you magically turn into a plant, she'll get bored of you soon. She always moves on to her next project. I can't even believe she proposed this insanity."

"Good," I retort. "I bet you can't cook anyway."

His mouth drops open. "You do realize I'm a Michelin-starred chef."

"You mean you *were*. But now you're not and haven't been for two years. I bet I can cook you out of this kitchen."

His hazel eyes blaze with fury. And it's kind of sexy. "Do you want to make a wager on that?" he asks.

I'm going for the jugular. "Oh, did I bruise your itty-bitty ego?"

"My ego isn't small; it's huge," he says, and my gaze involuntarily shoots to his crotch.

Why did he have to say that? I shake off my thoughts and collect my wits. I stick out my hand. "Deal. You're cooking for me. I'm cooking for you. Let the best man or woman win, Anti-Keanu."

"What?"

"You're nothing like Keanu."

"You don't make any sense." He grips my hand. "You're going to lose. Here's the deal. If I don't like what you prepare, you're staying away from my mother, and if your restaurant isn't a success, well, you know her terms."

"Deal," I say, and we shake. "Let the cooking games begin."

We're still gripping hands and staring each other down when Garrance sashays into the kitchen with Juju. "Wonderful! The two of you have met and are already getting along. I had a good feeling about this." She pauses, looks me up and down. "Kate, what on earth are you wearing?"

I rip my hand from Charles's. "I wasn't expecting anybody today. And it's hot."

"You should wear more clothes. It's not very ladylike," she says with a tsk. "And I probably should have called to tell you that Charles was back. It slipped my mind. That's why I'm here."

"You also didn't tell me Charles lived in the building."

"It never occurred to me to do so," she says. "Is it a problem?"

Charles nods. "Yes, Ibu, it is. We've already met, and we don't get along."

"We really don't like each other," I add. "At all." I pause. "Wait, what's an ibu?"

"'Mother' in Indonesian," says Garrance. "Now, back to the discussion at hand."

"I can't work with her," says Charles.

I throw my hands in the air. "Voilà! I can't work with him. Problem solved."

Garrance shakes her head from side to side. "*Tant pis*. We can't always get what we want, and, if I have anything to say on the subject, you *are* going to work together." She turns on her heel. "Come, follow me, we're going to sort out what's happened between the two of you in the dining room. Now!"

Charles whispers, "I don't know what you did to get her under your spell, but working together is out of the question."

"I agree," I say with another low growl.

"After you," he says.

I push by him. "Don't look at my ass, you ass."

"Don't forget about our deal."

I look over my shoulder as we head to the table Garrance and Juju are seated at. I catch him glancing at my second-best feature. Admittedly, I put the thought in his head because, from what I've heard echoing in the vents, he's a horndog. The second I sit down at the table, Juju jumps in my lap, purrs.

Charles grimaces. "The gros con actually likes you."

"We had a rough start, but we're friends now," I say as Charles reaches out to pet Juju's head. Juju hisses and I say *Good kitty* in my head. "And he clearly hates you."

I whisper to Juju, "Did you just call him a gros con too? I agree."

Normally cool, calm, and collected, Garrance slams her hand on the table. Both Charles and I jolt. Juju jumps off my lap.

"Enough with this childish bickering. Kate, you're twenty-eight years old. Charles, you're turning thirty-five in a few months. Both of you are acting like extremely immature teenagers." She catches her breath. "I want to know what started this animosity between the two of you. Because, correct me if I'm wrong, when I walked into the kitchen, you were shaking hands."

"We made a bet," says Charles with a snort.

"And?" questions Garrance, motioning for him to continue.

After Charles explains the deal we'd made, I jump in and explain our hellacious backstory, how he barreled over me on the street, and then I throw him under the bus. "He has a revolving door of women. And I can hear them going at it all night long in my apartment. Through the vent. He's a disgusting man with very loose morals." I glare at Charles. "There's no way in hell we can work together."

Charles blurts out a wicked laugh. "Ha! Don't listen to her, Ibu, unless it's for the pure and simple fact we can't work together. At any rate, there were no women in my apartment."

"Porn?" I question with a snort. "Figures."

"Non, it was an actress I asked to do me a favor. A phone call. It was my way to get you back for spilling wine on my duvet and all your stomping around."

"Oh my god," I say, sitting back in my chair, shaking my head with disbelief. After I get over the initial shock of his deception, my lips twist into an awkward smile. "So, the other night—"

"I just placed my iPhone by the vent—"

"She's a really good actress," I say with a snort. "Really good."

He smiles for the first time. And my stomach drops. His dimples. His perfect teeth. So much better than the sexy scowl. Charles throws his head back in laughter. "I can't believe you thought it was real, especially after last night."

"Not funny," I say, even though it kind of is. "Annoying."

He sits back in his chair, a smug grin on his face. "You're annoying."

Garrance clears her throat. "All bets—except the one I'm going to propose—are off." She meets my eyes. "Kate, you promised you'd let Charles into your kitchen. That deal sticks." She whips her head to face Charles. "And, Charles, you promised to stop philandering around without purpose. Your sabbatical is over." She nods her head to make a point. "Finally, you are both doing this for me. Until this afternoon, right now, I've been the happiest I've ever been."

"What's your interest in this"—he waves a dismissive hand toward me—"girl."

"We've spent some time together, and our passions align, don't they, Kate?"

I nod, wanting to keep Garrance on my side. "They definitely do."

Charles's posture goes rigid and he scowls. I tilt my head and offer him a satisfied half smile.

Garrance takes our hands within hers, squeezing tightly. "I'm asking for the two of you to work together for two weeks. One week as we prepare for the grand reopening and one week after. If the two of you can't work things out, then you can go your separate ways. My bet is that the two of you will get along. If you don't, I'll stop insisting and you're on your own." She pauses. "Charles, if you don't get back to life, you'll be cut off from the estate. We're under Singaporean inheritance laws, not French, as you know. And I also want you more involved with Tenang." She then places her focus on me. "Kate, as you know, I'll close the restaurant down. That's my deal. That's my bet. Take it or leave it."

"I don't get your reasoning, Ibu," says Charles. "It doesn't make sense why you've become personally invested in her. She's not worth it."

"I'll tell you why. And she is." Garrance takes a sip of water. "Kate, her restaurant, has brought me back to life, the reason I'd said no to Starbucks. I saw her proposal, liked it, and I wanted to become involved. For some time now, I'd lost my passion for creating things. And I think you did too." She pauses when Charles gulps, his Adam's apple bobbing up and down. "You're a chef, a very good one, a great one. And getting back into the kitchen with Kate will spark up your passion, just like creating with her has done for me."

Knowing of his loss, my heart goes out to him for a moment. Maybe he's not such a jerk after all. Just bruised and a little banged up.

"I'll try," he says, defeated.

"Great," says Garrance. She meets my eyes. "Kate?"

I sigh. "Fine. I'll try too, but I'm only doing this for you, Garrance."

And for my dream.

"Good," she says, smoothing out her skirt. "First step: Kate, make us a cocktail. I need one right now. Second: I want the two of you to apologize to each other. And the third: carry on with your bet that isn't a bet anymore and make me something to eat. I'm starving."

Charles looks up, offers a weak smile. "Don't argue with my mother."

"I won't," I say, and then whisper in his ear. "Just you."

He blurts out a laugh as I head over to the bar to make our drinks. On the way, I'm thinking about his smile, and I nearly trip. I pull out the kitchen torch, preparing to make flaming hurricane cocktails, because my mind is on fire. I set to work, and our drinks are ready in four minutes.

"Step right up," I say.

I light the top of the drinks. The flames rise, Charles's face illuminates in the glow. Maybe he does have an orange aura? The sparks settle down. We toast, take a sip.

"This is pretty good," says Charles, licking his lips. "But it's missing something."

"What?"

"Ginger," he says.

"Maybe," I say. "But it might overpower the taste. So it's a hard no."

Garrance laughs, leans over. "And, now it's time for step two, because I'm looking forward to step three."

She's not letting us out of this.

"I'm sorry I ran into you," says Charles with a slight eye roll. "I was on my way to clear up some loose ends with my father's estate. I was in a very bad mood. And you were in the middle of the sidewalk during rush hour."

"I'm sorry I called you a dick," I say, and Garrance cringes. "Sorry, Garrance. And I'm sorry my friend and I were so loud. We were just letting off steam."

"I'm sorry I placed my pretend phone sex by the vent," he says. "You pissed me off, and it was my immature way of getting back at you."

Our eyes meet. I have to look away. His smile slays me. Damn that dimple.

"I'm sorry I stained your duvet. It's not my fault the building has porous floors." I squint. "Maybe you should do something about that? You do own the building. And maybe you could get the electric volet on the side of the street fixed?"

"Take it up with management."

I huff. "I thought that's what I was doing right now."

Garrance interrupts us. "You both realize how ridiculous this sounds, don't you? There have been some very odd misunderstandings, but no reason to be at each other's throats. Now that everything has been cleared up, please, I beg you, I can't listen to this drivel anymore. I'm hungry."

Charles laughs. "We've got you, Ibu." On the way into the kitchen, he latches on to my wrist and says, "I'm looking forward to seeing what you can do."

"Too bad," I reply. "I've already prepped and prepared the meal."

"So you don't want me to be your sous-chef?"

My hair, my spine tingles. "You'd really work under my direction? Under me?"

"No," he says, his eyes meeting mine. "I like to be the one in control."

"Me too," I say, ripping my arm from his grip. I point. "Go keep your mother company in the dining room. I've got this."

"You'd better hope so."

I clench my teeth. "Is that a threat?"

He shoots me a wicked grin and turns on his heel. "Think what you want."

With a heavy sigh, I head into the kitchen to finish up the meal I'd started this morning. Thankfully, everything, for the most part, is prepared. All I have to do is heat up the tortillas, my special version made with duck fat instead of lard, roll in the roasted chicken, already marinated in my sauce, with some cheese, cover it with more sauce, and bake the beauties in the oven. The black beans and rice are ready to go to—once I infuse more kaffir lime juice into the mixture.

I add a little more heat to Charles's plate—serrano chili pepper. The big fat baby of a man-child probably can't handle spices. I garnish the dish—a little crème fraîche, some cilantro, and avocado cubes. He'll probably hate it. But I don't care. Okay. I do care, a little bit. I want him to squirm.

After plating, I set three dishes on a serving platter, throwing napkins and cutlery haphazardly on the side, and I make my way out to the dining room. Charles sniffs the air. Garrance smiles.

"Here," I say, setting a plate in front of each of them, "bon appétit."

Within thirty seconds, Charles has eaten everything. "Is there more?" he asks. "This was so damn good. Simple in the best of ways. And elegant in others."

I wasn't expecting a compliment. I shoot him a surprised smile and hand him my meal. I hope he doesn't notice the lack of heat. "Don't worry. There's more. For me."

I'm about to head back into the kitchen so I can eat too when Charles taps my back. "I'm sorry I misjudged you, Kate. I'm sorry about what I said to you." He offers an apologetic smile. "But you have to understand, I'm really overprotective of my mother. So many people have tried to take advantage of her. She's assured me that you're not one of them."

This guy is good at backpedaling. Garrance is nodding and beaming from ear to ear. But something in Charles's eyes, a darkness, tells me that he isn't being honest with me. He's a conniving bastard, saying nice things to me for Garrance's benefit.

"Apology accepted," I say. "And I need to eat because I'm getting hangry."

"Hangry?"

"American slang. Hungry and angry at the same time."

"Wouldn't want that."

I eye him curiously. This time, his smile isn't fake: it's completely genuine. Damn him. I head to the kitchen, grab another plate, and sit back down with them. The first bite is heaven on my tongue—all the flavors coming together, the cheese melting. And, oh, the chocolaty finish.

Charles takes another bite of the enchilada, licks his lips. "I'm really enjoying this meal. Urfa biber flakes?"

What's up with the switch in his personality? Two compliments after his threat? He's obviously setting me up.

"Well, they're not Justin Bieber flakes," I say with a slight chortle, and his brows pinch together with confusion.

Oh my god. That was such a Dad joke, and he clearly didn't get it. His gaze meets mine.

"Yes, urfa biber—your mother gave me some. She thought I'd like using it." I lift my chin. "And I did."

"It's delicious, Kate. Really." He grins again, but it feels off, sarcastic, a hint of darkness in his eyes. "I think we've settled our differences."

Did we? It's like he's playing a role.

Garrance hasn't paid attention to one word we've exchanged, or so I think. Charles kisses her on the cheek as I finish eating. She looks at her phone and gets up from her chair, grabbing Juju with a slight grunt. "Thank you, Kate, for a truly delicious meal. My car is here. I'll stop by for lunch in two days' time, to make sure you haven't killed each other." She eyes the orchids and then blows us a kiss as she heads out the door. "I'll also take care of the plants."

One thousand points for Garrance—the spice master with a deviously wicked and masterful mind. But now I'm alone with Charles, which has me unnerved. In silence, we clean up, shooting each other an occasional glance.

"I'm exhausted from my trip, can barely keep my eyes open. Jet lag is brutal," he says after starting the dishwasher. "I'll see you tomorrow. The meal I'm planning has a lot of prep work involved."

"Tomorrow it is. I've already shown you mine. You'll show me yours."

Palm to face. How did I make a simple sentence sound dirty?

"Can I walk you home?"

"Sure," I respond. "We're both going the same way."

I turn off the lights, lock up, and we meander onto the street, our faces lit up by the hues of the setting sun. As Charles opens the door to our building, his face twists into a wicked grin and he says, "You can definitely cook, but I wouldn't get too comfortable. I still think you're taking advantage of her generous nature."

I don't respond to this obvious dig because it's at this moment that I realize Charles and I are playing a serious game of chess. And I'm going to do everything in my power to win the game. Wanting to get away from him, I race up the stairs, my head pounding. "See you tomorrow. Nine a.m."

"Can't wait, Crazy Kate," he calls, his words echoing in the stairwell.

CHAPTER THIRTEEN

Frenemies or Friends?

IT'S EIGHT IN the morning, and I've barely slept because I've had Charles on my mind. In a sick and twisted way, I like the way we argue. I like the tension, so thick, I'd need a butcher knife to cut through it. And I can't believe he'd faked loud sex by placing his phone by the vent to get under my skin. Hilarious. Oh boy, did he get me. Wait. On second thought, that's really messed up. Who goes to that extent to piss somebody off?

I'm not in a good place, questioning myself—always questioning. How do I control my kitchen, my dream, when I can't even control my thoughts? Where is my mise en place?

For every step I take forward, every stop on my life map, I keep ending up back at point A. Maybe my stops are out of order? Because I'm right back at square one—hating him and fantasizing about him—his lips and his damn vanilla scent. I've seriously got to stop thinking about licking his neck. I need to focus on my restaurant, my dream.

I throw on a pair of tight workout pants, a baggy T-shirt, and my

Crocs. I look at my phone, realizing I don't have time for yoga. I also have three missed calls and texts from my dad and Mark. I make a mental note to check them later.

When I head out the door, I find Charles pacing in front of the restaurant, a crate of ingredients at his feet. He sees me and taps his watch. "You're late."

"Thanks for stating the obvious," I say, doing my best not to think about how good he looks in a tight black T-shirt and jeans. I can see his tattoo clearly, the way the lotus flower snakes down his inner forearm to a delicate point of water drops.

"Let's just get this over with," he says.

I open the door to the restaurant while brushing off the fact I'd just been fantasizing about having his arms wrapped around me. "Don't forget. We promised your mother two weeks."

Charles picks up his crate and follows me into the space. "Are you ready to see what a real chef can do?"

"Maybe show me what a real man can do first," I say. Wow. That came out so wrong. "I mean, I hope you're not intimidated by female chefs."

"I think it's great women are making their marks in what was once a male-dominated industry."

Good answer. And one I'm not expecting.

He places his crate on the prep table. I lean over, trying to look in. "What's all that?"

"My tools, my knives, and a few of my go-to ingredients—a few things to prep for tomorrow's meal."

I nod. "So, you're moving in?"

"At least for two weeks."

"We're really going to do this?"

"We're going to try." His dimples pucker. "Where are your chef's coats? Toques?" he asks.

"There aren't any," I say. "This isn't a Michelin-starred restaurant. We wear aprons and caps. Not highbrow enough for you?"

"Not at all," he responds. "Stars come with too much pressure."

"They come with fame and glory too," I respond.

"I'm not into that. At all," he says, with a frown. "Believe me, as
time went on, cooking became less fun."

I walk over to the locker, open it, and toss him the goods. After
he puts on the cap, he tucks his hair behind his ears, and then he
puts on the apron, tying it loosely around his waist. I hate how cute
he looks in this uniform.

"You're now a marked man."

"*Quoi?*" he questions, facing me with an eyebrow raised.

"You're wearing the logo of my restaurant."

"I actually think it's pretty cool," he says, and I go quiet, eyeing
him with suspicion. "So, gila, I'd like to know what kind of cheese
you used in the enchiladas."

I narrow my eyes. "Why? Did you think it was good-a?"

"No, it definitely wasn't Gouda."

"That was a joke," I say with a smirk. "Good-a? Gouda? Get it?"

"No, I really don't understand your humor."

"Maybe because you don't have a sense of humor."

"I assure you I do," he says with irritation. "The cheese?"

"Queso blanco is near to impossible to find in France so I used
Halloumi."

"It was nice," he says, and I recoil.

Is he trying to butter me up with compliments? I have to find out
his agenda. "Thanks," I say, throwing on my apron and cap.

"If we're going to work together, tell me about your concept," he
continues.

"*Raffiné*, a little bit on the gourmet side of things. Fresh ingredients. Exotic flavors with a French twist."

"I like the idea of refined cooking with a bit of fusion," he says, and now I'm really perplexed by his demeanor. "I need to see what we're working with. Can I see your proposed menu?"

I untack one from the board, handing it over.

As he scrutinizes the menu, Charles paces, shaking his head with apparent disgust. "Refined. You want refined? This menu needs to change. A raw bar? In the summer? You do realize the best oysters are in season during the 'r' months? Mussels too."

He's immediately put me on the defense. "There are still good oysters to be found. And you haven't tasted my mussels."

"Not for anybody with a true palate or who knows them. Only tourists."

And now I want to slap him. "What's wrong with tourists?"

"You need to attract the locals to sustain a business." He slams his hand on the prep table. "This menu is wrong in so many ways."

Heat flares on my neck. "My restaurant. My menu."

"Are you always such a control freak?"

"I am when I know I'm right."

"You have far too many choices. It's a mash of everything." He scowls, shakes his head. "And half of your offerings aren't even in season." He points to an entrée, taps his finger like a hammer. "Figs? Figs? They aren't in season until August. It's only just the beginning of June."

I glare. "I found figs. Delicious ones."

"And you're probably paying a premium for them." He lifts his shoulders. "And they're probably not from France. Are you insane?"

I slam my fist onto the prep table and then brace myself, leaning forward. "I'm not insane. But you're a pompous jerk. If you can't work with my menu, I can't work with you."

"Wait, Kate," he says, clasping his hand on my shoulder before I storm off. "We promised my mother two weeks, and that's exactly what we're going to do. I had a long talk with her last night. Can't we come up with a happy medium? Instead of hell, maybe we can try to get along."

I'm not expecting this response and need a second to think. I hold up a finger. "Give me a minute. I'll be right back."

I take off my apron to go the bathroom. Sitting on the seat, I'm wondering what he's up to. He'd pulled the bait and switch last night, pretending to be nice and then launched into devil mode. What's his next move? I wash my hands and splash water on my face, readying myself.

When I return to the kitchen, I throw my apron back on and eggs fly out of the pockets, splattering on the walls. Charles can't meet my furious eyes because he's hunched over in laughter, wheezing, "I told you I had a sense of humor."

"How old are you? Twelve?" I ask, but he doesn't answer because he can barely breathe. "I'm sure this isn't what they do at Michelin restaurants."

He snorts. "No, no, never, but I read about this haze in one of the trade magazines and thought it would be fun to try it out."

"Not funny," I say, placing my hands on my hips. "And you're cleaning up this mess."

"Oui, Kate. I will," he says, grabbing some kitchen towels. He can barely stand he's laughing so hard.

"Why are you doing this to me?" I sob. "This is my dream. It's not a joke."

What I really want to say is that *I'm* not a joke.

He sets the towel down on the prep table and walks over to me, placing his hands on my shoulders. "I'm sorry, Kate. I thought you thought I didn't have a sense of humor, and I wanted to prove you wrong. I really didn't mean to upset you. Well, I wanted to irk you, but not this much."

I take a step back and wipe my runny nose with the sleeve of my shirt. "I don't believe you."

"Okay. Let's start over. Can we have some fun in the kitchen, maybe even laugh a little bit? Make my mother's deal a little less torturous for both of us?"

"Sounds like a plan," I say. "For now. But no more pranks."

He takes a step closer and grips my hands. "Alors, we're good?"

Please back off. And stop smiling at me. Go back to being mean.

I release my hands from his, wipe them on my apron, and point to yolks and eggshells on the floor. "We're good if you clean this up."

"Deal," he says, dropping to his knees and wiping the eggs off the floor.

My eyes focus on his arms, the way he's scrubbing.

When he's finished mopping up the mess, he faces me and squints. "I'm wondering, what made you want to become a chef?"

"Food has always been my passion." I let out a breath and avoid his gaze. "I love creating, experiencing, and tasting. For me, food is better than sex, and way more adventurous and innocent at the same time. I lose myself in finding the balance of the flavors, finding a way to invoke all the senses." I pause, meet his eyes. "What about you?"

"You took the words right out of my mouth," he says, leaning forward on the prep table. "I feel the same way, mostly." He chuckles. "But better than sex? No way."

This is a conversation I want to avoid, because all I'm thinking about right now is Charles picking me up, placing me on the prep counter, and ripping off my clothes. Angry sex. Passionate sex. Movie sex. But this isn't a movie, this is my life, and I'm fighting for my dream.

Lowering my lashes, I mumble, "Right, right, right," and then change the subject. "Look, I'm open to your ideas, but I get final approval. Okay?"

"Kate, it's your restaurant. You're in control of everything. And I'd really like to understand your vision." He smiles, flashing beautiful pearly whites. "I think we should start off with a tour of your castle. I need to know everything about this kitchen."

He holds out his hand for a fist bump. I hope we're no longer sworn enemies, but I'm definitely being pushed into the friend zone. And my mind, my body, is screaming for more.

"Come on," I say with a nervous breath. "Let me show you around."

After the tour, where he murmurs his approval, we head back to the prep station. I clasp my hands together. "Do you need help?"

"And let you in on my secrets?"

I shrug. "I'm a chef. I'd figure it out anyway. And I already saw the lemongrass."

He raises a brow, shoots me a slight scowl. "Is that a slight because I didn't know what cheese you used in the enchiladas?"

"Whoa, I don't think anybody could have figured it out with the sauce."

"The sauce was nice."

This is going much better than I thought—almost too perfectly. It's almost as if we "get" each other. Because of his compliment I'm pretty sure I look deranged, but he hasn't called me crazy yet—a good sign.

"So, what are we cooking for your mom?"

"One of her favorite dishes—nasi campur, a traditional dish from Jakarta, where my father was born." He pauses, flashes a wicked grin. "You'll love it."

"What if I don't?"

"Then there's something wrong with your taste buds." He grins again. "I assure you that you'll be licking your plate."

After giving me a sexy smirk, he unpacks the crate, unloading spices and ingredients, and says, "Nasi campur is one of Indonesia's national dishes—very traditional. The name means 'mixed rice,' and it's typically served with a variety of local dishes, such as chicken satay, beef rendang, prawn crackers." He slams a whole chicken on the counter. "Can you handle this, Chef?"

My eyes go wide—from the fact he called me chef, which is a sign of respect, and also the fact this chicken still has downy white feathers on it, the head, the feet—everything. I point. "You couldn't have had the butcher take care of this?"

"I wanted to see what you could do. You're a chef. Get plucking. Unless you're scared. Or not a real chef."

"Right now, I want to pluck you." And, damn, that came out so wrong. My face goes hot. I unroll my knives, picking up the biggest cleaver before he can respond and cut off the chicken's neck and head with a swift whack. I look up at Charles. "Don't mess with me. My knives are always sharp."

Charles picks up the head of the chicken and, moving the beak, he says, "Kiss me, Kate."

Oh my god. I want to.

As he chases me around, I'm laughing, and I'm not thinking about chicken. I'm staring at his full lips. His laughter rocks the kitchen, and I snap out of the fantasy that is about to set in.

"Kate, I told you I had a sense of humor," he says, wheezing.

"You're not funny," I say with a snort. I grip the chicken, pull, and then throw a handful of feathers in the air. They float around us, al-most suspended in the air, and our eyes meet again.

"But I am. You're laughing." Charles's laughter booms. "I don't think you've ever plucked a chicken. You're supposed to scald it in hot water first for about a minute." He throws the chicken head into the garbage, picks up the unplucked chicken, puts it in a bucket, and walks over to the walk-in cooler. "We'll take care of this later." He pulls out a butcher paper–covered package from the crate and sets it on the prep table. "This is the chicken we're using for the satay, butcher-prepared. And I've already made the peanut sauce."

I shoot him a mock glare. "I know how to devein a foie gras like the best of them and how to break down a chicken into eight parts, but they didn't teach me that at Le Cordon Bleu."

"Yeah, I know they didn't." His eyes stop watering and he straightens up, his breath still ragged. "I learned my chicken-stripping skills in Jakarta with my grandparents. My *nenek* was a force to be reckoned with in the kitchen. She's one of the reasons I became a chef, taught me everything I know—told me a real man could cook, which was obviously a dig to my *kakek*."

"Pluck off," I say as he threads slices of chicken filets onto the lemongrass.

"Pluck you," he says with a sexy chuckle. "My mother was right. I really did need to get back into the kitchen."

"This isn't what I had in mind."

"Me neither," he says, hip bumping me. "But it's kind of fun messing with you."

"You're right," I respond. "You do have a sense of humor. It's sick and twisted."

For a moment, I watch his hands, the way they move, the way they know exactly what they are doing. He grabs a knife and chops up a cucumber into paper-thin slices, not even needing a mandoline. His skills surpass mine.

I'm staring at his lotus tattoo, the way it ripples when he flexes his muscles, wondering if he has any more. I get my meandering thoughts back on track. "Did you have a nice time visiting with your family?"

He sighs. "Yes. And no. It's just so much harder seeing them without my dad."

"You grew up in Jakarta and Singapore, right?"

Charles nods, and his body tenses. He stops chopping fresh herbs and meets my eyes. "Kind of—I grew up all over Southeast Asia, thanks to Tenang Resorts. My roots, where I spent the most time, were planted in Singapore, but my dad is Chinese Indonesian."

"Why'd you decide on Paris?"

"My mother is here." He offers a sad laugh. "Somebody has to keep an eye on her now that my dad can't." He eyes the carrots. "Can you get back to grating?"

A few layers of what was once a stinky onion reveal themselves. Charles respects and protects the women in his life. My heart rate picks up a beat or two.

THE REST OF the day goes by—no pranks, no digs, no animosity, but there is tension. Sexual tension as we cut and dice, our hands touching a few times as we reach for ingredients. I'm wondering if Charles feels it too.

After storing all the prepared goods in the walk-in, he grins. "Today was fun."

"Yeah, it was," I agree.

"My mother texted me that she'll be coming by at one tomorrow, so I was thinking we should meet here at eleven? Plenty of time to finish up and cook."

"Okey dokey," I say, an idea coming to mind. "Hey, are you free before that?"

"I am. Why?"

"I want to take you somewhere." I lift up my chin, my mouth in a half smile. "I think you'll like it."

He takes off his apron and baseball cap, hanging them up in the locker. As he smooths back his hair, he says, "You barely know me—"

"I know enough about you to know you'll like what I have in

mind," I say, tilting my head to the side. "Are you not up for a challenge?"

"When you put it that way, I'm intrigued," he says, turning to face me, a curious eyebrow lifted. "I'm in."

"Good," I say with a perfunctory nod. "Meet me downstairs on the street at nine. Don't be late."

"Yes, Chef," he says, and a small part of me wonders if he's being sarcastic with this show of respect.

I'll find out tomorrow because, although it seems we buried the hatchet, I don't trust him as far as I can throw him, meaning not at all.

CHAPTER FOURTEEN

Smashed

EVER SINCE I'D mentioned it to Caro, I've been aching to go back to the rage room to let out some extra tension and stress. And I have a feeling Charles needs to let off a little steam too. My heart beats in anticipation of seeing him again—not just for his looks, but the banter. Whether I liked it or not, I'd had fun with him in the kitchen. I step onto the sidewalk, and he offers a wave from the corner. Today, like yesterday, his hair is pulled back into a short ponytail, and he's wearing black. I'm wearing a navy T-shirt and boyfriend-style blue jeans, and my blond ponytail is messy.

"It's a twenty-minute walk from here," I say, making my approach and blowing a rogue hair away from my nose, instead of exchanging les bises, though I do consider kissing his cheek for a moment. "On y va. Our reservation is at nine thirty."

His gaze meets mine, and he looks supremely confused. "Reservation? Are we eating somewhere?"

"Nope. We're not. You'll see." My pace is brisk as we traipse down Rue Dieu. I shoot him a side-glance. "What's your favorite color?"

"This is what you want to know about me?" he asks, and I nod.

"This is only the warm-up. Believe me, we'll talk more soon," I say. "We could discuss the weather if you'd like? I mean, it's seriously a nice day."

Charles nudges me to the side.

"What? You don't like idle chitchat?"

"Look behind you," he says, and I do.

I'd just missed stepping into a giant mound of dog crap. I bat my eyelashes. "Thank you." I grin and then start singing "Holding Out for a Hero" softly, my pace picking up. I add a little booty shake.

"I don't think you need a hero," he says with a laugh. "I think you're trying to torture me."

"What?" I exclaim, stopping midstep. "My voice isn't bad. Oded agrees, and I'm taking his critique over yours. He's a musician. You're just . . . ," I begin, my voice trailing off as he meets my gaze. His eyes are liquid, hypnotic, and intense.

"I'm what?"

I have to recover from this without sounding like a complete psychopath or before telling him how beautiful I think he is. I scratch my head and put one foot in front of the other. "Supposed to answer my question."

He rolls his eyes. "Fine. For clothes, I prefer black, but I love all shades of blue, especially peacock, navy, and teal." He pauses. "I also like the color of your eyes, clear like the sky—"

I stumble, tripping over my own two feet. "You noticed my eyes?"

"Of course, we were together for most of the day." He nudges my side with his elbow. "They're much prettier when you're not glaring at me. And you?"

I'm thrown for a loop. Is he asking if I like his liquid-brown with a hint of green and completely hypnotic eyes? Probably not. But my answer would be yes. "And me what?"

"What's your favorite color?"

"Oh, right," I say with a nervous giggle. "Orange. Orange is my favorite color." And now I sound like Buddy from the movie *Elf*. I pick up my pace. "But I like blue too."

He bounds up to me. "Why are you walking so fast?"

"We need to be on time," I say with a slight pant. "Okay. Next question. Favorite movie."

"All the *Die Hard*s. Anything with Jackie Chan—" He stops mid-sentence and points to a man riding a bicycle, his tie-dyed outfit out of this world, with at least fifty stuffed animals piled precariously on the back, zooming down the street with music blaring—Mika's "Relax, Take It Easy." "And I thought you were bizarre."

"I'm not bizarre. I'm creative. Different strokes for different folks and all that. And wait a sec." I stop walking to catch my breath. "Back to your previous statement. Please don't tell me you that you don't like romances or romantic comedies. Because they are kind of my jam."

"I love them, in fact," he says. "But only the old ones—the ones my mother and I watched together."

He loves them? He can't be this perfect. "Which ones?"

"*Bringing Up Baby, Breakfast at Tiffany's, Casablanca,* and *Buona Sera, Mrs. Campbell*—"

My throat catches. He's mentioned most of my all-time favorites. "There's a big cat in *Bringing Up Baby*. A leopard—"

"I know," he says with a chuckle. "I like big cats. I just don't get along with Juju. I think he's jealous of me."

"And are you jealous of him?"

"Don't be ridiculous."

We pass by Place de la République, where, go figure, there's another manifestation—this one for climate change. The large crowd holds up signs and chants "*Nous ne sommes pas vos marionnettes*" and the police—dressed in riot gear with shields—are out in full force doing their best to keep the crowd under control. When I first moved to France, these kinds of public demonstrations scared the crap out of me, but they've become part of my life, almost weekly occurrences, ranging from the gilet jaunes to anti-vaxxers to political rallies. Sometimes they're peaceful; oftentimes they are not, the police using tear gas to disperse the masses. One time, I'd gotten off the Metro after they'd smoked up the place and, boy, did my eyes and throat burn for hours. Thankfully, there were volunteers from civil security leading people out of the station through the haze.

As we walk through the square, I examine the sculpture of Marianne, one of the symbols of France, topped on a chalky white seventy-foot-high monument representing *liberté*, *égalité*, and *fraternité*, holding an olive branch.

Charles grabs my arm, leading me away from the crowd. "I'm all for climate change, but I really hope this isn't where you wanted to bring me."

I shake my head. "The olive branch I'm presenting you is about ten minutes from here."

"Olive branch?"

"You'll see," I reply, turning on my heel. "Let's go."

Finally, after rounding a few more corners of busy Parisian streets, passing buildings covered with wild graffiti, I'm out of breath when we arrive to our destination, stopping in front of an old kebab restaurant in an alley. "We're here," I say.

Charles places his hands on his hips. "You can't be serious. I thought we weren't eating."

"We're not," I reply. "This is going to be the best thing you've done all week, maybe all year. Follow me."

Charles shakes his head and holds up his hands in utter confusion. I lead him across the street to a brick building. We walk into the lobby and Charles eyes the yellow-painted brick wall with the words in black: "RAGE ROOM: CHOOSE YOUR WEAPON." A baseball bat, a golf club, an ax, and a crowbar are mounted underneath these words. In front of us stands a reception desk and, down the hall, a bar.

"What is this place?" asks Charles.

"Sssh. Just go with it. Trust me, you'll like it." I walk up to reception. "Bonjour, I made a nine thirty reservation, the full-madness deal, for two people under Jenkins."

"Right. Prepaid," says the host, a young guy in his twenties with tattoos on his neck and tribal piercings. "*Suivez-moi.*"

Charles raises his eyebrows. I shrug.

We follow our host into a decayed and decrepit room. The host hands us goggles, plastic face masks, gloves, protective vests, and coveralls. "*Amusez-vous,*" he says, and leaves the room, closing the door behind him.

I suit up, looking a lot like the police we'd passed at Place de la République, as Charles watches me with a look of utter shock. Then I grab an ax.

"Choose your weapon," I say, stroking the blade.

He places his hands on his hips, his forearms flexing. "Is this a gladiator thing where we fight to the death? I mean, as much as you may have annoyed me, I don't want to hurt you."

I laugh. "Do you see any lions?"

"No, I see a bunch of crappy shit."

"Exactly. And we're going to smash the hell out of them, get all our aggressions out," I say, and his eyes light up. He surveys the room—the bottles, the television screens, the computers, the plates. "Now, get ready. And then choose your weapon."

"This could be fun," he says, his smile slowly reaching his eyes, and then he shimmies into the coveralls.

"Right? This is the reason I brought you here. But I have a rule."

He snorts and picks up a baseball bat, knocks his feet with it as if he's preparing for a home run. "Of course you do."

I snap on my vest. "After we break or smash anything, we tell each other our reasons for doing so."

"Is this your idea of couples therapy?" he says, leaning into me with a hip bump.

I stand rigid for a moment, trying to balance my thoughts, my words, before I pull a Kate—spouting off nonsense. I remind myself: I'm the one in charge here. I lift up my chin and face him.

"Kind of, but we're not a couple," I reply, hoping my voice doesn't betray my thoughts. I clear my throat. "If we're really going to work together, even if it's for a short time, I thought this might be a good way to get any lingering frustrations out."

"Okay. I'm game," he says, rubbing his chin. "Ladies first."

"Put your face mask on. I'm going medieval." I pick up a plate, throw it the air, and smash it with the ax, bits of porcelain flying. I turn to face him, placing the ax blade down on the floor, and balancing my weight on the handle. "I hated you when I met you. And I still think, even though you're being somewhat nice now, you're up to something."

I throw another plate, shattering it on the wall.

Through his visor, I see his eyes narrow. He places a bottle on the table, swings, and crash—an explosion of glass.

"I don't trust anybody, Kate, especially when I think they're taking advantage of my mother."

I pick up a vase, set it on the table, and whack it with the ax. I yell, "I don't have a choice. She offered to help. And if I don't succeed, my dream will die. The kitchen is my life. And I don't have a life outside the kitchen."

I wheeze and whack. And then my gaze meets his, and I lift my shoulders innocently. "Your turn."

Charles takes a step back. "Whoa. Remind me to never get on your bad side."

"You already have."

"I apologized."

"It wasn't sincere."

"It is now," he says. "What do you mean you don't have a life outside the kitchen? What do you do for fun?"

"I clomp around my apartment and sing with my friends," I say. "I also smash things."

His eyebrows furrow. "Kate, believe me, there's more to life than just cooking."

"Maybe for others," I say. "But not for me. Not right now."

"Okay, my turn." He throws a plate into the air, smashes it. "What are you after?"

I push his back. "I'm after my dream, you jerk."

"I'm not a jerk, and I'm going again," he says with a nod, placing the TV screen onto the table. "When I first met you, you just caught me on the worst of days. I told you I was dealing with family estate stuff." He pauses and then lifts the bat over his shoulder and bashes the screen over and over again. "I really fucking miss my father and my grandfather. It should have been me on the plane. I'm the one who should have died."

I wasn't expecting this kind of emotionally charged outburst from him. I slowly back away into a corner of the room. He's going apeshit, beating the television until there is nothing left but bits and pieces of scrap on the concrete floor. I remain silent, not knowing what to say, my jaw open. I just let him breathe, watching his chest rise and fall as he sinks to his knees. And I'm thinking, *Wow, there's more to him than just his sexy looks and talent in the kitchen; he's sensitive and not afraid to share his feelings.*

Finally, he looks up and shoots me a melancholy grin. "Damn, Kate, that felt really good. Thank you for this."

I walk over to him and place a hesitant hand on his shoulder. "Why do you think it should have been you? On the plane?"

"Because I turned my back on the family business to follow my dream," he says after swallowing, his eyes tearing. "If I hadn't become a chef, it would have been me on the plane."

"I'm sure your dad understood you were following your own path, not his," I begin, and then let out a breath. "The plane crash wasn't your fault."

"Wait," he says, meeting my eyes. "You knew about it?"

"Yes," I say with a guilty shrug. "I may have thought your mother was a mobster. So yeah, I kind of googled her. And she kind of told me about her life one day. She also said she couldn't imagine if she lost her son, that no parent should ever have to experience that kind of pain."

He squeezes his eyes shut, processing my words, and then blurts out an unrestrained laugh. "Wait, you thought my ibu was involved with the Mafia?"

"I know it sounds ridiculous. But, in my defense, when I met her, she told me about the old owner of the restaurant disappearing, and then, minutes later, a piano almost killed me."

Charles grips his belly. He's laughing so hard, he's crying. "And," he wheezes, "to think I thought you were after her money when you thought she was after your life. I can't even—"

I nudge him with my toe. "It's not that funny."

"But it is."

"Gah! Would you just get up?" I offer a hand, and he takes it. With a struggle, I pull him up from the ground. "We only have ten more minutes and I need to smash more things. I'm frustrated with the restaurant. I'm mad my dad didn't show up to the opening." I huff. "This isn't a joke. I've got a lot of aggression to get out."

Once he makes it to his feet, he meets my eyes. "You know what, Crazy Kate? I get it. And I kind of get you now."

His smile may melt me into butter.

"Don't call me crazy." I pause and hold up my ax. "I'm serious."

"After today, believe me, I won't."

"So, now that you know I'm not after anything but my dream, can we be friends?" I ask, and he smiles.

"Definitely."

"I guess I should stop calling you Anti-Keanu, then."

"I may still call you Crazy Kate. It's got a ring to it," he says, and I shoot him a mock glare. He nudges my shoulder like I'm his kid sister. "By the way, I'd like to pay for this. How much did this set you back?"

"A couple hundred euros," I say.

"Worth every centime." He smashes a pile of bottles. "I'm paying."

"But you're not. I've already paid."

The truth: I would have preferred spending this money to ensure the success of my restaurant, maybe buy more plants, but if I'm being forced to work with him (not that I mind so much anymore), I'm looking at this as a very solid investment. And it paid off. After we got our aggressions out, we came to a meeting of the minds, and I'd learned he had his own issues and trauma to work through.

"What if I insist?"

"I'd say no."

He sucks in a breath, and his eyes widen with surprise. "Wow. This is a first. Merci, Kate."

As I assess his words, I tilt my head. "Nobody has ever treated you?"

"No," he says, shaking his head. "The world is full of users and opportunists." He picks up his bat and swings it, smashing a computer screen. He takes in a deep breath and turns to me. "Promise me, Kate, that you aren't one of them, because if you are, I'll make your life hell."

For crying out loud, we're back to this again?

I clench my teeth and pick up a bottle, throwing it against the wall. "I'm not a user. And I'm not after anything from you or your mother. And if I fucking have to explain myself and my dream to you again," I begin, and then smash another bottle, "I'm going to kill you." Out of breath, I place my hands on my hips. "The door is there. If you don't trust me and my intentions, just go."

"I don't want to," he says, crossing his arms across his chest. "I just needed to know you really didn't ask for her help." He steps forward and holds out his hand. "Truce?"

I grip his hand. We shake. "For now, unless you're about to make another bet?"

"No, no bets, Kate, unless we're wagering on ensuring your dream."

My heart is pounding, beating frantically like the wings of a hummingbird in flight. "Are you for real?"

"I am."

"We'll see," I say, grabbing another plate and smashing it.

CHAPTER FIFTEEN

====

Double Trouble

WE'RE BACK IN the kitchen, cooking up a storm, when a cough comes from the doorway. "Chef, sorry to disturb you," says Albert, the only staff member of mine who didn't quit and was lucky to have weeks of paid vacation. "I'm here for my check and wanted to know when you're reopening."

"Right, right, right," I say, looking at Charles. I have no clue. "What's the plan?"

"In a week," says Charles.

"*Génial*," says Albert. "Have you hired a new staff, or are the others coming back?"

My face pales. "I . . . no, they're not."

Albert shuffles his feet. "I was wondering if I could be a server instead of a busboy and dishwasher. I don't have much experience, but I'm a quick learner. And I know the ordering and reservations systems."

"Sure, sure, sure," I say, rubbing my temples with my fingertips.

"Thanks, Chef," says Albert. "Just let me know when the reopening is scheduled and I'll be here."

He bounds out of the kitchen, leaving me to face Charles, his arms crossed over his chest.

"Kate, you don't have a full staff?" he asks, and I shake my head. "No hostess? No bartender? No servers? No line cooks?"

I want to crawl into the walk-in cooler and lock myself in it. "Everybody but Albert quit."

He clicks his tongue, a *tsk, tsk, tsk*. "This is serious, Kate."

"I know," I say, shuddering because he's right. "I thought Oded and I could handle everything for the time being. What with no customers."

"We're in a new situation now. And we have to be prepared for it."

I catch my breath. He said *we*. And damn. An idea comes to mind. Why didn't I think of this before? I prop my elbows on the prep table, raise a brow.

"I'll see if Le Cordon Bleu has any recent graduates who want to come into the kitchen, maybe a few of them wouldn't mind starting out as servers or roustabouts. All the people we'll call in will be *stagiaires*. They'll practically work for free."

He eyes me warily. "Good idea," he says, and by the nod of his head, I think he's more impressed with me. I'm not the lackey he initially thought I was with a mishmash menu and no staff.

"Can we postpone the opening?"

"No," he says. "My mother has already sent out the invitations. With this list of hers, there's no backing down now."

"That's right," says Garrance.

"We'll help," says my mom.

Charles and I shoot each other shocked looks, our eyes darting back and forth.

Both of our mothers stand in the doorway, and I have no idea for how long. Or why they've been spending so much time together. And why they have such large shopping bags set at their feet.

"I'll be an interim hostess until you find somebody more suitable," says Garrance. "I only have to attend a few board meetings for Tenang, and I'm not one to look down on hard work."

"And I'll tend the bar," says my mom. "I had so much fun with our experiments." She points, her gaze darting between Charles and me. "Isn't that Anti—"

"Yes, Mom. Mom, meet Charles, Garrance's son." I cringe. "Charles, this is my mother."

Mom mouths, "He's gorgeous," and thankfully Charles doesn't see.

"Please call me Cri-Cri," says my mom with a big, dopey smile. "And we're both here to help shed off some of the negative energy." She does a strange wiggly move, shaking her arms and fingers. "Lovely to meet you. Garrance speaks the world of you."

Garrance nods her head in agreement, her silky black hair glimmering. "I do in regards to both of you. And we're here to offer our support."

My mom drumrolls her hands on the prep station.

"We ordered new aprons and caps for the staff." Garrance pulls out one of each, and my eyes lock on to to the color: red. "Both of us find black so very drab, and red symbolizes—"

"Luck and success," I say with a sigh, taking an apron. "And I need all of it I can get."

"I'm certain the two of you will create with passion," says Garrance.

"Yes," agrees my mom. "After all, Kate, a Cancer, was born in the year of the dog, and Charles, as you told me, is a Virgo, born in the year of the rabbit—a perfect celestial match. Plus, you're seven years apart in age. Such a lucky number! Whatever you make together will surely be heavenly."

"Are you staying for lunch, Cri-Cri?" I ask, clasping my hands together.

Please leave before you open your mouth again and embarrass me more.

"No, as much as I'd love to, I can't," she says, and I let out an internal sigh of relief. "I made an appointment to get a manicure and pedicure—the ones where fish eat the dead skin off your feet. I just wanted to pop by." She nods to the bags. "Don't forget to put the new uniforms away."

After my mother breezes out of the kitchen, Garrance places her hands on her hips. "I didn't expect the two of you to work things out. But I'm so happy you did," she says. "I'm going to take care of the orchids. And I'm expecting my meal when I'm done. Negotiating with me is not an option." She waggles a finger, turns, and then meets my eyes. "I'm expecting something out of this world—not a typical nasi campur. Kate, this may be on you." She holds out a bag. "It's cardamom from India, the finest in the world. Use it how you see fit."

Garrance leaves us, and Charles and I stand immobile, eyes locked. "Well, you've now met my mom," I say, breaking the silence.

"Just what I've always dreamed of. We have two meddling women in our world," he says with a low, sexy laugh. "Um, your mother seems very spiritual."

"You don't even want to know."

"She's interesting. Based on my first impression, I like her," he says. "And I'm glad my mother has a friend. How long have they been conspiring together?"

"Honestly, no clue. They met at the first disastrous opening and must have exchanged numbers. I have no idea what they are up to."

He grins. "Probably no good."

I nod, making a mental list in my head.

1. Make sure to lock the front door
2. Take away your mother's key

"True," I say, pulling out my phone. "I'm calling Le Cordon Bleu to see if I can get this staffing situation sorted out."

Pacing, I call up the school. After eavesdropping on my call, Charles takes off his cap and swipes a lock of hair out of his eyes.

"And?"

"We're good," I say. "They're sending over candidates in a few days."

He makes a dramatic movement, sweeping his hand across his forehead. "Phew."

"The director said wonderful things about you, that you're very talented," I say, and then smell the cardamom Garrance had given me, and I'm instantly put into a trance from green, earthy, and perfumed aromas. It's like all my troubles are gone. I'm in India, envisioning dances and beautiful saris and delicious naan bread baked on hot coals.

Charles taps me on the shoulder. "Kate, where did you go?"

I wobble. "I think I was in Mumbai for a second. Maybe Chennai? I don't know. I've never been to India. I've just seen pictures in magazines."

He places his hands on my shoulders. "Spices transport you?"

"Yes," I say, still a little bit out of it. "Hers do."

He grips my shoulders, pulls me in closer. I smell his vanilla scent, and my knees turn to butter. "And I now know why my mother likes you. It makes perfect sense. She was right."

"About what?" I ask, breathing him.

"Working together and letting go of the bad energy. I know we can do this." His eyes spark with a passionate fire, and he smiles, his dimple puckering. I might melt like fondue. "Let's create a meal for her—the best one she's ever had."

He leans against the stove, his sexy, smoldering hazel eyes meeting mine.

My neck goes hot. I race over to the prep station and pick up the bag of cardamom, breathe it in—earthy, sweet, smoky, and nutty. Big mistake. Because I'm now licking his muscled chest in one of my deranged fantasies, which is so wrong. I throw the bag down, and the grains scatter on the countertop. Charles saunters over and places a hand on my shoulder. "Kate, everything okay?"

"Cool, cool, cool," I say. I shrug off his touch, dip around his shoulder, noticing how V-shaped he is. "I was thinking we add this into the peanut sauce for the satay."

"Good idea," he says. "Grind it. Nice and fine."

Stop. Stop talking with your lilting English accent. Stop smiling.

I'm staring at his hands, his lips, his eyelashes. My mind, my thoughts, and my body are about to explode.

"Kate, can you pass me the chilis? My mother likes things spicy."

"So do I," I say, reaching for it. Our hands touch as I hand him the spice.

I shiver.

"Me too," he says with a teasing growl. "And I know you added more pepper into my dish the other day. Good thing I can handle the heat."

I can't. It's getting way too hot in here. *Be mean*, I pray. I'm silent as I watch him slice and dice. Oh, the things he's doing with hands with such expertise and I wonder what they'd feel like on me. I need to cool off. Maybe I'll go into the walk-in and lie down.

He points to a cabbage, a red pepper, and a couple of carrots on the prep station. "Along with the cukes, I'd like to make a shredded salad."

"I have some kaffir limes," I say.

"She gave you some?" he asks.

"Yep," I say. "Yep, yep."

"She must really like you." He picks up an onion, dices it in two seconds. "You know what? You're kind of growing on me too."

"Like mold?" I ask.

"No, you smell too good," he says, turning his back to me. "I know your kitchen is well equipped. I hope you have a rice steamer."

"Duh," I say, mentally kicking myself for my unprofessional response. "Of course I do."

I walk over to the cabinet and step up onto my toes, but I can't reach the damn contraption. Charles steps behind me, reaches over my head, and grabs it before it tumbles on my head. For two brief seconds, his body presses into mine, his hands steadying my waist. I swear he's breathing me in. And I'm doing the same. He grabs the steamer, sets it on the counter. But he only shifts slightly, and there's clearly something wrong with my legs; they won't budge. I think I may be paralyzed.

"Did my mother make you the perfume you're wearing?" he asks, his breath on my neck.

"Uh, yeah, she did."

"The base notes smell delicious on you," he says, his voice husky and hot.

My spine tingles. A drop of perspiration beads on my forehead. I clamp my lips together before I tell him he smells delicious too and that he's invaded my thoughts ever since I first met him on the street.

Focus, Kate. CONTROL!

I duck under his arm and whip around, regaining my composure. "Let's get cooking, shall we?"

His expression is as shocked as mine is. His hand brushes across his face, his beautiful stubbled chin with the perfect two-day growth.

Finally, we plate the dish on a banana leaf, setting the rice in the middle and surrounding it with the vegetables, meats, and sauces. He looks up as he places the garnish, a thick cucumber slice carved into a lotus flower and a couple of carrots shaped into leaves, each detail intricate, each cut precise.

"Where did you learn to do that?" I ask.

"When we lived in Thailand. You should see what I can do with a mango," he says with a wink. "I can teach you the art of carving if you'd like."

"Um, yeah," I say, and shake the thoughts of what we could do with mango juice dripping down my breasts. "It's quite impressive."

And so are you.

"It's a date," he says, and my heart does a back flip. "But now we have to serve my mother, the queen. Trust me, Kate, you don't want to see her when she's hangry."

I snort out a laugh. "Hangry?"

"I may speak English, Indonesian, Mandarin, French, and Singlish fluently, but you're teaching me a new language, Kate."

"I bet I can teach you a lot of things," I say, lifting up my chin and meeting his gaze.

"And I bet I can teach you a few things too."

My heart flutters and I'm losing focus. I turn around and pick up the platter. "No more bets. Let's just get lunch served."

"A MOTHER KNOWS best," says Garrance. She takes a bite of the satay and then the rice. She daintily dabs her lips with a napkin, eyeing the dish. "This is the best nasi campur I've ever had, and believe me, I know. I knew the two of you could come together."

I clear my throat. Why did she have to say that? And Charles has to stop looking at me underneath those long eyelashes of his.

"Kate, I told you my son could cook. What do you think?"

I take a bite of the beef rendang. "It's good," I say with an involuntarily sigh. In fact, it's delicious—all the flavors hit me in waves. My upper lip is sweating. "But it may need less heat."

Garrance's phone rings. She answers it and then leaps up from her chair. "Kate, I have just the thing to cool you down." She claps and races to the front door. "It's a wonderful surprise."

My gaze locks on to Charles. "What's going on?"

Charles shrugs. "No clue."

To my surprise, a man wheels in a very big aquarium. "Where do I put this?"

"Behind the bar," says Garrance.

"What?" I exclaim.

Garrance tilts her head and pops her lips. "You didn't have a water element. And now you do." She instructs the deliveryman on where to install it.

This woman is trying to take over my vision. Granted, I actually adore the idea, but how much input of hers do I need to take? How much is it going to cost me? I sit back in my chair, a bit numb, my eyes meeting Charles's. "I didn't ask for this. You have to know I didn't."

"Welcome to my world," he says in a whisper and then stands up. "Ibu, this is Kate's restaurant, not yours."

Garrance's eyes focus like a laser onto mine. "Kate, do you not like the fish tank?"

"Uh, yes," I say. "It's an interesting component—"

"Wonderful. After Charles and I handle some business over at Tenang, the two of you are going to pick out fish today," says Garrance. She clasps her hands, smiles. "The more tropical, the better."

She eyes her watch and stands up. "Charles, we have to leave now. The board meeting starts in fifteen minutes."

Charles groans and then whispers, "Sorry about all of this. Can you handle cleaning up? I'll be back in a few hours."

"Sure."

After they leave, I wonder what the hell I've gotten myself into.

CHAPTER SIXTEEN

An Aria Is Not a Song

CHARLES HAS LEFT his knives and carving tools in the kitchen, and I'm more than curious. I unroll his knife bag, finding that they are all Japanese—Syosaku with hammered high-carbon stainless steel blades with handles made out of magnolia wood. The carving tools, on the other hand, are French—Bruneau, and he even has a special julienne tool and herb scissors made by the same mark. After running my fingers across the smooth handles, I put the knives back in order, feeling like a culinary spy.

Dreams, as mentioned, start with a vision, obtainable goals. Regardless of my fantasies about Charles, which is all that they are, and the desire probably unreciprocated, I'm focusing on opening up the doors of my restaurant to success, not my heart. I head to the bar and pull out my notebook to look at my latest list.

1. Hire a new staff
2. Keep it together, Kate. Don't overlook any details.
3. Stop thinking about Charles unless you are cooking together

Yep. That last note to myself didn't work. I look at the clock on the wall, wondering when he'll return. It's now a little past two in the afternoon. Antsy, I decide to take a walk to gather my meandering thoughts.

One foot follows the other, and I'm making my way to Le Jardin Villemin, busy with families—children running around in the play area, mothers and fathers laughing. Feeling melancholy, I sit on a bench. I want so much more. I'm so confused and out of sorts I don't even want to play my game of guess who would eat what.

My gaze drops down, and my eyes lock on to the cover of a tabloid magazine somebody left behind. I jolt out of my seat, standing upright in shock. On the cover, a picture of Charles is displayed, his arms crossed, his lotus tattoo exhibited in fine detail. The headline: CHARLES LIN-TRUFFAUT, FRANCE AND SINGAPORE'S MOST ELI-GIBLE BACHELOR.

I back away from the bench, wanting to hide. I feel like I'm in the scene of the movie *Music and Lyrics* when Sophie (played by Drew Barrymore) sees her abominable ex-boyfriend's book in a shop and she freaks out like I'm doing now. The look in Charles's eyes is so intense . . . it's almost as if he's watching my every move. But I'm not. I collide into a baby carriage and whip around to face a young woman.

"*Ça va?*" she asks, a look of concern pinching her face.

"I'm fine, fine, fine," I say, coming up with the most logical excuse for my odd behavior that I can think of. "I saw a rat." I point. "It leapt onto the bench and then scurried into those bushes. Over there."

"Ah, oui," she says, pushing her baby on as I peek into the carriage. The baby is adorable with chubby little legs like sausages. The mother, noticing me gawking, covers her baby with a blanket, blocking my view. "Rodents are a real problem with the canal. And the city. It's a good thing they are scared of humans."

No, they aren't. Definitely not. Still, I'm not about to tell a stranger about my incident with the rat when I was fifteen. Plus, she's already walked on. I'm left standing alone, the pages of the magazine flapping in the breeze. I look to the left, to the right. Nobody is watching. I race up to the bench, grab the magazine, and roll it, back cover facing the sun. Then, like a rat, I scurry as fast as I can to my apartment.

Charles Lin-Truffaut is so out of my league it's not even funny, and I really have to push the fantasies of him to the side. We're just cooking together, that's all, and I'm focusing on the success of my restaurant. Right?

I'M PACING IN the dining room, waiting for Charles to return. For a distraction, I put on some music and stretch out onto the floor, twisting my legs from one side to the other, allowing my spine to crack. Slowly, I move from a couple of sun salutations to mountain pose to warrior pose to tree pose. I'm in a zone. I'm finding my breath. And I'm in downward dog when, over the music, I hear, "Um, hello? I'm sorry to bother you," says a sultry woman's voice.

Shit. My ass is in the air, facing whoever is in the restaurant in all its bootylicious glory. I wonder how long she's been watching me. I snap to a standing position.

"Can I help you?" I say, focusing in on my unexpected visitor, taking in a quick breath and almost choking.

She's gorgeous, with mile-long legs, long black hair, a perfect smile, complete with a curvy but slim figure that most women would kill for. I'm trying to find her flaws—but nope, her breasts are definitely real, and it doesn't look like she's had anything else done. She's naturally beautiful—full lips and sexy, bedroom eyes. She towers over me in her spiked heels, and her outfit—a brown leather jacket over a slinky dress—is straight off the runway. People aren't supposed to be this good-looking in real life.

"I was looking for Charles Lin-Truffaut. Is he, by chance, here?" she says, and I stop gawking.

"No, he stepped out. And you are?"

"Aria."

My throat constricts. "And h-how do you know Charles?"

"Oh, I'm just an old friend from Singapore. Our paths didn't cross when he was in town," she says. "I found out he was working at a bistro, and I wanted to see it for myself." She surveys the space, her nose lifted. "Where are the customers?"

"We're reopening soon. In a week," I say, and her eyes narrow. She gives me the once-over, and the way she does it I feel naked, exposed.

"Oh, are you and Charles a thing?" she asks, lifting up her chin.

"Um, no, we're just cooking together," I say. This woman makes me nervous. She's like a cat, one that could strike at any moment. "You should come to the opening."

Why did I just say that?

"I'd love to." She looks at her watch. "I have to run. Oh, the life of a model." She pauses when my jaw drops, me feeling like a model idiot, and offers a half smile. "Do me a favor and don't tell Charles I stopped by. I want to surprise him, okay?"

"Uh, okay?"

She hands me a card. "Email me the details of the event, and I can assure you'll have a well-heeled crowd, uh, your name is—?"

"Kate." Crazy Kate for even thinking I could capture Charles's attention for a millisecond—not with women like this around. Something in my gut tells me she and Charles are more than just friends.

After she leaves, I pull out my phone and google her: Aria. Singapore. Search. Bam—a match—thousands of them. Like Madonna, she only goes by one name. I can't stop scrolling, flipping through pictures in horror. *Vogue* covers. *Cosmo* covers. *Maxim* covers. I'm nothing like her at all. I feel like a toad.

Someone taps me on the shoulder, and I close out of the browser immediately. It's Charles.

"What were you doing?"

"Before, a little yoga. Now, a little research," I say with a slight pant. I want to tell him about Aria stopping by, but I refrain because I'm seething with jealousy and the wrong words might come out. "It helps me to focus on my breathing."

"*Formidable*. Along with mixed martial arts, I practice too. Flexibility is important." He grins, a dimple puckering. "What's your favorite position?"

"All of them—especially reverse warrior." Damn. He does mixed martial arts. And he knows his way around the kitchen. With a blush creeping on my cheeks, I change the subject before I bring up the books—all the positions—my mom introduced me to.

"By the way, I spoke with my mother." He brushes a hand through his thick hair. "She just wants to feel needed and appreciated, especially after the death of my father." He pauses and takes in a deep breath. "She said she'll back off if you want her to. And so will I."

So, he questioned the menu and was a supreme jerk at first and Garrance installed a fish tank without asking me. I can't do *everything* on my own. I can adapt and adjust.

"I don't want her to. Or you to." I rock back and forth in my sneakers. "Ready to go catch us some fish for the tank? Maybe you'll find the gill of your dreams?" I say, my off-brand humor making me feel less vulnerable.

"Maybe I've already met her," he says with a shrug and turns for the kitchen.

My heart drops in my stomach like a weight. Surely, he's referring to Aria. "Where are you going?"

"I have to grab my knives."

"Your knives? Why?"

"You ask too many questions. You'll see."

Charles waits for me on the street, a backpack slung over one shoulder. He's on his phone, and he raises a finger. Two seconds. As I lock up, a shadow envelopes me. I turn, expecting to see Charles with an accusation that I fondled his gear, but it's Pierre Lavigne.

"Sorry to bother you, mademoiselle," he says, his lips puffed out. "But I miss my table. When will the restaurant reopen again?"

I know he misses his wife—the restaurant his last happy connection to her.

"In a week," I say. "But I tell you what. We're testing a few things out and will open it just for you. That is, if you don't mind an empty restaurant. And eating a few new things at lunchtime."

His blue eyes light up. "Mind? It would make me the happiest man in the world! Merci, mademoiselle."

"Please call me Kate," I say. "We'll see you tomorrow at noon. Consider your table reserved."

Pierre kisses me on the cheek, turns, and rounds the corner with a bounce in his step. I smile, and then I notice Charles watching me. He tucks his phone into the pocket of his jeans and swaggers over. "That was really kind of you. You're full of surprises. On y va. I may have a surprise for you."

"Are you going to throw me into a tank of piranhas?"

"You're funny, Kate."

He leads us down the street, and my heart sinks again. I feel like I've been reduced to being the comedic sidekick.

Charles walks with a brisk pace, and I'm finding it hard to keep up with him. Instead of turning toward the Metro, we're walking alongside the canal. I keep noticing the women gawking at him and giving me the stink eye, probably wondering what he's doing with a girl like me.

"Did you know that canal was built in the early 1800s to supply

Paris with fresh water?" he asks, and I shake my head. "Have you ever cruised the underground portion?"

"No," I say, wondering what he's up to.

His hand clasps on to my wrist, and he leads me through a throng of tourists. "I haven't either, which is why we're doing it today. Well, the one under la Bastille. There are three."

"I'm not a fan of confined spaces. I get a bit claustrophobic."

"Today, you're getting over your fears," he says, stopping in front of a boat at Quai de Valmy. It's sleek and white. "I booked us a private ride."

My heart is about to leap out of my chest. "What about the fish? We need to get fish."

"The store is located in the Marais, not far from our final stop." He jumps on board and holds out his hand. "Come on, I thought this would be interesting and fun. Plus, we can talk about what you want to do with the menu."

I stand rigid, nerves setting in. "The Metro would have been easier."

"It's also confined. And too many people."

"But it's safe."

"Trust me, Kate, so is this. And I've already paid, so there's that." He tilts his head. "It's also an apology for when I called you a crazy tourist. We're going to be crazy tourists together."

I gulp and take his hand, falling into him when I lose my balance. He grips my waist, steadying me, and he doesn't let go at first. When I find myself nuzzling his neck, breathing in his vanilla scent, I take a step back.

"Were you just sniffing me?"

Busted.

I try to hide the blush creeping on my cheeks and turn, pretending to check out the view. "Uh, no. I mean, why would I do that?" I point to a tree. "Look, a squirrel! So cute. I love French squirrels and their fuzzy ears."

"I don't see a squirrel," he says.

Because there isn't one.

Charles mumbles something I can't understand in Indonesian and then salutes the captain. He takes my hand and leads me to the upper deck. We're soon sitting at a table decorated with white linens and flowers. To the side, a buffet is set up with a variety of fruits and a chilled bottle of champagne in a silver bucket. Admittedly, my heart is fluttering like a caged bird from his close proximity. This is definitely the most romantic thing any man has ever done for me— minus the actual romance unless I count the fantasies picking at my brain.

After the crew unmoors the boat, a server pops up from out of nowhere and offers us a glass of champagne. Charles sets a paper bag on the table. "Have a taste," he says. "They're delicious."

I reach into the bag and pull out a dried fruit—dark red and pur- plish with wrinkled skin. "Is this a date?"

Charles leans forward and meets my eyes. "No, Kate, it's not a date."

As a dash of disappointment sets in, I clear my throat. "What is it?"

"It's a jujube fruit," Charles continues. "I brought them back from Indonesia. It may look like a date, but it isn't. It's a species from the Ziziphus in the buckthorn family. Packed with antioxidants, it calms the mind and strengthens the body."

"Oh," I say. I take one and place it in my mouth, savoring the sweet, apple-like flavor, only to realize I'm now chewing on the pit. With a pop of his lips, Charles blows his into the water, so I do the same. Unfortunately, my aim is so off the pit hits Charles smack-dab in the forehead. How classy.

"Sorry."

"It's okay." He dabs his head with a napkin, and I cringe. "They're good, aren't they?"

I clear my throat, searching for something, anything, to thwart my embarrassment. "I really don't feel like a tourist. It's more like lifestyles of the rich and famous."

"Because we're not *actually* tourists," he says with a grin. "And we have around two hours, so we're going to work." He steps up and heads over to the table, returning with two small watermelons and cutting boards. He sets them on the table. "I'm going to teach you to carve on the journey."

"Why?" I ask.

"Because I said I would," he says, pointing up to the arch of a *passerelle* as we float under it. "Call me crazy, but I'm kind of having fun with you."

"Okay, gila," I say with a snort, and he lets out a low laugh that sends shimmers up my spine. It takes some effort, but I pull myself together. "I'm looking forward to this."

He pulls out his carving knives from the bag, setting them on the table. "Getting back into the kitchen is, in fact, making me happy. And I haven't felt that way for a very long time. I have to let go of my grief and move on. My mom was right. You're helping me do it."

I tap my clavicle. "Me?"

"Yeah, you." He surveys the boat, then meets my eyes. "Smashing my pain really helped me to let it out. I think I'd held it in for far too long." He lets out a steady breath. "I took my sabbatical from cooking and everything partially because of grief, but, truth be told, I'd lost the spark for creating way before that. And you'll probably think that I'm being untruthful when I say this, but I really prefer a much simpler life."

We're slowly cruising the canal, going through one of the swinging bridges. I scrutinize our luxurious surroundings and flutter my hand. "And this is your idea of simple?"

"In my world it is." He laughs, his hazel eyes gleaming. He grabs a knife and points to the watermelon. "It's time for your lesson in *kae sa luk.*"

My heart stutters. "Which is?"

"'Fruit carving' in Thai," he says, shaking his head.

"So, we're really going to do this?"

"Carve? Yes." He hands me a carving knife. "We're starting with something easy—a dahlia pattern."

"But I've never done this before."

"Follow my lead." Charles trims off the green skin on one side of his watermelon and then places it on the cutting board so it's standing upright. He winks. "I have faith in you, Kate. Do what I just did—just take off the first layer, and don't cut into the flesh," he says, and I do. "Good." He takes a circle tool and makes an impression in the center and then lightly scores it with the carving tool, followed by another circle around the first one. He lifts the meat out and smooths the sides with his knife. "Now we're going to make the petals for the first flower." He looks up. "Kate, are you following along?"

I'm not. I'm way too busy looking at the graceful way in which he moves his hands. I'm breathing him in. A light breeze blows strands of my hair into my face. Charles sets his tool down and brushes it away.

He gets up and stands behind me, leaning into me. His hand clasps on to mine and he cuts with me. "Like this," he says, and then he takes his seat. "See, it's easy."

I let out a grunt and grip my thighs together. I never knew carving fruit could be so sexy. My hand shakes as I try to concentrate on the task. Petal unfolding after petal, layer after layer, dipping the knife in, shaping the leaves. We work for about half an hour, Charles's gorgeous lips pinched in concentration, me doing my best. Finally, we're finished, and I let out the breath I've been holding in. His watermelon is a true masterpiece, perfect.

He lifts up mine, inspects it, and smiles, his dimples puckering. "Not bad for a first attempt. If you'd butchered it, I'd have lost a little faith in you."

"So, I passed the test?" I ask, my voice shaky. "You're sticking around?"

"I am. Like I told you, I'm having fun," he responds. "If you'll have me."

It's a good thing he can't read my mind. "Right," I say with a gulp. "I guess we should talk about your salary—"

"I'm not doing this for money," he says with a wave of his hand. Before I can argue with him, he continues, "And perfect timing. We're about to go underground." He clinks my glass of champagne, and I pick it up. We toast, his eyes meeting mine. "Cheers."

"But—"

"No money."

I don't know what I did to have so many people helping me out—especially a guy as talented as he is. But I'm not going to look a gift horse in the mouth—one with such beautiful and very kissable lips. The boat glides into the vaulted tunnel. Rays of sunlight from a few openings in the ceiling bounce on the water, making the light magical, ethereal. I'm rendered speechless.

The light becomes brighter as we make our way out of the tunnel and we're cruising along the Seine. In the distance, I can see the Eiffel Tower, a speck of beauty, a symbol of Paris. We edge closer to Île de la Cité, getting up close to the Notre-Dame cathedral, still under construction after a ferocious blaze caused by faulty wiring nearly destroyed the historic monument in 2019. It's set to reopen in 2024, and I make a mental note to visit it again, considering the last time I'd explored the beautiful structure with its French Gothic architecture and catacombs was when I'd first moved to Paris.

"I've never seen Paris like this," I say with a sigh.

"Neither have I," says Charles. "It's kind of fun being a tourist."

I roll my eyes. "Most tourists don't carve watermelons on privately hired boats."

"True," he says as the boat pulls over to the side. Charles wraps the melons in plastic wrap, tucks them into his backpack, and stands up. "We're getting off here."

"Thank you for today," I say.

"The day isn't over yet." Charles jumps onto the dock and turns to walk away. "Come on, Crazy Kate, it's time to catch us some fish."

Yep. This is the date that isn't a date. And, my god, how I'm wishing it is.

CHAPTER SEVENTEEN

If I Were His Girlfriend

I'M AT HOME, thinking about Charles and looking at the fish he bought me for my apartment. I'd been drawn to an orange Siamese fighter fish with fins that moved like a graceful flamenco dancer, and I'd wanted one for the big tank in the restaurant until Charles explained that he (or she) would kill all the other fishes we'd picked out—tropical delights in all the colors of the rainbow, some spotted like leopards, all being delivered to the restaurant tomorrow morning.

I tap on the glass. "I'm going to name you Frushi. French sushi. Don't worry, nobody is going to eat you. The sea bass, on the other hand, that's another story."

Frushi shows off, wiggling his featherlike tail and fins, which look like they're made of inky silk, as he swims through the tiny castle and live plants I'd purchased for his new home. I watch, enamored with his grace, thinking back to the boat ride. Oh my, the way Charles handled his knives when he carved the fruit, the way he caressed the melon. I can't help it. I'm imagining his hands on me, on my breasts.

I'm a woman, and I have needs I've surely ignored, but having a boy-friend isn't a priority of mine: I'm focused on my dream.

Still, I can't stop thinking about our day, how romantic it was—the boat ride, carving the melons, winding through the streets of Paris to pick out the fish, his buying me Frushi. I love the way he teases me. I love his hands, his tattoo, and, most of all, I love the way he looks at me, his dimpled smile meeting his eyes. More than just devastatingly handsome, he's talented and shares the same passions as I do. Plus, he's kind and funny and sensitive.

I lightly tap Frushi's bowl, needing to talk to somebody. "I think I like him—like, really like him. I mean, I hated him at first. I thought he was such a jerk. But he really isn't. He's sweet and talented, not to mention drop-dead gorgeous. Do you think I stand a chance?"

Frushi swims up to me and opens his mouth as if to respond. Then, he swims away, orange tail flicking me off.

"That's what I thought," I say. "And I've completely lost it. I'm talking to a fish."

With a loud sigh, I sprinkle some pellets and brine shrimp into Frushi's bowl, and then get up to open the window. An aroma, cin-namon, envelops me—sweet, hot, and spicy. Charles is cooking something, and these scents are exactly how I'd describe my grow-ing feelings for him. I wonder whom in the world he's cooking for—probably some gorgeous model. Maybe even Aria. Before we parted ways, he'd asked for the chicken he'd put in the walk-in—the one I didn't know how to pluck.

The delicious smells emanating from his apartment become stronger, causing my knees to go weak. I wish Oded were home be-cause he gives such wonderful and positive advice, but he's been practicing with the symphony and the restaurant has been closed.

It dawns on me. I let the kitchen take over my life. Maybe Charles only represents the inner desires I've held close to my chest because, after Michael, I thought I wasn't worthy of love. The only thing I'm not insecure with is food and creating recipes. Maybe that's why I threw myself into cooking, this dream of mine.

The magazine sits on my coffee table, Charles staring me down. I want so very badly to read the article, but I can't because I'm thinking about his breath on my neck when we were carving the watermelon. I'm still staring at his face when a knock comes at my door.

And then I'm gazing at him in the flesh, the scents of cinnamon permeating my nostrils.

"Hey, you," he says, holding out a turquoise blue Le Creuset Dutch oven. "I was wondering what you were doing for dinner." He eyes the pot and then meets my eyes. "I might have made you something."

I stand silent, shifting my weight from one foot to the other.

"Aren't you going to invite me in?" he asks. "I thought we'd share a meal together. It's the chicken from the other day, now plucked and cooked. We should talk about your plans for the menu."

I parrot him. "My plans?"

He gives me a look like I'm crazy. "Of course, it's your restaurant."

Right. "Come on in."

I step to the side and sniff the air, my knees wobbling. "What did you make? It smells divine."

"Roasted cinnamon chicken with caramelized onions and carrots. It's Ceylon cinnamon from Sri Lanka. We have a resort there." He heads straight for the kitchen, setting the dish down. "It's a simple recipe I've been working on—nothing fancy. Do you have wine? A white?"

"Yep, yep, yep." I brush by him and open the fridge, all flustered. I'm bending over when I ask, "Will a Sancerre do?"

"Perfect." Thankfully, he takes the bottle from my hands before it slips from my grip. "It's dry and will balance out the dish. *Un tire-bouchon?*"

I point. "In the drawer right there."

A few minutes later, we're sitting at my small dining room set from IKEA, and I'm wondering what in the world is going on, especially after he says, "Let me serve you."

"Er, okay."

Charles gets out of his chair and, before heading into the kitchen, he pauses at the coffee table. He picks the magazine up and opens his mouth with surprise. "Where did you get this?"

His eyes hold such a fury in them they make me recoil. But I didn't do anything wrong. I straighten my posture, formulate my words. "I didn't buy it. I found it. In the park. On a bench."

He flips through the pages. "I'm going to kill my ex-fiancée. That petite salope."

A smile crosses my lips. *Ex*-fiancée. "Does she have a name?"

"She does. Aria," he says, and I hold back a laugh. Charles glowers at me. "Kate, this isn't funny. I lead a very private life—no photos ever."

I want to tell him. "Um—"

"She had a photographer take pictures of us three years ago at one of her modeling shoots. For us, she'd said." He slams the magazine down. "I should have known better."

I have to tell him she'd stopped by, but I don't want to ruin my moment, my chance with him. Not telling him something that would further piss him off is a form of protection, right?

"Did you read the article?" he asks, and I shake my head. "She told the press about my family's *exact* net worth." He paces. "This is not only bad for me but bad for my mother."

"Why?"

"Because of the vultures—the people who take advantage of us and the reason I didn't trust you at first."

"Again. Why? You can't be that rich."

"Kate, you wouldn't understand, and I don't expect you to." He slumps on the couch. "My father and grandfather started up Tenang Resorts with the money they made in oil." He hands me the magazine, open to the article, tapping the headline. "We've flown under the radar until this."

With my jaw dropped, my eyes scan the words. "Oh," I say, locking onto the b-word. "Billionaire? It's true?"

"Yep."

"Oh."

"It will be *you* making your mark once the restaurant opens again—none of this crap." He grips my hands. "Kate, I love being back in the kitchen, and my ibu is in rare form, the happiest I've seen her since the accident. But you have to promise me that my name and my mother's won't be associated with the restaurant. More than anything, I want to keep a low profile. So does my mother."

"Let me get this straight." I'm so confused. "You want to be totally incognito?"

"A ghost." He points to the magazine and then meets my eyes.

No wonder they need me. A no-name bistro. A woman people wouldn't even blink at. I'm not sure if I should be insulted or thrilled at the prospect. I wring my hands and clear my throat. "You can count on me. And now that that's settled, can we eat?"

"That we can do."

As Charles serves the dish, his hand grazes mine. I shudder and I swear he feels the spark of electricity too because he looks away before sitting down. We're about to dig into the meal when the doorbell buzzes.

"Are you expecting someone? A boyfriend?" he asks.

"No. I'm as single as they come." I point to the fish and get up to answer the intercom. I swear Charles is trying to hide a smile. "Me and Frushi are flying solo."

"Frushi? You named the fish Frushi?"

"French sushi," I say, and he laughs. I press the intercom button. "Who's there?"

"It's your mother! Let me up."

My eyes lock on to Charles's as I buzz her in. "Oh boy, get ready for a tornado."

In typical Mom fashion, she bounds into the apartment. "Kate, I really wish this building had an elevator. I mean, we're not living in medieval times. I'm sorry I haven't called you back, but the couple I told you about, the man with erectile dysfunction, booked an all-day appointment." She shrugs off her coat. "I think my lessons are working. Oooh, what did you cook? It smells amazing. Vegetarian, I hope."

"Nope," says Charles. "Chicken. But you'll love the carrots."

Mom's jaw goes slack as she takes in Charles's presence. "Am I interrupting anything?"

Kind of.

"No, not at all. Kate and I were working on something together," says Charles.

"On what?" Mom wiggles her brows. "I know your mother has brought Kate joy. Are you?"

What is up with her and her innuendos? "Mom!"

"It's Cri-Cri, Kiki!"

I slap my palm to my forehead. "Stop calling me that!"

Charles stands up, a look of bewilderment on his face, and he pulls out a chair. What a gentleman. "Cri-Cri, please join us for dinner."

My eyes shoot daggers in his direction.

"Why, I'd love to, but only if I'm not imposing."

You are.

"Not at all," says Charles with a wink in my direction.

"No chicken for me. Just carrots," says Mom, grabbing a glass and taking a seat at the table. She leans forward and pours herself a healthy serving of wine as Charles serves her a plate.

"Let me know what you think," he says.

"She will," I mumble. "And she eats turkey on Thanksgiving."

Mom huffs and takes a bite of the carrots, her eyes going wide. "Mmmm—I knew it. It's perfection. You two really do work well together—the perfect mix."

"I can't take credit for the meal," I say. "It's all Charles's doing."

"Maybe," says Mom. "But the way you use spices is just like this. And just as good."

"That's true," says Charles. "Her reinvention of a mole sauce with urfa biber had my taste buds dancing."

"It did?" I ask.

"Don't get a big head and go all prima donna on me."

"Kate?" Mom chuffs and chews. "She's as easy as it gets."

Charles's eyes go wide, and I choke on my chicken. "Cri-Cri!"

"I meant easygoing." She dabs her lips with a napkin. "How are your plans coming along?"

"We're still ironing out a few details," says Charles, nudging my shoulder. "I'm trying to convince Kate that a raw bar in the summer is a terrible idea."

"I agree," says my mom. "Even I know that oysters are in season during the 'r' months." She purses her lips and leans forward. "Then again, oysters are an aphrodisiac—the amino acids stimulate sexual desire."

"Cri-Cri! Does everything have to be about sex?"

"Yes," she says. "It does."

My eyes meet Charles's amused gaze. I let out an irritated grunt. "My mother is a sex therapist."

"A very good one," says my mom. "I have three books to my name and a fourth one coming out soon—*The Chronicles of a Voracious*—"

"Not a dinner conversation, Cri-Cri," I say, my cheeks flushing. She seriously has no filter. I throw back my glass of wine and dig into the chicken. "This is absolutely delicious, Charles."

"Merci," he says, leaning back in his chair, arms crossed, clearly amused.

For a few minutes, we eat and, in between bites, I tell Mom about our day.

Finally, Mom stands to leave. She dabs her lips with a napkin and then shakes out her hair. "Oh, to be young again. Don't do anything I wouldn't do," she says with a wiggle of her brows and closes the door behind her.

Charles blurts out a laugh. "What *exactly* wouldn't your mother do?"

For a moment, I'm at a loss for words, trying to swallow down all the embarrassment. I could kill my mother with her innuendos.

"Well, she wouldn't plan a menu. The woman barely knows how to boil water." I get up to clear the table, placing the dishes in the sink. "We have work to do."

"Right," says Charles. "We have to name our food babies."

I come back to the table with a menu, my notebook, and two pens. I shove his shoulder. "You're not funny."

"But I am." His eyes glimmer with mischief and I avert my gaze. "Where do we start?"

"With this," I say, opening up my notebook, and take my seat.

Charles hunches over the menu, crossing things out items, and chuckling. "Now, I get why you named your fish Frushi. Frexican? Frasian? Fruban?"

I grit my teeth. "Don't make fun of me."

"I'm not, but nobody, unless they know you, will get this fusion concept of yours—especially the French."

"The American tourists will," I say defensively.

"We're in France," he says. "You have to cater to the locals and to tourists from other countries as well, remember?" He rubs his eyes. "You also have to slim down the offerings—there's way too many choices, which will only lead to confusion. And the raw bar has to go, at least during the summer—"

Annoyance sets it. "My concept. My restaurant. I'm the one in control."

Charles ignores me and flips through my notebook. "I never said you weren't. Maybe you should lose some of this control of yours. These lists? Sure, they're a good start, but what happens when something unexpected hits?" His eyes scan my pages and he looks up. His finger taps a line. "What's this?"

I peer over his shoulder.

Find a way to get rid of my annoying neighbor. And stop looking at his lips.

And, now, I'm more embarrassed than I am angry, especially after Charles asks, "What's wrong with my lips?"

"Nothing," I say, grabbing the notebook from his hands. "That was when I hated you and wanted to punch you in the mouth."

He does his best to hide his smirk. "I really hope you don't hate me anymore."

"I don't. And I'm open to your ideas," I say, backpedaling. "Let's get to the menu. But all final decisions are mine."

"Are you always such a control freak?"

"I am when it comes to my dream." But, when it comes to Charles and his lips, I find myself spiraling out of control, like a car spinning on an ice patch.

"I get that," he says. "So, let's come up with a doable menu—a happy medium—where the food babies don't have weird names."

I snort. "You're not going to let me live that one down, are you?"

"Nope," he says.

Hours later with me hemming and hawing, we've finally come to terms and I'm happy with the menu. Charles is helping me clean up, soaping up the plates, and the scents still emanating from the remaining sauce in the Dutch oven bring on another involuntary fantasy, me with cinnamon sugar–covered lips, and him licking it off. Just as he's about to undress me, a plate slips from my hands and shatters on the floor. *Good one, Kate.* I grab a dustbin and brush from the closet. "I've got this. Thank you for the meal. And for getting the menu on track."

"Are you kicking me out already?"

Does he want to stay?

"Um, did you want a nightcap? Go over the menu again?"

"Non, I'm pretty tired. We had a long day." He kisses me on the forehead, but it feels purely platonic. "Bonne nuit, Kate. It was nice getting to know your mother a little better. But, before I make the long journey home, I have a question. Why does she call you Kiki?"

My teeth clench together. "I don't want to get into it now. I'll tell you tomorrow."

"Tomorrow it is," he says, turning to leave. I watch him walk to the stairwell and close the door.

After he leaves, I'm alone, sexually repressed and a little depressed.

CHAPTER EIGHTEEN

This Is My Ship, and I May Be Wrecked

THE FOLLOWING MORNING, I'm a couple of minutes late because I actually took the time to tame my wild hair from a frizzy mess into a slicked-back bun. I wait outside the bistro for a few minutes, but Charles doesn't show. Panic and disappointment set in; he'd ghosted me. Figures, he's all talk, no action, probably his plan all along to get my hopes up and ditch me, leaving me to face Garrance's wrath. With a loud moan, I open the restaurant and walk into the kitchen, to find him unloading ingredients. My heart skips a beat when he looks up and smiles.

"Uh, how did you get in?" I ask, and he holds up a set of keys. I bite down on my bottom lip. "Ri-ight. I forgot you own the building. But aren't you supposed to ask tenants for permission to enter the premises?"

"Not if they're late and working together," he says with a wink. "I hope you don't mind, but I wanted to get an early start." He pauses and tilts his head to the side. "You changed your hair. It looks nice."

I'm going to have a heart attack. He actually noticed something about me and gave me a compliment. Do I tell him how great he looks wearing my apron and how he should wear nothing else under it? My thoughts are turning wicked, and I have to pull myself together.

"I brushed it," I respond, my cheeks growing warm. "You look radishing today too."

Charles blurts out a laugh. "Was that a food pun?"

"Uh, I'm terrible with compliments."

"But I look radishing?" he says with a grin.

Always. From the first moment I met you. "You look clean."

Damn me and my self-defense mechanisms.

"Amazing what a shower can do, huh?"

"Right," I say, eyeing the clock on the wall. It's nine. "Ready to meet the brigade?"

"I'll be there in a second."

"Okay." I nod and then head to the front to find six eager people bouncing in front of the restaurant. I creak open the door and stand to the side, listening in on their conversation.

"I can't believe we have a chance to work with Charles Lin-Truffaut. He's an absolute legend."

"I know, right? But who is this other chef? The American?"

"Kate something. I've never heard of her."

"Why is Charles the chef at a bistro?"

"Maybe it's his new restaurant? This is so exciting. I'll do anything—even bus tables."

My heart sinks. Nobody cares about me, the nobody who can't do anything right. Bistro Exotique really doesn't feel like it's mine anymore. Maybe this was Garrance's plan all along. I turn, thinking about hiding in the kitchen, and run into Charles.

He gives me a surprised look. "Kate, you really should watch your step. This is the third time you've run into me. Where are you going?"

My words come out with an irritated tone. "I was going to leave you with your staff and your restaurant."

He raises his hands in defense. "Kate, it's *your* bistro, not mine."

"Doesn't feel that way."

He lifts my chin, meets my eyes. "Kate, I'm only here for the ride and enjoying every moment I spend cooking with you. This is your concept, your place."

"I still don't understand why a 'legend' like you wants to work here," I say, using air quotes. "Isn't it beneath you?"

"How many times do I have to explain myself?" he asks. "When I received the stars, cooking, which is my passion, wasn't fun, and I didn't enjoy it anymore. And I told you I'm enjoying my time with you." He grins. "How many times do you think I pranked my brigade? The answer is zero. I never had fun there. I'd probably have been charged for cruelty in a workplace environment."

I let out a huff. "So, I could file charges against you?"

"For a kitchen prank?" he says with a snort, his dimple puckering. His smile becomes wider, and he takes a step closer, eyes me up and down, and then he whispers in my ear, his voice low and so sexy. "What if I tell you that I think you're pretty cute when you're flustered?"

Wait. Does he *like* me? I must be dreaming. I want to squeal, but instead, I blush and rely on humor to hide my true feelings. "I'm definitely going to have to talk to the owner about that one. We have policies in place regarding sexual harassment, you know."

"We could break them."

"What are you saying?"

"I think you had me that first day I walked into the kitchen. I've been dreaming about seeing you in those shorts again." He takes my hand and squeezes it. "I also like your smile. And your corny jokes. And, while we're at it, I also like the fact you didn't know about my family's wealth and didn't treat me differently."

My throat catches. And, as my frazzled nerves set in, I say the most asinine thing. "Oh yeah, about that. Can I borrow a million?"

Charles cringes.

"I was kidding. I hope you know that."

He lets out a soft laugh. "I know. I had to mess with you. You should see the expression on your face—like a sad puppy."

A vision of Aria pops into my head. Instead of telling him about her, I dig for information. "I figured you be attracted to those model types—you know, all skinny and refined."

"Believe me, Kate, I went through that phase, but I discovered something."

"What?"

"They don't eat, and I'm all about food. I like a woman with meat on her bones, a woman who shares the same passions as mine."

He always says the right thing.

As much as I fantasize about Charles, I'm not sure I'm ready for anything more. Fantasies can't hurt me because they're just in my head. Still, I can't help but wonder where this is going. "So, what do we do now?"

"Take things one day at a time. See what happens."

I raise my brows, confused. "With us? Or the restaurant?"

"So, there's an 'us' now?" he asks, and I practically choke on my tongue.

Did I imagine the whole conversation? Misread him? Flushed, I say, "I— I'm sorry. I thought we might have felt the same way. I feel so, so, so stupid right now."

His laughter starts out soft, and then it booms. He places a hand on the small of my back and pulls me toward him. "I really like messing with you, Kate." He places a soft kiss on my neck. "I also forgot to mention that I can't stop thinking about your scent."

Before I turn into a puddle, I pull away. "This isn't a prank?"

"Non, and, honestly, it's taking every ounce of my self-control to not kiss those gorgeous lips of yours."

My heart does a backflip. My legs shake. I think I'm going to hyperventilate from wanton desire.

Do it. Do it. Do it.

But now is not the time, nor the place.

My gaze leaps to the group standing outside, and Charles places his hands on my shoulders, gives them a light squeeze. "Remember, this is your ship, your brigade. I'm only along for the ride."

"Give me a second." A second to gather my wits, my thoughts, my mind. I hold up my phone. "Before we let them in, I have to make a quick call."

With a shaky finger, I punch in Albert's number. After hanging up, I open the front door, and I'm about to greet the chattering bunch of recent Le Cordon Bleu graduates when a bulky guy with red hair rushes up to Charles. "Chef Lin-Truffaut, it's a true honor to work with a legendary chef like you."

Charles meets my gaze and then turns to the group. "Let me make something clear to all of you. Bistro Exotique is not my restaurant. I'm simply the sous-chef. Call me Charles." He indicates to me with a swift nod. "The title of chef is reserved for Kate."

Mumbles of shock and murmurs of "Charles Lin-Truffaut is a sous-chef?" follow us into the foyer. I'm so happy I could twirl, and you'd have to smack the wide smile off my face.

"Chef, why don't you take it from here?" says Charles.

My waning confidence is back. I clap my hands together. "Thank you all for coming. Everybody, come in, take a seat at the bar, and I'll explain how things are going to work. Since you're all aspiring chefs, we're going to rotate responsibilities of who does what on a nightly basis, which will give you an inside look as to how all the cogs of the wheel in a restaurant really work. With that said, every night two of you will cook on the line; two of you will be servers; and one of you will bus tables, do the dishes, and other general roustabout work like prepping, taking out the garbage, et cetera. Sound good?"

"Oui, Chef," comes the response.

Charles leans against the bar, looking so sexy in his jeans. He smiles and motions for me to carry on.

Focus. Kate, focus.

"Good." I take in a breath. "We're keeping things a little simpler with four signature dishes as well as three daily specials, including one entrée in addition to the five, as well as a couple of desserts. It's a sit-down service." I hand out menus, listing the offerings and ingredients, all seasonal and exotic for the opening night. "Please look this over."

Albert bounds into the restaurant, and I acknowledge him with a hearty introduction. "This is Albert, our head server. He'll train you one by one on how to use the reservation, ordering, and payment systems."

"Head server?" mouths Albert, and I nod.

He beams from ear to ear, and so do I. Kate is back in action and raring to go—maybe in more ways than one—although the thought of Charles and me kissing is a tad bit terrifying.

After we're finished with our training, Charles pulls me to the side. "You might want to bolt out of here a little earlier."

"Why?"

"My mother just called. She's having a car pick you, me, and Oded up at six. We're all having dinner tonight at Tenang."

ON THE DRIVE to the hotel, Oded and Charles hum "Les Champs Elysées" as we circle the famous Arc de Triomphe on Place Charles de Gaulle, Charles's voice low and sexy. Paris, the sights and the sounds, never gets old. The air is crisp and cool—perfect. Finally, we pull up to an enormous cake-white and creamy building with wrought iron Juliet balconies.

"How many rooms are there?" asks Oded.

Charles responds, "One hundred eighty-five for guests and five permanent residences—one of them my mother's."

"Wow," I say as the driver opens the door.

The Tenang Hotel Paris is the most luxurious property I've ever stepped foot in. I'm wearing a black sheath dress and matching flats, my hair tied back into a tight chignon and, although I'm dressed up, I feel underdressed. Modern crystal chandeliers hang from the ceiling, the floors inlaid marble, the floral arrangements enormous. I inhale the aromas of frangipani piping in the room and know Garrance has worked her magic here. My mom and Garrance wait in the lobby, and the entire staff buzzes around Garrance, practically bowing and curtsying.

Three peacocks, all male, strut around, tails fanned in all of their feathery glory. Garrance smiles and points, "Kate, those are Yin and Yang's little ones."

"Yin and Yang?" questions my mom.

"My peacocks. I have two in my greenhouse."

"It's on the roof across the street from the bistro," I add.

"Oh my," says Mom.

Garrance leads us to the lounge. Even at this early hour, the place is packed with Parisian fashionistas. A hostess dressed safari-chic welcomes our group and leads us to a table, located on the side, right in the middle of the room. She lifts up the velvet rope, and we saunter in. After taking in the space, the wood-paneled walls, lit up seductively, the bar carved into a wave, I sink into a cushy leather chair, Charles next to me.

With all these glamorous people eyeing us, I'm feeling out of my element.

"Isn't that an actress? Marion Cotillard?" asks my mom.

"*Probablement*," says Garrance. "A lot of famous people come here."

I gulp.

"Kate," continues Garrance. "While we eat, I want you to focus on the music, the kind I think you should incorporate at the bistro. I hope it's okay, but I've ordered a couple of my favorite dishes for us." She turns to my mother. "As I recall, you are a pescatarian?"

"I am," says Mom with a smile. "So nice of you to remember."

"Having grown up in hospitality, I remember everything." Garrance winks. "Did you bring your cards?" she asks, and Mom nods.

Oded, like me, fidgets in his chair. He whispers, "Have you ever been to a place like this?"

"No," I say. "Never."

"It's a little too much for me," says Charles. "I prefer the bistro."

I close my eyes for a moment, listening to the music. The first beat is intriguing—electro-ethnic, soon changing to something slightly tribal—loungy, clubby, exotic, and soothing at the same time. The server brings over a bottle of champagne, shows the label to Garrance. "The Krug 1982, as you requested, Madame."

Holy guacamole. This bottle costs more than sixteen hundred euros.

Garrance nods and the server pops the bottle open, serves us, and after placing it in an ice bucket, leaves. "Shall we toast?"

We clink our glasses together, meeting one another's eyes, as one must do in France or will be considered rude. "Santé."

"Kate, what do you think of the music so far?" asks Garrance.

"It's incredible."

"My husband was in charge of finding the right DJs and producers to make the compilations. He wanted to create the right vibe, like the Buddha-Bar Paris and Hotel Costes had done. A zen-lounge vibe, hip and exotic." She takes a sip of her champagne. "But I think ours is better. Plus, they're more current."

I gulp. "It's an awesome idea, but I can't afford a DJ or a producer."

She pulls out a USB stick from her purse. "You don't have to. Here," she says, handing it over. "This has more than six hundred songs on it. It's everything we play in this lounge."

I'm confused. "Isn't it illegal for me to pirate another lounge's music?"

"Darling, no, we sell the compilations. Anyone can use this music anywhere they see fit."

"Thank you. You've done so much for me. But you have to stop giving me things."

"No, I don't," she says, turning to my mom. "Back to the reading—" she begins, and then coughs up her champagne, her eyes wide.

We all turn to see what's captured her attention. I bite down on my bottom lip, and my spine goes rigid. Aria, just your run-of-the-mill supermodel, sits at the bar beside an older and extremely elegant woman, presumably her mother—what with the same high cheekbones and beautiful smile. My heart sinks when they make their approach, and my eyes leap to Charles. His jaw is tense, and he's wringing his hands, looking as if he's trying not to punch something.

"Charlotte. Aria," says Garrance curtly. "What an unpleasant surprise. Please tell me you're not staying at Tenang."

"Of course we are," says the older woman. "It's the best hotel in Paris but, honestly, a little shabbier now that Peter isn't running it."

Garrance's fists clench into tiny balls. She lifts her chin. "I'm surprised you can afford the rates."

"Oh, darling, I can, but this time it's Aria's treat. She's a celebrity, you know."

Garrance takes a sip of champagne and dramatically rolls her eyes. "I'll make sure to have your rooms fumigated."

A heavy moment of silence passes, the women glaring at each other.

A hand touches my shoulder. I look down at manicured nails encrusted with small diamonds. "Kate, lovely to see you again."

"You know her?" asks Charles with a surprised gasp.

"I stopped by the bistro the other day." Her dark eyes narrow into slits and she shoots me a wicked grin. "Did Kate not tell you? I told her to."

The bitch has clearly set me up, and I don't get a chance to respond because Garrance slams down her glass, rushes toward the ladies' room, my mother in tow, and Oded gets up, excusing himself. Charles shoots me a look and stands up.

"What the hell are you doing here, Aria?" he demands.

"In Paris? Catching up on our haute couture," she replies with a dainty giggle.

Charles lets out an animal-like grunt. "To spend the money my mother gave you? I'm surprised there's any left."

"I'm not here to shop," she says, recoiling. "I'm taking part in a couple of fashion shows, runway, you know, and a couple of shoots with Maison de la Barguelonne. Anyway, enough about me. We heard about you and the restaurant, and I wanted to drop by to say a quick bonjour."

My eavesdropping ears ring at the mention of Maison de la Barguelonne. I should leave and call Caro, but I'm rooted to my seat.

"Bonjour," he says, his voice gruff.

Charlotte nudges Aria in the ribs, and Aria grabs his arm. "Why are you being so cold?"

"You know why," he hisses. "She paid you off. You left. End of story."

"But it isn't," she says, and her mother nods. "I'm assuming that your mother never told you I didn't cash the check. But why would she? She hates me. I tried getting in touch with you, but you never answered my calls."

"I blocked your number," says Charles.

"Well, now we can set things right," she says. "That's the other reason I'm in Paris. I miss you from the moon, stars, and back again."

I want to vomit.

"No, Aria," he says, running his hands through his hair. "Too much time has passed. There's nothing between us. I'm over you."

"Time we lost and can now get back." She smiles and bats her lashes, runs a hand down Charles's arm. "I'm not over you. We were so good together. Can you at least give me a chance to explain what happened? At the very least, you owe me that."

Charles visibly exhales. "Fine. But not here. And not now. Come by my place tomorrow, around seven. I live in the same building as the restaurant. I guess you know where it is," he says, his eyes shooting daggers at me. "Ring the buzzer for the second floor." He turns on his heel and storms out of the lounge. "I'm not hungry anymore."

Aria and her mother head back to the bar. Alone, uncomfortable, and not knowing what to do, I'm relieved when my cell phone buzzes.

> Mom: I'm with Garrance in her suite. She's really
> upset. Oded is taking a taxi home. Bill is taken
> care of. Car will take you home. Call u tomorrow.
> Love u.

I'm feeling my heart break one tiny piece at a time. I'm shattered. There is no way on earth I can compete with Aria; they have too much history. I grab my purse and race to the bathroom to stop the tears before they explode, the last thing I need is public humiliation.

For a few minutes, I sit on a toilet seat, wiping my runny nose and tears, my head pounding. And then, right when my fingers unravel my tight chignon, I hear it, her twinkly laugh.

"This went way better than I thought it would," says Aria.

"France and Singapore's most eligible and wealthiest bachelor is going to be yours," says her mother. "You better not blow it."

"Oh, I won't," says Aria. "Charles has never been able to resist my charms, and this time I'm not letting go." She lets out a low laugh. "I can't believe he fell for the whole 'I never cashed the check' play."

"And he can never find out you did," says Charlotte. "As I told you, I have good word from my circle in Singapore that he and Garrance may be on bad terms. She's the one who forced him to cook with that girl at that dreaded bistro. It's up to you to drive them further apart."

"As if she could possibly compete with me."

"I saw the way he was looking at her. What if she can?"

"I'll destroy the reputation of the bistro, and she'll blame him." She laughs again, and I'm clenching my teeth so hard I think they'll break. "I've already contacted my connections in the press. They're just waiting for the word."

The sound of heels clicking. A door closing. Rendered immobile, it takes me a few minutes to pull out my phone because my hands are shaking.

ME: I am so upset.

MOM: Come up to Garrance's.
Penthouse.

CHAPTER NINETEEN

New Look, Same Me

MY MOM OPENS the door to Garrance's. I'm shaken up but still can't stop myself from taking in the luxury of this enormous suite with an awestruck gasp—the sparkling chandeliers, the living room with its plush furniture, the fully stocked bar, and the sitting area with the flickering fireplace. I can't believe she lives here. Once over the glitz and glamour of my surroundings, I catch my breath and clench my fists. "You're not going to believe this. Aria and Charlotte—"

Garrance sneers. "What about those horrid women?"

I take in a deep breath. "I overheard them talking when I was in the bathroom—"

Garrance ushers me to a chair.

My mom pours me a glass of lemon-cucumber-mint water. "Tell us everything," she says, sitting beside me, and after chugging the drink, choking a little bit because I drank it so fast, I relay the conversation I heard.

"This isn't good," says Garrance, tapping her chin. "We have to do something."

"I know," I say. "She's not only after him, she's after me."

"Like mother, like daughter—both of them unscrupulous gold diggers." She frowns. "I assure you that Aria indeed cashed that check. And then she asked for more. As if 250,000 euros wasn't enough."

"I don't get why you paid her off in the first place," says my mom.

"I knew she was up to no good, and so I hired a private investigator to dig into her life a bit more, and he discovered that she was having an affair with Nicolas, the son of the founder of Maison de la Barguelonne, the whole time she and Charles were together and engaged to be married."

My jaw drops. "Whoa! That conniving bitch!"

Before I clasp my hand over my mouth and apologize, I remember her swearing parrots. She's heard worse.

"Yes, she is. Anyway, rather than hurting Charles with the news of her unfaithfulness, I offered her a deal and she took it." says Garrance, shaking her head with sadness. She takes in a breath, lets it out slowly. "It wasn't my finest moment, but I'm a mother, and I was desperate to protect my son from being hurt. I know I was wrong to intervene, but I couldn't stop myself, and honestly, and even though Charles could handle the situation on his own, I'm glad I did it."

"I am too," says my mother, latching on to my hand. "I'd do anything to protect Kate."

I shoot my mother a sideways glance. "I don't need protection."

"Honey, we all need somebody to look out for our best interests."

"Maybe," I say. "But going behind somebody's back without telling them what you're doing first is five degrees north of shady." I meet Garrance's eyes. "Does he know what you did?"

"Darling, of course," says Garrance. "He was livid, wouldn't speak to me for three months until I told him what I'd found out and that I had another motive."

"Which was?" asks my mom.

"You see, her mother, Charlotte, is the nastiest seed of them all. She was my best friend in Singapore. Well, until she found out I was dating Peter. When we got engaged, she started a rumor that I was barren in the hopes of stealing him away from me." Garrance leans forward, her eyes twinkling, and she lets out a little wicked huff. "Little did she know I was two months pregnant with Charles—"

Mom and I gasp, motioning for her to carry on.

"I was so thin, even at four months, when Peter and I married, I hid the pregnancy well. But Charles was born five months later and Charlotte started up another rumor, that I fell pregnant to trap Peter into marrying me, that I was a whore. I lost most, if not all my friends, and that's when I turned to creating perfumes and cultivating spices."

My mother grips her hand. "She's pure evil."

"They both are." She lets out a long sigh. "I only told one person about Charles's anger with me—Nina, one of the women I've kept in touch with in Singapore. I had lunch with her on my last trip, and I told her about the restaurant and how I wanted Charles to become involved." She throws up her hands. "I thought she was a friend. Clearly, she isn't."

"I'm so sorry," I say, trying my best to swallow back my anger, for her, for me. "What do we do? Why did he invite her over? Does he still have feelings for her? I don't get it."

"I don't get it either, Kate. She's always had a strange hold over him," Garrance says, and I squeeze my eyes shut. "But he told me about his growing feelings for you. And I was so happy. So was your mother."

For a few minutes, we sit in silence, me tapping my leg, Garrance huffing and puffing.

Mom leans forward. "I've got it! We could poison both of them."

Her eyes dart from side to side. "Garrance! What else do you grow? Anything lethal?"

"Jeez, Mom, we're not murderers," I say. "Tone your ideas down a notch."

"I agree," says Garrance.

"It was a joke," says my mom. "To lighten up the mood because it's so heavy right now. And stop calling me Mom."

"Okay, Ibu," I say, and Garrance snickers.

"She's stopping by his place tomorrow," I continue, a thought hitting me like a lightning bolt. "I know this might be a terrible idea, and a little off, probably totally unethical, but we might be able to listen in on their conversation through the vent."

Garrance's eyes light up. "We need all the ammunition we can get."

"Believe it or not, Kate, I'm a really wise woman and not just about sex but matters of the heart," says my mom. "I'm in too."

She's right. And I need my wacky mom because my heart is breaking. Juju jumps onto my lap, and I squeeze him. My mom and Garrance share another look and nod perfunctorily.

"Tomorrow's your day off, right?" asks my mom, leaning forward.

"Yes. Why?"

"Your mother and I were talking."

My eyes volley between the two of them. "About me?"

"Yes," says my mom. "You need a serious makeover. Now don't be insulted, but your California 'beach waves' look like seaweed, and your eyebrows are unruly, not to mention the way you dress—"

I thought I looked nice—or at least presentable.

"You should take pride in your appearance," continues Garrance. "One reflects what they put out to the world, n'est-ce pas?"

I slump into my seat, floored. It's bad enough that Aria is throwing herself at Charles, but I never thought I was this much of a hot mess. "If this is your idea of a pep talk, it's making me feel like shit."

"Oh, Kate, you're absolutely beautiful," says my mom, and Garrance nods her head in agreement. "But you need to get out of the kitchen sometimes and take care of yourself."

"I'm not changing myself for a man," I say with a growl. "I'm happy with the way I am."

"Non," says Garrance. "The makeover is for you, and you'll still be you."

"Just a little more polished and less grubby," says my mom, and I glare at her. "Kate, like Garrance said, you need to take care of yourself. You're young and beautiful—"

"You forgot grubby and unpolished," I say with a groan. I twirl my hair. My mom is right—it does look like seaweed.

"We're not picking on you," she says. "We think it will make you feel good. So, what do you say? Are you in?"

"It's for the restaurant, too," says Garrance, and my ears perk up.

In a way, it does sound fun to be pampered and preened. And, my neck is so tight from stress I could really use a massage. "I guess so," I say.

"Good, because I already booked you an appointment for a Brazilian blowout tomorrow morning." She coughs and then mumbles, "And a Brazilian wax."

"Mom!"

"It's for you. I can only imagine the situation"—she rotates her finger in front of crotch—"you have going on down there."

I brush her hand away. "Geez, Louise."

Garrance smiles. "I'll meet up with the two of you for shopping in the afternoon. I made an appointment for us at Maison de la Barguelonne with your friend Caro."

"I can't afford anything there."

Garrance smiles, and in a firm but friendly voice says, "Good thing we can. Saying no to us isn't an option."

"I'm not getting out of this, am I?"

"Non," they say in unison.

"Fine," I say, gnawing on my cuticles. "I guess two mothers know best. But if I come out looking like a freak, I'm blaming you."

"Bon, it's settled," says Garrance with an excited squeal. "I'll have my driver pick you up in the morning."

My mom swats my hand. "I've booked you a manicure and pedicure too."

Looking at my butchered nails, I think this seems oddly planned out, like they've been talking about me behind my back for quite a while. I'm curious, and I'm in front of them now. "How much time have the two of you been spending together?"

"A lot," says my mom. "We have something in common. We both love our children and want the best for them."

Garrance squeezes my mom's hand. "I finally have a true friend I can count on and who I can talk to openly and honestly with." She smiles at me. "Kate, that goes for you too."

"What time is that girl going to Charles's?" asks my mom.

"Around seven."

"We should be done with your appointments around six. I'll keep a lookout from the window of my atelier. When the coast is clear, I'll come by with your mother. Sound like a plan?"

A demented one. But a plan it is. I nod.

GARRANCE'S CHAUFFEURED CAR whips my mom and me through the streets of Paris. We pass the Jardin des Tuileries, already bustling with tourists, some wearing berets and striped shirts (don't do that unless it's for fun), the Louvre, people posing in front of it with their thumbs and forefingers pinched as if they're holding the glass triangular structure, the Ferris wheel, and finally cross over Pont Neuf.

As we pass Notre-Dame, I think about the boat trip with Charles, his scent, the way his hands expertly carved the melon.

"Are you excited?" asks my mom. She squeezes my thigh.

"Meh."

"You should be excited. This is going to be so much fun," she squeals. "We haven't had a real mom-daughter day in such a long time."

I slump in my seat, my gaze watching the blurry Parisian streets. We pass an old woman walking a dog—a fluffy little one. "I hope they let animals into the salon, because I feel like a beast."

Mom gasps. "It was never our intention to make you feel that way."

My eyes meet hers. "I know, Mom, but you're right. I haven't been taking care of myself. And when all those perfect, gorgeous girls trotted around like groomed ponies in their high heels at the lounge they made me feel like crap. I figured, why bother?"

"Because you're worth it."

"Are you quoting an ad?"

"Er, maybe," she says with a laugh. "But, honey, don't compare yourself to other women—especially the models in magazine ads. They're airbrushed and tampered with and far from perfect in real life, designed to make us feel bad." She pauses. "Half of my clients are beautiful women, but they feel worthless. We need to empower women, make them shine, harness their true beauty, bring back inner confidence."

I face her. "Then why today? Why are you trying to change me?"

Mom laughs. "I'm not trying to change you. Honey, can you even run a brush through your hair?"

Point taken.

"I want you to care about yourself first. When you feel good about yourself, only positive things will come your way. I hate seeing you feeling down and insecure. Aside from your delicious meals, you have so much to offer the world. But you've been holding back on exposing all the facets of yourself."

"Maybe," I say glumly. "I guess I spend way too much time in the kitchen."

Like Charles, I'd been flying under the radar, keeping people at a distance, trying to keep my head down. Maybe it really is my time to shine.

"Mom," I say, gripping her hand. "Bring on the works. But I'm still going to be me."

"Oh, honey, you'll always be you—sweet, beautiful, smart, talented—"

"Just not as grubby," I say with a laugh.

FOUR HOURS LATER, my hair has been highlighted and straightened, my nails and toes manicured. I've been plucked, shucked, waxed, and left out to dry, me screaming, "Putain, this hurts," the whole time, the staff at Le Salon grimacing. The only things I've liked about this day so far was our lunch, the endless champagne, the body massages, and when the shampoo stylist massaged my scalp. I drooled with delight, the stress melting away. All the good stuff made the pain worth it.

A makeup artist is in the process of applying the finishing touches on my face.

"I didn't do much. Just a little foundation to balance out your ruddy complexion, a little blush to highlight your cheekbones, a coating of mascara to bring out your beautiful eyes, a balm to smooth out your dry lips, and some gloss."

At least there are one or two compliments hidden among the snarky monologue. She wheels the chair around so I can face the mirror. I can barely recognize myself.

My hair is slick as a seal—a blond one. My eyes look huge and sparkly, full of light. My eyebrows look awesome, trimmed and manicured into arches I didn't know I had. My lips are plump, maybe even sexy. I check out my nails, my toes. I'm me, but not me, because I feel smoking-hot, from the top of my head to my feet. I grin as my mother peers over my shoulder.

"What do you think?" she asks.

"I'm speechless. And happy."

"Good," she says. "I've already taken care of the bill."

"Mom!"

"Don't worry about it. I told you about my book advance. And I'm enjoying bringing a little joie de vivre to my daughter." She kisses my cheek. "And, don't forget, there's more. Garrance is waiting for us at Maison de la Barguelonne."

A FEW MINUTES later, the car pulls up to a beautiful stone Haussmannian building, still in the sixth arrondissement and we could have walked—literally—around the corner, but my mom insisted we show up in style. I've seen where Caro works, but I've never been inside—too much of a hassle with approvals and forms and background checks.

Caro and Garrance greet us in the lobby.

"Ooh-la-la," says Caro, fanning her face. "I almost didn't recognize you. You look amazing! I can't believe they were able to tame your hair."

Garrance and my mom share another one of their looks. And now I know Caro's been in on the plan too.

"Okay," says Caro. "The staff, Garrance, and I have picked out a couple of outfits for you from our prêt-a-porter collection—not too over-the-top, but things you will definitely like." She pauses. "And wait until you see the lingerie—"

"What? Lingerie?" I clench my teeth. "I'm not doing this for a man."

Caro places her hands on her hips. "Of course you're not. This is all for you. There's nothing wrong with feeling sexy and good about yourself—even when wearing raggedy sweatpants with holes in them, the ones we're hoping you'll throw away when you see your new stylish wardrobe." She turns on her heel. "Follow me, you're all signed in."

OVER CHAMPAGNE, OYSTERS, and caviar, I've been outfitted and then reoutfitted again for three humiliating hours. Regardless of being stripped down in front of everybody, I love the clothes—the wardrobe comprised of some hip athleisure pieces, a couple of dresses, light cashmere sweaters, silk blouses, and slimming pants.

When we're finished, Caro bounds over to me. "The driver has loaded everything into the car. You're all set," she says, kissing me on the cheek.

"I guess I should get changed."

"Into what? You look fabulous in that dress. And—"

My mom and Garrance giggle. I know my friend. "You might have thrown what I was wearing away?"

Caro's lips pinch to the side. "Don't be mad. Think of it as a favor."

"You're a good friend." I look to my mom and Garrance, a tear creeping down my cheek. "You all are. I don't know what I did to deserve all of this, the kindness. I didn't earn it."

"Kate, you nourish all of our souls with your kind heart," says Garrance with a wink. "We all feel the love you have for us in every dish you create."

The women in my world nod.

"Caro, are you going to be part of the mission tonight?" I ask.

"I'm trying out online dating and have a first date," says Caro. "First one since Hugo the Horrible." She clasps her hand on to mine, pushing something into it. "But I'll be with you in spirit. I made you a mix of our favorite songs. You have to play them in order."

"But I want to do something for you," I say, looking at a USB stick.

"Enjoy your night off. You deserve to be pampered. And we enjoyed doing it today. Now, pamper yourself."

She doesn't follow her statement with a perverse comment. Something is up.

Before we leave the atelier, Garrance reaches into her purse and pulls out a small black metal container from it. "Kate, this is for the restaurant. Open it."

I take the oval tin and lift the lid to find strands of saffron glowing red. In fact, all of our faces sparkle from the light.

"It's the finest of saffron, from Kashmir, worth its weight in gold," she continues, her eyes twinkling. "I'm expecting you'll use it wisely to create something magical."

"Today was magic," I say, kissing her cheek. "*Merci pour tout.*"

"This is only the beginning," she says.

THE INTERCOM BUZZES a little after seven, and I let my mom and Garrance up, leaving the door open, and then uncork a bottle of wine—red and spicy like my mood. My mom and Garrance are dressed nearly identically—all in black with super large sunglasses and hats.

Mom says, "The coast was clear. We made it here unnoticed. I feel like Mata Hari."

I hand them each a glass. "And that explains your ridiculous outfits."

"Have you heard anything yet?" asks Garrance.

"Nope," I reply. "Not a peep."

"It's a beautiful evening out," says Garrance, looking around the apartment. "Maybe they're on the terrace. Open your window."

I slump onto the couch. "This is a bad idea. I don't think I can do this."

My mom and Garrance share a surprised look. "Why?"

I take a sip of wine, swallow it down. "A woman like Aria is more his type."

"Don't say that," says Garrance forcefully. "She's a waste of the air he breathes. And he never talked to me about the women in his life with such a spark in his eyes. He told me how much he loves spending time with you, how you make him laugh. And, the two of us"—she nods to my mom—"saw the way the two of you look at each other."

My throat constricts. "It's too late."

"It's never too late," says my mom. "Do you want to fight for him or not?"

My eyes narrow into a glare. "I thought the makeover was for me."

"It was," says my mom.

"I don't know," I say, thinking about all the fun we had together in the kitchen, the way we banter, the way my knees melt and my body quivers when he's around. I throw my hands up with defeat. "It doesn't matter. Perfect Aria is back in the picture now. I can't compete with her."

"Nonsense. You can. And you will. That horrible trollop is not worthy of Charles. You are. Now, open the window," Garrance demands with a challenging eyebrow raised.

For a moment, I sit in silence, writing a pros and cons list in my head.

Pros: Funny, sexy as hell, killer body, talented chef, smart, gets
     my sense of humor, romantic, confident, courageous, shows
     his vulnerability, and, for the most part, honest
Cons: Can be mean as a venomous snake, a bit egotistical (but I
     like that), has a sick and twisted sense of humor (but I like
     that too)

"Kate, don't just sit there," says my mom.

Damn it. I've completely fallen for him. But the real question pecking at my brain is: Has he really fallen for me too like he'd said? With my heart racing, I get up and crack the window open, and the conversation from the floor below is as a clear as the night sky.

"Charles, I'm so glad you agreed to see me," says Aria, her voice low and throaty. "Did you miss me as much as I missed you?"

No answer. A pause. The sound of a drink being poured—the fizz of champagne. "Tell me what you want, Aria."

"I told you. I want to go back to the way things were. We were so damn good together—the sex, the laughter, the conversations— especially the sex. Orgasm after orgasm, the way you made me scream—"

"Putain, Aria!" he hisses. "Don't touch me."

"Why? You used to like this when we were together."

I want to scream. My nails dig into the palms of my hands.

"That succubus," whispers Garrance. "She's trying to seduce him. I—"

"Sssh," whispers my mom. "They might hear you."

Another long pause. Garrance latches on to my hand, squeezing it. I'm holding on to her for dear life because my knees are going to go out from under me.

"Cut the crap, Aria. You're just here to talk, so talk."

"Fine. Be that way."

"Were you being honest with me when you said you didn't cash the check?"

"Of course. I'd never lie to you."

"Is that so?"

"Charles, stop glaring. You're way more handsome when you smile."

"Oh," says my mom, her voice hushed. She rubs her hands together. "This is getting good."

"I'm in control of the family account, the one from which my mother wrote a check for two hundred and fifty thousand euros made out to one Aria Chan. Don't look so surprised." A pause. "So, if you didn't cash the check, who did?"

"I—I—I—"

"Need to get out my sight right now. This whole time, my ibu knew exactly what you were all about, and she was right to pay you off. You're just like your loathsome mother. And I can't believe you planted that story in the tabloids. But what's done is done."

I hear the sound of scrambling. Garrance smiles, and my heart does a back flip.

"So I cashed the check. Big deal. You need someone like me, from the same upbringing and social status—"

"You're nothing but a social climber."

"I'm most certainly not. I'm good for you."

"A cheater is good for me? I don't think so. Explain Nicolas de la Barguelonne." He laughs. "It's no wonder your modeling career took off the way it did."

Silence.

Garrance grips my hand and whispers, "My son is smart."

"I have no idea what you're talking about," says Aria, her voice low. "You're being ridiculous."

"Putain, Aria. I'm not an idiot. I saw the tabloid photos of you with him, heard the rumors. I just wish my mother had talked to me *before* paying you off. She really wasted that money. I hope you invested it wisely."

A glass shatters. "Why the hell did you invite me over?"

"I know how you get. I didn't want you making a scene at the hotel." A pause. "And I didn't invite you over. You invited yourself. There's the door. You can show yourself out."

"You are going to regret this!"

"But I won't."

Heels clomp on the floor, stomps echo in the vent, and I don't bother holding back my smile. Hope flutters in my chest. Maybe there's a chance for us? Once it's quiet, my mom gingerly lowers the window.

"Well, that was easy. We didn't have to do anything to rid ourselves of the enemies," says Garrance, her smile lighting up her face.

Her cell phone buzzes. She holds up a finger. "One second."

"No, darling, you're not bothering me. I'm glad you called." A pause. "I'm not home right now. I'm with Kate's mother." Another pause. "I'd love to meet for lunch tomorrow. Does the lounge work?" Garrance breathes out a happy sigh. "Okay, you're right, darling. We do need talk privately. I'll order up room service. Yes, I'll tell Kate's mother to tell Kate you'll be coming in the afternoon." She clicks the line to a close, raises a triumphant brow, and claps her hands together.

"He's probably mad at me because I didn't tell him she stopped by," I say with a sigh. "You should have seen the way he glared at me."

"If he is, he'll get over it," says Garrance.

"How can you be so sure?"

"I know my son."

They both put their sunglasses back on. My mom creeps into the hallway. "The coast is clear," she whispers. "Kate, I'll call you tomorrow." I watch them slink down the stairs, trying to hold back their giggles.

After they leave, I check out my reflection in the bathroom mirror. Oh, pluck me. I look awesome. And, oh, pluck me harder. Charles might despise me because I withheld information from him and I've fallen for him—hard.

ACT THREE

In France, cooking is a serious art form

and a national sport.

—Julia Child

CHAPTER TWENTY

Any Press Is Good Press

IT'S TWO IN the afternoon, and I'm waiting for Charles on the terrace, a cup of coffee in hand. I'd set up a table outside and my nerves are on fire, wondering how his lunch with Garrance went, wondering how he feels about me. He jumps out of the back seat of Garrance's car, a scowl on his face. Well, stick a fork in me, I'm done, there's my answer.

"You're mad at me," I say when he makes his approach.

"Kate," he says, placing his hands on his hips and shaking his head slowly. "I'm not mad at you. But I need to know why you didn't tell me Aria stopped by the bistro." He sits down at the table, joining me. "The truth."

The truth? I was seething with jealousy and hoping she'd go away, vanish into one of her shiny magazine covers never to be seen again.

"She asked me not to. She said she wanted to surprise you, that you be thrilled to see her. I didn't know about your history. And I was enjoying spending time with you. And she's so perfect—"

He squints. "Are you wearing makeup?"

"Is this a tangent?"

"Maybe."

"You don't like my new look?"

"I do," he says. "You look gorgeous, but—"

"But what?"

"I think you're naturally beautiful, one of the reasons I was attracted to you in the first place."

Is he telling me he appreciated how I was? My heart is going to explode out of my chest. I can't move my lips.

He rubs his eyes with his fingertips. "Some people are downright ugly. Like Aria. You're attractive from the inside out. Look, I know what a manipulative bitch she can be—that's the reason I stormed out of the lounge, not because of you. And, if we're being honest, I was completely blindsided. I wish you would have told me so I could have been prepared."

I suck in my breath with joy and then guilt, hoping he doesn't know we spied on him. I have no idea what he and Garrance talked about.

"Okay, I'll start with another truth." I let out a breath. "I know all about Aria and what she did. Don't be mad, but I overheard her and her mother talking at the restaurant. And I also overheard your conversation on the terrace. So did our mothers."

Charles lets out a soft laugh. "I was wondering if you'd tell me about your spy mission. My mother did."

My jaw drops. "She did?"

"She did—crazy getup and all. In fact," he says with a laugh, "I saw her and your mother heading up to your place. I knew they were up to something."

"Oh," I say, blushing.

"Look, Kate, when I make a commitment to something, I'm one hundred percent in. You and I have a good thing going on. Don't we?"

I shoot him a hesitant smile. "We do."

"Aria is a nightmare from my past. I didn't even look her up when I was in Singapore. Word got out that she was trying to track me down, so I went to places she'd never dare to step foot in." He drums his fingers on the table. "So you can imagine my surprise when she'd said you'd met."

"I'm sorry," I say, feeling terrible. "I should have told you."

"Don't apologize." He leans forward and clasps my hands with his, making circles with his thumbs. "I understand why you didn't."

"We're good?"

"Yeah, we're good."

My cell phone buzzes, and I glance at the screen, before picking it up. It's a Google alert about the bistro. I pull up the article and when I read the headline my throat constricts: WHY IS BILLIONAIRE MICHELIN-STARRED CHEF CHARLES LIN-TRUFFAUT SLUMMING IT AT A NO-NAME BISTRO?

My hand shakes as I read the article. This is so bad. Charles leans forward. "Kate, is something wrong?"

"Yes," I say, holding out my phone.

I watch Charles seething as he scans the words. He grips his hair. "Fucking Aria. She told the press about me. Again. Probably her revenge for me shutting her down last night."

My bottom lip quivers. There is some truth in the article and insecurities peck at my brain. "Are you slumming it with me for fun? I mean, I'm not a game, Charles. I'm a real person."

He recoils as if I've slapped him across the face, his eyes darkening. "I told you that running a three-star establishment nearly crushed my spirit and I feel like myself at the bistro with you, didn't I? Do you not trust me?"

Charles gets up and paces on the sidewalk. I go silent for a moment. He has me pegged. Aside from cooking, I *am* insecure and I know that I really need to work on my confidence with life outside of the kitchen, especially with women like Aria lurking around. Still, I have to give him the benefit of the doubt.

"I do trust you," I mumble. "But I didn't at first."

"I'm crazy about you, Kate. And, if you couldn't tell from her reaction last night, the way she eyed you up and down, Aria is extremely jealous of you."

"Me? No, I don't think so."

"Take a good look in the mirror, Kate. Not only are you beautiful, you're real. She's fake—her laugh, her colored contact lenses, her hair—"

"Her hair?"

"Extensions." He shudders. "So disgusting finding clumps of it in the shower."

He places my phone on the table, huffing, his face turning red with anger. "I hate the fucking tabloids—goddamn pieces of merde. This is the reason why I like living a quiet life. I'm sorry to bring you into my messed-up world."

"But you didn't."

"Actually, Kate, thanks to Aria, I did. I suggest you buckle up and get ready for a media storm."

My phone starts dinging—one loud beep after the other.

As if on cue, five cars screech up in front of the restaurant. A bevy of men and women dressed in black swarm toward us like maddened bees, cameras in hand. "There he is! It's true. Charles Lin-Truffaut is actually working at a bistro!"

My ears ring, the clicks from the cameras almost deafening, one pushed into my face. Spots dance in front of my eyes, and I feel like I'm in a horror film. I can't move.

"I got the shot," says one.

"Charles, is this your girlfriend?" asks another one, pointing. "What's her name?"

"Fuck off, you pieces of shit," says Charles.

After slamming his fist on the table, Charles places one hand over his face and with the other he latches on to my arm, pulling me into the restaurant. He releases his grip on my wrist, locks the door, and lowers the volets. The restaurant loses its natural glow from the sun, so I flick on the lights, my legs shaking. I sink into a chair, massaging my throbbing temples.

"Don't answer any of their questions," says Charles. "Kate, this is bad. They're going to hound me, which also means they'll be coming after you. The maggots travel in packs and can be quite aggressive." He pulls out his phone. "I'm going to call in a security detail."

"They can't be *that* dangerous," I say.

"Don't worry. My guys are good *gendarmes* and they'll keep them at bay. Thankfully, the senate approved that off-duty police can carry weapons a few years ago." He kisses me on the cheek, breathes me in. "This mess won't affect the opening. And I'll just keep cover in the kitchen."

I'm seriously regretting opening up the wall. I point to the open kitchen and Charles says, "I'll stay toward the back."

"What about me?"

"Do you have any skeletons in your past?"

"No," I say. "I'm as clean as they come."

"You'll be fine. But they will find out who you are and try to get shots of you."

My phone begins dinging nonstop with alerts, and I put it on silent. Now I know what it feels like to be hunted.

Charles lets out a sigh. "I've tried my best to fly under the radar, especially after my father and grandfather died. That's part of the reason I took my sabbatical from the kitchen, from everything— even the Tenang business. My mother has been handling everything on my behalf, which wasn't fair to her. But I had my reasons.

And I'm doing what I can now." He gulps. "After the crash, one of the tabloids wrote I should have been on that plane, but that I was probably bruléeing when it burst into a fiery blaze. Remember? That's why I lost it at the rage room."

A tear slides down my cheek. I wipe it away and take his hand, squeezing it. "What the tabloid wrote was terrible. You know it's not your fault. And nobody thinks it is."

"Maybe." He blows out the air between his lips. "Honestly, the pain and guilt started to ease at your bistro. I meant what I said—I feel like myself when I'm with you—happy. You make me smile. You make me laugh."

My heart skips a thousand beats in one second. He isn't talking about the meals we're creating together or how cooking makes him happy, but me.

"Can we focus on that?" I ask.

"I'll try," he says. "But if I get moody or become snappish, please, just remember my anger isn't directed at you."

"You know what helps me out when I'm stressed?" I ask, and he raises a brow. "The kitchen."

"The kitchen?" he asks, and I nod. "Great minds think alike. Which recipe?"

"You haven't tasted my mussels yet."

He shoots me the side-eye and places his hands on his hips. "I can't believe you convinced me to keep something that isn't technically in season on the menu."

"This is a bistro. You can't have a true French bistro without mussels. My menu, my rules."

"I guess I'm learning to break the rules."

Charles follows me to the prep area, and I point to the walk-in cooler. "Get the mussels."

"It's a good thing I'm used to be being bossed around. You should meet my grandmother. She'd like you. A lot." He pauses and then mumbles, "I kind of like being told what to do."

As he's commandeering the mussels, I race around wildly to gather the ingredients: kaffir lime leaves and limes, coconut milk, coconut sugar, galanga, lemongrass, spicy red peppers, straw mushrooms, garlic, green onions, ginger, and coriander.

When he returns, he clears his throat and his hand snakes over the ingredients. "I know what you're up to. I spent a lot of time in Thailand, having lived there. Your recipe is based off of tom kha gai, but instead of chicken you're using mussels," he says, and I nod. "Would you be open to using my mother's lemongrass and limes?"

"These are her limes," I say.

"Good," he responds. "The lemongrass?"

"I bought it at the market."

He picks up the thin, green-yellow rods and dumps them into the garbage, turns, and heads to his crate, pulling out a new batch. "We just brought the plants back from our trip. She's growing them, I think, for us. Have you seen her roof garden?"

Us. "I have," I say, my brain fritzing out for a second. "I met the swearing parrots."

"Yeah, she's still mad at me for teaching them those words." He chuckles. "I think it's hysterical." He heads over to the spice rack. "Would you mind if we added some turmeric? It'll be better, I swear. If it isn't, you can have your way with me."

My jaw goes slack. *Focus, Kate. Focus.*

"Let's do it," I say breathlessly, and quickly recover. "I mean, great idea. Turmeric is anti-inflammatory."

After Charles rinses and scrubs the mussels, side by side, we prepare the meal. While I slice the galanga, Charles braises the shallots, ginger, and fennel, adding in the lemongrass. I'm in a trance, now in Thailand. With him. We're floating in a pond filled with lotus flowers, the water warm, and I'm getting ready for a spiritual awakening—

"The galanga," says Charles, and our hands touch as I pass it over. He adds it to the pan and a moment later, after adding in the coconut milk and squeezing the lime juice, he holds out a spoon. "Taste this."

The flavor is warm, with a little heat and sweetness, infused with the citrusy lemongrass, ginger, and garlic. I let out a soft moan.

"What do you think?"

"I think you're incredible," I say, quickly recovering. "Um, this sauce is heaven on my tongue. My palate is awake." I will my legs to stop quivering. "I can't wait to see how everything comes together."

"Yes, Chef," he says with a wink. "But this is your recipe. I've only made one adjustment to it."

"Right," I say with a shudder.

TWENTY MINUTES LATER, we sit in the dining room, eating, drooling, and swooning, the flavors of the mussels—rich, potent, steamy, and sexy. He dabs his mouth with a napkin. "This was incredible, Kate, and you've proven me wrong about serving mussels. But it's missing something."

My heart jolts. "What?"

"Bread," he says, "to soak in this delicious sauce."

"Oh my goodness," I say, standing up, knocking over my chair. "I forgot about my sourdough! They've been proofing for weeks in the walk-in! And I haven't fed my starter!"

Charles shakes his head. "I understand homemade pita and tortillas, but please don't tell me you think you can make fresh bread every day."

"I can do anything I set my mind on doing—"

"And when are you going to sleep?" He pauses. "Lose a little control. You can't do everything."

"But—"

He holds up his phone. "I'm calling my guy—the best baker in all of Paris. And then we'll trash your bread."

And, damn it, he's right. Moreover, so is my mother. She's always been right and I hate admitting that to myself. I have to lose a little control, stop being so uptight, and ride the winds of change.

AFTER WE CLEAR the table and clean up, Charles's phone buzzes. He looks at the screen and then walks into the dining room to open the electric volets. He calls for me. I step out to join him to survey the windows, surprised at the view. Four or five buff armed guards dressed in blue uniforms with shielded helmets pace in front of the bistro. There is no sign of the paparazzi.

"The locusts aren't permitted to step foot on private property, which includes your terrace," says Charles. "The guards will be working in twelve-hour shifts, keeping them at bay." He clasps his hands on my shoulders. "I hope things calm down before the reopening. Good news. If they don't get photos of me, they'll have nothing to report."

"How do we get back home? We have to go outside."

He holds up a key. "Haven't you used the back stairwell?"

"No," I say. "I didn't even know there was one."

"You know that locked door in the back of the kitchen?"

"Yes."

"That's it." He nudges my side. "We don't let renters use it. One of the benefits of owning the building. I'll walk you home."

"Oh," I say, hoping it isn't dark and festered with rats. "Makes sense. But this doesn't. What about the customers, the staff, the guests for opening night?"

Charles unlocks the door, and we meander up the steps. It's dark, but thankfully, no critters lurk in the shadows.

"The guards have a guest list for opening night and a list of our brigade. If they're not on the list, they won't get in. All customers will need a reservation, and the taking of photos will not be permitted."

This is beyond my comprehension, having to go through lengths like this. Plus, the stairwell is dark and musty. I'm careful to put one foot in front of the other. "I'd be scared as hell walking up to a restaurant with armed guards."

"Right now, this is the safest bistro in all of Paris." He pauses. "I had the publicity manager at Tenang send out a press release for us."

"I guess you thought of everything," I say. "Except for one thing."

"What's that?"

"Do you have an extra key for the back stairwell?"

"I do," he says. He reaches into the pocket of his jeans, pulling out the key chain. He unlatches a spare and hands it over.

"Thanks. I'd like to do something for you tonight, if you don't have plans." I rock on my heels. "Can you meet me at the restaurant? Around seven? I may have a surprise for you," I say. "I mean, that's if you're not sick of me."

"I like surprises," he whispers in my ear, his breath hot. "And I don't think I could ever get sick of you. I'll see you then."

CHAPTER TWENTY-ONE

It's Getting Hot in Here

WITH ALL THE drama, I kind of want to relax, but I'm inspired to create something for Charles to thank him and also to create something for the women in my life to really show my love. Before heading back to the kitchen, I decide to wear a dress with some sexy lingerie under it—for me. I snake down the back stairwell with a shiver to the restaurant.

I push the USB stick Caro gave me into the sound system, blaring Bruno Mars's "Uptown Funk," and dance into the walk-in, remembering the time when I made Caro shuffle down the street, shaking her booty. I laugh, surveying what's on hand: lobster, scallops, sea bass, and shrimp on ice. Bok choy. Watercress. Edible flowers. Fresh herbs. The idea hits me—a deconstructed bouillabaisse, celebrating in-season seafood with a twist—a saffron sauce and a saffron-infused lemon risotto.

I dance back into the kitchen, spinning as I throw on an apron, and then chop to the beat.

The seafood I've commandeered thaws on the prep counter, and I gather the rest of the ingredients for the sauce, namely white wine, butter, and cream, and the song changes to Fergie's "Glamorous." I open the tin of saffron—it glows as brightly as my heart does—and sing along, feeling glamorous myself.

"'G-L-A-M-O-R.'" Pause. "'O-U-S.'"

I smell the strong leathery and earthy threads and my thoughts meander to Charles—sweet and musky. I lick my lips, thinking about him. Shaking my head, I close the lid before another strange fantasy sweeps me off my feet and set to making the risotto side dish.

Once the rice is in the oven, I crack the shell off the lobster, sear all the seafood, and make the sauce.

Soon, it's time to incorporate the saffron. Hesitantly, I open up the lid again. I've never visited Kashmir and all of a sudden I'm there with him, running through a field of vibrant purple flowers. Scarved women dressed in browns and turquoises and oranges smile and wave. And then I'm swimming in crystal clear waters—naked. But before this involuntary fantasy gets too hot and heavy, a charred scent fills my nose, bringing me back to the present. The scallops are beyond seared; they're completely burned.

I don't let this get me down because, although I was distracted, I'm inspired, and I know I can do this.

As they say, merde happens.

Forty minutes later, the meal, now with perfect scallops, is nearly complete and the kitchen smells like heaven, the aroma emitting almost unexplainable. As I prepare poached pears in white wine with ginger and saffron, along with a fresh mascarpone whipped cream for dessert, Iggy Azalea's "Fancy" plays and I sing along at the top of my lungs.

In the midst of whipping the cream, I'm belting out the lyrics and shaking my ass to the beat, when somebody clears their throat—loudly.

"Kate?" says Charles.

I whip around to face him, blender in hand, my mouth dropped open with embarrassment.

He sniffs the air, eyes me up and down. "What are you up to?"

"A little somethin'-somethin'," I say, placing the blender down and waving to the prep station. "Your mother gave me some saffron. And I'm using it. I'm making you a special dinner tonight."

He takes a step toward me, smiling. I take a step back.

"Nobody has ever cooked something special for me. Ever. You sure you're up for the challenge?"

I snap my fingers. "Piece of cake. You know I can cook."

"I know you can." He nods. "But you were singing—"

"I was," I respond, preparing myself for an insult.

"Your voice is actually kind of nice," he says taking another step forward. "And you look really good in that dress. Really good. The color orange really suits you." He takes another step forward. I take another step backward—a tango of nerves dancing around in my brain. He looks really good too, in slim-cut black pants and a teal cashmere sweater that highlights his muscles, his scruff perfectly trimmed.

Before he gets any closer and my heart jumps out of my chest, I point to the doorway. "I'm just finishing up. Go make us some drinks and I'll meet you in the dining room. You know where the bar is."

"Oui, Chef," he says, shooting me another sexy grin, his eyelashes fluttering, and then he turns on his heel. Under his breath he mumbles, "I can't believe my ibu parted with some of her prized saffron. She must really like you, and I kind of like you too."

He exits the kitchen, and I leap for joy—not too high, just a little bounce. Then I plate the dishes, already enraptured by how it will taste. As a final garnish, I sprinkle on a few threads of saffron, the red strands glowing hot like the brightest point of the sun, and then add some edible flowers. My head is pounding and whirling, and I don't know if it's my nerves or my random fantasy or what. Quickly, I scramble over to the medicine cabinet and grab an ibuprofen.

With a perfectly plated dish, I enter the dining room as gracefully as I can and set the plates down on the table. As I flip my straightened hair over my shoulder, Charles gasps. "Kate, this meal looks worthy of Michelin stars."

"I'm not after stars," I say.

"Good," he says, picking up his fork. "But if this tastes as good as it looks, they might shoot in your direction." He looks up. "Is it me? Or is the restaurant glowing red?"

"It's you," I say, looking around. But it isn't him. I see the glow too. Something strange is happening. A heat grips me in a vise, starting at my toes and rushing to my head. Even my hair tingles.

"I have to taste this," he says, holding up a finger. I stare at his plate as he takes a forkful of the risotto with a small slice of the lobster. "Oh mon dieu, I feel like I've died and I've gone to heaven. This is seriously—"

"Magic?"

"Yes." His hands clasp mine and I pull them away. "Kate, would you please eat or at least look at me?"

"Nope. I can't—not hungry."

"Can you put the music back on?"

I pull the remote out from the pocket in my dress and click over to the next song: Ed Sheeran's "Shape of You."

"I love this song," he says. "And I have a deal."

"Not another one." My eyes meet his, he grins, and then I look away. I scramble out of my seat and hold up a finger. "Let me grab the dessert."

"Okay," he says, pointing to his plate. "But I've barely started this gorgeous meal. And you haven't touched yours—"

As I bolt to the kitchen, I yell, "New rule. Dessert first."

"Your kitchen. Your rules," he replies with a chuckle.

I place my hands on the prep table, willing my heart to stop racing, and exhale a deep breath. He probably thinks I'm a total and complete psychopath. I'm feeling so out of sorts—sick to my stomach. But the kitchen always brings back my confidence, puts me on track.

My hands shake as I plate the pears. I place a dollop of the whipped cream on a plate, followed by a pear, and cover it in the wine sauce, trying to get my act together. I sprinkle a couple more threads of saffron on the pears. It's gorgeous, this work of art. Straightening my posture, I return to the dining room, two beautiful desserts plated in each hand.

"So, dessert first?" Charles questions as I sit down, placing a plate in front of him.

"Why not?" I respond. "We're going to be rule breakers tonight."

"I'm up for that," he says with a sly grin. "Now, about my deal. I want to be honest with you." He pauses and chews as I gulp. "My mother can be more than meddlesome, and she's forced herself and her ideas on me—but, and I hate to say this, she's always been right. It took a lot of soul-searching for me to see this."

I can't meet his eyes, so I take a bite of the pear and . . . holy flavors! What in the world did I create? Was I cooking my heart out? Because it's right here—on the plate before me. I take a sip of my drink—a little liquid courage. "What is this?"

"It's a passion fruit cocktail made with a rum and a few secret ingredients, complete with a sugared rim." He leans forward. "Changing the subject?"

"Maybe." I dig into the pear, wanting more. "Honestly, I don't remember what we were talking about."

"We were talking about my deal."

I watch his fork cut into the pear, dip it into the saffron sauce. "And?"

"Putain, this is so good!" He pauses and meets my eyes. "I'm not mad at my mother anymore. I'm glad she did what she did—everything. She's only been looking out after my best interests. And that includes bringing you into my life."

I take another sip of my drink. "What do you mean by that?"

"You really want to know?"

"Maybe," I say, tapping my fork on the table. "Maybe not."

He clasps my hand, stopping my thumping. "I think you'll like what I have to say."

I meet his gaze, my foot tapping underneath the table. "What do you have to say?"

"I'm glad you and my mother are friends. She's so happy. And I want to be close to you too. Kate, I'm far from perfect. Grief has a funny way of eating you up from the inside." His Adam's apple bobs up and down. "I want to let my guard down with you. Kate, I've fallen hard for you. That's why I was so angry the other night and stormed off."

He's fallen for *me*? For a moment, I can't speak, my words catching in my throat, my thoughts scrambled in my brain.

"You've fallen for me?" I finally say.

"I have." He squeezes my hand. "And I'm thinking you feel the same way too. But I could be wrong."

"I, uh, I—"

The song changes to Sixpence None the Richer's "Kiss Me," featured in the movie *She's All That*, where the big man on campus (Freddie Prinze Jr.) falls for a dorky unpopular girl (Rachael Leigh Cook) after she gets a makeover.

"What do you want from me? What's your new deal?"

"Honesty."

"So we're going to be honest now?"

"That's my hope. You can't build a relationship on distrust. I just told you how I feel about you."

This is getting intense. My neck flames with heat. And I can't help the insecurity pecking at my brain: perfect Aria comes to mind.

"Did you love her?" I ask.

"Who?"

"Aria," I respond, my voice low.

He leans back in his chair. "At first, I thought I did. But she blinded me with her seduction tactics, and I couldn't see straight."

"And what do you see now?"

"A future with you."

Just stop it.

I probably watch too many rom-coms on repeat, and I can't stop the words from sliding out of my mouth. "I'm not here for your amusement, Charles. Did you make a bet that you could change me? I need to know. Are you going to stick around?"

"Kate, I never asked or wanted you to change," he says, running his thumbs on my hands. "I'm sticking around, if you'll have me. But there's something I need to do first."

Charles stands up and pulls me into his chest, his vanilla scent invading every pore. He whispers into my ear, "I really want to kiss you, Kate."

I nod, my lips parted, and Charles leans into me, his mouth finding mine. He bites my bottom lip softly, and, after a moment of extreme bliss, I take a step back, my mind spinning.

"Obviously, I do feel the same way about you. There's your answer. But I t-t-think we should t-take things between us slow," I stutter. "I mean, we are w working together. "

"A bonus. Don't you think?"

"We'll see."

"Yeah, we'll see."

One of his hands run up my neck and through my hair, the other supporting my waist. I'm held up by a dizzying suspension, feeling like I could sprout wings and fly. Time stands still and the only thing I can think about is the taste of his mouth, his tongue, spicy and sweet from the saffron, and how I hunger for more. His hand cups my ass, and he leans into me, kissing my neck. My hips grind into him. This kiss, this moment, really proves I'd never experienced passion like this before. It's more than a connection between bodies; it's like a recipe with the perfect balance of ingredients.

Over his shoulder, I swear the remains of our desserts glow red—like my beating heart.

I pull away, biting down on my lips, now swollen with passion, and try to collect myself, my breath. "Your mother is absolutely right."

Charles's jaw drops with mortification. "About what?"

"Spices and senses really do transport you. Because, for a moment there, I was on another planet, just breathing you in and tasting you."

I'm so dizzy, almost delirious.

"I was lost in your scent too. You smell so good. Taste even better." Charles straightens out his shirt and takes in a deep breath. "I have another rule, and this isn't negotiable: never bring up our mothers after a hot make-out session."

My shoulders quiver with laughter. "Deal."

"So we're good?" he asks.

"Duh," I say. How profound.

"Can I walk you home?"

"Front door or back?" I ask. *Gah!* Damn me and my big mouth. "I mean, now that the paparazzi is here, we have to sneak around."

"I know what you meant, Kate," he says with a snort. "And I don't care if they catch us because I'm the happiest I've ever been."

"You're over the quiet life?"

"Only with you by my side." He smooths out my hair. "I'm really glad I met you."

"I'm really glad we're spicing things up," I respond.

We walk into the stairwell and meander up the steps.

"I'm all about heat, but are you just using me for sex?" he says, pulling me aside and whispering in my ear. "I mean, I'm fine with that."

This is moving too fast for me.

"As much as I want to dive right in, it's been a long time since I've been in a relationship," I say, placing a hand on his chest. "I've been burned before. I think I should probably head home."

"I get it. I know we still have some things to sort out, but let's take this one day at a time. I'm sure you can make it home okay," he says with a nod. "I'd walk you up, but there's too much temptation, so I'll see you tomorrow. *Bonne nuit, ma belle.*"

"Good night," I respond, and turn, heading up the steps, placing one foot after the other.

My body, my heart, my soul is on fire. How in the world am I going to get any sleep tonight? I also have the worst headache, the kind where it feels like tiny fists are punching the back of my eyes. I try to swallow but can't.

"Wait, Kate," he says, and I turn. "One more kiss."

A chill shimmies down my spine and I fall into him.

"Kate," he says, "You are so hot."

"So are you," I mumble. "Better call the firefighters."

He takes a step back and places a hand on my forehead. "No, I'm serious. You're burning up."

A sour taste fills my mouth. My stomach gurgles. "Bathroom!

Now!" I exclaim, and he latches his arm into mine, quickly unlocks the door, and leads me into his apartment. We make it the bathroom just in time before I retch out the contents of my stomach into the toilet. Charles holds back my hair and rubs my back as my shoulders shake.

He hands me a towel to wipe off my face. I can't bring myself to look at the toilet or flush it, because I'm slumped over it. I hear him fumbling around in a cabinet. "I'm taking your temperature," he says, stroking my head.

A ding. Charles takes the thermometer. "Putain, 39.5 degrees!"

"In Fahrenheit?" I manage to mumble.

"Over 103." He races out of the bathroom. "Stay here. Don't move. I'm calling our family doctor."

Like I can go anywhere. I'm a puddle.

Charles returns a minute later and turns on the water. "He'll be here in about thirty minutes. In the meantime, I'm supposed to run you a lukewarm bath and give you an ibuprofen to start trying to break the fever."

My tongue sticks to the roof off my mouth. "I already took one about a half hour ago."

"Symptoms?"

"A wild headache," I say. "Maybe some lower back pain. But I always have that thanks to the ladies."

And then I throw up again.

When I'm finished, Charles props me up and then flushes the toilet. "Kate, I have to undress you. Unless you want to ruin your beautiful silk dress."

This is so not how I envisioned the night to go.

"I don't want you to see me naked," I say, my bottom lip trembling. "Not now, not like this."

"Keep your undergarments on," he says, lifting my dress over my head. "Whoa. God, you're gorgeous."

He picks me up and gingerly places me in the bathtub. Instantly, my teeth start chattering. "I'm getting in with you," he says, and I jolt.

"I'll keep my boxers on. It'll be like we're in bathing suits. On a holiday at a beach."

He whips his socks and his jeans off, and then his T-shirt, his body sheer and cut perfection. Those abs—an eight-pack, or, as they say in France, *le bar du chocolat*. Those legs. The tattoo of two tigers anchored on his hairless and sculpted chest. And I'm too sick, too delirious, to explore every delicious detail. Charles lifts my back and slides behind me. He wraps his arms around my waist and I sink into his embrace, snuggling into the warmth of his body.

"I think you have food poisoning," he whispers.

"Oh no," I moan. "They served oysters at Maison de la Barguelonne."

"Kate, why in the world would you eat them when you know they're not in season—the waters have been especially warm this year, climate change and all that, and bacteria thrives in uncooked seafood."

"I couldn't help myself."

"Did anybody else eat them? Our mothers?"

"No," I say. "Even Caro raised her nose at them."

He lets out a sigh of relief. "Good," he says. "And you've stopped shaking. Let's get you out of this tub, dried off, and in bed. The doctor should be here any minute."

I burst into tears as he slinks out of the water. "I'm sorry I ruined our evening."

For a moment, he doesn't say anything. He grabs a towel and

picks me up, wrapping it around my body. "Don't apologize. It brought us closer together. And there's a bonus. I'm not letting you of my sight, and you'll wake up beside me." He pauses when I grimace. "Let me take care of you."

"Okay," I say. "Thank you."

As he turns to carry me to the bedroom, I glance at my reflection in the mirror—black mascara streams down my cheeks. If I'm not able to clean myself up, he'll be taking care of a nightmare from a horror film with horrendous vomit breath.

"Charles," I say with a whimper. "Can you please put me down? I need to wash my face."

"Are you sure you'll be okay?"

"Yes," I say with a pause. "And do you have any mouthwash?"

THE DOCTOR HAS come and gone. I'm supposed to keep hydrated, starting off with ice chips, and to call if my temperature doesn't break by the morning. I'm wearing one of Charles's T-shirts and a pair of his boxer shorts, curled up in his bed.

"I'll never forget this evening," whispers Charles, pulling me closer.

Neither will I. "Can I have a do-over?"

"I'm counting on it," he says. "When you're feeling better. And, on that, I'll take care of the restaurant tomorrow. You're staying in bed."

"Sure you don't want to kick me out?"

"Nah," he says with a laugh. "You smell much, much better. And every sweet has its sour." He kisses my neck and breathes me in. "Can I ask you a question?"

"Sure," I say. "Anything."

"Did you buy that sexy lace ensemble for me?"

"No," I say matter-of-factly. "Our moms did. And it wasn't for you, it was for me."

He flops onto his back and groans. "I really hope you know how weird that sounds."

We both burst into laughter and, once we settle down, he draws me close, me the little spoon and him the big one.

CHAPTER TWENTY-TWO

Ocular Reconnaissance

THE FOLLOWING MORNING, I'm feeling better and I get out of bed while Charles is showering. Instead of yielding to the temptation of seeing him naked, I wander around his bedroom, not having had a good look at it before. Complete with an enormous and extremely organized walk-in closet, it's the size of my place with a carved-wood king-sized bed and matching dresser, a small library and desk, two comfy lounge chairs, and a luxurious day bed, all the fabrics, save for the pristine white duvet, in shades of blue. A couple of photos decorating the walls catch my eye, and I step closer to get a better look—a picture of him graduating from Le Cordon Bleu, Garrance and his father by his side, and a couple of others from when he was much younger with his dad. They're in tropical places—fishing, laughing, and on a huge yacht.

"Snooping?" asks Charles with a soft growl, and I jump in surprise.

"No, no, no," I say with embarrassment, pointing to the photos.

"Just looking at the pictures on the walls." My throat catches as I survey his wet body, glistening with water droplets, wearing nothing but a towel. I look away and fiddle with his T-shirt that I'm still wearing. "Why? Do you have something to hide?"

"I'll tell you all my deepest and darkest secrets." He takes a step toward me and pushes me onto the bed. "If you tell me yours— starting with what are you doing up?"

I prop myself up onto my elbows. "I'm feeling fine. You don't have to take care of me."

"But I want to." He steps over and places a hand on my forehead. "Your temperature seems to be normal, but I'm going to check it." He turns and heads into the bathroom, returning with a thermometer and handing it over.

I stick it under my armpit and eye him, part of me hoping his towel drops to the floor. Sadly, he adjusts it, tucking it back over. My eyes lock on to his body, his chest, rising and falling.

"Didn't I tell you that it's rude to stare?" he asks with a wicked grin.

I haven't even looked in the mirror yet. I'm sure I look like hell warmed over. But, save for distracting him, there's nothing I can do about it.

"Pot, kettle," I say, as he flops down next to me. I trace the lines of the tattoo on his chest—two tigers facing off with symbols and words. "I thought you didn't like cats. When did you get this?"

"Oh, I love cats. Just not my mother's," he says. "As for the tattoo, I think I told you that I practice mixed martial arts. I got this one when my family lived in Thailand, setting up one of the resorts, when I was eighteen and practicing Muay Thai. This design has traditional symbols of Sak Yant—twin tigers, five lines, nine peaks, and eight directions, all deeply rooted in ancient Buddhist and Hindu practices and representing forces like power, strength, fearlessness, protection, and wealth."

"You definitely have all those attributes," I say, enraptured by the design and the softness of his skin. Everything about him is so sensual—from his lips to his toes and whatever he's hiding under the towel. "Do you still practice?"

"I do," he says. "It's a great way—and a little bit healthier than a rage room—to let stress out."

"I thought you loved the rage room."

"I did," he says with a grin. "I can't wait to go back there with you—unless you want me to teach you a little kickboxing or self-defense?"

"I'm game, although I do know how to take care of myself."

"I never said you didn't, but if you haven't taken any self-defense courses, it's always good to be prepared."

The thermometer dings, and Charles takes it from my hand when I pull it out from under my shirt. "It's still a little elevated—"

"My heart rate?"

"No, your temperature," he says, raising an eyebrow. "And don't get any funny ideas. You're still not coming into the kitchen today."

Not what I was thinking about.

He looks at the clock on the nightstand. "As much as I want to stay with you, the deliveries will be here any minute. And I've got to get dressed."

He walks toward the closet, dropping the towel from his waist.

I flop down onto the bed with a giggle. To think I'd called him an ass before was meant to be an insult. Nope, his is sculpted perfection, worthy of a museum. Michelangelo's David would be seething with jealousy.

A few minutes later, Charles walks back into the bedroom, unfortunately, dressed. "Are you staying here today?"

"I think I'll head back to my apartment," I say, clearing my throat. "I have to feed Frushi." And call Caro. And get my head together.

He puffs out his bottom lip with disappointment. "Oh well, at least a man can dream about having a beautiful woman waiting for him in bed." He pauses. "I'll bring you some broth at noon."

"Broth?" I question. "What if I'm hungrier for more?"

"And maybe some crackers," he says, not picking up on or ignoring my lame innuendo. "Doctor's orders."

We leave his apartment and we're standing in front of my door when I realize I've forgotten my shoes and clothes. "My things—"

"Aren't going anywhere. But, unfortunately, I have to." He pulls me toward him. "Just not before doing this."

When his lips touch mine, oh, yes, my appetite has definitely come back, and then he leaves me craving his touch.

BACK IN MY apartment, I slump on the couch. Am I ready? My body says yes; my mind says no. To my surprise, a large, silky gray form crawls out from under a chair and I jump up onto the couch, knocking over everything on my coffee table, screaming bloody murder. "A rat! A rat! A fucking rat!"

Orange eyes blink at me with astonishment. So do the jewels on his collar.

"Oh my god. How did you get in here?"

Juju flicks his tail toward the window I'd left open, and I peek through the curtains. There are no lights on at Garrance's shop. He must have snuck out again, but how did he get in here?

"You are one wily cat," I say, petting his head and he purrs.

I curl up on the couch, Juju by my side. He rolls onto his back, and I stroke his chin. That's when I notice his paws are wet. "Please, tell me you didn't eat Frushi."

I get up to find my fish hiding in his castle right as my phone buzzes.

> GARRANCE: Sorry, my darling, to bother you.
> I thought Juju was in the car when I left my
> workshop, but I can't find him. Is he at the
> restaurant?

> ME: Don't worry. He's curled up on my
> couch. I don't know how he got into
> my apartment, but he did.

> GARRANCE: Oh, thank heavens.

Three dots blink as she types.

> GARRANCE: Would you mind keeping an eye on
> him? I'm back at the hotel and I'm taking care of
> Jezebel. I'll pick him up sometime tomorrow.

> ME: No problem.

Who is Jezebel?

> GARRANCE: Close the windows. He's like
> Houdini—an escape artist. Just put some
> magazines or papers on the floor. He'll go there.
> Thank you, Kate.

I close out of messages, my head pounding, and then grab an ibuprofen from the medicine cabinet, washing the pill down with water.

"Well, Juju," I say, scratching under his chin. "You're going to be my wing-cat and cuddle buddy today."

He meows and follows me into my bedroom.

A FEW HOURS later, I'm feeling one hundred percent. Today, I'm heading back to the kitchen for day one of the staff training.

Charles raises a brow when I walk in. "You should be in bed."

"No, I shouldn't. I should be here," I say. "I'm feeling better, and the reopening is in two days. Plus, it's the first day of training."

He feels my forehead. "You seem normal."

"That's a nice compliment. Thank you."

"But if you start feeling woozy—"

"I'll go home."

Albert stomps into the kitchen. "What's going on? Why are there armed guards outside?" he asks. "And all those photographers? Is somebody famous coming in?"

"Long story," I say, my eyes meeting Charles's. "I'll explain everything when the rest of the staff arrives."

I have no idea what to say. I can barely come to grips with the situation myself. I feel like I've been dropped headfirst into a bad reality TV show.

I'm in the midst of updating the staff, and they all seem pretty excited that the restaurant is in the eye of the storm. I overhear some of them chatting, hoping to get photos worthy of Instagram and high-fiving one another, until Charles says, "Don't forget you all signed NDAs and you'll be held liable if you talk to the press."

A collective groan fills the kitchen. Questions ensue.

"Is the restaurant staying open?"

"Are you really a billionaire?"

"What if somebody takes a photo of us?"

"Yes. None of your business. And, as for the last question, I, nor any of you, can control that," says Charles. "Just try to stay away from the photographers, and don't answer any questions."

One of the female servers surreptitiously attempts to put on lipstick. I catch her, and she shoves the tube into the pocket of her apron.

Shit on a cracker, I'm irritated as hell, the gravity of this weight of a mess pulling my mood down. This restaurant is my life, not the attention of a media frenzy. I poured my heart and soul into my dream. And now my plans have changed so drastically I'm not sure if I can adapt and adjust. But I have to. I roll my neck, cracking it, and get back to prepping, Charles by my side.

"I'm really sorry, Kate," he says.

I shoot him the side-eye and brace my hands on the prep station. "Would you please stop apologizing?"

"I don't take this situation lightly."

"And I'm not going to let this situation mess with my dream."

"We're going to cook our hearts out." He whispers, "Kate, you already have mine. Just don't serve it up on a platter."

I can't bring myself to look at Charles because when I do, he smiles and all I can think about is kissing him. As we make a home-made Mexican-inspired chocolate sauce for the vanilla ice cream, our arms brush together as I hand over the urfa biber flakes. He stirs the pot, the aromas mingling together, all sweet and spicy, and now, thanks to his recording in the vent and the words I'd heard, I'm imagining us together.

"Kate, taste this," says Charles, snapping me out of my fantasy. He holds out a spoon laden with sauce, I take a tiny mouthful, and then lick my lips. Charles flashes a sexy smile. "Almost better than sex, huh?"

He has to be a mind reader. "I wouldn't know," I mumble.

"What?"

"Oh, nothing," I say, twirling my ponytail and not meeting his eyes.

"I can't wait for this day to be over," he says with a groan. "Now that you're feeling better, do you want to come over to my place when we're finished?"

Merde. In my head they're fine, but I'm not ready to act out my fantasies in real time—not to mention the devastating fact I'm wearing granny panties. I gulp. "Okay. Cool, cool, cool." I raise a finger. "I'll be back in a second. There's something I forgot to do."

I race to the bathroom to call Caro. She picks up on the first ring. Breathless and panicked, I explain the turn of events, including my underwear dilemma, concluding with: "You know me. I don't know about these things. I've slept next to him, and I've kissed him, but my vagina isn't voracious. I think it has cobwebs."

Caro snorts out a laugh. "Kate, he's not going to expect you to sleep with him."

I bite down on my bottom lip. "He isn't?"

"Don't worry about it. Take things slow. Kiss him if you want to, don't if you don't."

"Oh, I do want to kiss him, and I already have. Aside from food, he's all I think about."

"This is so unlike you," she says.

"I know. And that's what scares me."

"Stop overthinking," she says. "For once."

Friends for more than thirteen years, she knows me and my military-like ways. "I hate you," I say.

"I love you," she says, and we laugh before hanging up.

AFTER THE STAFF leaves, Charles and I finish cleaning up the restaurant, me gulping like a fish out of water. We're alone together, me facing the sink. I'm washing pots and pans slowly, trying to post-pone our date. Technically, this is our fourth rendezvous if I count the boat cruise, the dinner he'd made me, and the one I'd made him. Caro could be wrong; he may be expecting more than just a kiss.

"Ready?" he asks, holding out the chocolate sauce.

No.

"Yes," I say, bouncing on my heels.

"Kate, is something wrong? You're acting jittery. I'm not going to bite you."

My lips pinch together, and he whispers, "Unless you want me to."

I usually have a comeback for everything, but not this. He un-locks the door to the stairwell, holding it open for me. "Let's go re-lax. I have some ice cream in the freezer. And a bottle of champagne chilling in the fridge."

"I need to feed the fish first," I say, stalling. "And clean myself up a bit. I'll meet you there in a few."

"Great," he says, giving me a peck on the cheek. "You know where I live. See you soon."

As I walk up the steps, I'm trying so hard to control my feelings, but it's a moot point. I've fallen for him, and this all too new for me. My mind is swimming with confusion. More than anything, I want to take our relationship to the next level, but it means taking a risk. Do I let go of fear and surrender to emotions I can't control? Move forward instead of pulling the breaks?

A line from one of my favorite old movies, *Auntie Mame*, pops into my head: "Live! Life is a banquet and most poor suckers are starving to death."

I'm hungry, ravenous. I've been starved for love. And I'm going to blow into the winds of change. Well, after I get my mise en place prepped—this time meaning me, not ingredients—and stop my heart from racing.

CHAPTER TWENTY-THREE

Hotter than a Jalapeño

Taking a deep breath, and now wearing black lingerie and a casual but slinky midnight-blue dress with matching ballet flats, I pick up Juju and meander slowly down the stairs. Juju is so heavy it's almost as if he's grounding me so the butterflies in my stomach don't carry me away. Hesitantly, I knock on Charles's door. No answer. I bang harder—possibly too hard.

"Whoa, whoa, whoa," I can hear Charles say. "Somebody is impatient." The door creaks open and his eyes lock onto Juju. "What is he doing here?"

"Uh, he kind of snuck into my apartment, and I promised your mother I'd watch him."

He sighs, and Juju hisses. "I've begrudgingly watched the furry asshole in the past and may have some things—food, bowls, litter," he says. "Put him down, follow me, and I'll give you a quick tour. You've seen my bedroom, but you haven't seen the rest of the place."

If I think on it, his statement is beyond bizarre. I walk in and set Juju on the floor as Charles closes the door. He glares at Juju. "Cat, you know the drill. If you piss on my furniture like last time, I'll drop you off at an animal shelter."

I gasp. "You wouldn't really do that."

Charles laughs. "No, but I would lock him in the bathroom."

Out of it the previous night, I hadn't taken a good look around. His apartment is huge—five or six times the size of mine and, considering it covers the entire second floor, is not all that surprising. What is surprising is his taste. I'd expected a bachelor pad with leather couches and a big-screen TV, not rustic chic with hints of Asiatic elements like the wooden bookcases and tables, the dark armoire with silver details, and the Balinese carvings decorating the walls—everything streamlined and elegant with a dash of modern.

"This way," he says, walking down the hallway. I follow him, Juju following me. "Now, this first room usually has women gasping—"

My knees are about to go out from under me. "You have a red room?"

"Huh?"

"*Fifty Shades of Grey*? You know, Christian and Anastasia? Butt plugs and whips. I have to confess, I don't think I'd be into that."

"I have absolutely no idea what you're talking about, and this room is gray," he says, opening the door. "Honestly, at the mention of butt plugs, my cheeks clenched and I don't want to know." He waves a hand. "This is my gym. Go on in," he says, and Juju does, flicking his tail.

I enter the room, my mouth dropped open. "It's bigger than my entire apartment."

"The benefit of taking over the entire floor." He points to a corner. "I even have some yoga mats, a Pilates reformer, and some other things besides weights and my treadmill if you ever want to work out here." He pauses. "Not that you need to."

"Right, I'm in peak form."

"You are to me."

My nerves set in, and I have to change the subject. "I'm wondering how I ruined your duvet. By my calculations, my apartment is above the living room."

"Because I hand-washed it and it was drying on a rack there—more open windows." He shrugs. "And, no worries, I got the stain out." He clasps his hand on to mine. "Let's have some champagne, shall we?" he says, leading me into his kitchen.

I follow him, taking everything in, the dark polished floors, the large center island made of concrete, and, damn, the peacock-blue La Cornue stove. I point. "How in the world did you get this up here?"

He shrugs. "Big windows and an extra-large terrace."

"I've always wanted one."

"You can use it any time. *Ma cuisine est ta cuisine.*" He smiles, reaches into a cabinet, his T-shirt riding up and exposing his toned stomach. He places two coupe à champagne glasses on the table. "Take a seat. Relax. I'll pop open the bottle. Are you hungry?"

Yes. But not for food.

"Not really," I manage to squeak out. Like creating recipes, the attraction I feel toward him isn't rational—it's a craving taking over my entire body and, although I know my way around the kitchen, I honestly don't know what I'm doing with him. I'm out of my realm.

Charles pours us a glass, the champagne golden and fizzy. "I think the menu we came up with is incredible."

"Yep, yep, yep," I say, taking my glass. I down half of it in one sip.

Charles meets my eyes. "You realize we're supposed to toast first."

"Oh, right. Sorry, sorry, sorry," I say, kicking myself. I'm a three-word wonder. I force a smile and hold up my glass. "Santé."

Charles takes the seat beside me and we clink. "Here's to the success of Bistro Exotique. And to you."

His knee touches mine. I move my leg and chug the rest of my champagne, letting out a loud hiccup. "Kate, seriously, what's wrong? You're not even meeting my eyes—and you know that's the golden rule when toasting in France." Charles sets his glass down, walks over to the stereo, and flicks it on, the song Ed Sheeran's "Perfect," and then he moves toward me and holds out his hand. "Can I have this dance?"

I nod. Wow, he's really pulling out all the stops. I'm on my feet, barefoot, and our bodies sway rhythmically to the music, my head resting on his chest.

My neck goes rigid when his hands wrap around my shoulder blades. His fingertips circle softly at first, and then he applies more pressure, moving his hands down my spine to my lower back, pushing firmly. He works his way back up to my neck, kneading the muscles with his thumbs and forefingers. All I can think about is how he knows exactly what he's doing, how this is definitely foreplay, and I tense up even more.

"I can't do this," I say, my breath coming hard and heavy, and I scramble to the far side of the room.

"Do what?"

"This. I'm not very experienced. Actually, I have practically zero experience." I should shut the hell up, but I launch into a nervous babble. "You'd think because my mom is a sex therapist, I'd be open to the idea—"

Charles laughs softly. "I don't want to have to sex with you."

I clasp my hands on my head. "What? You don't?"

"No, we're working together. We have to take this—us—slow." He pauses. "But I really, really want to kiss you again, Kate. Are you okay with that?"

He's actually asking for consent? I can't help but to grin. "I'm more than okay," I say, leaning forward and practically falling down.

"Good," he says, one hand clasping on to the back of my neck, the other cupping the base of my spine. "Because I've been dying to do this all day."

Our eyes meet and the look in his gaze is so intense, I shut mine. He pulls me forward and leans into me, his mouth finding mine. He lightly nibbles my bottom lip, and I let out a moan. He whispers into my mouth. "A little bite isn't that bad, is it?"

"No," I say.

His mouth, his lips, become more ravenous, and our heated breaths become one, his chocolaty and spicy. His hands envelope my jaw-line as he pulls me into him even more. Our tongues explore each other's, gentle and demanding, and my hands slide down his sides. The kiss is urgent, fervent, and so utterly delicious. I'm clinging onto his back now, light-headed and dizzy. Wild tremors rush down my spine right into my loins. I grip him tighter, about to lose my breath as I breathe him in.

He pulls away, groaning softly. "Do you want me to stop?"

"No," I say breathlessly.

"Let's get comfortable on the couch."

I can only nod. He picks me up in his strong muscled arms, and I stroke his tattoo as he carries me into the living room.

The next kiss is better and more intense than the first—the kind that makes me see fireworks, the kind that makes me want to explode. Every nerve in my body throbs, the weight of his body pressing against mine, his hardness. My hands explore his back as he kisses my neck. It's like I'm starving and thirsty and I want to eat him, drink him in. This is too good, too much, too delicious. Between the taste of his mouth and his scent, I think I'm going to pass out.

I push on his chest, and he pulls away, breathing heavily, and then I fan myself dramatically with my hand. "Is it hot in here or what?"

He blurts out a laugh and sinks into the couch, his head tilted back. "Oui, it is. I'm burning up."

I let out an unrestrained donkey-like giggle. "I know you're a pretty big dill, but that kiss was getting intense."

He offers a slight grin. "Did you just use an herb pun?"

"Pickle. Dill pickles," I say, feeling the blush creep along my cheeks. "I use puns when I'm feeling out of sorts."

"I thought we were good," he says. "I make you feel out of sorts?"

Yes. "No, not at all. It's just really hot in here. Could you talk to management about putting in AC?"

"You're funny," he says, and I flinch.

"I usually go for ice cream when I want to cool down. I made coconut last night—my special blend. Want some?" he asks, and I nod like a bobblehead. He kisses me on the forehead and then lets out another chuckle. "That kiss though. I thought you said you were inexperienced."

I smooth out my hair and shoot him a nervous smile. "I guess I'm a quick learner."

He grins again and says, "I'll happily be your teacher."

Before I melt onto the couch, Charles stands up and then heads into the kitchen, leaving me to catch my breath. We're supposed to be working together, not this. But I can still taste his kiss on my lips. Maybe the ice cream will cool down my lustful thoughts.

A few moments later, he saunters back into the living room and places two bowls on the coffee table, perfect cloudlike mounds of white balls with a smattering of toasted coconut flakes, the scents of the tropics immediately embracing me. "Spoon?" he asks, sitting down next to me, his hair messed up.

"Thank you," I say, taking it from his hand and digging right in.

The coconut flavor is intoxicating, followed by notes of vanilla. The texture is creamy and cold and warm and soft at the same time. I let out a soft moan, and he wipes the corner of my mouth with his thumb, his gaze locked on to mine.

"It's delicious," I say, trying to gather my thoughts. Once I find my breath, I swallow back another bite of the ice cream. Damn, it's so silky and tasty. "Um, we should put this on the menu. For sure."

I spoon in a third mouthful of the ice cream and, as I swallow it down, bizarre visions flash in my mind's eye. Charles and I making passionate love, me gripping his back. A wedding, me with wildflowers of blues and purples in my hair, Charles waiting for me at the altar. Me, holding a beautiful baby swaddled in pink and Charles smiling a dimpled smile as he looks over us. I'm completely sober, but I feel drunk—high as a kite. A baby? Why is my head even going there? Why does this keep happening?

I blink the visions away and set the spoon down into the bowl. "The vanilla? Where did you get it?"

"My mother. Why?"

Garrance's ingredients are really messing with my head, but if I tell him that, he'll think I'm nuts. I clear my throat and meet his eyes. "Just wondering."

Charles raises a brow.

"Thank you. This was nice," I say, and stand up, wringing my hands. "I should go."

"You're leaving? You didn't even finish your bowl."

"It was delicious, but I can't."

"Did I do something wrong?"

"No," I say, and it's the truth. He's done everything right, but it's all too much for my mental bandwidth right now.

He eyes me curiously, his brows pinched together. "Do you want me to walk you home?"

"That's okay. I'm only one flight up. I'm good." I rock back and forth on my heels, trying to come up with a logical excuse for bolting. "I've just got a lot on my mind. You know, with the opening. I really need a solid night's rest."

Charles tilts his head to the side. "I get it. And I'll see you tomorrow, Kate," he says, squeezing my hand. "Tonight was amazing. And so are you."

I can't focus, so I squint and turn on my heel, heading for the door. "Thanks for the ice cream. See you tomorrow."

I don't wait for his response, and I race out of the apartment.

On the way up the stairwell, I lean against the wall, trying to catch my breath, my heart racing. My step falters, and I nearly tumble down the stairs. Why do I feel this way, like I'm walking on a cloud? Why is there an ethereal glow in the hallway? A smoky haze? I take in a deep breath, trying to calm my mind. I close my eyes and wave my hands, trying to get rid of the white puffs floating in front of me. These visions? They must be happening because I'm stressed out, not going crazy. Garrance's ingredients are only that—ingredients. Then again, this isn't the first time that strange sensations have washed over me since Garrance and Charles came into my life. But there is no such thing as magic. Food doesn't bring on fantasies or transport you like it's been doing to me. I'm probably overtired. I need to take better care of myself. For now, I'll just put one foot forward in front of the other and try to get some sleep. First priority: the restaurant. Right? I open my eyes and the haze is gone. I stumble into my apartment and flop onto my bed fully clothed, tossing and turning all night.

THE FOLLOWING DAY, Charles and I bumble around the kitchen, knocking into each other, spilling herbs, and making a general mess. When our hands touch, we jump apart as if we've been electrocuted, and the staff gives us odd looks—especially after I drop a plate of risotto on the floor.

"I can't stop thinking about our kisses last night," he whispers.

"Neither can I."

"Did you want to come over tonight?"

"I do. I really do," I say, thinking about everything that's transpired. "But I don't think it's a good idea. Tomorrow night is important. I can't handle any distractions."

He blows out the air between his lips. "I can't either. But you're really the best of distractions, Kate."

Funny, when I'd first seen him on the street I'd thought the same thing about him. I'm just hoping this—what's happening between us—isn't temporary.

WE'VE BEEN SLICING and dicing and filleting like mad, Charles shooting me an occasional dimpled grin, and it's as good time as any for a little break. I pull out my phone and, listening to Charles's advice, delete all the Google alerts—at least one hundred of them—and then check my messages.

CARO: What are you wearing to the opening?

ME: What I wore last time.

CARO: No, you're not. I'm leaving work early and bringing you something else. I'll be there at five.

ME: Thanks. But you don't have to.

CARO: But I am.

ME: I'll let the guards know.

Caro calls me a few seconds later. "What's going on?"

I explain what went down. She sighs, "Alors, as they say, any press is good press."

I'm not sure about that. We hang up, and I scroll down to the next message.

> DAD: Sweetie, I was going to try and come, but can't. Proud of you. Love you.

> ME: Love you too.

Kind of a lame response, but it's all I can come up with. I shake off my disappointment and read the next message.

> MARK: Looking forward to the reopening!

> ME: Is Eloise coming? I'll have to add her to the list.

Three dots blink. I wait.

> MARK: We broke up.

> ME: What?

> MARK: Will tell you what happened in person.

I put my phone back in my apron's pocket and rub my temples. The opening could be a bomb of epic proportions. Or it could be a hit. We've been working so hard, and the menu is phenomenal. Or is it? Why am I still doubting myself?

I've got this. I do.

My gaze shoots to Charles as he preps. We've got this.

Don't we?

Needing to shake off negativity energy, I decide to prepare one of the desserts—something sweet to take away the sour taste of fear infiltrating my mouth. I'm going to tackle the strawberry and lavender sorbet—the herb from Garrance's rooftop garden, the strawberries sweet and juicy. Thankfully, the recipe is easy—especially when you have three Thermomix machines at your disposal.

After commandeering most of the ingredients, I smell the lavender Garrance had bestowed upon us and another fantasy sets in. Charles and I are running through a field bursting with purple flowers in the South of France, smiling and laughing. We're kissing, softly at first, and then we're naked, exploring each other's bodies, his rippled stomach, and floating on a cloud made from the fragrance of the lavender—sweet and woodsy—

"Kate, where'd you go? You look all dreamy," says Charles.

"Nowhere. Just thinking," I say.

"You're sexy as hell when you think. You bite those full lips of yours and it's kind of distracting when I'm trying to work. I almost cut my hand—"

"Sorry," I say. "I won't do it again."

"No, please do. It reminds me of our first kiss."

He's really the best of distractions, but I need to focus.

After regaining my composure, I dismiss the staff, giving them a last-minute "We can do this" pep talk, my heart racing. Charles leans against the prep station. "So, we're making the sorbet tonight?"

I nod, offering Charles a weird smile, turn, and then shuffle to the bar to grab some prosecco—a secret ingredient to reduce the base's freezing point and improve its texture. "It has to set," I say over my shoulder.

When I return, Charles stands at my station and he says, "Come here. You have to taste this."

I set the bottle down and step up to him. He holds out a berry, but before I can reach for it, he places it in his mouth, half sticking out. He pulls me toward him and raises his brows. I'm so into this. My lips part and we're like human forms of Lady and the Tramp—our lips touching, a quick chew, and our tongues meet. I'm not trembling from fear of the paparazzi anymore but from full-blown lust. When we separate, Charles licks his lips and traces my mouth with his finger. "That was the best damn strawberry I've ever eaten. You're delicious, Kate—"

I place a hand on his chest. "So are you, but we've got to chill out."

"I get it, Kate," he says, a glimmer sparking his eyes.

"Yep, yep, yep," I say. "And right now it's time to make the sorbet."

"Yes, Chef," he responds with a perfunctory nod and a sly smile.

The opening has to be on point. And I'm going to do everything in my power to take hold of my dream. After a little wavering, confident Kate is back in action. She has to be; I have too much riding on this.

CHAPTER TWENTY-FOUR

Tantric Food; It's a Thing

THE BISTRO PIPES Garrance's scents, the lounge music is playing, the fish are swimming in their tank behind the bar, the orchids are watered, and the menu is prepped. We're running a sit-down service tonight for Paris's elite and a few of my guests. Charles didn't invite anybody, and when I'd asked him why he'd just shrugged and said, "I've barely spoken to any of them in two years," and he'd left it at that. Knowing of the timing, and his pain from the loss of his father and grandfather, I didn't press him.

It's just after four when my mom and Garrance join us for the family meal—both of them unfashionably late. I'm seriously regretting accepting their offers to help, since Garrance is a bit flighty and my mom might scare people away if she advises them on their sex lives as she pours drinks. The two of them corner Charles and me.

"It's madness and mayhem outside," says my mom. "So very exciting. I've been reading about everything online."

Garrance shoots me an empathetic look. "I'm sorry to bring you into our world, but it could be good for the restaurant."

Charles crosses his arms over his chest, and Garrance turns her head away, lowering her gaze. "This isn't good at all, Ibu. Until now, we've led private lives, and Aria has outed us to the world. We'll never have a moment of peace." Charles clenches his fists. "I had to hire police to keep the paparazzi away."

"Maybe you should have thought about that before your billionaire, hot-chef article was released," says Garrance.

"I had nothing to do with that piece."

"You posed for pictures."

"For Aria," he says with a mumble. "Three years ago."

I gulp. Damn Aria, haunting me again.

"That explains everything," says Garrance.

My mother scratches her neck and clears her throat.

"I've just lost my appetite," says Charles, turning to face me. "Kate, I've got to cool off, take a shower, do anything before I punch something. I'll be back at five so you can get ready. Can you take things from here?"

"Yes," I say, and he bolts to the back of the kitchen, leaving me stupefied.

Garrance straightens her posture and reaches into her purse, handing over a sack. "Here are some more vanilla beans. I noticed yours weren't producing pods just yet. These are from my own personal collection, and I'm thinking we need to tone down the heat tonight."

You think?

Garrance turns to my mother. "Cri-Cri, do you want to help me out with Kate's orchids and then have a drink together, maybe feed the beautiful fish in the tank, before the festivities start?"

My mother says yes, and by the expression on her face, I'm sure she wants to get away from my glare. Sometimes mothers do *not* know best, and my heart aches for Charles.

I don't have time to collect my thoughts. Albert races up to me. "Chef, we're all waiting for the meal," he says. "We all still have a ton to do, and we're starving."

"I'll be right there," I say, forcing a smile.

My mom's laughter echoes in the dining room. I stand in the doorway to find Mom and Garrance sitting at the bar, laughing conspiratorially. "Do you think it will work?" asks Garrance, Juju sitting in the barstool next to her like a furry king on his throne.

My mom and Garrance clink glasses. "It's already working—the perfect chemistry," says my mom.

I shake my head and clear my throat. "What are the two of you up to?"

Juju meows and jumps off his barstool and then snakes around my ankles, purring.

"Oh, Kate, we have a wonderful new invention," says my mom. She straightens up in her seat and squints in concentration. "We just came up with a new drink using the seeds from Garrance's vanilla beans. It's delicious. Want to try it?"

"No," I say with suspicion. I can smell the drink from where I stand, wafting up to my nostrils; it's his scent. "It's time for the family meal. Are you eating with us?"

"No," says Garrance. "We're saving our appetites for the big event."

They are definitely keeping something from me. But hungry stomachs and a busy night await.

FINALLY, IT'S ALMOST go time. I'm showered and now wearing the dress Caro brought over—a peacock-blue chiffon number from this season's Madeleine Bouchard collection. Again, it's like it's made for me—a perfect fit. When I enter the kitchen, Charles is still in a foul mood, barking out orders to the staff.

"Charles," I say. "Can you tone down the anger in your voice? We're all working together. Aren't we?"

"We are," says Charles, looking up and taking in my presence. His hands fly to his heart. "Whoa, ooh-la-la. You look amazing. That shade of blue really brings out the color in your eyes."

"Merci," I say. "But I know I'm not glamorous." I want to add *like Aria*, but hold my tongue. Instead of fanning the flames of my insecurities or letting him know that I'd googled her again like a jealous girlfriend, I smooth out my dress and change the subject. "The paparazzi will get bored and move on, right? And it could be good for the restaurant," I say, and he rolls his eyes. "So it's not that bad."

"It's catastrophic," he says. "The press is going to be all over me like vultures picking at prey."

Before I can respond, Albert rushes up to me. "Chef, all of the guests are seated."

"Right," I say. "Merci, Albert."

Charles meets my curious gaze. "Look, we'll talk about this later. Right now, it's time for your opening speech. I'll man the kitchen. You're not cooking tonight, and you'll take all the credit for the dishes. Your restaurant, your recipes. Just pretend I'm not here."

Easier said than done. My life has become a telenovela with a reality TV show twist, complete with the hot, broody guy. Now, I have to act out my part: confident, not crazy, Kate.

BISTRO EXOTIQUE IS packed, every table filled with fashionistas dressed to the nines. To my surprise, I give the opening speech without stumbling over the words, mostly because I keep them simple.

"Welcome to Bistro Exotique, where our offerings will surely open your minds and palates. I hope you enjoy everything we've lovingly prepared for you. Merci. And bon appétit."

Applause. Forks clink on glasses. When I finish, a couple of air kisses from the people I'd invited, namely Oded, Caro, Mark, and Pierre. Juju sits at the bar like a Buddha wearing a sapphire collar, his orange eyes laser focused on me. He blinks. My gaze latches on to my mom as she makes a smoke bubble and pops it for a guest. I watch the haze of white roll across the bar.

This is all a bit surreal.

Garrance meanders up to me, her long skirt swooshing. She whispers, "You really should mingle with the guests—from table to table. These people are *very* important. Answer any questions they may have." She grasps my hand, placing something in it. "Put this on. I had it made for you."

"I have a question," I say, locking my gaze onto Juju. "Am I one of your pet projects?"

"Don't be silly, Kate. You really say the most ridiculous things." She points to Juju. "I already have a pet. And I adore him as much as I adore you."

Gee, thanks.

She turns on her heel and walks up to a table of "very important people" before I can respond. I look at the palm of my hand to find a sapphire-encrusted hummingbird brooch—the logo of my restaurant. Wide-eyed, I stare at the sparkling jewels, debating whether I should accept this extravagant gift. Maybe she's accessorizing me like Juju? But a part of me kind of loves the brooch.

As I'm pinning it to the bustline of my dress, Caro and Mark bound up to me.

"This is so much better than your first opening, Kate," says Caro, and I flinch. "I can't believe who's here." She tilts her head. "Marion Cotillard? Catherine Deneuve? Jean Dujardin? How on earth did you get them to come?"

Holy high rollers.

"I didn't," I say with a gulp. "Garrance did."

"Must be good to have friends from the upper echelons of society," says Mark. "That explains the armed guards outside."

"Not exactly," I say with a shudder. "The paparazzi, the guards—this is all due to Charles's ex, Aria."

I explain what went down.

"Who cares? Aria is a bitch, and she can't snuff out your glow. She got wasted before one of the fashion shows and face-planted on the runway. We're never hiring her again," says Caro. "Enough about her, not worth another word. Focus on the good. This opening is sensational. *Absolument*. People are going to be talking about it for months."

A noise distracts me. I turn my head to find the source: my mother is tapping the hang drum to a funk remix of Lilly Wood and the Prick's "Prayer in C," her head swaying from side to side, her long gray hair swinging on her back. Oded sits at the bar, gazing at her with a goofy smile on his face, looking like a lovesick teenager.

"Gah!" I exclaim, pointing. "My mom is so embarrassing."

"Nah," says Mark. "People love her. Even the fish are swimming to the music."

Time to change the subject. "Mark, tell me what happened with Eloise. I thought things were great between the two of you."

"Not much to tell," he says, his Aussie accent rising and falling. "She left me for another guy—the chief physician in charge of her rotation. I'd suspected it for a while, confronted her, and she packed her bags."

Woah. This is a complete surprise. Eloise was one of those squeaky-clean quiet types. Or so I'd thought. Albert catches my eye, and he waves his hands, mouthing, "Service is about to start."

I exhale a deep breath. "Guys, I'm so glad you're here. You're bringing normalcy to this evening. Sadly, I really want to hang out with you so you can update me on everything, but, according to Garrance, I have to mingle with the guests."

"That's right. You do," says Caro, linking her arm into Mark's. "Why don't we go have Cri-Cri make us a drink, and I'll tell you my sad, pathetic story."

"What story?" asks Mark.

"I caught my fiancé fucking a model at one of our shows." She lifts her thin shoulders. "Suffice it to say, he's no longer my fiancé."

"Damn. That's harsh."

Caro focuses on me, and then she winks. "Kate, ignore us tonight. But if we get bombed drowning our sorrows, call us Ubers. Right now, you have to mingle like a very well-dressed trained monkey. By the way, you look absolutely stunning."

"You do," says Mark. "And that brooch is gorgeous too."

They walk away and my hands leap to the pin. I take a deep breath and slowly walk from table to table to personally introduce myself and welcome the guests.

DURING DESSERT, I'M in the midst of giving a closing speech, but the patrons barely acknowledge my presence, some of them drooling, their heads tilted back. I've never seen anything like this before; it's as if the entire restaurant is having a collective foodgasm— moans and groans and gasps of delight echoing from every corner of the room. I make my way over to my mother and Oded. They stop playing the hang drum.

"This is so weird," I say, meeting my mom's eyes. "Please tell me you weren't dolling out sex advice."

She shoots me a closed-mouthed, guilty grin.

"Cri-Cri!" I growl. "I asked you not to do that. Look at everybody now."

"I had absolutely nothing to do with this experience. It was your meals. And I think it's amazing. Somehow you've created tantric food. Just look at their faces."

Oded says, "It's the most amazing meal I've ever had."

Mom goes back to beating the hang drum to an electro-tribal beat. They both ignore me.

Frustrated, I wander from the table to table, eavesdropping.

"*That meal! I was in Sri Lanka and I was making love to you on the sand.*"

"*I was by the sea. Did you smell the ocean? Feel the waves?*"

"*I remembered our trip to Mexico. And I had a fantasy of licking the spicy chocolate sauce off your body.*"

"*This sorbet! The lavender—the strawberries! I want to taste the flavors on your mouth.*"

Couples are kissing, holding hands, and giggling. Ties are loosened. I'd never intended on creating a food orgy, and I stand in shock until Garrance latches her arm on to mine.

She says, "I told you my spices, my scents, are magic. They transport you to another time, another place." She grins and waves a manicured hand to the tables. "You and Charles created this atmosphere with your chemistry—the love, the heat, the anger, the passion in your cooking. My spices are only the catalyst."

My head whips to the bar. My mom holds up a drink, the scent of vanilla washing over me, fantasies of sex with Charles picking at my brain.

"Enjoy the night," says Garrance. She air-kisses my cheek and then meanders back to her table.

With my jaw slack, I race to the kitchen and grab Charles by the arm. "We're getting the hell out of Dodge. Now."

"What's going on? Are there complaints?"

I'm shaking. "No, it's an absolute freak show out there."

Charles steps up to me and steadies my wobble. "Kate, are you okay? Everything seems normal to me. People are enjoying themselves, eating and talking."

I hunch over, placing my hands on my knees. Did I imagine everything? Am I that stressed out and tired? Rivulets of sweat pour down my back, dampening my dress. "I—I—I," I wheeze. "I don't know what happened."

Charles lifts my chin up. "Where did you get that brooch? You weren't wearing it before."

"Your mother gave it to me."

He shakes his head, eyes closed. "You do realize it's a bribe."

"For what?"

"By keeping you close to her she thinks she'll be closer to me." He scowls. "Let's get this night over and done with. Right now, go do your thing."

The look in Charles's eyes is so cold, I freeze. "Which is?"

"Ensuring the success of the restaurant. Say goodbye to the guests. I'll see you tomorrow. I'll close up."

My hand flies to the brooch. "I really don't understand why you're acting this way."

"I'm not acting."

"You're mad at me."

"No," he says. "I'm mad at myself. Just go. You've gotten what you wanted."

I turn on my heel and bite down on my lip, trying to figure out what happened, trying to give myself a pep talk.

I'm happy the opening—strange as it was—went well, but Charles's demeanor has shifted like the tides, twisting my gut with dread. The restaurant will be fine, but I'm not, because I'd finally opened up my heart, went for a relationship outside the kitchen, and it appears as if my decision has completely backfired in my face.

CHAPTER TWENTY-FIVE

A Bitter Taste

THE FOLLOWING WEEK, life is almost back to normal—the paparazzi have given up trying to snag photos of Charles and, soon, the guards are gone. We'd hired a new bartender and hostess—Charles's idea because he's sick of meddling mothers. But aside from cooking with Charles, we haven't spent any time outside the kitchen together. On far too many occasions, I've thought we were going to lean in for a kiss, but one of us backs away (him) or drops something (me). He'd said he needed time to think, to get his head together. But it's more than that. I can feel it in my bones.

The word about the restaurant has spread like a grease fire. A few of the recent headlines:

"Rekindle Your Romance at Bistro Exotique"
"Passion Is the Main Ingredient at Bistro Exotique"
"Fantasies and Fantastical Food Await at Bistro Exotique"

And the worst one:

"Heat Up at Bistro Exotique with Hot Chef Charles-Lin Truffaut"

Gaggles of beautiful women flock to the restaurant, dressed to the nines in low-cut dresses, their hair perfectly coiffed, their makeup flawless. They sit at the bar, hoping to catch a glimpse of Charles, doing things like laughing loud or exposing their cleavage to capture his eye. And it does wander. I'm seriously regretting my decision of having an open-kitchen concept, not when I can see and hear everything.

"Is he on the menu?"

"He's single, he can cook, and he's a billionaire."

"He's so gorgeous."

"Oh, the things I would do to him."

"Forget about the fish, he's the catch of the day."

Even worse, Charles seems to be reveling in the attention. Instead of keeping a low profile, like he'd said he'd wanted, he steps out of the kitchen when these succubae of Paris's femme fatales ask to meet him. And he smiles his dimpled smile as they take pictures with him.

I don't even know where I stand.

I'm sick of his excuses, him saying he's tired or that he needs to concentrate. And, considering nobody asks to meet me, this certainly doesn't feel like my restaurant. He's the one basking in all the glory when I'm hot and sweaty and cooking, my hair matted on my forehead.

Almost a week later, it's Sunday's dinner service, and I've had it. After a gorgeous woman with silky chestnut hair scribbles something on a napkin, presumably her phone number, Charles pockets the paper and responds, "Wouldn't you like to know?"

I slam my knife on the prep table. All eyes at the bar are now on me. Charles swaggers into the kitchen. "Kate, is something wrong?"

To avoid prying eyes and ears, I walk to the back of the kitchen, and he follows.

"I don't know," I say with a huff. I whip around to face him. "Maybe ask one of your girlfriends."

He laughs and pulls out the paper in his pocket, ripping it up. He throws the scraps into the bin. "Food groupies mean nothing to me."

"Doesn't look that way."

"Seriously, Kate," he says with a shrug. "I'm just being polite. Don't tell me you're jealous."

Yes. Seething. Boiling over.

"No," I snap. "I'm not."

"Doesn't look that way," he says, parroting me and I glare at him. "What's wrong?"

Is he serious? "I don't know what's going on with us. I thought we were headed somewhere and obviously we're not. You've barely spoken two words to me in a week unless it's to pass the salt. It's like you're avoiding me." I pause to catch my breath. "And this really doesn't feel like my restaurant, what with all the people fawning over you and not me. Tell me, what did I do?"

He shrugs helplessly. "Kate, I can't control how a bunch of crazy women act."

I push his shoulders with both of my hands, shoving him a little too forcefully. "But you can control how you act. You're ghosting me."

"I've been with you every day."

"No. You're just around me, haunting me like an evil spirit."

"I'm not evil, Kate," he says, lowering his lashes.

For a moment, I go silent, remembering our conversation on opening night. "What's going on? The truth. Don't feed me a bunch of baloney."

He nods and lets out a sad sigh. "When I saw the brooch my mother gave you, the past hit me on the head. And it's something I can't shake off. You made a deal with her just like Aria did, didn't you? What does she want?"

Did he really think that?

"It was a gift, not a bribe or a payoff."

"Same thing in my mind," he says.

"I'll give it back."

"It's too late, Kate, you already accepted it."

My bottom lip quivers. "I—"

I can't finish my sentence because the hostess interrupts our conversation. "Excuse me, Charles, but somebody wants to see you."

Charles shakes his head and meets my eyes. There is no spark, no passion, in them. It's like I'm a stranger. "We'll talk more later, okay?"

"Sure," I say, gulping.

He turns on his heel, leaving me feeling like a complete shit—somebody who's only after his family's money. No wonder he's been keeping his distance. I take a moment to collect myself, to stop the tears from falling. With shaky legs and a heavy heart, I meander back to my station. I grab a white onion, thinking this is how I feel—bitter, not sweet.

When Charles reenters the kitchen, I look up. His face pinches with concern. "Are you crying?"

"No," I say, trying to keep my voice from quivering. "Just chopping onions. My eyes are really sensitive." I grit my teeth.

He sets to finish plating his dish with edible flowers, ignoring me by turning his back.

As I stumble to the bar to grab some limes for my dish, I knock over a glass, and it shatters on the ground. It may be wrong of me to go behind Charles's back, but I need to talk to Garrance. Now. This is serious, and my blood is boiling in anger. After grabbing a dustpan and a brush, I throw out the glass shards in a bin.

"Charles?" I say.

"What?" he says. "Did you cut yourself?"

"No," I say. "We're out of kaffir limes. I need to get more from your mom. Can you handle the kitchen for a few minutes?"

"Do what you have to do," he says, and returns to plating. "And, yes, I can handle the kitchen."

BEFORE DASHING ACROSS the street, I scramble up to my apartment to grab the brooch, which I'm now definitely giving back. As much as I love it, the pin has driven a wedge between Charles and me, and I need to lift it. I'm practically hyperventilating when Garrance buzzes me in.

She opens the door, tilts her head. "Kate! Darling, what a lovely surprise!"

I hunch over and place my hands on my knees, wheezing.

"Is something wrong?"

I hold up a finger, trying to catch my breath, and hand her the brooch. I meet her concerned face. "Yes." *Pant.* "Horrible. I think Charles hates me." *Pant, pant.* "He thinks you bribed me."

"Kate, consider it a token of our friendship, not a payoff. I wanted you to have it. You do realize this was Aria and Charlotte's plan all along—to drive you apart. You were a threat."

"Me?"

"I saw the way they looked at you. And I wasn't born yesterday."

"Any idea of how I can win him back?"

"Just be honest with him, like you are with me." She holds out the brooch. "Keep it."

I clasp my hand on to hers and kiss her cheek. "I can't accept this gift. Your friendship is all I need," I say, and tears form in the corners of her eyes as she clutches the brooch. Our gazes meet and I nod.

"You're keeping this. Garrance, I have to get back to the kitchen before Charles wonders why I've been gone so long." I clench my teeth and mumble, "I may have told him I was picking up some kaffir limes from you. So in addition to your friendship, uh, I kind of need some limes."

Garrance stands up, heading to her counter. "That I can do. And, don't worry, Charles just needs time to calm down. Aria really pulled a number on him."

WHEN I SLINK back into the kitchen, Charles points to a bunch of limes set by my station. "Have fun commiserating with my mother?"

"I—I—"

Want to vomit.

I drop my basket of limes on the floor and they roll around by my feet. "Let me explain."

"I don't want to talk now. It's not the time or the place. I'm busy." He slams his knife into a potato. "We'll talk later."

"I'd like to talk now."

"I don't," he says, eyeing the staff.

Our line cooks share a look, and when I glare at them, they get back to cooking.

LIVID, AFTER CLOSING up the service, Charles and I speaking only in grunts and glares, I pace in my apartment, venting to Frushi.

"Can you believe what a supreme jerk he is? I mean, it's like he's sticking around to torture me." I shake my finger. "He told me I was in cahoots with his mother. Just because she gave me a beautiful brooch. How dare he!" I lean toward the tank. "What do you think?"

I tap the bowl. Frushi flicks me off with his tail and swims into his castle. Even my fish has ghosted me—there but not present.

I slump on the couch, seething. In the end, Charles was no different from Michael. But this time the hurt cuts worse, and I can't stop my tears from falling. I'm ugly crying when the knock comes at my door.

"Go away," I yell.

"Kate, it's Charles, we need to talk."

"I have absolutely nothing to say to you."

"Just let me in." He taps the door again. "Please."

Trying to pull myself together, I wipe away my tears with the sleeve of my shirt and open the door. He takes a step toward me. I take a step back. "I know you returned the brooch." He holds out his hand and opens it, the sapphire-encrusted hummingbird sparkling. "I want you to have it."

My eyes narrow into slits. "So now you're trying to bribe me?"

"Is it working?" He brushes his hair back, and I want to run my fingers through it, clasp on to it.

Yes.

"Not really," I say, my throat catching, my knees shaking. "You really hurt me, Charles."

"I know," he says, blinking. "I took my anger out on you, when I shouldn't have. Can you give me a few minutes to explain?"

I cross my arms over my chest, kind of enjoying seeing him squirm. "The same time you gave to me? Which was none, by the way." I take in a deep breath. "I've told you from the beginning that I was never taking advantage of your mother. Everything she's done for me was of her own accord. I've never asked her for anything." I pause. "Except for kaffir limes and a couple of dresses. In fact, she and my mother bought me a whole new wardrobe because they wanted to. Does that bother you?"

Charles runs his hands down his face. "No, because you look really good in those dresses. Really good. Orange really suits you, so does blue." He takes another step forward. I take another step backward.

I remind myself that Charles has a lot of explaining to do. I remind myself that I'm not going to jump right back into how things were between us, no matter how much I want to. I straighten my posture, reminding myself I can't and won't become swept away by the fantasy of him because his actions spoke louder than his words and he ruined it.

Which means I have to avoid his eyes. And his lips. Hell, I shouldn't look at him at all. Instead, I look at my feet.

"You want to explain, so explain."

"Kate, I'm so sorry. You don't know how many people have tried taking things from us. It's a constant battle." He holds up the brooch. "This pin set me off, had my mind reeling right back to the past with Aria and how she took advantage of my family, of me."

"I am nothing like her," I hiss.

"I know," he says. Charles takes my hand, pressing the pin into my palm. "And I'm glad you and my mother are friends. She's so happy." His lips pinch together and then he sucks in a deep breath. "I want to be close to you too. Kate, I'm far from perfect. I'm sorry I screwed things up."

I eye the brooch and look up, noticing the watery look in his eyes. I'm a goner. "As much I want to get back on track, it's going to take some work on your part."

"I'm willing to do anything," he begins. "Can we try for a fresh start? I don't want to lose you because I was paranoid and angry. Can we press the rewind button?"

My mouth twists. Like Jerry Maguire, he had me at hello. *Great willpower, Kate.*

"Fine. But not to the part with your sex tapes in the vent or when you were a supreme jerk. Or when you ghosted me and treated me like merde. We have to skip those parts." I brush my hair over my shoulder and lift my chin. "I have some rules."

"Don't dance with a bear?"

I push his shoulder. "Nope, no kissing, nothing. We're going to take things slow. You make my head spin. And I don't want to get hurt again."

He grins his dimpled smile. "You make my head spin too." Then his smile falters, his eyes searing into mine. "You're serious? No kissing?" he asks, and I nod. "This is going to kill me, Kate."

Yeah, me too.

Why on earth did I tell him no kissing?

"There's something I need to do." Charles pulls me into his chest, his vanilla scent invading every pore. He whispers into my ear, "You didn't say no hugging, and I've missed holding you, Kate."

I pull away, my lips parted, and Charles leans into me, his mouth on mine. His tongue runs across my lips, and his mouth latches on to me. I'm yielding into his embrace with so much desire it hurts. Still, I'm not ready to become swept up in him again, as much as I want him. He bites my bottom lip softly and whispers, "Yeah, that rule was stupid as hell."

"I agree," I say, wanting to take control of the situation, my pasta-like legs not al dente but overcooked.

"Are you mad at your mom?" I ask, placing a hand on his chest, pushing him slightly away, and his jaw drops with horror. "You've said bringing up our mothers cool things down."

He chuckles. "No, she's my mother. I'm used to her meddling, and I love her." He pauses. "She's not the only woman in my life I feel love for. There's my nenek, my aunties, and, oh yeah, you." He kisses my knuckles. "I've really fallen for you, Kate, and it scares me."

My heart stutters. "I'm scared too. What do we do?"

"We see what happens."

"Good idea. But as for tonight, what's happening is that I'm going to bed. Alone." I push him toward the door and then kiss him on the cheek. "Bonne nuit, I'll see you tomorrow."

He grins. "Okay. But tomorrow is Monday—our day off. Do you have plans?"

"Are you asking me out?"

"Yes," he says, batting his lashes. "Pick you up at noon?"

"I'll meet you downstairs," I say before closing the door and leaning against the wood, my heart racing, my mind spinning. If I'm not mistaken, he'd told me he loved me. And, for crying out loud, I've fallen in love too.

CHAPTER TWENTY-SIX

Cool as a Cucumber

IN THE MORNING, I pull my hair into a slick ponytail and then shimmy into a red lace bra with sassy matching, high-waisted boy shorts. Before dressing, I check myself out in the mirror. Hot damn, call the fire department. I look good, the way the shorts ride up a little in the back making my ass look perky, the way the bra holds the twins up. Smiling, I dab on some mulberry lipstick, a little blush, and some mascara, and then smack my lips.

"Looking good, Kate," I say.

Feeling good, I think.

Now to figure out what to wear. I go through the bags I still have yet to unpack, opting for a pair of black skinny sweatpants that tie at the waist and have deep pockets—so cute and flattering I'd also picked them up in charcoal, navy, and light gray—paired with a tight white tank top and a slouchy midsleeve T-shirt in dusty violet, the boat neckline cut on a bias so it reveals one of my shoulders. The final touch: hip black suede gym shoes with a ribbon detail, so comfortable because they support my high arches.

After feeding Frushi and throwing my ratty Keds into the garbage can, I sashay down the stairs, shaking my shoulders and humming Beyoncé's "Run the World (Girls)."

I'm getting ready for the day, telling myself I can't let this get to my head. Despite my attraction for him and his smoldering kisses, I can't let my mind float into the clouds filled with fantasies of what we could be. We'd cleared the air last night, but what if he snaps again?

When I open the front door, I find Charles waiting for me on the street.

"Kate," he says, his face registering his surprise. "You look . . . nice."

I shoot him a mock glare. "What are you inferring?"

"You always look incredible," he whispers. I turn to face him, and I swear he blushes before looking down. "I like your shoes." He runs his hand through his hair, coughs.

He's nervous.

If Charles only knew what I was wearing under my athleisurewear.

"What are we doing today?"

"It's gorgeous out. I thought we'd just wander around and maybe have a picnic in the park." He lifts his backpack. "I may have prepared something. Okay with you?"

I eye the baguette sticking out from his bag. "Sounds good."

We make our way to the canal, heading to Jardin Villemin. He's not acting like himself at all. Nervous and fidgety. Check. Not meeting my eyes. Check. It's like our personalities have been switched. It's time to test the waters.

"Do you think we should start up lunch services next month? You know, before the influx of tourists invade Paris?"

"Sure, sure, sure," he responds. "Whatever you think."

There are still a few details to iron out, and I know we're not quite ready.

"Yeah," I say, pressing further. "And I'm thinking we should bring back the raw bar."

"Great, great, great," he says. "Good idea."

Agreeing with everything I say? Triple check. I cross my arms over my chest. "No, the raw bar isn't a good idea until the fall. You were right—oysters should only be served during the 'r' months. If I never see an oyster again, I'm fine by that. And we're not quite ready for lunch services. We don't even have a staff for it." I clasp onto his arm. "What's going on? You're acting so weird."

He finally meets my eyes, his eyebrows knitted. "Kate, I didn't tell you everything last night. And I wanted to."

My throat constricts, and I brace myself for a bomb. He probably has second thoughts about me—about us. I take a step back. "What?" I ask.

"Kate, when I'd said I'd fallen for you, I wasn't being one hundred percent honest. I know it's fast, but I've more than fallen for you. I can control my body, my urges, but I can't control my heart. I've fallen in love with you."

I'm rendered speechless. Shocked, almost like I've been electrocuted. My jaw goes slack, and I shake my head from side to side. My heart might leap out of my ribcage.

"You don't have to say it back. I know it's a lot to take in. But I'm hoping you may feel the same way." He pauses. "You're the last thought I have before I go to bed and the first thought I have in the morning."

I gulp. I've never said these three little words to anybody but my parents before. "I'm in love—" I begin, and he blinks. "With your cooking, definitely. Maybe your stubbornness. Your pranks? Not so much, although you did make me laugh when you made the chicken head talk—"

His hands clasp on to mine. "Kate, I love your sense of humor, but would you be serious for a moment? I just poured my heart out to you. Do we have a chance?"

"I'd like that very much," I say, batting my lashes.

"Good," he says, pulling me in for the sweetest of kisses. I'm too swept up in the moment to care about PDA. Hand in hand, we meander slowly to the park.

Charles spreads out a blanket on a grassy patch, urging me to sit, and then unloads a bottle of champagne, a bowl of strawberries, a variety of cheeses, and a massive slice of pâté de campagne. He settles down next to me. "I thought we'd keep things simple today."

"Perfect," I say. "Sometimes simple is best."

"I'm sorry I made things complicated."

"Stop apologizing," I say, leaning back and propping myself on my elbows, staring into the cloudless sky. "Let's talk about life. I know your mother, but I don't know anything about your dad really."

"He was my idol—strict, but always up for an adventure." He sighs. "If he wasn't, I wouldn't have had all the opportunities I'd had, like living all over the world, experiencing new cultures and foods. I did go to business school in Singapore, but he saw how miserable I was. It was my dad who urged me to follow my passion."

"You're lucky to have been close with him," I say, gripping his hand. "I barely even talk to mine."

"Why?"

"He's just too busy for me."

"When's the last time you called him?"

"We text," I say. "And he can call me."

"Kate," he says. "The phone works both ways. Did you ever think you might have been too busy for him? It's important to stay connected. You never know what can happen until it's too late. Make sure to tell him that you love him."

My throat hitches. I turn toward Charles.

A tear slides down his cheek, and he wipes it away. "I miss mine every day. And I never got to say goodbye or tell him I loved him."

I don't know what I should do. Hug him? Comfort him? Tell him everything will be all right? Instead, I sigh. "You're right. I'll call him."

"Good," he says with a sexy wink, "now let's eat some strawberries."

I DON'T KNOW when or how the paparazzi snagged a picture of me looking ravishing, if I say so myself, and of me and Charles in an almost kiss, but when I wake up the following day, thanks to an onslaught of Google alerts, I discover our faces plastered all over the internet, the headlines a bit nuts and, honestly, soul soaring.

"Bistro Exotique, the Brainchild of Kate Jenkins"

"Charles Lin-Truffaut Is Cooking Things Up with the Hottest Chef in Town"

"Passion: The Main Ingredient at Kate Jenkins's Bistro Exotique"

Charles and I are setting up the terrace when Oded rounds the corner. "I don't have rehearsal until this evening. Your mom, Garrance, and I have dinner plans," he says, his cheeks turning crimson. He runs a hand across his cheek. "Do you think I should shave? Change my clothes?"

Nobody has ever asked me for this kind of advice.

"Are you asking me what my mom is attracted to?"

"Maybe," he says, not meeting my amused gaze. "She's an incredible woman. I probably shouldn't be telling you this, but you know her best, and I'm hoping I stand a chance."

"I thought you were dating," I say, confused.

"We've been seeing a lot of each other. I'd like something more—a relationship with her. Is that okay with you?"

"Of course," I say. "As long as she's happy."

"Any advice?"

"Just be yourself," I say.

"Not good enough." Oded fumbles with his keys. "I need to clean myself up."

He races into the apartment building.

Charles walks behind me and grasps my waist. "Somebody is crushing hard on somebody."

I turn to face him. "We need to crush other things," I say, pressing my body into his.

He wiggles his brows. "Oh, yeah?"

"Garlic," I say, pulling away and entering the restaurant.

KITCHEN LIFE IS getting steamy. Charles looks up from prepping his mise en place for two seconds, blows me a kiss, and then his hand swipes a bowl of salt and the grains scatter on the counter.

"I can't take it anymore," he says, lifting me up onto the prep station. My legs wrap around his waist, as his kiss starts off slow and then turns hungry. Vegetables scatter, cherry tomatoes rolling onto the floor. Dishes break. Not one burner is on, but the kitchen gets hotter. Oh, and hotter. Hello, volcano. His hand latches around my ponytail, titling my head back. His mouth finds my neck, and he covers it with his kisses, slowly making his way down to my exposed shoulder, his finger running along my clavicle.

A cough comes from the doorway. "I see the two of you have settled your differences."

I leap off the counter, pushing into Charles, and we almost fall down. Mortified, we turn to face Garrance and my mother.

"Not exactly sanitary," says my mom with a giggle. "But there's no controlling passion."

"We're both looking forward to your saffron dish, Kate. Charles told me it was magic," says Garrance, lifting up a manicured brow. She nods to the floor. "Why don't the two of you clean up this mess—yourselves included, hmmm? Cri-Cri and I are going to tend to the orchids."

As the meddlesome duo meanders to the dining room, whispering, Charles sighs, "We need to change the locks."

I burst out laughing. "We also have to make sure that never happens again."

"Never?" he says with a pout.

"Not never—just not in this kitchen." I hand him a broom. "You sweep, I'll sanitize."

"We make a good team." He grins his dimpled smile and kisses my forehead. "Can you come over tonight?"

I spray the counter, my heart racing. "Yeah, I kind of want to jump your bones." And damn it. My face is hot to the touch as I clasp my cheeks. "I said that out loud, didn't I?"

"Nothing wrong with saying what's on your mind. I'd be lying if I said I wasn't thinking the exact same thing."

"So, we're going to be honest about everything now?"

"Oui," he says. "And it's a hard no on the raw bar. Or opening up for lunch services unless you hire another chef. I want to spend quality time with you, every waking moment, because that's what partners do."

"You're not just talking about the restaurant, are you?"

"Non, Kate, you know I'm not. Together, we create magic."

"Sure you're not going to get sick of me?"

"No, gila, I'm not. It's impossible. You keep me on my toes."

This time I don't bite his head off when he calls me crazy. Because I *am* crazy—a fool falling head over heels in love.

THE RESTAURANT IS packed. My mom, Garrance, and Oded are swooning over the deconstructed saffron-infused bouillabaisse, a clean-shaven Oded laughing a little too loudly at everything my mother says. Juju sits at the bar, eyeing the fish with malicious intent. I wander into the dining room, Charles joining me. Before we make our approach, the rest of the guests applaud and we greet them before moving on to our mothers.

"Kate, this was incredible," says Garrance, waving her hand over the dish. "You've outdone yourself."

"Yes," agrees my mom. "Completely orgas—"

"Cri-Cri!"

"What, Kate? It was divine. I knew you and Charles would come together—"

"Mom! Just stop! Don't say another word—"

"Honestly, I didn't say anything bad." She dabs her lips with a napkin. "The two of you obviously have chemistry." She grins wickedly and smirks. "At least in the kitchen. Maybe elsewhere too."

Charles clears his throat.

Mom lifts her shoulders innocently. "What? I saw what I saw."

"Unfortunately," says Garrance, "I did too."

"What happened?" asks Oded.

Turning, I storm to the kitchen, my face flushed with embarrassment, Charles following. "Sometimes she's too much," I say.

"So is mine," he says. "Do you think we could sell them on eBay?"

*   *   *

WE FINISH PREPPING for tonight's service, me shooting Charles the occasional sideways glance. Part of me wants to restrain my emotions, the other part just wants to let go and allow the winds of change to blow me—right into his bed. Nervous and out of sorts, I wipe off my hands and hang up my apron.

"Where are you going?" asks Charles.

"Just taking a little break," I say. "I also have to call my dad."

"Oh?" he says, his hazel eyes lighting up.

"Do you want me to stay? I mean, I can call him later."

"Stop procrastinating." He rolls a kitchen towel into a makeshift whip and snaps it softly on my butt and then points. "Go, call your dad."

I raise my hands in mock defense. "Fine, fine, fine, you win."

"Good," he says with a laugh. "Oh, and as much as I love my mother keeping tabs on me, I'm still having the locks changed to the restaurant, if you're okay with that. She has to stop popping up unexpectedly. She almost gave me a heart attack this morning."

"Only this morning? Mine gives me one every time she opens her mouth," I say. "Would it be terrible if we banned them from coming here?"

"Yes," he says with a laugh. "We only have one mother."

"Funny," I reply with a snort. "Because I feel like I have two."

He clasps my shoulders. "You're lucky, Kate. I'm glad my mother adores you. I'm betting my father would have too," he says, his eyes darkening. "Now, go call yours."

Right. It's something I've been putting off. I exit the restaurant and slink up the steps to my apartment, staring at the phone before dialing. Why do I blame him when I should also blame myself?

We all lead busy lives. I'd been so consumed by my dream, from attending cooking school, to climbing up the ranks, to get where I am today. Part of me, even with my lists, had lost a true sense of direction. Finally, I dial, and he picks up on the first ring.

"Dad?" I say, sinking on the couch. "It's me. Kate."

"Oh, honey, I'm glad you caught me. I was just headed out the door for a big meeting. But I have a few minutes."

"You only have a minute? For your daughter?"

He sighs. "I'm sorry, honey, I always have time for you," he says, and it's my turn to sigh. "What's wrong, Katie-Bug?"

"I just wanted to call you to tell you that I love you. And that I miss you."

I'd blown off my father countless times—too focused on achieving my goals. But the truth is, I'm learning the art of letting go, to become swept up in the winds of change. I can't control everything, especially when it comes to my feelings, and I want to fall into bliss— letting light and life in.

"I'm glad. And I love you too. I'm so sorry I had to cancel my Paris trip for the first opening. I had to put out a five-alarm fire or lose everything. As for the second one, I just didn't have enough notice. As much as I wanted to be there for you, I couldn't swing it." He pauses. "I'm so very, very proud of you, and I should call more. I just get so wrapped up in everything, all the deals . . ."

"I get it, Dad. And I haven't been the most communicative person on the planet either. I get wrapped up in my stuff too."

"But that's not the only reason you're calling. I can tell. Your voice is all shaky. What else is going on? Is it the restaurant?"

"No, everything is going great," I say, letting out a breath. I tuck my knees to my chin. "I've fallen in love, and it happened so quickly. It's like I can't control my thoughts or anything."

"Does he feel the same way about you?"

"Yes."

"Well, if he didn't, I was going to say he's an idiot," says Dad with a chuckle. "Love is tricky, demanding, transformative, and it happens when we least expect it, like it did with your mother and me."

"But you're not together anymore. And I don't want to get hurt," I mumble. "Is it true you were embarrassed by Mom?"

"Who said that?"

"She did."

"Not true." He lets out a breath. "When I met your mother, she was so free-spirited, it was like I'd captured a wild butterfly. When our marriage ended, and you were, for the most part grown up, I knew she needed to spread her wings and fly. I'll always love her."

"You will?"

"Of course, Kate. We're just cut from different molds, and over the years we realized that, aside from you, we didn't have much in common. The only thing worse than love is not knowing it at all, closing ourselves and our hearts off." He pauses. "So tell me about this guy," he says, and I do, leaving out the hot kisses and the fact I'm thinking about sleeping with him.

When I'm finished, Dad says, "Well, you and Charles definitely got off on the wrong foot, that goes without saying, but it sounds like he's being honest with you now, so my suggestion is for you to be honest with yourself."

"And?"

"Remember when I taught you how to swim?"

"Yes," I say with a laugh. Why was I only thinking of bad memories with regards to my dad? He was always there for me growing up—teaching me to swim, ride a bike, to read.

"You can't just have one foot in the pool if you want to learn how to swim, you have to dive right in. Don't think with your head but with your heart. "

I'm about to say, *Too bad my body has a mind of its own*, but refrain. I'm talking with my conservative dad, not my wacky mother, and he might flip out.

"Whatever you decide, you'll do the right thing. I'm glad you called." He pauses. "We really should talk more, and that's my fault."

I have fingers. I could dial in a phone number. I could visit him. "It's mine too."

I swallow. "Are you seeing anybody?"

"I am. Like me, she's in banking and also divorced. We're going to try to get to Paris in a couple of months. Can you spare some time for your old man? I'd really love for the two of you to meet."

"Definitely. Thanks, Dad," I say. "I'm looking forward to it."

"I love you, Katie-Bug."

"Love you too, Dad."

The line clicks to a close. I'm thrilled for him and the conversation we'd just had.

Funny, I'm more like my mom than I'd thought—a notion that makes me laugh like a psychotic hyena. Later tonight, I'm taking a risk and diving right into the deep end with Charles. Before I head back to the kitchen, I spray on the perfume Garrance made me—on my wrists, on my neck, and, well, why the heck not, a little dash somewhere else.

CHAPTER TWENTY-SEVEN

Good Things Come to Those Who Wait

I'M BACK IN the kitchen, bossing around the line cooks and the servers, when Charles steps over. His eyebrows furrow with concern. "How'd the talk go with your dad? Not good?"

"Oh, that, it went great. Great, great, great. You were right. I needed to talk to him." I go back to cracking the shell off a lobster, seeing we've included my latest meal as tonight's special. Charles doesn't move and leans into me, breathing my scent in.

"Why are you barking at the brigade?"

"Because one of the line cooks almost started a fire, and I needed to control the situation." I shrug and take a step back. "Can you stop staring at me with those sexy bedroom eyes? I'm trying to work. And we can't have a repeat of what happened when our mothers caught us—"

His upper lip lifts into a confused smile. "Why not? You smell so good. And I can't stop thinking about your lips on mine. I know we just ate, but I'm still hungry—"

"Curb your appetite, mister." I nod toward the staff. "There are people around."

"What happens in the kitchen stays in the kitchen."

He grins, surely liking the fact I'm all flustered. Once again, our demeanors have shifted like the tides, and I'm the nervous one. "That's not the expression. And I'm not breaking rule number six."

"Rule number six?"

"It's new. No monkey business when we're cooking."

He pounds his chest with two fists. "I didn't know you had a thing for monkeys. But I can work with it. Me, Tarzan. You, Jane," he says, with an *oooh-ooh-oof*.

I snort and nudge his chest. "Not funny."

"Then why are you laughing?"

"Because you're driving me bananas." I pause. "Just beet it."

"What are rules one through five? I forget, gila," he says, and my nose pinches.

I pull out my list I keep in my pocket:

1. No food puns
2. No kitchen pranks
3. Always be honest
4. Don't dance with a bear
5. Lock the front door when the restaurant isn't open

"We're back to this again?" he asks, and I nod. He swipes the list from my hand, rips it up, and throws the paper into the air like confetti. "Rule number seven: no more lists."

"What are you trying to do to me?"

"Keep you grounded," he says. "You don't need this crazy list. You're still coming over tonight, right?"

"Yep, yep, yep," I say. "But if you're going for roe-mance, then you may want to consider some caviar. And, cod, I don't think I can get any punnier."

"Oh, Kate, by my calculations, you've broken rule number one three times in less than a minute. I may have to reprimand you," he says, and my eyes go wide with horror. "I'm just kidding. But you better prepare yourself, because I'm going to surprise you tonight. I've thought of everything."

I have no idea what he's planned, and now my knees are shaking.

"Chef, I'm sorry to bother you," says the hostess, slinking up to us. "A few of the guests are insisting on meeting you."

"Me?" I tap my collarbone and then point to Charles. "I'm sure you mean him."

"No, you," she says with a roll of her eyes and sashays away. "Unless Charles changed his name to Kate."

My eyes lock on to Charles's. "Can you remind me why we hired her? She's kind of surly."

"We?"

"Yeah, we. Isn't it clear we've been doing everything together? We're partners."

He smiles. "We are. And we hired her because she gives off that snobby bourgeoisie vibe people seem to love—the kind of personality that makes people think if they're not a part of something, they're being excluded. Plus, she Instagrams shots of the restaurant every two seconds, so there's that. I could live without the ones of her in them—she makes duck lips."

My eyes narrow. "Did you have anything to do with the press this morning? Hot Chef Kate? And the photos?"

"It's your restaurant, Kate. I wanted to take the attention off me—it wasn't fair to you. Would you be mad if I dangled a carrot or two?"

"We'll see," I say, turning on my heel and head into the dining room.

A few minutes later, I storm back into the kitchen, right up to Charles, completely flipping out. "I'm going to kill you."

"Why?"

"A couple asked me if I was open to new experiences as they cornered me. A woman gave me her number along with a sexual innuendo. And then a man asked me if I was out of sugar and if he could buy me some. I said no, and he said, 'Too bad. I was hoping to be your sugar daddy.'"

Charles snorts. "I told you food groupies were weird. And now you have some. Welcome to the world of being a superstar chef."

"That isn't the worst of it. A woman came running into the restaurant, blaming me—our food—for her impending divorce. Her husband, apparently, has never experienced passion. She spat at my shoes, and Albert had to drag her out, kicking and screaming. What in the world is in your mother's spices? We have to stop using them."

"Kate, they're just spices. You can find them on every shelf at a grocery store—maybe not as good, but spices all the same."

"No, hers are different."

"Maybe," he says. "Only because they're better."

"They. Are. Magical."

"Look, most of us have a memories of a dish that takes us back to the past. And these memories are vivid and evocative, creating a much more powerful effect. Our meals, the dishes we're creating, bring on new sensations—an awakening of sorts for certain people, albeit nostalgia or something else. Food brings on emotions—and we're doing things right if we're bringing them out in people."

"Food is about the balance of flavors and textures and taste, not emotion."

Charles grips my shoulders. "Kate, when you cook, how are you doing it? With anger or with love?"

"Probably a little of both sometimes." I gasp. "What are you saying? People are eating my emotions? Like in that movie with Sarah Michelle Gellar? *Simply Irresistible*? She was a chef, like me, with a flailing restaurant, and there was a rich guy, like you. And a crab."

He snickers. "This is real life, not the movies. And I have absolutely no idea what you're talking about." He pauses. "All I'm saying is good food—the kind we're creating together—brings out emotions and feelings."

I meet his amused eyes and blurt out, "Your mom isn't drugging people?"

"She may smuggle plants in from Asia, but she's as clean as they come. She can barely handle one glass of champagne."

I saw the movie *The Craft*. "Magic? Is there witchcraft involved?"

"Are you serious?" he cackles, and rubs his hands together. "A little of eye of newt? Hmm, what else can we put into the cauldron? Aha! I know! The toe of a frog and some fenny snake. Whipped up into a frothy boil—"

"Then explain us," I demand.

"I can't. I fell for you. Does falling in love need an explanation?"

"I guess not," I say.

His expression turns serious. "Did you tell your dad about me?"

"Maybe," I say, and his eyes light up. "Totally." I rewind the conversation we'd just had in my head. He probably thinks I'm insane. "You still think I'm crazy, don't you?"

He pinches his fingers together. "Just a little bit. But that's why I'm falling deeper and harder in love with you every day. You're funny, quirky," he begins, and I cringe until he says, "And so damn hot—especially when you're pouting and gnawing on your bottom lip." He eyes the clock. "It's almost time to close up. You're still coming to my place?"

"Yes," I manage to squeak out.

I've never been more excited or nervous about anything or anybody in my entire life.

"Why don't you leave now? I'll finish up," he says. "I'll meet you at mine in a half hour."

WHEN I ENTER Charles's apartment, he could have knocked me over with a feather. The room is lit by candles, hundreds of them twinkling and flickering. A bowl of strawberries sits on the coffee table in a silver bowl, a bottle of chilled champagne by its side. A small tin of caviar with what appears to be homemade blini by its side. Vases of flowers—roses and lilacs and peonies—cover every corner of the room.

"When did you do all this?" I ask, getting the chills.

"This morning before the deliveries, I had deliveries of my own," he says. "All I had to do was light the candles." He pours me a glass of champagne. "Have a seat, Kate. I'll be right back."

"Where are you going?"

"Kick your shoes off, relax," he says, and kisses my cheek.

My heart races, and my ears tingle, and the butterflies in my stomach are back in full force.

Charles returns a minute later. He walks over to the stereo and flicks it on, the song Ed Sheeran's "Shivers," and then he moves toward me and holds out his hand. I get up from the couch and fall into his embrace. As we rock back and forth to the beat, our bodies swaying to the music, my spine tingles, and as the chorus sets in I realize I do want it all.

"I love holding you, Kate. And there's so much more I want to do," he whispers.

Aside from the physical attraction, he makes me feel safe—physically and emotionally.

Our tongues find each other's. Our bodies rhythmically grinding. He kisses his way down my neck and then I stop him, my breath heavy.

He squeezes my arms gently and then lifts up my chin. My eyes meet his. "Are you not ready for this? For the next step?" he asks.

I am so ready to fall into love, to let go and go with the flow. "Yes," I say breathlessly. "I want you. All of you."

Charles places a tender kiss on my cheek and then picks me up, carrying me to the bedroom.

A FEW WEEKS pass and it's the middle of July. Bistro Exotique is still as full as my heart, Charles and I now not only business partners with the restaurant but also in bed. Don't worry: one can still eat at Bistro Exotique without fear of our sexcapades, his kitchen our new playground where we re-create the bread-and-butter scene from 9½ Weeks—often.

While in the midst of prepping for the dinner service, my phone dings. I pull it out from the pocket of my apron to read the latest headline: LOVE MATCHES (AND MISMATCHES) AT BISTRO EXOTIQUE COME WITH PASSION-FILLED MEALS.

"Another alert?" asks Charles, and I nod. "With all the press, the place is going to be packed. Are you ready for the height of tourist season?"

"Ready as I'll ever be," I say, holding up the phone and showing him the latest. "People may think that they'll find love here."

"Why not? We did."

"People have also gotten divorced."

"Yes, but in the end, everybody is happy."

"True," I say, thinking about all the positive changes that have taken place—with me and all the people in my world. Ciao, negativity. Bonjour, love.

Oded is officially dating my mother. Caro is trying her hand at online dating. Mark is taking a break from romance and wants to embark on a few weeks of adventure traveling, his ex not into rock climbing or bungee jumping.

"I was thinking . . . ," I begin.

"Oh no," says Charles. "Tell me, you're not considering bringing back the raw bar?"

I grimace. "No, if I never see another oyster again, that's fine by me. Kind of snuffed out the sparks of romance that first night." I tilt my head to the side. "But I am thinking about something fun, maybe even sexy." I have his full attention now. He sets his knife down and raises his eyebrows. "We should go somewhere the last two weeks in November."

"What about the bistro?"

"It will be here when we get back, and I'm sure the staff can manage without us."

He lets out a surprised breath. "You're saying that *you* can give up that kind of control? You?"

I take a step toward him and wrap my hands around his waist, pulling him in for a slow and delicious kiss. "I already have."

"Okay, you sexy rule breaker," he says, his dimple flashing. His hands slide up and down my hips. "Where did you want to go?"

"Jakarta to meet your grandparents. Singapore to see where you grew up—" I pause. Save for one, we'd discussed most of these ideas before. "And Thailand for a Sak Yant tattoo—the five-line Ha Taew blessings."

"You are full of surprises, Kate," he says, his brow crinkling. "I'll set up the trip. But I'm still a little irked about something," he says with a sigh. "I don't know why my mother insisted on giving us two of Jezebel's kittens as a housewarming gift. Who is going to watch them?"

"Not a problem. Oded already offered. And they're Juju's kittens too."

"Exactly," he says with a shudder.

"Well, Keanu is adorable and Katniss is—"

"Trouble. I caught her climbing the curtains the other day."

"Oh, I thought that was me after we had sex. My bad," I respond, referring to the French expression of having an orgasm, and he laughs. "At least your mom didn't give us a painting of a vulva."

He shrugs. "I don't know. I kind of like it. I thought it was a flower."

"It's not," I say. "And it's going up in the laundry room, where nobody but us can see it."

Charles nudges me. "Cool, cool, cool." He meanders over to the walk-in. Over his shoulder, he says, "Your dad and his girlfriend will be here next week, right?"

"Yes, you know this."

"And I'm meeting them?"

"You know that too."

He places his hands on the prep table. "I have a confession to make."

I brace myself. "What?"

"That dish, the one you made with the saffron?"

"Yeah?"

"When I ate the first bite, I was whisked away into a fantasy—a happy life and a future with you. Maybe you're right. Maybe there is something special about my mother's spices—"

Do I tell him about all my fantasies? Nah, I'm living them now. I smile and get back to chopping up the tarragon, inhaling the sweet, grassy aroma. I let myself fall in love. I let myself float into bliss. I have my dream and it came with more happiness than I had ever imagined.

"Or maybe we just have the perfect chemistry," I say.

Through it all, Charles and I learned that letting go of negativity leads to happier futures (and better food and sex). As for Garrance, her work is complete; she's found happiness for Charles and me, her and my mother's plan all along. Magic? Some may say. But love is the greatest magic of all—and a required ingredient for everyone.

What's next for Bistro Exotique and Charles and me? Only time will tell. But I'm ready to adapt and adjust, keeping myself open to all the possibilities—even the unexpected—while savoring every single, delicious moment. I may even lose a little more control.

Bon appétit.

The
Spice Master
at Bistro Exotique

SAMANTHA VÉRANT

Questions for Discussion

1. Kate has two wildly wacky and eccentric women in her life: her mother, Cri-Cri, and Garrance—both of them quite direct (and a bit bizarre) with their approaches to the world. Do you think their influence on Kate helped her to grow as a person? Or did they step out of bounds with their advice? What's the best or worst advice the women in your own life have given you that you've chosen to take or ignore?

2. In the beginning of the novel, Kate makes it clear that her one and only true love is the kitchen, but when Charles (a.k.a. Anti-Keanu) steps into her world, she loses herself within fantasies of being with him even though, based on her first impressions of him, he's a supreme jerk. Have you ever been attracted to someone who seemed completely wrong for you at first? Also, have you ever put the promise of love to the side when fighting for your own dreams?

3. Kate is surprised so many people come to her aid, especially after so many catastrophes. Why do you think she attracts so much positivity—people like Oded, Caro, Garrance,

and Cri-Cri fully supporting her dream? Have you had people supporting you and your dreams when things aren't going your way?

4. What did you think of the rage room scene, when Kate and Charles still distrust each other but kind of work things out? Do you think a situation like this would help or hinder a relationship to develop? Have you ever been to a rage room? If not, would you go to one?

5. Charles and Kate's relationship moves from being enemies to working together to falling in love. Was this a natural progression for you? What would you change in the course of their dynamics?

6. Charles's and Kate's worlds get upended when Aria pops up, bringing up bad memories not only for Charles but also for Garrance. After hearing her reasoning, do you think Garrance was right to do what she did? Or should she have let Charles figure out his life on his own? Do mothers always know best?

7. Charles has always been wary of people taking advantage of him and his family because of their wealth. Was Kate wrong to accept the brooch from Garrance? What did you think about his reaction and eventual redemption?

8. A huge theme featured throughout the book is how food can transport you. Do you have a favorite meal that recalls memories? What is it? And does it bring on good memories or bad ones? Do you believe what Kate experienced was magic from Garrance's spices or did it come from within herself? Or was it the chemistry with Charles?

The Recipes and
a Note from the Chef

Dear Reader,

Please remember, recipes are only guidelines, and none of the dishes I make are typical. In France, it's difficult to find a lot of ingredients, so we use what we have on hand, what's in season, and we make the recipes our own while keeping the general method intact.

As Jacques Pépin has said: "Cooking is about the art of adjustment."

Sometimes in France, when searching for ingredients, we definitely need to adapt and adjust. I also use a lot of spices—most of which can be found online or at specialty grocery stores. Use your spices wisely! (I highly suggest urfa biber flakes! They are a game changer!)

Charles's satay is inspired by his time in Indonesia and Thailand, and not exactly a typical addition to a traditional nasi campur. He got creative!

In a restaurant in France, the meal may start with an entrée (the first small plate/starter), followed by le plat principal (main course), then the cheese and/or salad course, and, finally, dessert.

With that said, I hope you enjoy the recipes Charles and I have chosen to share with you. Use them as guidelines and make them your own.

Bon appétit!

Chef Kate

(and Charles)

KATE'S CARPACCIO DE NOIX DE ST. JACQUES

(SCALLOP CARPACCIO)

ENTRÉE

Serves 4 to 6 (small portions)

Prep time: 20 minutes

The equipment: sharp knife and/or mandoline (highly suggested)

INGREDIENTS

12–16 fresh sea scallops (2–3 per person)

2 large avocados

2 large mangoes

Juice of ½ lemon

½ large cucumber

4 shallots

Juice of 3 limes

Chili powder

Coconut sugar

Finely minced cilantro or flat parsley (garnish)

Pomegranate seeds (garnish)

Lime wedges

TECHNIQUE

1. Wash the scallops, pat dry, and then place in the freezer for 15 to 20 minutes to make them easier to slice.

2. Slice the avocados and mangoes in half, getting rid of the

pits. Peel. Slice paper-thin with a mandoline or sharp knife. Sprinkle with a bit of the lemon juice so they don't brown. Set aside.

3. Slice the cucumber and shallots, also paper-thin, with a mandoline or sharp knife. Set aside.

4. Take the scallops out of the freezer and slice as thinly as possible, around ⅛-inch thick, with a sharp knife. Place the slices in a bowl and squeeze the juice of 3 limes over them. Mix. Place in the refrigerator. Let rest for 5 to 10 minutes so the juices of the lime "cook" the scallops.

PLATING

1. Alternate a mango, scallop, avocado, cucumber, and shallot slices on a small plate.

2. Sprinkle a little chili powder and coconut sugar (a pinch or two).

3. Garnish with finely minced cilantro (or parsley) and pomegranate seeds.

4. Chill in the fridge until ready to serve . . . or serve immediately, a lime wedge on the side.

KATE'S ROASTED RED PEPPER AND GARLIC HUMMUS

(SERVED WITH GARLIC NAAN, A CRUDITÉ PLATTER,
AND PAN-FRIED PADRON PEPPERS)

ENTRÉE

Prep time: 30 minutes

Cooking time: 20–45 minutes*

Rest time: Overnight if using dried chickpeas

The equipment: baking tray, parchment paper, food processor, cast-iron or nonstick skillet, rolling pin

INGREDIENTS FOR THE HUMMUS

(makes about 3 1/2 cups)

    2 cups chickpeas, preferably cooked fresh* (1¼ cups dried—the volume will increase) but can use canned

    1½ large red peppers, deseeded and sliced into 1-inch strips

    8 garlic cloves, skin on (or more cloves to your taste)

    Olive oil

    Sea salt

    Juice of 3–4 lemons

    ¼–½ cup tahini (depending on taste preferences, add more if desired)

    6 tablespoons ice water

    2–3 tablespoons urfa biber flakes (depending on taste preferences, add more or less if desired)

    Fresh ground pepper

OPTIONAL GARNISH

A couple of chickpeas (set aside some!)
Paprika
Olive oil
Finely minced cilantro
More urfa biber flakes, to taste
Lemon wedges

TECHNIQUE

1. If using dried (not canned) chickpeas, soak them, covering them in cold water (2 inches above) the night before.
   Drain the following day. Bring slightly salted water to a
   boil, add the chickpeas, and turn the heat down and simmer for 30–45 minutes, perhaps longer, removing any foam
   with a spoon. The chickpeas are done if they easily break
   apart when pressed together with your fingers.

2. While the chickpeas are simmering, preheat the oven to
   400°F. Line a baking pan with parchment paper. Place the
   sliced peppers and garlic cloves on it. Drizzle with olive oil
   and a pinch or two of sea salt. Roast for around 25 minutes,
   flipping the peppers over midway. Check to make sure the
   peppers don't get too charred. If they do, you can scrape
   them with a knife or leave as is.

3. Drain the chickpeas. Rinse. Let cool. Take the peppers and
   garlic out of the oven and let cool to room temperature.
   Take the skin off the garlic.

4. Place the chickpeas, peppers, and garlic in a food processor with 4 tablespoons olive oil, the juice of 2 lemons,
   and the tahini. Blend until creamy, adding in more olive oil

and lemon juice as desired. Add in the ice water 1 table-spoon at a time. Blend. Add in the urfa biber flakes 1 tablespoon at a time and blend, tasting in between, until to your preference. Add salt and fresh ground pepper to taste. Keep refrigerated until ready to serve. (Will keep for 4 days.)

PLATING

In a bowl, garnishing as desired.

INGREDIENTS FOR THE NAAN

(makes 10–12)

   ¼ cup warm water
   3 teaspoons granulated sugar
   2¼ teaspoons active dry yeast
   ¾ cup warm milk
   ¾ cup Greek yogurt
   ¼ cup sunflower oil, plus extra for cooking
   4 cloves garlic, minced
   ¼ cup finely minced parsley
   4 cups all-purpose flour, plus extra
   2 teaspoons baking powder
   2 teaspoons salt
   4 tablespoons (½ stick) unsalted butter, melted

TECHNIQUE

1. Whisk the water, sugar, and yeast together and let sit for 5 to 10 minutes, until the mixture begins to bubble.
2. Add in the milk, yogurt, oil, minced garlic, parsley, flour, baking powder, and salt. Mix with your hands until the

dough comes together into a shaggy ball. If the dough is too wet, add in more flour, 1 tablespoon at a time.

3. Turn the dough out onto lightly floured surface. Knead the dough until smooth.

4. Place the dough in the bowl and cover with plastic wrap or a damp kitchen towel. Let rest at room temperature for about 1 hour, until the dough has increased in size.

5. On a lightly floured work board, divide the dough into ten to twelve equal pieces. Roll into balls. So the dough balls don't get dry, lightly coat with oil using a pastry brush. Cover with plastic wrap for 30 minutes, removing plastic wrap before cooking.

6. Heat a large cast-iron skillet over medium-high heat.

7. Using a rolling pin, roll one piece of the dough balls into a large oval, about ⅛ inch thick, on a lightly floured surface.

8. Place on a hot skillet and cook the naan until bubbles form on the top, about 1 to 2 minutes. Flip again, cooking the other side for one more minute.

9. Remove the naan from the skillet. Using a pastry brush, lightly coat both sides with the melted butter, and place on a plate, covering with a clean kitchen towel or plastic wrap. Repeat with the remaining naan. If preparing in advance, store the cooked naan in a plastic container or ziplock bag for up to two days in the refrigerator. Reheat in an oven set to 400°F for 3 minutes.

INGREDIENTS FOR THE CRUDITÉ PLATTER

Whatever vegetables you prefer—carrot strips, baby carrots, cherry tomatoes, tiny dipping peppers, radishes, endive . . . the list goes on! Highly recommended braised padron peppers.

INGREDIENTS FOR THE PAN-FRIED PADRON PEPPERS

Olive oil
Padron peppers
Sea salt

TECHNIQUE

1. Coat the bottom of a pan with olive oil. Heat.
2. Add peppers and braise until slightly charred.
3. Sprinkle with salt.

PLATING

Set a bowl of hummus on a serving platter. Surround with the vegetables of your choice, including the peppers (if using), and sliced pieces (3-inch strips) of the naan bread.

KATE'S ISRAELI COUSCOUS SUMMER SALAD AND GRAINS OF PARADISE ENCRUSTED STEAK

PLAT PRINCIPAL

Serves 4

Prep time: 30 minutes

Cooking time: 20 minutes

The equipment: cast-iron or nonstick pan

INGREDIENTS FOR THE COUSCOUS SALAD

1½ cups Israeli couscous

Unsalted butter

Olive oil

¾ cup fennel, diced

¾ cup jarred/canned artichoke bottoms, diced

½ cup slivered almonds, toasted

1 cup cherry tomatoes, sliced in rounds

2 cups crumbled Feta cheese

1 cup de-pitted green or black olives, sliced in rounds

1 cup diced preserved lemons (quick and easy recipe follows)

½ cup finely chopped mint

1 teaspoon ground cumin

1 teaspoon ground cinnamon

1 teaspoon ground turmeric

1 teaspoon sumac (optional)

Red pepper flakes (optional, to taste)

Olive oil

Juice of 2–3 lemons to taste

Sea salt or kosher salt and fresh ground pepper to taste

TECHNIQUE

1. In a medium-sized pot, cook the Israeli couscous to the package's instructions.
2. While the couscous cooks, add a knob of butter with a dash of olive oil to a pan on a burner set to medium-high. Once the butter is melted, add in the fennel, cooking until tender, about 3 minutes. Add in the artichoke bottoms and cook for another 3 minutes (until warm).
3. When the couscous is ready, drain and rinse.
4. Combine the remaining ingredients and spices in a bowl, mixing well. Set aside.

INGREDIENTS FOR THE STEAK

4 filet mignons (or rib eye)

3 tablespoons mixed colors peppercorns, coarsely ground

1 tablespoon grains of paradise, coarsely ground

Pinch or two of sea salt to taste

3 tablespoons unsalted butter

TECHNIQUE

1. Let the steak rest at room temperature for 20 minutes.
2. Combine the peppercorns and grains of paradise on a plate.
3. Press the steak in the mix, including the sides. Sprinkle with a little sea salt.
4. Heat up a cast-iron skillet over medium-high heat. Add the butter. Once melted, add the steaks and sear each side until

golden brown, 3–4 minutes each side for medium rare. Transfer to a plate and cover with aluminum foil to keep warm while plating. Slice before serving.

Optional garnish: Chopped chives, edible flowers

PLATING

Serve the steak slices over the Israeli couscous salad, garnish as desired, and enjoy.

PRESERVED LEMONS

If you are unable to find preserved lemons at your local grocery store and you don't want to wait a month to make them from scratch, here's a quick and easy recipe that emulates the same flavors. The lemons should be prepped the day before you want to use them. Note: they are also great in salads. They can be stored for 2 weeks in the refrigerator.

Makes around 1¹/2 cups
Prep time: 10 minutes
Rest time: 12–24 hours
The equipment: 1 medium-sized mason jar

INGREDIENTS

6–8 Meyer lemons
2½ tablespoons sea salt or kosher salt
5 tablespoons sugar
Juice of 1 lemon
1 sprig fresh rosemary (optional)

TECHNIQUE

Wash the lemons thoroughly, slice into thin rounds, and then quarter the slices. In a bowl, toss the lemon slices with the salt, sugar, and lemon juice. Place the mixture in a mason jar with a sprig of rosemary, if using. Place the jar in the refrigerator for a minimum of 12 hours. Store any leftover lemon slices in a plastic container with a little water to use in other recipes or your favorite tea.

CHARLES'S CHICKEN SATAY AND VEGETABLE SLAW

ENTRÉE OR PLAT PRINCIPAL

Makes 12 skewers with enough sauce for more
Prep time: 30 minutes
Cooking time: 10 minutes

INGREDIENTS FOR THE SATAY

4 chicken breasts, sliced lengthwise in 1½-inch strips
3 tablespoons sunflower oil, plus extra
1 tablespoon curry powder, mild or hot depending on taste
2 tablespoons coconut oil, plus extra
1 tablespoon finely minced garlic
1 tablespoon finely minced fresh ginger
2 cups coconut milk
¼ cup peanut butter
2 tablespoons sweet soy sauce
1 tablespoon coconut sugar
1 teaspoon ground cardamom
1 teaspoon chili powder (optional)
4–6 stalks lemongrass, sliced lengthwise into halves or quarters,
    depending on size
¼ cup finely minced cilantro or flat parsley

INGREDIENTS FOR THE SLAW

1 cup thinly sliced and diced red pepper

1 cup fresh soy sprouts

1 cup thinly sliced cucumbers, quartered

½ cup julienned carrots

2 tablespoons coconut sugar

1 tablespoon finely minced mint

½ cup rice wine vinegar, plus more if desired

½ tablespoon red pepper flakes (optional)

TECHNIQUE

1. Place cut chicken strips in a bowl. Cover with the sunflower oil and curry. Toss. Put in the refrigerator to marinate for a minimum of three hours or overnight.

2. Make the slaw. Combine all slaw ingredients in a bowl, toss. Place in the refrigerator until ready to serve.

3. Heat up the coconut oil in a medium-sized pot, burner set to medium-high heat. Add the garlic and fresh ginger, cooking until fragrant, about two minutes. Add in the coconut milk, stirring and bringing the mixture to a simmer. Whisk in the peanut butter. Add in the soy sauce, coconut sugar, cardamom, and chili powder (if using). Mix well. Simmer for 2 more minutes, then take the pot off the heat and set aside. Cover the pot to keep it warm.

4. Take the marinated chicken out of the refrigerator and thread the slices onto the lemongrass. Using a pastry brush, lightly coat the chicken with the peanut sauce.

5. Heat up a nonstick or grill pan over medium-high heat,

lightly coating with the oil of your choice (sunflower or coconut). Place the chicken slices in the pan and cook for 4 minutes each side.

PLATING

Serve the skewers, garnished with cilantro or parsley, with small bowls of the peanut sauce, steamed rice, and the slaw.

POACHED PEARS IN WHITE WINE WITH GINGER AND SAFFRON AND SERVED WITH A MASCARPONE-INFUSED WHIPPED CREAM

Serves 4

Prep time: 15 minutes

Cooking time: 20 minutes

The equipment: handheld blender

INGREDIENTS FOR THE PEARS

2½ cups white wine (a muscadet), plus more if needed

¾ cup granulated sugar

1 teaspoon coconut sugar

Juice of 1 lemon

2 teaspoons freshly grated ginger

1½ teaspoons saffron

1 teaspoon honey

Pinch of sea salt

4 pears (ripe, not mushy but firm), peeled, stems intact

INGREDIENTS FOR THE CREAM

1 cup heavy cream (cold)

¾ cup granulated sugar

½ cup mascarpone

1 teaspoon vanilla extract, or the seeds from a vanilla bean pod

TECHNIQUE

1. In a medium-sized saucepan, combine the wine, sugar, coconut sugar, lemon juice, ginger, saffron, honey, and salt. Bring to a simmer/slight boil and peel your pears. Place the pears in the pot. Lower heat to a slight simmer and cook the pears for around 20 to 25 minutes, turning occasionally with a slotted spoon, until the pears are easily pierced with a knife.

2. While the pears are cooking, make the whipped cream. In a medium-sized bowl, pour in the heavy cream and the sugar and whip on medium-high until soft peaks form, around 10 minutes. Add in the mascarpone and vanilla, blending for 2–3 minutes, until medium peaks form. The mixture shouldn't be too soft or curdled. Check the consistency as you go, turning off the blender. Place the bowl in the refrigerator until ready to serve.

3. Once the pears are cooked, using a slotted spoon, take them out, place them on a plate, and cover the plate in plastic wrap. Let them chill in your refrigerator.

4. Bring the sauce to a boil. Whisk, and let the sauce reduce by half, about 10 minutes. Remove from the heat.

PLATING

This recipe can be made in advance. Heat up the sauce slightly. Take the pears out of the refrigerator, warming until room temperature. Add a cloud of the cream, followed by the pear, and then drizzle with the sauce.

CHARLES'S COCONUT ICE CREAM

DESSERT

Serves 6–8

Prep time: 30 minutes

Rest time (with a little work): 5–6 hours

The equipment: Large mixing bowl, handheld blender, 9 x 5 loaf pan (or other receptacle around this size that you can put in the freezer)

INGREDIENTS

1¾ cups heavy cream (cold)

½ cup granulated sugar

½ cup powdered sugar

2 cups coconut cream

1 cup coconut milk (cold)

½ cup sweetened condensed milk (cold)

Pinch of sea salt

2–3 teaspoons vanilla extract

The seeds of 1 vanilla bean pod

TOPPING

1 tablespoon unsalted butter

½ cup shredded coconut

TECHNIQUE

1. In a large mixing bowl, whip the heavy cream and both sugars (granulated and powdered) with a handheld blender, moving from slow to medium-high speed, until soft peaks form, around 10 minutes. Add in the coconut cream (which is more dense), and continuing whipping on medium-high until smooth. Add in the coconut milk, condensed milk, salt, vanilla extract, and vanilla seeds. Mix together with a spoon or blender set on low.

2. Pour the mixture into your loaf pan (or other receptacle) and place in the freezer for 1 hour. Stir with a fork and restir in 1 to 2 hours. For a creamier ice cream, stir every 30 minutes—a total of 5 hours.

3. Ten minutes before serving, take it out of the freezer and stir the mixture, letting it rest on your counter.

4. Prep the coconut topping. In a pan, melt the butter and then add the shredded coconut, toasting for about 2 minutes. Let cool.

PLATING

Serve the ice cream in bowls with the shredded coconut topping. The coconut ice cream can be placed in the freezer in the container covered with plastic wrap, or transferred to a plastic storage container with a lid. Best enjoyed within 3 days, but can last up to 5.

ACKNOWLEDGMENTS

Once again, a brigade made this book happen. Hopefully, the writing is seasoned with the right amount of salt, pepper, and/or sugar for your tastes. I had so much fun writing this novel and cooking up the recipes. I hope you enjoy it too.

Let's cut to the cheese.

My agents, Kimberly Witherspoon and Jessica Mileo, are phenomenal—especially Jessica, who gave me supremely detailed edits. She's the best alpha reader ever, and she whipped my manuscript into shape!

I want to thank my dream team at Berkley—Cindy Hwang and Angela Kim; I adore both of you. Thank you for guiding this manuscript into the fun, heartfelt, and magical book it was meant to be. I love being a Berkley author, especially with the ongoing support from Jessica Plummer and Tara O'Conner, my marketing and PR team. Thank you. To the copy editor, Erica Ferguson, thank you for doing such a stellar job fine-tuning my words.

What about this gorgeous cover? I let out a squeal when I saw it the first time! Who am I kidding? I'm still squealing. Thank you to

Katie Anderson, the art director, and cover designer Lila Selle. You talented gals captured the magic. And my cat, Juju, who doesn't know he's a character in the book, loves the way you slimmed him down. Damn. Do I have to buy him a diamond collar? Thank you to the interior page designer, Katy Riegel, for making everything look so pretty and fun.

Thank you to my fantastic beta readers—Lori Nelson Spielman, Barbara Conrey, and Liv Arnold. Seriously, pass the chili peppers because you all helped to spice up this manuscript.

Thank you to Oksana Ritchie and Susy Nataly for inspiring the concept behind this book. One of them has a spice dealer. One of them grows exotic plants. Both of them hold my heart. I'm blessed to have such amazing friends.

Thank you to Elle Marr and Lauren Ho for reading my proposal way back when. Thank you to the debut 2020s for the ongoing support. Thank you to Mary O'Leary, who gives me tips on all things cooking and chef-y. (That's a word now.) And a huge merci goes out to the incomparable Bobbi Dumas! Thank you for listening to me ramble on about this book and for guiding me through the magical art that is tarot.

Merci to my husband, Jean-Luc, and my stepkids, Max and Elvire. Thank you for tasting and eating all of the recipes I created and letting me know your thoughts about them. On second thought, maybe they should be thanking me.

Finally, thank you, dear reader, for choosing this book. I've loved connecting with all of you on my writing journey and I'm so thankful to have you in my life. Merci! Merci beaucoup. Happy reading! Happy eating! I think it's time for a group hug!

Samantha Vérant is a travel addict, a self-professed oenophile, and a determined, if occasionally unconventional, at-home French chef. She lives in southwestern France, where she's married to a sexy French rocket scientist she met in 1989 (but ignored for twenty years), a stepmom to two incredible kids, and the adoptive mother to a ridiculously adorable French cat. When she's not trekking from Provence to the Pyrénées, embracing her inner Julia Child, or searching out ingredients and spices, Sam is making her best effort to re-learn those dreaded conjugations.

CONNECT ONLINE

SamanthaVerant.com

 AuthorSamanthaVerant

 Samantha_Verant

 Samantha_Verant

Ready to find
your next great read?

Let us help.

Visit prh.com/nextread